Raise Dragon

L.A. Kristiansen

Best Wishes

[signature]

Ringwood Publishing
Glasgow

Issued in 2021
by
Ringwood Publishing

Flat 0/1 314 Meadowside Quay Walk, Glasgow
G11 6AY

www.ringwoodpublishing.com
e-mail: mail@ringwoodpublishing.com

ISBN: 978-1-901514-76-6

British Library Cataloguing-in Publication Data
A catalogue record for this book is available from the
British Library

Printed and bound in the UK
by Lonsdale Direct Solutions

Dedication

To my wonderful D (1929-2021) who gave me strength, patience, determination and drive.

And for Trevor and Mark who left the world too early. I miss them all.

Prologue

Escape from Acre, 17th to 18th May 1291

Well, Geoff, it was not your day to die, Geoffroi de Charnay mused. *But I wonder if tonight will be the last time you look at the night sky.* His weary eyes swept the heavens, and he stretched out his bloodied and bruised hands as if to touch them. He was nearly forty years old and felt older, but he was an experienced knight, as shown in his pitted hands and scarred face and body.

Is my death written in the stars?

His concentration was broken by the sounds of two figures slipping quietly under cover of night across the esplanade.

Their shadows were cast long and narrow against the light sandstone blocks that made up the field of fire. Two horses stood in the open by the entrance to the castle keep, uneasily digging into the dry ground and trying to swat biting insects with their tails. The fleeing men, obscured by the debris of bodies, stones, and dead horses, stepped softly and spoke only in hand signals, but their moving forms broke the static edges of the destruction around them.

De Charnay knew they must be Templars; everyone else had been killed or had fled. The dark, almost blood-red crosses on the tabards of the two figures were tattered but still distinguishable despite the gore of battle.

Both were large men, with broad shoulders and strong hands for wielding sword and axe. They each carried a large, bulging sack made of soft leather that looked like it had been hastily over-packed.

A white tabard caught on the jagged edges of the debris

1

and tore, the lost fabric waving a sad farewell. Their sword blades reflected what light there was and, just once, de Charnay thought he caught sight of a fine sword with a fire opal embedded in the pommel. Their valuable weapons were tightly grasped in their right hands, held away from their lightly armoured bodies to stop any noise from awakening the remains of the garrison. They were fleeing - leaving the darkness, their brother knights, and their shame behind them.

Distant fires and failing torches peppered the darkness. Only the humming of crickets and the neighing and nickering of the horses broke the silence.

De Charnay watched with morbid fascination as they moved with purpose towards the entrance to the castle crypt and the exit to the harbour.

An intense scream tore through the air, and the men turned and paused.

The screaming intensified, and de Charnay watched one of the knights retching behind a dead horse. He shook the vomit from his filthy beard. The entrance to the crypt was but a few feet away, but the knight paused and squatted, hiding behind one half of the heavy open doors, before he gathered enough courage to move. His companion pushed him towards the doors, the harbour, and the escape. Their argument was silent, but the fear was clear.

De Charnay covered his ears to muffle the continued high-pitched screams as a man begged for his suffering to end. He held his ears tighter, and his eyes filled with tears as the cries grew stronger. He felt ashamed, as the tears were not only for the screaming man's suffering, but also for himself.

The Mamluks were torturing a prisoner they had captured during their last assault. They rarely took prisoners, and especially not Templar captives or any holy crusading knights. Mercy was a stranger to both sides.

The Mamluks were not without honour. They had a code that respected brave soldiers and warriors, treating their views with tolerance and their actions with forgiveness as the Koran dictated - but that was only for pilgrims and pressed soldiers.

De Charnay was no coward or zealot, but his morale was sapped. He was hungry and exhausted, though he could still fight despite his haggard, thin frame making him vulnerable and weary. His body was an illustration of all these things. He had not seen proper food in weeks. His stomach churned, mostly from hunger but also from fear.

He considered these men's escape, this act of desertion, understandable if not forgiveable. He thought he recognised them as they disappeared through the keep doors, but his mind was tired and, in any case, it did not matter who they were.

Many of the ephemeral glory-seeking Crusaders had left earlier with Henry the King of Cyprus a week since.

He recognised that his faith was under stress, but it was still strong, and his loyalty to the Templar Order was even stronger. Those who had decided to stay had chosen to die in defence of Christ, and he had resigned himself to that fate.

He pitied those who had left. Faith had left them in their hour of need. He would try to sleep and block out the screams and pleas of the dying, to conserve his strength and reinforce his faith, for he would need to draw on them both in the morning.

Suddenly, he put names to the faces.

'I remember you now,' he muttered. Talking to himself proved he had not lost his mind.

Otto de Grandison and William de Beaujeu: two knights with the most noble of pedigrees, but unlikely bedfellows indeed. Grandison was for the English King, and the vomiting one, William de Beaujeu, the French. In any other place they would have killed each other, but they had found a reason to put their differences aside. *Survival makes even the most stoic forgive their enemies.* De Charnay scoffed.

They were of his kind. He had seen and learned many things since he had arrived in the Holy Land that had shaken all his values and loyalties. He was not the only one to have changed in how he saw the world order. He did not care who was king in France or England, as his Lord was of the heavenly type, and for that reason he would not run away.

Acre had been under siege for months, and the defenders were fewer and dying in greater numbers. The Templars had fought bravely for so long, and he wished he could think of something other than defeat and death, but he knew that Acre would fall to the Mamluks tomorrow.

The lull that had allowed these men to escape had been expensively purchased by the life of the tortured man - and men like him. However, de Grandison and de Beaujeu were the sort of knights drawn to this land for advancement, patronage, and hubris, not faith or belief. That was why the Crusaders were losing.

De Charnay had noticed their heavy sacks and concluded they were motivated by the avarice and greed of third-rate brigands. They had forgotten why they were there.

'How dispiriting,' he announced as he turned away and began to look at the stars once again. He started to smile. *Yes, far more interesting.*

*

The two deserters fell through the heavy but fractured doors of the keep, stumbling and tumbling down the stairs as they headed towards the harbour. Their fear of this dark place was only surpassed by the horror of the alternative above them.

They did not look around as they made their way to a pilot's boat moored by the outer wall of the harbour. Only the creaking of the masts and wooden decks gave its presence away.

They threw their leather bags onto the deck and swiftly followed them, only just avoiding landing on a large hemp sack, tied securely at both ends. Without a word, the crew began rowing quietly out of the harbour towards a sea barge until a breeze filled the sails and took them away from Acre towards the open sea.

*

De Charnay slept deeply, hidden amongst the blackened rocks under the stars, unperturbed by thoughts of the final battle that would take place that day. There was nothing he could do to change the situation, and he was not a man to worry about something that had no solution.

As the day broke, he felt nauseous, but not from fear. He wondered if this was the feeling everyone had when they knew they faced death.

There was a surreal calmness around him on that warm May morning in Acre. Some defenders were quietly whimpering with their injuries, some were screaming with the audible weariness of a body near death, and others just wanted to contemplate what was to come, making peace with God in contemplative prayer. All amongst a bloody sea of human flotsam gently lapping at the feet of the Tower of the Flies as it dozed within the ravaged keep.

The night's background noise had stopped, but de Charnay knew this was but a signpost for the final attack.

Suddenly, noise exploded all around him. Arrows thudded into the ground, making de Charnay jump as they skimmed the very air that he breathed.

He grabbed his sword as the Mamluks attacked once again. Trumpets and drums rang out as men and horses rushed towards the remaining defences, ordered by the Sultan Khalil to take the city, and offer no quarter.

Cries of triumph and of pain. Swords crashing on shields. Death screams. The air filled with the smell of burning flesh and blackened iron, mixing unpleasantly with the salt-laden acid air of the harbour. Acrid and bitter smoke rose into the May sky and filled the battlements as the last knights of the Crusade battled the Mamluks for each grain of sand, each

5

stone, for their lives and their eternal souls.

De Charnay watched as Acre fell. First the Tower of the Patriarch, the Tower of the Germans, and the Tower of the English, undermined by the tunnelling efforts of the Mamluk engineers. More stone blocks cascaded towards the ground, and huge swathes of dust and sand rose into the sky.

De Charnay climbed up onto a fractured wall and saw that a group of men had been buried alive under a pile of huge stones. Some of the dying were only visible by their flailing limbs, thrashing in their final throes as attackers stabbed between their legs, halting the death dance as they quickly bled out.

His nostrils filled with sand and the metallic smell of fresh blood, mingled with shit from voided bowels. Screams and prayers died as the Mamluks pulled and twisted their swords from the groins of dying defenders, wiping their weapons on the hated cloaks bearing the red cross.

He watched as the Mamluks charged the next defensive line of knights, screaming 'God is great'. There seemed to be no end to the screaming. The resistance was dogged and desperate. This was not going to be an easy victory, and that made the Mamluks even more determined.

The sun was dimmed by smoke as human and animal screams rang out amongst the clash of swords and the rush of arrows that pierced the flesh of man and beast. A gory mist of blood-coated men and horses alike. Men struggled to see the setting sun, and some gasped through blood-filled lungs as they fought for air.

De Charnay could barely lift his sword arm, speckled with bruises, blood, and guts. His breath was shallow, and he struggled to fill his lungs with air that did not taste of blood and sand. Wave after wave of attackers had been held off by a dwindling band of defenders, and the heat had sucked away what energy he had left. His respite had been a couple of minutes following each attack as they had regrouped, and he was fighting two or three assailants at a time, missing death by tighter margins as their numbers increased. He recognised he was exhausted, everything hurt, and his power was waning like the day.

He had lost count of the men he had killed. He could not carry on any longer; his hands were swollen, his energy almost depleted. A saddled horse, one of the few uninjured horses, darted towards him, and he grabbed its harness and used it to shield himself from attackers as he had been trained. His bloodstained white tabard was a terrible testament to his success, but he could not take much more of this intense fighting.

Beneath his helmet, he could feel the sweat run down his forehead towards a deep gash just above his right cheekbone.

He was a broad man, weathered and experienced, and had the presence of one who would not die easily, but every man had his limit, and he knew he was near his. He was surprised at how much the salty sweat stung, and at the depth of the pain. In all the chaos, he had time to think how stupid it was to care about a small wound of no significance when his death was mere minutes away.

The air was now saturated with a sticky mix of blood, sweat, and dust that oozed into his and his horse's eyes. The horse panicked and stumbled on the debris, and they both went down. De Charnay's helmet fell off and rolled several feet away. His instincts told him he had to get to his feet, or it would be the end. His boots slid in what looked like entrails and, desperate to stand, he danced like a man at the gallows, trying to cling on for a few more seconds of life.

The horse rolled onto its side, got enough purchase to get to its feet, and put its front leg, and its full weight, onto de Charnay's left foot. He felt a rush of what he thought was blood. He pissed himself, such was the suddenness and intensity of the pain.

The bones of his foot had no form; they were loose in the

skin, and he was nauseous, almost fainting. The horse bolted off towards a gap in the wall as de Charnay pulled himself onto his knees with all his remaining strength. He used his sword as a crutch to get to his feet.

His struggle attracted the attention of two Mamluk besiegers armed with swords and bows. They watched the bolting horse, likely wondering where it had come from, and then turned to see de Charnay defenceless and broken.

One of the archers removed his bow from his shoulder, took an arrow from his quiver, and lined up a shot at the knight's exposed head.

De Charnay saw the archer through the dust, but he could not run, and his heart pumped harder as he waited for death. He prayed and looked skywards for his last sight of the heavens; an arrow fired from behind him thudded into the Mamluk bowman. A second arrow hit the other attacker. Both men fell with arrows protruding from their chests, dead before they hit the ground.

The killing of the Mamluks was as skilful as it was clinical. Turning, the astonished knight saw the face of his salvation: a red-haired soldier, running towards him while returning his bow to his left shoulder.

De Charnay mouthed '*Merci*' as his rescuer bundled him towards cover, behind the stout but fractured doors directly above the harbour - the same escape route used the previous evening by Otto de Grandison and William de Beaujeu. It was the only way out.

The soldier cried out over the din of battle. 'Get your fucking head down, and don't ask any questions.'

De Charnay was out of immediate danger, his exposed skin burning and bleeding as it scraped across the ground.

They stumbled towards the staircase that led to the harbour.

'*Je ne peux pas aller plus loin,*' de Charnay blurted in French, shaking with the pain. 'Mon pied est cassé.'

'I understand French, but prefer English.'

The archer then lifted him up, and they both crashed through the wooden doors, tumbling down the first four steps before their bodies came to a fortunate halt at the top of a large descending staircase. They could only guess at the distance to the bottom, as there was a deep void. The smell of rotting flesh was overpowering, and both men gagged.

The first steep flight of steps was partially lit by a ray of late-day sunlight that had penetrated a gap in the door. It did not reach the exit and could not show them the way out, but they could hear that the sea was nearby. The second flight of steps was steeper and as black as pitch.

The archer snatched a dwindling torch from the grasp of a dead Mamluk and bundled de Charnay down the steps, almost carrying him to compensate for his swelling foot. The pain was intense.

'Please, stop.' De Charnay said. 'I am going to be sick.' Acidic bile rose into his throat.

The archer did not stop and was promptly covered in vomit - de Charnay would apologise to him later if he lived long enough.

De Charnay tried to make sense of everything. Who was this man who had risked his life for him? Could he be a Mamluk looking for ransom? That did not make sense: no Mamluk would ever give quarter to a Templar and kill his own men in the process.

The descent towards the harbour had been frenzied, and he struggled to keep his footing. The stairs became wet and treacherous underfoot, and his pain was so great that he could not bear it any longer. He fell hard to the floor of the bottom landing and cried *'S'il vous plaît. Arrêtez!'*

De Charnay said it with such conviction that the archer momentarily stopped and, for the first time, looked him in the eye.

He was a head and a half taller than de Charnay. He could

9

have been a slave, freed to fight in the Mamluk army, but this man did not have the presence of a slave.

De Charnay could see - even through the sweat, blood, and dust coating the archer's face - that his skin was reddened from the sun.

His hair was long, a shade of reddish-blond bleached paler by the baking sun. His eyes were a rich green, his lips pale. De Charnay had seen that this man was an experienced fighter and knew he was in good hands, but where had his rescuer come from?

Most of those defenders who had remained were Templars, French, or Almogavars from the border country between France and Spain. He had not seen this soldier before, but he had seen his type. His tabard was covered in filth, but de Charnay could just make out the white cross on the blue background, and he remembered where he had seen it before. His mind was muddled, but he thought he knew now that the archer was *Écossais* - from Scotland.

'Stop … please, stop. I am a broken man,' he said in hesitant English whilst sliding in the sticky, putrid mess. 'Who are you?'

*

The archer looked at de Charnay; this was not the time for a conversation.

'Fuck that!' he said, dragging de Charnay towards the sound of water.

The torch failed. It no longer brought light, but it was metal and might be useful.

Noises came from above, and he was not going to wait around to discover whether they were from friend or foe. He could hear the voices getting closer. They had to hurry if they were to escape.

He would answer the questions later. His job for now was to stay alive and get Geoffroi de Charnay out of Acre.

His Grace's instructions were clear: 'Get him out alive

and intact.' The archer, John Wishart, would do precisely that.

He pushed de Charnay through an archway and out into the evening air. Sunlight was fading, replaced by a brightening moon. Both men squinted to see what was waiting outside for them. They moved quickly away from the exit, using the torch to bar the door handles.

'I knew it would be useful,' Wishart murmured.

Holding de Charnay by the waist, Wishart pulled him around the outer wall of the crypt, towards the dock and out of sight. It would only be a short time before their enemies followed. He could see that de Charnay's shock had left him dazed and malleable. It was easy enough for John to manoeuvre him as they moved towards their escape.

Wishart assessed the harbour wall and its height above sea level. The drop below was survivable.

Wishart was lightly armed and not weighed down by chain mail and armour, and de Charnay had shed most of his armour and mail during the fighting. If they hit the water, they could use the small outgoing tide to take them away. They needed to be further up the coast and away from the pursuing Mamluks, but more pressing needs required an immediate solution. The pursuers were now battering against the exit door.

Wishart climbed onto the top of the harbour wall and was surprised to see the top pennant of a mast before him. A small, heavily laden barge had drifted around the corner to within a few feet of the harbour.

He could see that it was lying extremely low in the water, and the main deck was only about ten feet above the waterline. There were numerous boxes, linens, and barrels on the back deck, so he thought he could easily drop de Charnay there while he jumped onto the main deck. He had no time to measure the drop, or for any other niceties. If they could make it to the small harbour wall and jump onto the barge, they could hide from their pursuers at least for a minute or two.

They did not have a choice. This was not just a chance; it was their only chance. He recognised the sail as belonging to a supply barge of the Templar fleet; it seemed noticeably quiet. Where was the crew?

It was strange that no one was on the deck preventing a collision with the stone wall of the harbour. But he did not have time to figure it out.

Wishart heard a commotion behind him. He had no more time. They were going over the harbour wall and into the water, and if there was a boat to break the fall, so much the better.

De Charnay kept trying to speak, but everything came out as gibberish. Wishart chose to ignore him as he pushed him towards a small flight of steps that led to the top of the harbour's perimeter wall.

The Mamluks had now broken through the door, and the tips of their swords caught the fading light and reflected it on the stone floor. They were directly above Wishart and de Charnay, but for the moment, they did not appear to see them.

One of the Mamluks shouted in Arabic, arming his bow and gesturing to the barge below.

The barge was now about six feet away and twenty feet down from the harbour wall.

'Jump,' Wishart screamed as he pushed de Charnay off the wall and onto the deck.

Both landed heavily with a dull thud onto a pile of what looked like assorted linen and barrels.

'Shit! That hurt … and I can't swim!' De Charnay cried. Thuds resonated from the front of the barge as several throwing axes cut into the deck, followed by the sound of arrows whistling and punching into the masts.

'I would rather die with a sword in my hand than drown

like a rat.'

'Aye, right,' Wishart said, dismissing his pleading. 'Shut up and get down. We have no time for pointless heroics. Or do you want to be one dead fucking knight?'

*

De Charnay saw stars, but his fall had been broken - he was bruised but unharmed. Whatever he had fallen on looked familiar, and he could sense that his hands were covered in a sticky substance of metal, salt, sweat, and meat. He recognised the smell of death and the slaughterhouse; it was a sour odour, and it came from something wrapped carefully in woollen bales. The landing had felt warm to the touch. De Charnay brought his right hand towards his face and saw a bloodstain on his arm. The blood, though black, was yet to crust. His head began to spin, and he felt consciousness drain away as he passed out. His head fell against a bloodied corpse.

*

Wishart hid behind the chests littering the deck. Arrows and axes continued to rain down from above him, and he could see figures on top of the wall, but with each new wave, the barge and its cargo were carried further out to sea. They were still not safe.

Wishart reached for his sword, but it must have fallen out of its scabbard when he jumped on deck. His hand came to rest on a broken oar that might function as an effective club. If it came to it, he would use this to beat the shit out of the Mamluks.

The current was changing, and the barge was drifting away from the harbour wall. Safety was more certain with each wave, but Wishart could see that one of the Mamluks was hastily undressing and looked to be getting ready to attempt the leap onto the ship. Wishart gripped the oar tightly and scrambled around on the deck for any other weapon or

13

shield. He had to keep low to avoid the arrows. He looked over to de Charnay and saw he was not moving.

In his clumsy fall, de Charnay had somehow buried himself amongst the wool and sailcloth and was largely out of sight, protected from the weapons flying towards the deck. Wishart hoped that de Charnay was not dead, and that God was still with him.

In a few seconds, the Mamluk had stripped down and was naked with a dagger between his teeth; but even in these few seconds, the ship had moved further away from the wall.

The Mamluk would have to be quite an athlete to leap twenty feet onto the ship, but Wishart had seen extraordinary physical feats in battle before.

The arrows stopped as the Mamluk ran at high speed to leap across to the barge. His arms and legs flailed like wings to extend his travelling distance. Wishart watched from behind a barrel as the Mamluk appeared to travel further and faster than he could have imagined. Time seemed to slow.

Wishart cried out to the crew, but there was no response. If the barge were boarded, they would all be killed.

Maybe they are drunk. They could be sleeping it off under the canvas that covered three-quarters of the deck.

The Mamluk hit the stern and tried to hold onto the rail, but his fingers slipped, and he crashed, groaning, into the rudder of the barge and disappeared beneath the waves. Seeing the attempt at boarding had failed, Wishart ducked further under cover as the hail of arrows and other missiles recommenced, but each flight became less and less effective as the barge drifted further and further out to sea. By now, most of the arrows were falling short, but occasionally one hit the mast. When this too stopped, Wishart felt safe enough to move around the deck.

As he stepped from his shelter, he noticed his leg was covered in dark, sticky fluid. He dipped his fingers in it, rubbed it between them, and confirmed it was blood - a lot of blood - and it was not his.

It was as if the crew had washed the deck in blood in some macabre ritual. It lay in pools.

What the hell happened here? It is a bloodbath.

Wishart could see de Charnay's head poking out from the linen that had been concealing him, and he pulled the canvas towards him to wipe his hands clean. An arm fell on his shoulder, followed by a limp body that had been balancing on a barrel, covered by the same canvas. The body landed face up on the deck.

Wishart jumped. 'Sweet Jesus.'

The man's face was contorted. He had been almost decapitated and had multiple stab wounds to the chest and abdomen. His intestines could be seen pushing out between the wounds. There were five deep knife wounds, and his leather jerkin had been pushed into each wound with considerable force.

Wishart continued to explore the deck in silence, swallowing hard. The horror hit him as if he had been struck in the gut. He felt a wave of dread as he uncovered two more male bodies, each one the subject of a frenzied knife attack. They were all lying across heavy wooden chests and barrels.

He stopped pulling back the remaining canvases and held the wooden club even more tightly. The killer or killers might still be on board, hiding beneath the remaining coverings. He was sensitive to every sound and listened attentively for any unusual noises. All he could hear was the creaking of the wooden barge and its masts, and the slap of water on wood. Everything seemed quiet, but he could not be sure.

Wishart continued searching the deck, but he was far more cautious now as he removed each covering. As he brushed the cargo chests, they held fast, and he could not easily move them to see if anyone were hiding. A crew would be needed to load and unload these.

One of the barrels had been split open by a Mamluk's

axe. The wooden staves holding it had shattered, spilling gold coins onto the deck.

Inside, he saw the glitter of a golden chalice proudly embellished with a large ruby the size of a hen's egg. Wishart moved closer to touch it. He could see gold and silver plate, and polished jewels as numerous as the seeds in a barrel of grain. He had never seen such wealth.

This was why the barge had lain so deeply in the water. It appeared to be full of gold and valuables, as if all the wealth of the world were concentrated in this one spot.

He spotted a billhook leaning between a chest and a barrel and exchanged his wooden club for it. Even the billhook was covered in blood. He cleaned the handle on his tabard and paused to try and make sense of what he was seeing.

He was a soldier, and he knew these men had been soldiers and sailors. They had known the risks of war, but the way they had been slain … it was as if the killers hadn't gotten enough from the simple act of killing, as if they had to make theatre of it. How had the killers kept the crew at bay as they stabbed them? There had to be more than one killer. One to kill and at least one to subdue.

There might have been great anger, pleasure, or secrecy involved in these killings. However, the gold alone would give most men the excuse they needed. No one appeared to have survived this orgy of death.

Wishart came across two more bodies, both killed with the same excessive violence. There were five dead men now, and the crew for this sort of barge comprised between eight and ten hands. The barge was missing its ancillary boat, so perhaps the murderers had escaped?

He looked for the other men, not knowing if he was going to uncover more bodies or a crewman hiding. Perhaps he would uncover a murderer too? This made Wishart nervous about finding anyone alive. How could he tell the innocent from the guilty?

Wishart could not rely on the tide to carry them to safety. The barge needed a crew to work the sails and the rudder, and he did not know the waters sufficiently well to know where the tides and currents would take them. Landing on shores controlled by the Mamluks or their allies was a risk he was not prepared to take.

He slid on the blood-soaked deck as the ship rolled. Lying in a gap hidden behind the largest chests were two more bodies - but these were different. Wishart knelt behind the first body, which was sitting against the largest chest. They had not been covered by the sail canvases: it looked as if the material had fallen onto them rather than being placed over them like the other bodies. They were Templar knights, still wearing their bloodstained tabards of white cotton with a large red cross on the front.

Both had died from sword wounds to the stomach. Their faces were caked with blood splatter and were unrecognisable. Matted hair distinguished one as fair and the other as being much darker. He touched their foreheads. The fair man was cold and had been dead for several hours. The darker-haired man was still warm and had died only recently.

They both had expensive swords in their hands, and each was wearing a large golden ring on his left index finger. Wishart took the rings off and held them up, but could not make anything out, so he placed them in a wooden pail that he found at his feet.

Something moved beneath one of the fallen sails. Immediately, Wishart drew the billhook back and cautiously pulled back some of the covering. Without thinking, he brought his right hand down and repeatedly hit the moving object. It screamed, but he carried on. Again, and again, he brought the metal billhook down and hit the moving canvas. The movement stopped, yet he still carried on in a frenzy of violence. He drew back the canvas to reveal the body of a large rat. Wishart felt genuine fear, and that was unusual.

Something terrible had taken place here.

'I am dying.' The groan was deep, guttural, and in broken English.

He turned quickly and raised his billhook to prepare to defend himself, but it was de Charnay. He was slowly coming around, defenceless, and oblivious to the bloody nightmare around him.

Wishart gestured to de Charnay to remain quiet and pushed him down. Shocked and surprised, de Charnay immediately suppressed his moans and sat down like a disciplined knave.

'Shush,' Wishart whispered.

*

De Charnay had so much to ask. He remembered jumping from the harbour and landing on the barge in a haze of pain, but every memory after that was missing.

The wind was gusting, and the barge was rolling as the current pushed it further out to sea. De Charnay had been a sailor in his youth, and he knew the wind and current were controlling the course. If the swell did not grow too much greater, he was content that the barge's natural buoyancy would keep them safe for the moment.

'God, my foot hurts,' he groaned.

He found the waves hypnotic, which was good. He was in great pain.

'I will explain, but we must be quiet now,' the red-haired archer said. 'Please, be silent and listen.'

'Why must I be silent?' De Charnay replied sheepishly as he gestured to the horizon. 'We're out at sea.'

'Yes, and we are also surrounded by dead bodies.' The archer pointed to the two dead knights. 'Besides those dead Templars, the crew has been murdered as well.'

De Charnay remembered the blood on the deck as he had landed on the barge.

The archer continued. 'We're on a floating slaughterhouse.

Can't you smell the blood? Look at your hands. There are seven dead men here with us on this ship, and no crew. These men were butchered on this ship, and the killers may still be here, hiding amongst these chests and barrels.'

Wishart handed de Charnay the wooden club. De Charnay held the club, desperate to know more. 'I need to know who you are. Why did you save my life, and why am I here? Do you know who I am?'

The archer paused to allow de Charnay to fill the silence, but he did not. At last, the archer reluctantly replied. 'Oh, I know very well who you are, sir. I was asked to get you out of Acre in one piece. You're Geoffroi de Charnay.' And he quickly added, 'I am John Wishart.'

De Charnay recognised the name, but said nothing.

A metal bucket, which had been hanging on the cross mast, fell onto a small hemp sack that was tied at each end. A noise filled the air, like a child whimpering.

Wishart moved quickly and cautiously towards the moving mass on the floor, clutching the billhook in his hand as de Charnay followed.

*

Wishart raised the bloodied billhook, ready to hit the squirming and trembling form. De Charnay dragged his foot behind him; the wooden club in his right hand was part weapon and part crutch. He stood guard as Wishart untied the sack at each end and pulled the hemp away to reveal a body - hog-tied, face-down, and frail.

Based on the ragged clothes and dishevelled appearance, de Charnay was certain that this man did not have the strength to kill Templar knights. In any case, what man would kill a crew and then tie himself up in a sack?

Wishart lowered the billhook and turned the body around. The figure was slender, and the face was covered with a leather mask that obscured his eyes and forehead. The hair sticking out the side of the mask was a vivid ginger in

19

patches and flecked with grey.

De Charnay noticed a small mark below the man's hairline by the left ear - a red clover birthmark. He had seen this mark before but could not place it.

The man was of middle age, thin, and gaunt, and judging from the signs of his skin and build, he had suffered severe and long-standing neglect. De Charnay hoped he would survive to tell them what had happened here.

Wishart tried to remove the mask, and the man cried out. The leather had stuck to a large gash on his head. There were several crusted wounds on his hands and feet that had bled profusely on being tied, and had been made worse by struggling. He had older injuries to his feet and hands, and a broad scar of toughened skin, white and translucent, had grown around each limb. The newer tight leather bindings had dug into these scars and had cut deeply into the skin. The wound on his forehead must have produced a deep concussion.

The gaunt man was slowly regaining consciousness and murmuring incoherently in French and English. His voice was faint, and he was obviously in pain. In his confused state, de Charnay thought he recognised a few words.

'Geoffrey … *Je suis* …' he mumbled, or so de Charnay thought.

Perhaps he was a Mamluk slave. From the evidence of his wrists and ankles, he had been in some sort of restraint for a long time. De Charnay saw a jewelled dagger next to the bound man and used it to cut his hands free and remove the bindings at his feet.

The captive was still only half-conscious from the severe blow to his head. Wishart turned to de Charnay, 'Help me get him up.'

De Charnay hobbled towards the water store and filled a cup. He intended to take it to the others, but realising his own thirst, he drank it quickly. Wishart remained with the captive and attempted to prop him up against one of the laden chests.

De Charnay refilled the cup and glanced around the deck, looking for anyone else. There was a small, covered sleeping area that was in disarray, but would be repairable. They would need to fix the roof and shelter there from the cool air that he knew swept across the sea.

Returning to the invalid, de Charnay sat down exhaustedly as Wishart stood up. 'I will check the rest of the deck and see if there are any other people alive,' Wishart said.

De Charnay nodded his agreement as Wishart cautiously threw the remaining canvases back and checked beneath them.

After a minute or perhaps two, he returned to de Charnay. 'There is no one else, just the three of us - but the ancillary boat is missing. The rope holding it to the side has been cut.'

De Charnay ignored Wishart's comment and focused on the barge, which was well out to sea. Its design seemed to give him a level of control he wasn't expecting, given the weight of its cargo.

The old man started to shout. 'Geoffrey … ma mère,' he groaned, making no sense.

'Here. Drink.' Wishart poured the water into the prisoner's mouth.

De Charnay studied him as he drank. He sensed that he knew him. There was something about him, a familiarity he could not place. He convinced himself he must have seen him in Acre, perhaps in the kitchens or the dungeons.

The man sat up, cowering, his hand covering the left side of his face. He was starved, beaten, weak, and scared. So why was he the only one left alive?

Night had now fallen, and the wind was cooling the air. Wisps of sea mist were beginning to form, weaving a white landscape across the black sea.

Wishart took it upon himself to make a cabin to protect them from sea and wind. He threw a sail over the remains of

21

the wooden frame that surrounded the sleeping platform and rearranged the woollen blankets that had been strewn around the decks. De Charnay, still lightheaded, helped him drag the old man into the shelter, where they lay down to sleep.

De Charnay was considering how they could control the vessel with so few men, but he still struggled to think straight. He could read the messages sent by the barge as it rolled with the current and the waves. His experience told him they were going out to sea and were safe for now in the darkness and fog. He allowed the barge to rock him to sleep.

*

As De Charnay and the invalid slept, Wishart paced the deck, taking time to think. *Where are we going to go?*

He had not anticipated taking to the sea so soon, rather an escape by land through the pilgrim route via Constantinople, perhaps picking a ship up there with the many Norwegian traders. Constantinople was hundreds of miles from here and now he was in these strange waters, with de Charnay injured, no crew, and an invalid and seven rotting corpses as unwelcome travel companions.

He would jettison the corpses tomorrow. The bad air and humours caused by the dead and the rotting could kill them all, but it was cool tonight, and he needed time to examine the dead and try to work out what had happened.

As the night lengthened, Wishart stripped all the bodies before carefully washing them with seawater as best he could and wrapping each one in a length of canvas - endless amounts of it seemed to cover the ship. He had seen men horribly mutilated before, but there was something malevolent about the way these men had died, and the task disturbed him.

He removed all their personal effects and threw them into a metal bucket. In the morning he would get de Charnay to help him lift them over the side of the ship and send them to their watery graves.

Wishart whispered a prayer over the corpses and made the sign of the cross. The foul metallic smell of blood still lingered. He would scrub the stench of death from the decks and, with de Charnay's help, sail the barge to safer waters, though he was not sure where those safer waters were. At least they now had two good swords from the dead knights.

Wishart sat on the deck next to the bound corpses, thinking as he washed and bound them, depleting what little energy he had left. Something bothered him about the contents of the buckets, something he had previously missed. He pulled out the two gold rings he had removed from the dead knights.

He lit a small, whale-oil lamp that was gently swinging in its holder, and unhooked and held the lamp close to each ring. They were bloodied, and he struggled to see the detail, but when he took them in his hand, he could feel the raised metal crest on the face of each ring.

He spat on each ring and wiped the blood away to reveal the enamelled crests. These were not the adornments of insignificant knights, but of people of standing - people who did not care about being noticed and who certainly had not expected to end up dead on a ship.

The first ring was scratched and beaten, but he could just make out a cross etching with five scallop shells.

He carefully placed it on the bottom of his woollen shirt, making sure it did not fall through the deck planks, and picked up the second ring from his lap. He repeated the cleaning and exposed a gold enamelled cross emblazoned with an imperial eagle.

He did not recognise the first ring, so he scrutinised the inside of the second ring for an inscription. The imperial eagle meant that it must have come from a German knight. He began to wonder what he had stumbled upon.

This whole scene did not make sense. There had been a fight here. Two well-equipped knights and a battle-hardened crew were dead, but the one man least equipped to survive was alive.

The barge ached with gold. Wishart knew it was worthy of a king or a tyrant, but which one? The world was full of them - stealing and killing for self-aggrandisement.

No good would come of being in possession of a cargo with such earthly value. The massacre here clearly signalled that someone did not want to leave anyone alive to tell the tale.

The clues were around him, but he was struggling to put the puzzle together.

He needed to organise his thoughts, and that required a clear head, so he had to sleep. Whoever was looking for the treasure would need to find them, and the sea was large, with many places to hide. Wishart walked around the sticky deck one last time. De Charnay and the old man were sound asleep, and likely to be so for a considerable time.

His last patrol completed, he lay down, clutching the dagger he had picked up earlier and setting the two swords by his side. Tomorrow he would look a little more closely at the corpses of the knights and question the survivor of the murderous affray. Hopefully, he could piece together what had happened and decide what they were going to do. It had been a long day, and his head buzzed with the memory of what had happened, but exhaustion finally overtook him, and sleep came.

*

The barge had been meandering sidewards, but the current was strong, taking the men and their cargo further away from Acre and their main reference point, the lighthouse above the Tower of the Flies. As night progressed and with changing temperatures, the current and tide had further strengthened. The barge was pushed faster, wave by wave, out into the open sea.

Off to the starboard side, just out of sight, a small-masted Byzantine ship, a chelandion, was sailing a rapid and deliberate course, following de Charnay and Wishart.

Eight pairs of men cut their oars effortlessly through the same currents. Sound travels fast on the sea, and each oar was covered with a felt cloth that suppressed the sound of the strokes as they dipped into each wave. A small sail made their progress swifter.

An imposingly tall man stood apart from the crew on a raised wooden platform by the bow, moving the rudder and dictating the course. His name was Axel Myhre, but the Byzantines called him Aurelian because of his flamboyance and his bright golden hair like a burst of fire. His muscular body was covered in dark green tattoos of Norse gods marking him out as a Norseman. More importantly, he was blessed with the patronage of the Emperor and led his Varangian guards. He stood upright with an unyielding arrogance, driving the crew to quicken their efforts.

On board, barely alive, were the weeping figures of Otto de Grandison and William de Beaujeu, their small pilot boat strapped to the side of the ship.

Aurelian watched as they squirmed in their iron restraints, wept, and told a tale of murder and the devil. He felt no pity. He was more interested in what these knights had been doing in the pilot boat from his treasure barge.

The chelandion was prepared for boarding the barge, but they had to catch it before it reached the fog banks that covered the coast.

The fog was becoming denser, reaching out like a divine benefactor, and pulling the barge quickly towards it. The Byzantines needed to board the barge before it disappeared into the fog and floundered on the sandbanks.

'Row quicker and harder, or I will return you to the dungeons I found you in!' Aurelian shouted. The whip crashed on the shoulders of the oarsmen. The crew were cowed. They understood this was no idle threat.

The barge was in darkness apart from a solitary lamp

25

that hung on the mast. The sea fog thickened and enveloped around the mast obscuring the light. Its form could only be glimpsed as it cut in and out of its white camouflage, ignorant of the danger it was in with its armed pursuer.

The chelandion was much faster and could have caught up with it, but there was no reference point. A few minutes travelling with this current could put them hundreds of yards in the wrong direction. The last strands of light from the barge's only lamp disappeared. It had escaped for now.

'Damn them!' Aurelian cried whipping the rowers again and again. The knights screamed as they too were beaten relentlessly. Aurelian took his frustration and anger out on everyone around him.

'Now I have to return home empty-handed and tell the Emperor we have failed!' he cursed the crew and whipped them harder. 'Brigands! I will lodge you all in the dungeons.'

Aurelian would search for the barge incessantly, and even though patience was a foreign virtue to him, he was wise enough to know that with treasure they could not run and hide forever. He would have to find the barge another time, using other means.

'Let us get out of here before we run into a sandbank or pirates.' He turned the sail and tiller northeast towards Byzantine lands as the disgruntled crew swapped positions and rowed away.

*

It was the evening of May 18, 1291, and unknown to those on the sea, the last Crusader foothold in the Holy Land had finally fallen to the Mamluks. This time there was no second chance for the Christians: the Mamluks had learned their lesson and gave no quarter. There would be no vestige of Christian rule left in the Holy Land. The final gate was breached, and the Tower of the Flies caught alight as the invaders, thwarted for so long, took revenge on anyone and anything still whole. The screams seemed to go on forever.

Plunder was replaced with destruction, and the walls were torched and cleansed with fire. The inferno lit up the sky, painting the early summer night with reds and ochres.

The sky was unusually full of birdsong, as they too were in flight, looking to escape the carnage and find a place of sanctuary.

Wishart was momentarily awoken by the flight of birds flocking above him, announcing the disaster that had befallen the city.

'I wonder what woke them up,' he murmured as he tried to focus his eyes.

He did not know that the siege had ended, and no more Christian knights had escaped. He and de Charnay had been the last survivors of the last Christian city in the Holy Land.

The end, when it came, was chaotic, uncontrollable, vindictive, and merciless in a time known for great violence. The sandy streets of Acre were now clumps of sand soaked with blood.

*

The waves were regular and soporific, but the early morning was also turning cold. The men on the barge pulled the sack and sailcloth tight around their bodies to keep warm. Nothing stirred as the vessel moved further out to sea. Even the songbirds had gone. Their calls were now faint as they headed back to the land.

Just as dawn broke, a scream tore through the early morning light. John Wishart jumped up, clutching the dagger in his right hand, and rushed towards the old man. He had been thrashing around and had freed himself from the sailcloth he had used for warmth. He kicked Wishart, who was surprised at the man's unexpected strength.

Wishart raised his voice. 'I'm not here to hurt you. Be calm, my friend.'

Waking from his nightmare, the man clung to Wishart like a child seeking protection and reassurance, weeping tears of pain and relief.

Silently, de Charnay stepped behind Wishart and placed his hand on his shoulder. Wishart whipped around, wielding the dagger that had been concealed in his sleeve and planting its point firmly above his navel. Only a split second of recognition stopped him from pushing the blade firmly upwards into de Charnay's heart.

De Charnay stood back in shock.

'Excuse me,' he murmured, the cold of the dagger still touching his stomach.

Wishart replaced the dagger inside his left sleeve.

He left the weeping man and walked to where he had spotted provisions tied to the side of the ship. He cut down a large chunk of dried meat and picked up some apples and a small wine flask.

While they ate voraciously, Wishart gave the heavy crested rings to de Charnay. He groaned as he sat down.

'Sir, I need your help. I'm hoping these rings might explain what happened.' Wishart placed them carefully in de Charnay's palm.

De Charnay examined the rings. Wishart sensed he recognised the seals as he scrutinised them.

'Where did you find these?' De Charnay asked as he turned the rings around and around between his thumb and middle finger.

'I took them from the two dead knights I found on the deck over there,' Wishart replied, pointing to a bloodstained patch near the front of the ship. 'I think these men were the last to die. One was still warm when I found them together. The others were very cold and seem to have died where I found them. The crew were unconscious before they were stabbed.'

'How do you know that?' De Charnay asked.

'The crewmen's shoes had no blood on their soles, and what's more interesting is that the knights were without shoes, but had bloodied feet. They were probably hiding amongst the treasure chests before they slaughtered everyone - or maybe it was someone else who did this. Don't you think it would be strange to stab people with your shoes off? The pilot boat is also missing. It might have drifted off, but more likely someone left here alive.'

Wishart nodded at the one survivor, who was still ravenously eating. The old man ignored the attention and was focused on the food as he rocked to and fro, excited and delighted by it as if it were a banquet fit for a king.

'I hope we can get some sense out of him, but I don't think that will happen any time soon. I need to know what happened because we have stumbled upon a secret that we were not meant to find. I'm sure you have noticed we have a mutilated crew for company and a barge bursting with treasure.' Wishart paused. He felt that de Charnay knew who the rings belonged to, but de Charnay said nothing and looked away.

The frustration in Wishart's voice was palpable. 'Oh, and just in case you were thinking it wasn't quite desperate enough, we've no charts, we're lost, and unless we work together, we will all end up dead.'

De Charnay hesitated, and Wishart understood he would have his own set of questions about his rescue from Acre and Wishart's motivations.

'Be reassured that I have been sent here to save and protect you,' Wishart said. 'Nothing else. These murders, this barge, and the treasure aren't part of my plan.'

The old man was oblivious to the conversation between Wishart and de Charnay. He stuffed meat into the gap between his threadbare shirt and his jerkin and did not move his head away from the food.

'Before I will tell you anything, I need to know more,' de Charnay said. 'Why did you come so far to rescue a stranger? An action for which, I may add, I am forever in your debt, John.'

The fog was beginning to lift as the sun's rays burned through the thick black line of the horizon, signalling the end of the night's dark hold.

'I saved you because I am a soldier and agent of His Grace, Bishop Wishart of Glasgow,' Wishart said, 'and he told me to find you, and remove you from any harm.'

De Charnay said nothing, but Wishart could see in his face that he recognised his brother's name and position. De Charnay seemed relieved by his response, and he sighed deeply.

'I can help you,' de Charnay said. 'I can sail this barge. I should have spoken earlier, but I did not know if I could trust you. I have sailed through these waters many times since I was a boy, and I need no charts to navigate a route away from Acre. My family were traders long before I joined the Templar Order, and I have an aptitude for remembering things. I studied the stars, you see, and can navigate as any captain would. The stars tell you where you are and point to the whole world if you have the whole world in your head.' De Charnay tapped his forehead as he spoke. 'And during the day, the currents and the colour of the water are all I need - and of course the sun, which is conveniently rising.'

He pointed to the west. 'God is with us indeed. The currents are pushing us west towards my lands, and towards safety. As you said, with a king's ransom and a dead crew on our hands, we need to land with secrecy. That will be difficult, as two of the dead men we travel with are not the sort of whose demise will go unnoticed.'

De Charnay spoke quietly as he placed the rings back in Wishart's hand. 'These two knights are strange shipmates. The ring with the golden cross emblazoned with the imperial eagle belongs to a German knight: Konrad von Feuchtwangen. Do not let that fool you, though; he is not working for any German tyrant, but for one much closer to your home: King Edward of England. He is the King's leading assassin, and he was out here to kill someone. Wherever there is an unexplained death that is convenient for the Plantagenet, you can be sure von Feuchtwangen's greasy finger are almost always on the corpse.' De Charnay paused. 'And we can discount ourselves as his target. If that were the case, we would not be here discussing his death over his cooling corpse. He was King Edward's trusted assassin - not because he was stupid or careless. If he were after us, we would already be dead.'

Wishart pressed. 'Don't hold back: I need to know everything, brother de Charnay. Please, the other knight. Who is he?'

'Ah, that makes this conundrum even more fascinating. The other ring, the one with the cross sable with five scallop shells, belongs to Jean de Grailly, an agent of the King of France, Philip IV "Le Bel". He is of the same profession as Konrad, but that is where the connection ends. A man devoted to his master in Paris, and with the mark of the assassin etched through his dark soul. The fact that these men were on the same ship means this ship and this treasure are no secret. I have no doubt King Philip and King Edward sent them here.' De Charnay paused and wiped the sweat away from his forehead.

'What I cannot work out is, why kill the crew? If you wanted the treasure, you would need the crew alive to escape Acre and get back home. Perhaps what we think is true is in fact false.' John had an enquiring, clever mind and it was clear he wanted to understand the story of these men he never knew; he grasped at least some of their possible motivations.

'What do you mean?' De Charnay asked.

'Konrad von Feuchtwagen and Jean de Grailly are assassins, not treasure hunters. The man with the scallop shell ring, the one you said was Jean de Grailly - he was still warm when I found him, so he died last, having probably killed the German and succumbed to his wounds. I am speculating. The only one who can confirm this is the old man here, who seems to have lost his wits.'

Wishart noticed de Charnay was unsteady, but he moved to the mast and pulled hard on the rope tied to it. The single red sail swung to the right as he pulled the rope further, and the light breeze caught hold of the sailcloth and pushed the barge westwards.

'The sun is rising,' de Charnay said. 'It will warm the air and strengthen the wind, and we can head straight towards the Venetian Lagoon.'

The barge was in full sail, and de Charnay tied the rope to a metal hook that was on the port side of the ship. Wishart simply stared as de Charnay moved with increasing confidence despite his groaning.

'I have told you about the rings. My guess is we have stumbled upon something big - something that started in the courts of France and England and, for some reason, has ended in this Godforsaken place. Perhaps Jean de Grailly was protecting the old man, given he is the only survivor. Seems a possibility, don't you think?'

Wishart nodded because he had no rationale to disagree, and it was an explanation where none was obvious.

De Charnay held the rudder tightly with both hands as the breeze strengthened, crashing the barge through the swell. The mist was clearing, and with a following wind, the heavy ship flattened each wave. De Charnay was getting every ounce of speed out of the cumbersome barge.

Wishart watched de Charnay work. He was surprised by the man's skill and deftness in handling the barge alone, but he felt sufficiently comfortable to ask for more information. 'Bishop Wishart asked me to put a question to you that might help explain why he sent me to rescue you. I am to ask you whether it is true about the Fair Maid of Brittany.'

De Charnay continued to steer the barge, but Wishart could see the question meant something important to him.

'What do *you* know about the Fair Maid of Brittany?' Asked de Charnay. Wishart felt immediately de Charnay's discomfort in his tone.

'I thought I was asking the questions,' Wishart replied. 'For what it's worth, I know nothing of this woman.'

De Charnay moved towards the mainsail, finessing the angle of the sail again so that the barge could push faster towards the west. Wishart remained seated, as his sea legs were rapidly escaping him.

The barge was now moving with considerable speed - so much so that the keel was creating a swell, and water and foam were beginning to wash the deck of its crimson coating.

'For generations, the Order has used my family to carry forbidden knowledge - notes so secret that pen and paper could not be used to capture their content. I was party to the secrets of all the kings and tyrants, taking their whispered words from court to court and plotter to plotter. It was the old King of Scotland, Alexander, who told me about the Fair Maid - the Pearl, or Damsel, of Brittany.' As he spoke, he brushed his tatty, bloody tabard down, smoothing the creased red cross down over his chest.

'The Fair Maid was the eldest daughter of Geoffrey, the fourth son of Henry II, King of England. You see, she was the next in line - not King John. King Edward's grandfather, John, was Henry's fifth son. There was some rumour that she married and that there may have been a child.'

'King Alexander never let facts cloud a good rumour,' Wishart scoffed. 'Sounds like a lie.'

'Yes, it does. Yet it came from the mouth of a King, and he believed it. So do I. You asked me if it was true about the Fair Maid of Brittany, and my answer is yes. It may just be court gossip, embarrassing yet threatening enough that King

Edward would want it silenced.'

Wishart understood now why the Bishop wanted de Charnay alive - to stir things up. King Alexander had died five years ago, and this secret with him. De Charnay must be one of the few people alive who had talked with the King about this matter.

'We will head to the nearest friendly port,' de Charnay said. 'If this wind keeps up, we will hit the Venetian coast soon - if we can avoid pirates and sandbanks.'

Wishart did not need to give his permission.

De Charnay continued. 'This barge is small, but it is heavily laden and will not escape attention. Fortunately, I have some friends who can help us.'

As he pulled hard on the rudder again, Wishart stumbled, and the old man cried out. It felt as if they had hit something solid, but it was nothing more than the waves, increasing in size and strength.

'The attention this treasure will attract will be as dangerous as the siege we have just escaped, so I suggest we land at night,' Wishart said. He did not know Venice and its politics, but their situation demanded the secrecy night provided.

'You are right,' de Charnay said, 'so I have a mind to sail up through a small tributary of the River Brenta to Padua,' he gestured with his hand to show how they would move fishlike up from the Adriatic.

'This barge has a shallow draught and is small enough to navigate the river, and the Paduans are no friends of the avaricious Venetian pirates, who would steal the skin off your back if there was a market for it. I have friends there who will keep us and our secret safe.' De Charnay paused as he fastened a rope to the mast.

'We will keep away from the Venetian coast until dark; otherwise, we will be fish bait for the Venetian galleys that prey on those who sail within sight of land. The worst thief is the doge himself!' de Charnay chuckled.

Wishart had the sense of this man's intelligence. It did not surprise him that the Bishop valued him. This was someone who might just be pragmatic enough to survive through charm and intelligence, and John Wishart valued those things too.

De Charnay pointed to the old man, who was eating an apple with all the skill and dexterity of a small child. 'I can't see us putting up much of a fight if we do get spotted. What do you think?'

'On the contrary. I am a wily, determined Scot - how can we fail? And the old man … is someone to protect. We are saving the meek. That's what your order is all about.'

Wishart laughed, and de Charnay smiled and nodded - then flinched in pain.

'My brother sent me thousands of miles to risk my life for you and bring you back,' Wishart said. 'You must matter a great deal!'

Wishart sensed de Charnay was scrutinising him. He wondered if de Charnay had recognised the Bishop in him.

'Let us make your rescue successful and get everyone and everything to a safe place.' De Charnay patted Wishart on the back, and he felt reassured.

The sun was becoming stronger, and the corpses, which had been washed and tied, were beginning to smell. Wishart's nostrils flared with the odour.

'I suggest we jettison these unfortunate souls immediately to the deep, or the Venetians will smell us coming.'

Wishart lifted each corpse over the side, and they sank quickly into the currents and swell. As he did, he observed de Charnay whispering a prayer for the dead.

At last, the old man finished eating. He began to chatter.

'Un faldestoed i unt fait tut d'or mer,
La siet li reis ki dulce France tient.
Blanche ad la barbe e tut flurit le chef,

Gent ad le cors e le cuntenant fier -
S'est k'il demandet, ne l'estoet enseigner.'

De Charnay started to translate the French into English.

'Upon a faldstool wrought in purest gold,
Sits Charlemagne, the King who rules all France.
White is his beard, and hoary is his head,
His stature noble and his countenance proud -
No need to point him out to any man.'

Wishart placed a hand on the man's shoulder. 'No peasant or serf would know the *Song of Roland*. Who are you? Where do you come from?'

The old man grasped Wishart's hand, rubbed it against his cheek, and started to weep again.

'Our travelling companion is truly an enigma - or so scarred by what has happened to him that he has lost his wits,' said de Charnay.

'That's why he needs our protection. I'll take him back to Scotland.'

*

The old man sang, and the Templar and his Scottish saviour drank, laughed, and talked - and drank some more as each night passed.

Fortune was protecting them and their secret whilst thwarting their pursuers. God was indeed on their side.

Chapter One

Glasgow, February 11th, 1306: The Storm Begins

The cathedral was the centre of the world for Bishop Wishart. As he looked upwards from the outside, he could see only too well the leaking roof in the bell tower that held his Bishop's chair. This sacred space was where his congregation and his priests did their praying.

The chants of the liturgy seemed to warm the bitingly cold air outside the leaking building. A small group of monks and novices had huddled together in the western transept to complete the required rituals that brought form, substance, and - for a short time - calm amidst the prevailing atmosphere of conflict and chaos. For many years now, this had been the only place where the clergy and the people could seek peace and sanctuary.

The Bishop was maturing in years like a fine wine, he thought, but he could not pretend he did not feel every chill. His cloak and vestments had once been fine and opulent, but he did not care for frippery now. He wore them for their warmth - but the damp climate still gnawed into his bones. There was a food stain on the front of his shirt, and he looked disappointedly at the result of his own clumsiness. He had more important things to worry him, however.

He had discovered, much to his indignation, that often, when he woke up, something in his body that had been performing perfectly adequately the previous day had decided not to function anymore. The superficial trappings of a bishop would not save him from this decay, but these were afflictions of his body, not his mind.

He had the mind of an athlete and the body of a pugnacious sixty-year-old cleric. He observed everything and missed nothing. He was smart as well as sharp, with green eyes, pale skin, and thick luxurious snow-white hair, which he liked to grow longer than a respectable churchman should. It was his one indulgence that he knew was frippery, but he decided even a bishop should never be perfect: that was the reserve of Christ, and he should have at least one flaw.

His outdoor cloak was open and hung untidily on his shoulders as he walked the short distance from his lodgings towards his cathedral. His cloak of thick, greased wool had kept the rain from penetrating his vestments, hose, and tunic. He only wished he could use the same method to protect his monks, priests, and congregation from the elements, never mind the ruinously expensive craftsmen who were extending his western transept and reconstructing his bell tower.

Just outside the transept door, the Molendinar Burn ran around the cathedral into the Clyde, creating a perfect spot for the only bridge across the Molendinar. Access to the bridge was indiscriminate, and it brought friends and enemies alike to the cathedral and its market, but in these difficult times, enemies were numerous and friends more difficult to find.

The money generated from the relics and the cult of Saint Kentigern allowed the Bishop to fix his cathedral and finance his rebellions. Their reverence and worship brought in money from pilgrims, traders, and much to his ironic satisfaction, the pious and not-so-pious English, who were his nosey neighbours. Their money was used to fight them. He found that amusing.

The English were too near for his liking - a short distance away in the castle across the square that separated his cathedral and his lodgings. He tweaked his nose at them every day as he passed. It was most unchristian, but he felt the better for it.

Scotland might be under occupation, but the Scottish

Church was still independent. If it remained, so did hope. Scotland was not finished just yet.

Bishop Wishart had supported many insurrections, and in the Wallace rebellion he had been lucky not to be executed. Wallace had been gone but a few months, and his quartered body still rotted on the gates of Berwick. That event had convinced the English that Scotland was defeated.

A myth had already grown that Wallace's finger bones pointed portentously to the north, as if in his death, he knew the war was not finished. Things were looking bad, and the embers of freedom were only just alight.

The English King was old and decaying, not far short of threescore and ten. He did not have long to live, and his son was an arrogant man who was full of hubris. Bishop Wishart's existence was dedicated to preserving the remaining support for independence and waiting for the elder English tyrant to die.

The elderly King's attempts to take over Scotland had been far more successful than his attempts to take over the nation's Church, and Wishart would continue to fight that with all his being. If the Church lost that battle, Scotland would lose everything and would be unable to reclaim the sovereignty that an independent Church brought. The English King wanted to destroy the one institution that was continuous and gave the nation hope. He also wanted to destroy Wishart. However, this was not so easy - even for a wily old fox like the King of England - for Scotland still had powerful allies in the Papacy and the French. Whilst Wishart knew these alliances were not to be relied upon, he never looked on providence as anything less than a gift from God, and he would make friends with the Devil himself if it would help Scotland remove the English from its soil.

It was beginning to rain again, and his thoughts turned back to the building site that had been his cathedral.

Bishop Wishart looked again at the bell tower, and he

heard the large raindrops echoing as they bounced off the darkening stone. He sighed. Water was slowly gouging at all the wall paintings and carvings and would soon weaken and crack the huge stone pillars that held the roof.

He could also hear his masons, including the remarkable Master Mathew - the head mason and architect - who was shouting orders and encouragement at his subordinates. He had some bad news to deliver to Master Mathew regarding his scaffolding, and it was a difficult message.

Wishart visualised the confrontation and rehearsed out loud what he was going to say. He could not explain that they were really doing God's work by helping the cause of independence. If his false explanation sounded convincing to himself, then he was sure Master Mathew would believe him too. He had lied to the best of them, even to kings, but he felt ashamed lying to an honest man like Mathew.

The stout wooden scaffolding poles were currently being transported north to Saint John's town of Perth to be converted into siege engines for a forthcoming battle at Cupar Castle. Scotland's enemies were many, and the castle's current occupants were the English garrison, assisted by Scottish traitors. Both were to be removed, and many sacrifices would need to be made if this new rebellion were to succeed. Wishart feared that by being honest with Mathew about his plans, he might put him at risk should he be arrested by the English. He had decided to lie to protect his dear friend and buy some time before he could secure additional wood to replace the timbers he had allocated to the Cupar siege.

He had other deadly weapons in reserve that he would not hesitate to use when the timing was right. He thought of his brother and his great friend Geoffroi de Charnay, and smiled.

Wishart could hear the masons, but he remained hidden in a spot outside the wall surrounding the nave and, most importantly, away from the judgemental eye of Master Mathew.

*

Master Mathew was sitting on a plank with his back to the Bishop some hundred feet up off the ground, looking downwards from the bell tower. He was a solid, powerfully built man with a ruddy complexion - a testament to years in the open air.

Mathew took his cloth satchel, which still contained the scant remains of his lunch of mutton and fruit. Picking up the bones and apple cores, he carefully placed them behind the stone he had just finished carving. With great effort, he pushed the stone back into place, entombing the food relics for a future generation to find. He knew his work would last for a thousand years if it was not destroyed by all the water leaking in through the roof. He needed to talk urgently with the Bishop.

Where was his new scaffolding? Every time he had gently introduced the subject, the Bishop had headed off in the other direction without answering his questions. He was even told that the English had paid for it, such was the pressing need.

He was sure that an order had been made and that stout oak beams had been sent from the forests of Cannock.

In the dim light of this late winter day, Mathew recognised one of the apprentices, and a plan sprang rapidly to mind.

The apprentice was taller than his peers, and Mathew could just make out the profile of Bishop Wishart's nephew, Jamie. He had the lithe frame of a teenager not quite ready for the muscles a mason's life puts on a body. His clothes framed his body rather than fitted it and were still too large for his slim, athletic legs. Mathew valued intelligence: intelligent men were the best masons, and Jamie had already surprised him with his inquiring mind and wit. He had the advantage of being well connected with the Church through his uncle. Contacts and intelligence were a powerful combination if used correctly. Perhaps Jamie could find out what had happened to the scaffolding without the necessity of confrontation.

The previous summer, Bishop Wishart had come to Mathew and asked that John Wishart's eldest son be taken on as an apprentice. His brother John had disappeared at the French court whilst working on the Auld Alliance. John Wishart had been selected as someone who could be trusted with political negotiations requiring cunning and strength of will. These traits were appreciated and respected by Philip and his advisors, Charles de Valois, and Guillaume de Nogaret.

France had no great love for Scotland and had signed the Auld Alliance out of fear and hatred towards England. Anything they could do to take Edward's attention away from France and direct it somewhere else suited them.

Bishop Wishart had sent his brother to France to remind Philip of the terms of the alliance, which stated that France would help Scotland when its sovereignty was attacked, but the French King was the definition of duplicitous. He did not take kindly to being reminded of his obligations.

John had not returned from France and was presumed dead. Bishop Wishart felt guilty, and for the love for his brother, he looked after the boy. Mathew believed the bishop could see John so clearly within the boy, and he wanted to keep him close by as a reminder of what he had lost.

*

Bishop Wishart was still watching through a gap surrounding the door that led to the nave. He listened as Mathew shouted towards his head mason.

'Master Peter, how much longer can we work without more scaffolding?'

Before Peter could answer, the door to the nave banged against the metal frame, and Bishop Wishart breezed in.

Wishart shouted up to him. 'Mathew! Mathew, my good friend!'

'I see you have returned from some travels, Your Grace?' Mathew said as he climbed down the rickety scaffolding which creaked its fragility as he moved. The Bishop was wearing his riding coat to broadcast the fact.

'Mathew, I have good news about the timbers for the bell tower. I am assured the wood will be here next week. Prepare for that, dear boy. I know you will manage until then. Do you have your latest plans for me to peruse?'

The Bishop was ashamed by his deception, but he felt justified. and he knew Mathew would accept his tale.

Wishart delved into his pocket and produced a pair of lenses. If he held them close to his eyes, they worked magic, and he could make out Master Mathew as clearly as if his eyes were forty years younger. 'Please, go on.'

'Your Grace, the plans are in the chapter house, if you'd follow me,' Mathew said. 'But we need that wood.'

Mathew walked away, continuing to speak, but Bishop Wishart was dawdling several yards behind him, no longer listening.

Bang, bang!

The wind blasted through the nave as metal clashed on metal, and they heard cries as three knights forced their way past a small group of priests and apprentices, pushing them out the way in their haste.

Bishop Wishart turned to see the commotion. The masons and their apprentices grasped their hammers and chisels, watching with suspicion. Out of the corner of his eye, the Bishop saw Mathew fleeing to one of the small chapels, running down the nave towards the high scaffolding.

After twenty years of schism, unexpected visitors - especially those brandishing swords still covered in dried blood - were never good news.

The knights ran towards Bishop Wishart with their

swords held high in their hands. He did not move or try to defend himself. He could immediately tell that something terrible had happened. The knights were covered with the evidence of a frantic ride.

He braced himself for the blow, but before he could exhale, all three knights fell to their knees, placing their swords on the ground. The leading knight then stood, picking his sword up and placing it in its sheath.

The Bishop could not identify him, so thick was the mix of dried blood and mud obscuring his face, and many of the candles had blown out, making it harder to see. He was a tall man with a broad neck, a large head, and heavy features. He had the gait of a confident man, but there was something about him that made him distinctive. Exhaling, Bishop Wishart pulled the man into an embrace.

'My God, Lord Bruce.' Looking beyond him, he tried not to cry out. 'And who are these men with you?' The Bishop asked his voice was strained and he sensed the danger.

'This is my old friend, William de Irwyne. For his loyalty I made him my armour bearer.'

The Bishop could not recognise a man he had seen grow up and had educated at this very cathedral. 'Will – Is that really you? I hear the English have increased the bounty on your head to twenty pounds of silver - they must fear you.'

'Yes, Your Grace - it appears I have been killing too many of their soldiers and getting away with it. With the help of my Lord Kirkpatrick.'

Will gestured to his right, where Kirkpatrick stood. His bloodied face and hair were still matted with brains and flesh. Wishart winced as he looked at the deep cuts on his forehead and cheek; some tragedy had taken place.

'And lastly, my Lord Roger Kirkpatrick, welcome. I see your deeds on your face, my Lord. Indeed, I see that you have all shared in some slaughter. The English will be increasing the price on all your heads.'

'Yes, Your Grace, the English man who gave me these wounds is now dead, I made certain of that,' Kirkpatrick bowed in acknowledgement.

'Roger, you are young for such elevation. Lord Bruce is an excellent judge in such things and your courage will be of great use for our cause.'

The Bishop embraced the knights, and the atmosphere seemed to lose its tension; on seeing this, the masons returned to work.

Chapter Two

Glasgow Cathedral, Feb 11th, 1306: Confession and Absolution

Mathew had returned to his high vantage point and could see that Lord Robert Bruce's voice was raised and that he was shaking with emotion. He tried to hear all the words and in doing so nearly toppled off the high scaffold.

Bishop Wishart stood with his head slightly bowed, nervously rubbing his forehead. He replied with such vehemence that his voice rose above the noise of the masons and the rainstorm that had now erupted outside the nave, as if nature had already anticipated the gravity of the event.

Wishart shouted in frustration. 'It's too soon! What were you thinking about?'

Mathew had rarely heard the Bishop raise his voice except in high mass and was always surprised how someone of his small stature and late-middle age could fill a whole cathedral.

Wishart measured every response and outcome, almost as a chess player anticipated five or ten moves ahead. He was a man of considerable composure and rarely showed emotion. He considered every word and gesture, but this outburst was uncontrolled. Mathew dared not move.

Mathew believed the Bishop never asked a question to which he did not already know the answer. Whatever had happened clearly surprised and scared Wishart.

Mathew could see that Wishart's pain was real, born of frustration and exasperation. The Bishop paced up and down, rubbing his brow and repeating his unanswerable pleas. 'It is too soon, far too soon. What were you thinking about, Robert?'

Wishart pulled Robert towards him. Was it out of affection, anger, or frustration? Mathew could not tell.

He tried not to make any sound, though his heart was pounding in his chest, forcing him to breathe deeply. He moved silently, following Lord Robert and Bishop Wishart as they walked towards the completed end of the nave, about three hundred feet away from his hiding place. He expected the scaffolding to give way at any moment. He would have to climb onto the roof timbers if his eavesdropping were to continue.

Kirkpatrick and de Irwyne remained close to the cathedral entrance and stood shivering from the draught. Wishart and Bruce were now well out of earshot of everyone, but Master Mathew's curiosity had gotten the better of him. He stepped from the scaffolding onto a wooden ledge above the nave with an agility that surprised him.

The Bishop removed his damp woollen cloak and threw it to the ground as he entered the small gate into his private chapel, out of sight of everyone - or so he thought.

'I wasn't expecting a visit,' he heard the Bishop say, 'and from the state of you and your escort, I knew the news was bad.'

Wishart moved closer and, in a voice that was only just under control, added, 'You have the evidence of this heinous deed on your person, and you brought this sacrilege into my cathedral? What drove you to do such a thing? You were to talk with Comyn, not kill him. We did not need to kill him now. He had already agreed to support you taking the throne, and we needed this truce in place until the time was right. You understood we were to deal with Comyn when Longshanks was dead.'

The Bruce retorted sharply. 'Comyn was never going to allow me to be King. He was already negotiating with

Longshanks's son.'

Mathew saw the Bishop look up, and for a moment he thought himself discovered.

'By killing John Comyn at the altar of Greyfriars Monastery, you managed to make a martyr of him, a hero for Longshanks to avenge, and opened the throne room for that degenerate son of his as heir to our kingdom. We will certainly lose what support we had from the Papacy and the French King. You could not have done a better job getting sympathy for the English King if you had designed it so!'

Mathew saw Wishart cross himself, and he leaned further out from his hiding place.

'Comyn was a traitor.' The Bruce preened self-righteously. 'I have letters from him to King Edward betraying us all! Lord de Monthermer might be Longshank's son-in-law, but he is our ally and warned me that the King meant to arrest me at last month's court in Winchester and give my lands to Comyn.'

The chants of the liturgy had begun, and they resonated as far as the private chapel where the two men argued.

'I was meant to be Longshanks's honoured guest,' Bruce said. 'Honoured guest? Bollocks. It was a trap, and that traitor Comyn wanted me arrested and out of the way - wanted my lands! I sent Will to tell Comyn to meet me. It was to talk ... only to talk. But then he showed me a copy of a letter for Longshanks betraying us all. He deserved to die.'

Even a lowly mason knew that when the heir to the Scottish crown had murdered his rival on the altar of a church, he would be damned by both the English and Scottish nobles. This would not be a secret for long - but what they did about it might be.

Mathew could just hear Bruce's voice, which was still raised but cracking with emotion.

'Comyn came to the meeting having already sent word to Longshanks. He had hidden a dagger under the altar cloth to kill me. I meant no harm, but he was there for a fight!'

The Bruce pulled a bloodstained parchment from his leather jerkin.

'Read this! See, it has Comyn's seal attached.' Bruce shoved the paper into the Bishop's hand.

Mathew could see the Bishop studying the letter.

'And in his own hand … Comyn wouldn't trust a steward to ask for your arrest and mine. He would be in fear of his own people betraying him.'

Wishart threw the letter down onto the floor. 'No doubt Longshanks planned to put Comyn on the throne as his puppet. He sold us all out, and you were to pay a traitor's death, Lord Robert. Damn his treachery!'

'He came to Greyfriars to taunt me, knowing Longshanks would make him the new King of Scots and get rid of me at the same time.'

The Bruce had his face a few inches from the Bishop. 'And he did not need you either, Your Grace! He had thrown his lot in with Longshanks and would use the English to gain his throne. Your independent Scottish Church would have been given up for his ambition.'

'Your outrage is understandable.' The Bishop lectured Lord Bruce, struggling to conceal his feelings that this action was biblically stupid. 'You needed to confront Comyn on his betrayal, but unseen, anonymous, without any trace back to you or me. Did you not consider the place and the implications? A King in waiting needs to think at length and act with caution. Otherwise, he will end up isolated and dead. You will force actions for which we are unprepared!'

Mathew could see the Bruce was now pacing around the small chapel, listening like a scolded child.

'The English cannot let this affront to their dignity go unavenged. You have provided the perfect excuse they require to destroy our reputation and ally with the Papacy and the French. Aymer de Valence is married to Comyn's sister and cousin to the King so it is doubly personal. I have no doubt King Edward will send another army to capture you and your supporters and will urge his brother-in-law King Philip to use his influence with the Pope, firstly to have you excommunicated, and secondly to have me removed from my seat and replaced by the Archbishop of York.'

The Bruce looked down at the floor as if he were embarrassed at his own rashness and stupidity.

'In one act, Robert, you have given the English the advantage. We are now in the position in which they want us - without a friend or ally in Europe.'

Mathew watched the argument, waiting for the opportunity to escape. His bladder, full of ale, was now demanding to be emptied.

'I can't undo what you've done, so I need to manage it,' Wishart snapped. 'I need to think. Where is Comyn now?'

'I thought I had killed him in the church, but I was brought word he was still alive, though gravely wounded. Lord Kirkpatrick went back and finished him off. His face is a bloodied testament to that!' Bruce wiped away the perspiration that was carrying blood and dirt into his eyes. 'Sir John Lindsay remained in Dumfries with some of my retinue. They fought Comyn's supporters in the burial ground. Roger, Will, and I left, and Lindsay was to make certain that none of Comyn's men survived.'

Wishart interrupted. 'Alea iacta est. The die has been cast, and we need to act decisively! Comyn's family will have dispatched a message to the English King, and it will be on its way to him in Winchester. The King will then send the news to the French court and then to the Papal Curia asking for your immediate excommunication – that will take about three weeks and Pope Clement will be compelled to act by return – a further four weeks.' The Bishop hesitated.

'That gives us about six or at best seven weeks to carry out my plan for your coronation before the bull for your excommunication arrives here and I am forbidden to anoint you on pain of my own damnation. We will have you crowned King within the month. You will leave for Scone immediately.'

Mathew gasped as he heard the Bishop promise to crown Lord Robert.

'My coronation ... Scone?' The Bruce replied in shock.

'That is where they crown Kings,' the Bishop said. 'You need the legitimacy of a legal coronation; your kingship must be legitimate and that can only happen in Scone. I will send a messenger to Bishop Lamberton and the other bishops to make ready. They know what to do. They have always known this day would come. I even have your robes prepared.'

Mathew saw that Bishop Wishart had calmed himself sufficiently that his shock at Bruce's act of violence and sacrilege had dissipated.

'Robert, you always knew to take the throne was the course God had set for you. Now you have a clear choice to become a King or a fugitive, and it has always been in my mind that you should become our King. I have planned this since the Fair Maid died.'

Mathew was amazed at how deeply the Bishop was involved in this rebellion. This declaration was unambiguous.

The Bruce knelt before Wishart, and the Bishop turned his back. Mathew could not clearly see what was going on, apart from the movement of the Bishop's right hand over Bruce's head.

Wishart spoke. 'Robert, the English already believe I corrupt the ears of noble and commoner alike, and I am already under threat of banishment from my flock and my land, but this act of absolution is sincere and properly done.'

The Bishop spoke the words of the absolution.

Robert Bruce stood up and kissed the Bishop on both cheeks. The Bishop dropped to the ground and knelt before

Bruce.

'On behalf of the Guardians and the people of Scotland, and before God, I acknowledge you as the true and undisputed King of the Scots. Do you accept the acclamation of God, the Church, and your people?' The Bishop's voice faltered as one large tear began to run from his right eye.

The Bruce's lips moved incoherently in response. He grabbed at the Bishop to make him stand, but the Bishop merely grabbed the Bruce's hand and kissed it.

Bruce paused and mumbled, 'Yes.'

'Go now, Lord Robert, and without a sound! Make haste to Perth, and I will send a messenger ahead of you to make the necessary arrangements. You must not remain here; I will meet you as soon as circumstances dictate. Go across the Molendinar at its ford, not over the bridge where you will be noticed. I, too, must make plans to leave: I suspect I'll shortly be the very centre of King Edward's vengeance.'

Master Mathew knew the real story would not be Comyn's murder, but the revelation of Bishop Wishart's absolution and planned coronation of Bruce. He saw the two men appear to seal the deal with an embrace that sanctioned a coronation and rebellion. This was significant indeed.

Lord Robert turned and left the private chapel, and quickly walked towards the heavy main door where his men were still standing. Mathew stood even tighter against the buttress, fearing discovery at any moment.

Bishop Wishart shouted after the fleeing knight. 'One small favour, Lord Robert!'

Lord Robert stopped. 'Anything, Your Grace,' he replied as the Bishop drew closer.

'Leave young Will de Irwyne behind. I have something important for him to do.'

Lord Robert thought for a second, then nodded. The Bishop followed him whilst Master Mathew remained silent and hidden in the ever-increasing shadow of darkness.

He watched as the Bishop put his arm around Lord Robert, and together with Roger Kirkpatrick, walked towards the cathedral door in the direction of the Molendinar Burn. The Bishop hesitated and stopped just as the others exited through the door before turning to look above where he had just walked and where Mathew was hiding. He darted behind a grotesque of a laughing devil. The Bishop stared hard for a moment, scrutinising the nave below before smiling and following Lord Kirkpatrick through the open door.

Master Mathew's heart pounded, but he remained still until he was sure his eavesdropping had not been discovered, then at last returned to the chapter house unnoticed by his fellow masons.

He tried to calm himself after what he had just heard, but that was proving hard as his heart raced. His masons would be asking him the mundane - about scaffolding and how they could keep working - and he had just heard the extraordinary: about murder, treason, and rebellion. He had to appear normal, or his men would notice and make comment. He had to switch his mind to his work and nothing else.

Anxiously he drew a plan on a small slate tablet he carried with him, then wiped his face and hands with a cloth he had removed from his mason's sack. He looked to the heavens and spoke softly, but he was still shaking.

'I am doing my best, Lord! My absolute best!'

Chapter Three

Great Hall, Winchester Castle, February 23rd, 1306: Raise Dragon

It was barely half past six on the morning after the royal banquet, and the hall was quiet apart from the soft-footed servants sweeping away the dirty rushes that covered the corridors between the great hall and the retiring rooms that lay beyond.

Edward Plantagenet, the first of that name, named for the Confessor and the fifth of the dynasty, sat alone by the fire. A grey-bearded man with his left eyelid drooping so that it was almost closed, clad in rich crimson velvet and a shirt of the finest embroidered silks, he stretched out his long limbs, yawned, and leaned back on his chair.

Putting the carver on its back legs, he made a soft squeaking noise as he gently rocked the chair back and forth. His gnarled hands gripped the arms of the chair tightly, exposing his pale, wrinkled knuckles stained with the liver spots of old age.

Within his left sleeve, a small, tightly rolled parchment was just visible above the richly embroidered gold edging.

He pulled out the document and, drawing a candle towards him, studied the script like a surgeon scrutinizing a tumour. He read it again and again before squeezing the small scroll back into his sleeve.

'God, give me revenge!' he screamed. 'Damn Bruce! That insolent dog will pay! And damn all the Scots back to hell. I will burn the land and kill their families.'

John Comyn had been his cousin by marriage, a loyal ally, and the brother-in-law of his champion knight, the heir to the Earl of Pembroke, Aymer de Valence. He was one of the King's family and not subject to the summary justice of Scottish rebels.

The previous month, Comyn had warned him here of Bruce's royal ambitions and had only escaped arrest by fleeing in the dead of night. Edward knew he had been warned by another traitor whom the King had yet to find.

Edward had a looking glass on his table and picked it up vainly, preening himself as he gazed on his face and considered what he saw. He had been self-conscious all his life, with a drooping left eyelid that had made him appear initially young and sinister, and now old and sinister.

You look magnificent in your velvets and ermine even at near seventy years old. Men tremble in your presence and that still feels good after all these years. All men except the Scots.

'Damn all these troublesome Scots!' he shouted knowing it was wiser to be quiet - retiring he was not. He had to react in an extreme manner and squash this rebellion: any procrastination would look weak. The vultures within the court were waiting for him to fail in Scotland; there was always somebody else ready to be King. He started a silent prayer and gazed towards the ceiling.

He glimpsed the round table that hung on the wall of the great hall above his throne for all to see, and reminding the court that his divine power lay in his descent and inheritance from the legendary King Arthur.

I am King Arthur, and I rule the whole of this island. You will regret the day you crossed me, Scottish bastard!

His blood was pumping hard, and it was difficult for him to keep calm. He threw the looking glass down, shattering its face into shards. What had gone wrong with his plans, so carefully crafted, to bribe or kill any Scot who challenged him?

The Scots should have lost their will to fight. The Scottish army had been humiliated at Dunbar, and not one castle of any substance remained in Scottish hands. He had even seen to it that the Scottish records had been burned so that there was no written history or memory that Scotland was a sovereign state. Someone was behind this plot.

He instinctively knew who was behind this. 'Wishart!' he cried with such anger that it made him clench his teeth.

You exhale the stench of rebellion and treachery and I know your creation Bruce is not acting alone. You will never have the independence you crave, especially if I am still your King.

He knew why he was so agitated. Intelligent men caused greater trouble than brave ones, and ones with a claim to the Scottish crown made for a dangerous rebellion. Bruce was astute, strong, and he had purposeful men around him. Wishart was his tutor and was more intelligent and thus even more dangerous.

He rested all four chair legs against the wooden floor and gestured to one of the servants, who was still removing the remnants of the banquet.

'You, bring me that plate of bread and cheese you have in your hand and get me wine. Now!'

The boy's hands shook as he placed the silver plate on a small wooden side table next to the King. Edward stretched his hand out towards the dish. His fingers showed the trappings of kingship, including a large gold ring with an engraved purple amethyst cabochon.

He had liberated the ring from the traitor Wallace. He liked to wear it when he met the King of France as it seemed to torment him, and the French had made numerous attempts to get the ring back, even as part of the recent truce.

Momentarily, he held the stone up to the light.

'I wonder why the trappings of the dead matter so much

to you, my dear brother-in-law,' he whispered.

'Fetch Lord Pembroke, now!' he ordered the serjeant at arms, who grabbed a lit torch from next to the main door leading out of the hall, almost dropping it in his haste. The King had begun to eat and was oblivious to his clumsiness.

The King greedily ate and drank as he waited for his cousin. He needed to eat when he was agitated, and his appetite was always healthy despite his tall lithe frame.

Within minutes of his order, the doors flung open and the serjeant of arms and Pembroke's steward walked briskly into the room.

Aymer de Valence strutted behind them brushing and straightening his hair and tabard with his hand. He had the arrogant gait of a bull-headed bully with a sense of entitlement that exceeded even the King's. Sallow-skinned, tall, and muscular, he was a generation younger than his cousin.

'Sire, my steward woke me on your orders. I surmised it must be important at this early hour, but I still beat him anyway.'

The King laughed out loud. 'Yes cousin – at this moment I need a brave man not a fair one.'

*

The steward stood silent, his head bowed and his eye red and swollen in the shape of a fist. Murdie MacBeith loathed everything about Aymer de Valence, but he had to put up with him. Such was the life of an indentured servant.

*

'Cousin, fetch a stool and sit; send your servant away.' The King raised his hand to point to the other side of the fireplace.

'Aymer de Valence sat on a backless stool as Edward passed him the message.

'No doubt you will recognise the writing on the outside, my Lord.'

The King watched him read the news of his brother-in-law's death at Bruce's hand. He could see de Valence's face reddening.

'I want you to make Bruce a fugitive from his kin and people. I want Wishart, his cabal, and any man and their families connected with the Bruce dead, and their heads brought before me.'

De Valence said nothing. He stood and kicked the stool into the air, launching it halfway across the hall. The veins in his neck stood bold, and he clenched the parchment in his hand.

The King placed his hand on the earl's arm. 'We had already sent word to the garrison in Glasgow to arrest Bishop Wishart following Bruce's escape from court, but this escalation raises him to a new level of treachery. Give no quarter, no chivalry, no mercy, no rules. I want you to "Raise Dragon", lay waste to Scotland and teach these rebels a lesson they will remember for a hundred years.'

De Valence clenched his fists by his side. 'Sire, he will be under arrest soon, but as for gathering up the rest, we will need a show of overwhelming force and assemble an army. We need to catch and kill Bruce before he gains momentum and is joined by other rebels.'

'Aymer, be cautious. We have a traitor in this court who works for Bruce's cause'. The King's face was flushed purple, and his voice trembled with rage; the earl was visibly shocked, 'Sire, no one in the English court would take the side of the Scots.'

'You are wrong Pembroke, remember Bruce fled just before I ordered his arrest, so now we will act quietly in assembling our northern cohorts. Keep my council and hide your anger, and by spring we will have the four thousand men at arms we require. I am sure the allies of Comyn will add their men and swell our numbers. I will write to Lady Comyn to that effect.'

The King looked for something amongst the items now messily strewn on his table and covered with glass from the shattered eyeglass. 'Indeed, I will find other, less orthodox, means to find this traitor. We must use someone nearer to the Scottish court to sniff him out. I have someone in mind. I will write to him in Scotland once I find pen and parchment.'

He threw most of the contents of the table adjacent on the floor taking no regards for the glass, diplomatic papers and death sentences.

'Damn it – fetch me writing materials!' The King stood, and all the servants took this as a signal to simultaneously leave the hall in pursuit of paper, pen and ink. The steward, the King's guards and serjeant remained - stationary and at attention.

The King embraced Aymer. That was unusual for him, who had little warmth for anyone, but he knew this gesture would add an extra seal on the deal and help Aymer understand how much the King needed him to be successful in capturing Bruce and Wishart.

'I remember that our fathers shared a mother and the same blood,' Edward said. 'Go, make haste, my cousin. I could only give this task to one such as you. Avenge our loss and bring me Bruce's head.'

As Valence went to leave, the King called him back purposely.

'I have word of Innes de Mayon, Wishart's agent in Rouen and an old acquaintance of your wife. Didn't they share a friendship?'

Valence nodded. 'Beatrice and he were close.'

The King had deliberately exploited an open sore and could see the pain and anger in Valence's face.

'He is back plotting with King Philip and Wishart and is to be found in Rouen,' Edward said. 'I am sure that, as part of your rounding up of Wishart's cabal, you will make sure he does not leave Rouen alive.'

Valence stopped and snarled. 'So, the great traitor, de Mayon, has been located. I will get our agents in Rouen to search for him and bring his head back to this court. My immediate retinue will leave within the hour.'

The King gestured for the earl to leave and returned to his desk. He thought on the rebellion, unable to accept that Wishart had acted simply to protect Bruce, who would certainly be a pariah for killing in a church. Convincing people to rally to Bruce and accept his coronation would be difficult for Wishart. Even the greatest Scottish patriots would struggle to condone such sacrilege whilst at the same time acclaiming a new King.

Why is Wishart acting now? He has been quiet for many years – he should have waited until I was cold. He felt such a surge of panic and anxiety that he felt light-headed. He took some long breaths to stop his hands shaking before concluding. *Innes de Mayon is half Breton and his father Knox a despicable traitor ... I wonder if those damn Bretons are behind this. And there is always great uncle Geoffrey, dead over a hundred years, yet his family still haunts my throne.*

He had been King for over thirty years, anointed by God, and no one was going to destroy him or his legacy, especially not a provincial Bishop and a second-rate rebel.

He grasped a pen and began to scribble a note to all his commanders in Scotland, ordering them to arrest any man over sixty-five found with Wishart, and put him in solitary confinement. It seemed a strange thing for him to write such an order, and in his own hand. After all, de Valence had been tasked with finding and arresting Wishart. He only wrote the most important state matters in such a manner, and this was urgent and critical to the continued success of his rule. This personal touch would not be missed by his subordinates, and its importance would not be misunderstood.

*

'We return presently to your estates, my Lord?' Murdie asked, trying to elicit information on his master's meeting.

'Yes, indeed; make sure the men are in the courtyard and battle-ready. Fetch my cloak first, and once you have woken the rabble, follow me to the stables!'

The earl entered the courtyard that led to the stables. Murdie was surprised to see him so agitated, and this only increased his curiosity.

A storm was gathering pace, but the earl did not seem to notice. As the door to the courtyard closed, Murdie could hear the earl kicking and shouting at his soldiers who were sleeping off their hangovers in the courtyard and stables.

'Get up now, you brigands, and prepare to move. We are going to Scotland!'

Murdie hurried towards the sleeping rooms to rouse the earl's remaining men at arms and prepare them for war.

Time was short, but he would stop for a little while and write a short note to Ralph de Monthermer, Lord Bruce's most loyal friend in the English court, telling tales of invasion, betrayal, and raising the pennant of the dragon. Lord Monthermer would know what to do with this information, and Murdie would be rewarded. He would write a second letter to his real master, Bishop Wishart, for which he did not expect a reward.

Murdie McBeith played the steward, but was no fool. He pulled out his dagger and, in its smooth blade, caught his reflection. His face was a little rounder than it had once been, but still handsome in a rustic way. He could not risk being recognised in doing his dangerous work and had disguised his youth with the face of a much older man.

He conceded that he had put on a few pounds, but it was worth it. He pushed Baron Monthermer's letter back into his woollen shirt to conceal it from prying eyes.

'You look older, my friend, but after five years in this ungodly place, I am not surprised you have aged.' He ran his hands through his thinning, greying hair, emphasising the statement.

Now he had a sense that his work was being rewarded. He had never seen the old King and his slimy cousin so riled.

He could barely conceal his smile as he heard the screams of Aymer de Valence bullying his troops.

Men fight for Bishop Wishart because they want to, but they fight for you, Aymer de Valence, and Edward Plantagenet because they must. And that is why we will win.

'Steward, attend!'

Replacing his dagger, he hurried past the room where more soldiers were resting. Grabbing a full piss pail conveniently left outside the door, he threw it over the snoring soldiers.

'Get up now, you bastards! Lord Valence awaits us in the courtyard!' McBeith screamed. The pail came flying back towards him, but before it reached its target, he was away.

Chapter Four

Glasgow Cathedral, March 12th, 1306: The Storm Breaks

The Bruce and Lord Kirkpatrick had been gone several weeks.

The Bishop sat alone in his private chapel, knowing that a vicious storm was imminent. The English King would know about Comyn's death, and the Bishop would soon be arrested. But the important thing was that Bruce was still free.

The coronation was set for March 25, about two weeks from now. Bruce was safely hidden, with many miles between him and the pursuing followers of Comyn.

He heard someone approaching, but was not alarmed. The steps sounded like the soft leather soles of a running monk. The Bishop was praying as the elderly brother entered the chapel, stumbling and dragging his left leg behind his.

The brother's wet cassock was heavy and had caught the brunt of the pouring rain, which was now clattering purposefully on the stone roof, dancing and dripping on the scaffolding. His hood fell from his head. Panicking, he placed the damp cloth back on his head, pulling the back tightly down.

'That is right, Brother Geoffrey, cover your head. You must not run around the cathedral without your hood. You mustn't catch cold.'

Brother Geoffrey called out anxiously to the Bishop. 'Your Grace, Your Grace, we have English messengers in the courtyard.'

His gait was clumsy and awkward, lacking any rhythm and coordination. He was a small man with a slight stoop and a pale pink complexion. His greying and thinning hair was streaked with pale red strands, and his thin, transparent skin was faintly wrinkled but tinged with an overly red complexion. His features were largely obscured by a woollen hood and eye patch that covered part of his face as well as his left eye. The Bishop had kept him working in the tannery attached to the cathedral grounds, where the smell ensured that there were very few visitors.

The Bishop sensed in his tone that these messengers were not the friendly kind, and held his arms out in an embrace, steadying Brother Geoffrey and holding him upright. 'Brother, catch your breath and tell me your news. Do the English have their swords drawn?'

Brother Geoffrey nodded.

'I was expecting them,' the Bishop said.

The soldiers were rounding up Bruce's supporters. If they had known he had absolved Bruce and was planning to crown him, the cathedral doors would be in pieces, and he would be on a gibbet. These visitors were on another quest and not one of King Robert Bruce.

Will de Irwyne entered the cathedral via the private chapel, avoiding the courtyard and the soldiers.

'Good morning, Will. It appears we have some English visitors,' the Bishop's voice had a worried edge to it.

From outside, the Bishop could hear the anxious stirring of the masons, who could see the soldiers from their scaffolds.

'Geoffrey, did you recognise them?' The Bishop spoke loudly, as it had begun to hail. 'Are these men from Glasgow Castle?'

'They wear the tunics of the castle.'

Bishop Wishart pulled the brother closer. 'No one saw you watching them, did they, dear Brother Geoffrey?'

Brother Geoffrey shook. 'N-n-no, Your Grace,' he

stammered. 'I was careful not to be seen by the soldiers.'

The Bishop kissed Geoffrey softly on the forehead and, taking his hand, walked towards his nephew Jamie, who was peering through the small oriel windows that overlooked the courtyard.

'Good morning, Your Grace.' Master Mathew removed his woollen cap and bowed slightly. 'The masons are worried by the soldiers.' The Bishop ignored his excuses. The work was of little interest to him. He pointed to his nephew. 'Come here, boy.'

Jamie hesitated, he stared at the grounds embarrassed to be singled out.

'Jamie, please go and receive the English soldiers whilst I remove Brother Geoffrey. Send them through to me in five minutes. I need a little time alone with Brother Geoffrey before they come to see me.'

Without waiting for Jamie's response, the Bishop took Brother Geoffrey's hand and walked back to the private chapel and the exit to his lodgings without a glance back to his young nephew.

*

Jamie feared that his uncle was placing too much trust in him with this dangerous task, but he needed to test himself. He did not know what was more powerful, his fear or his ambition, but he would soon find out, as he started to rehearse what he would say to the English soldiers.

He was not sure of himself. *Uncle, you would have been wiser to trust Master Mathew, he is far more qualified.*

The soldiers were now pounding the heavy wooden door with their sword pommels. His heart pounded, his hands began to sweat, and he thought his face was flushed yet the weather was cold. He tried to open the door, but it had swollen. 'Please, help by pushing rather than trying to batter it down,' he called to them. Jamie tried to appear calm, but his voice faltered, and his throat was dry.

The wooden door moaned, scraping on the cold, unyielding stone floor as the soldiers pushed their shields and swords through the increasing gap, almost pushing Jamie to the ground as they rushed into the nave.

'We have been ordered to see that the work progresses on the tower and to talk with the rogue Bishop Wishart,' the English sergeant snarled in Jamie's face.

Jamie bowed to him, hoping this humble act would diffuse the sergeant's anger and prevent any rash action.

'Sir, His Grace is at prayer within and cannot be disturbed.'

The sergeant shoved Jamie aside, corralling the rest of his troop behind him. Jamie could not run away, but he had found some courage deep inside himself. It was a strange, wonderful sensation.

'Please, sirs, follow me to the bell tower. God's house is well-served by His Grace King Edward's generosity.'

Jamie's grovelling reference to the English King's benefactor appeared to diffuse their hostility, and he managed to get the half dozen soldiers to follow him to the bell tower, which was covered in a skeletal frame of wooden scaffolds. Jamie pointed out the work he and his fellow masons were about, buying valuable time for the Bishop.

*

'Please be silent, dear Geoffrey. I know you are afraid when you see the English lions.' The Bishop placed his index finger to his lips.

They entered the Bishop's lodgings through a long, dark room that was only partially lit by a dwindling torch.

'This way.' The wall at the back was a dead end without an obvious way out.

Wishart pushed one panel of the wall, and a hinge gave way, exposing a secret compartment hiding a small, round metal handle. The Bishop pulled hard at the handle, which was stiff and tight. The door frame had been smeared with dark grease to absorb any light from the outside.

The door hid another room and, behind that, a narrow set of steps and a tunnel that led to the Molendinar tributary. From there, he could escape by river cog to the Clyde and out to sea.

'Brother Geoffrey, take this torch and follow the steps down towards the small cave at the end of the tunnel. Wait there.' The Bishop handed him the small torch from the receiving room.

Brother Geoffrey nodded.

'Don't be afraid,' the Bishop added. 'And remember, Brother, let no one see you, and keep the torch hidden.'

The elderly brother took the torch and, holding it tightly, limped towards the end of the tunnel.

The Bishop heard the approaching soldiers and firmly closed the hidden door blocking out any light from his receiving room.

The Bishop called to his servant. 'Hendor … Hendor, attend me now.'

The Bishop kicked the door with his foot. 'Wake up, you scoundrel! We have work to do!'

Hendor woke to the sound of an increasingly irritated Bishop. He was dreaming again of battles. His scarred face and hands ached with the cold, and his remaining three fingers on each hand had turned pink and mottled with a light blue vein. Whenever he looked at his hands and face, he was reminded of the battles at Stirling Bridge and Falkirk, his capture, torture - where he had been horribly scarred and almost lost his hands - and his tormentor Aymer de Valence.

The Bishop had rescued him from a life of seclusion and, as his loyal servant, he had discovered an equally rewarding vocation in the Bishop's service.

The receiving room was darker than usual. *Why is the small torch missing?* He felt his left sleeve for his dirk. *They don't walk on their own accord.*

A familiar voice interrupted him.

'Hendor, fetch a small oil lamp and prepare me an audience with our English friends. My wits are ready, and my bowels too.' The Bishop winked. 'And once you have brought them into the receiving room, can you put some more wood on the fire? Not too bright - I want the room to be subdued. Light the small oil lamps on the wall, but not the torches. I will go to the privy.'

*

Suddenly, the door to the Bishop lodgings burst open, and the English soldiers stormed through. Jamie felt the boot dig into the small of his back as Hendor turned to face them. From the ground, Jamie could see Hendor's hand feeling for the dirk concealed in his left sleeve.

Amongst them was a man clad in blue and white. 'I am the messenger of His Grace Aymer de Valence.' Jamie could see that Hendor recognised his emblem of gulls on a blue and white background, and struggled to keep his composure. The messenger took a few steps and removed a small scroll from the satchel. It was embossed with the lions of the English King.

'Where is Bishop Wishart? We were told he was here.'

'His Grace is withdrawn to the privy, but is available to speak to you through the door - or you can wait awhile.'

The messenger looked frustrated, and his temper was short. Jamie smirked as the obvious disrespect the Bishop was showing had riled the pompous messenger.

'I will wait out here.' The servant shuffled and stamped noisily. His humiliation at the provocation seemed to amuse Hendor too.

Hendor called through the wattle screen separating the room from the privy. 'Your Grace, a messenger from King Edward has arrived.'

'Ask the messenger to come closer, and I will speak to him,' the Bishop shouted, finishing the sentence off with several large farts.

Hendor suppressed a laugh. To insult the King's messenger was to insult the King, which was always the Bishop's intent.

'Conclude your business, Sir,' the messenger curtly replied.

'My master, Aymer de Valence, orders that you present yourself to the court of the King to answer certain charges on a most serious matter concerning your relationship with the traitor Robert Bruce. I will leave these soldiers here to help you pack and will return tomorrow to accompany you to King Edward's court at Winchester. It is only out of respect for the Church that we don't drag you out now.'

'Can I see the arrest warrant?' The Bishop calmly asked.

The messenger thrust the warrant into Hendor's hand, and he passed it through a gap in the wattle to the Bishop.

*

The Bishop smiled as he read the document. He was certain now that the news of his part in Bruce's absolution remained a secret; otherwise, he would have gone to England tied to a horse. The warrant was dated two days before Comyn's death and proved that he had implicated Wishart in his allegations of the Bruce's proposed rebellion. The King had yet to tie the Bishop to Comyn's murder. That was only a matter of time until the English King sent orders on that matter.

'Sir, I am of course a loyal servant and subject, and will willingly answer these charges. I have taken an oath of loyalty and intend to defend myself against these spurious accusations to the satisfaction of the King.'

'I am no traitor, and I will prove it to the King in person.' The Bishop would agree to anything to get the soldiers to leave, but he had no intention of fulfilling his commitments.

'We shall see tomorrow, cleric, and the King's law will deliver the justice you deserve!' The messenger's tone was mocking.

The sergeant at arms and his retinue moved to leave, but the sergeant turned and shouted back.

'I don't want you to get lonely, so I am leaving a few of my soldiers outside to keep you company.'

Chapter Five

Bishop Wishart Lodgings, Glasgow; March 12th, 1306: The Escape

Jamie Wishart did not react as the soldiers left. He did not want to betray his thoughts or intentions.

Hendor was stone-faced. Jamie did not know what to make of him, even though he had been a good friend of Jamie's father. The two of them had fought together at Stirling Bridge and Falkirk.

The privy screen opened, and the Bishop came into the reception room with a lamp, setting it down on a small table before sinking into a large carver chair, indicating to the two men that they should sit on the bench beside him.

He spoke softly and purposefully.

'I need you both to listen, as we don't have much time. I will be leaving this evening to follow Lord Bruce to Perth, and I need you to work for me.'

He turned to Jamie. 'I want you to leave with Will de Irwyne for France.'

Jamie swallowed hard; he had never travelled more than ten miles from Glasgow.

'Hendor, you will come with me to Perth and later follow Jamie to France and meet with our agents and friends working there. A new rebellion has started, and conflict with the English will be impossible to stop. I will be meeting the Bruce and then crowning him. The maelstrom that will follow will claim many victims, but it is something we have to do.'

Jamie gasped. This was high politics, and he was only

seventeen years old. Before he could think of what to say, Hendor interrupted.

'Why were the soldiers here?'

'To arrest me on the say-so of John Comyn.'

'But Comyn is dead,' Hendor replied.

'Yes, he is. I am being arrested on the word of Comyn as a supporter of Lord Bruce and suspected traitor. Whilst the soldiers know about Comyn's death, they were here to arrest me as an ally of Bruce. They do not yet know of my intentions to crown him. That would make me a proven traitor rather than a suspected one. Lord Bruce asked for and received my absolution, and now I need to prepare for that coming out. King Edward will wreak revenge on all of us.'

'Your Grace, the English do not normally need an excuse to take revenge on Scotland - I want the chance to fight for our country not meekly sit back and see us being ruled by a foreign tyrant.'

The Bishop smiled. 'I often forgot you are Sir Hendor Robertson, knighted at Stirling Bridge by Wallace.'

'I am with you and Hendor,' Jamie answered instinctively: he could not control his words.

'I am blessed to have such men as you in my service,' the Bishop's voice faltered, and he wiped a tear from his cheek. 'But we have important work to do. Look!'

The Bishop removed a large gold ring with an engraved amethyst from a velvet purse hidden beneath his cassock and placed it quietly on the desk in front of him.

Jamie had seen a similar ring before. It had belonged to his father, who had told Jamie that it had power and value, but had never explained why. Since his father had died, he had never found the opportunity to ask his uncle what had happened to it.

'That's my father's ring?' Jamie was irritated as his uncle had obviously not returned this to his mother and he had thought it lost.

The Bishop did not answer. 'Very soon, I will be leaving with Brother Geoffrey.' He seemed concerned only with the old monk. Jamie felt slighted and hurt.

Jamie looked around the room for Geoffrey and was surprised he was not there. He was normally close by his uncle. Jamie started to speak 'Your Grace ...'

The Bishop interrupted. 'Listen to me very carefully. In France, you will meet with an old and dear friend of mine. His name is Geoffroi de Charnay, the Preceptor of Normandy and second-in-command of the Templar Order: he is sympathetic to our cause. He will be found in the Paris Temple and is well known within the order. Be careful in how much attention you attract: we have friends and enemies in the French court, so act with discretion. The French are in an unstable truce with the English, and their spies will be interested in the mere fact that strangers from Scotland are seeking de Charnay.'

Jamie felt the Bishop push the ring into his right hand, closing his fingers around it.

'Take this ring with you. Show it to de Charnay, only him. Let no one see that you possess it. De Charnay will recognise its meaning and will understand why I have sent you. He has something for me, which we have great need of if my plans for Scotland are to be successful. This journey is a matter of great secrecy and importance, and it places you both in great danger. De Irwyne will meet with us tonight and take you to the port of Leith. There, you will take a ship to France and arrive one week from now. Will is one of our bravest knights and one of Lord Bruce's most trusted servants.'

The Bishop took Jamie's other hand. 'Jamie, listen to Will and learn from him! He is that rare beast, a man of education, courage, and wit. He will keep you alive and can be trusted in all circumstances. He thinks before he acts, and that is why he has lived so long with a price on his head. Now, prepare to leave. I've had your belongings brought from your dormitory.'

The Bishop pointed to a large woollen sack hidden in the shadows at the corner of the room.

'I knew this day would come, that the English would come for me, so do not be afraid.' The Bishop let go of Jamie's hand. Jamie tried to respond, organise his thoughts, but he didn't know where to start. *France, Will de Irwyne. Scone.*

'Hendor, I need you to help me get to Scone with Brother Geoffrey. We have a rendezvous with a consignment of wood that is currently on its way to Cupar Castle, and I need a man with your experience of siege machines to help me.'

Jamie had listened to his uncle with little understanding, but he felt an incredible sense of excitement mixed with stomach-churning anxiety. He was nervous of the responsibility the Bishop had given him. 'But why me, Uncle? … and I barely know Will de Irwyne.'

Hendor smiled, 'You have your father's heart and soul. You will be a formidable foe, but follow His Grace's instructions and learn from Will.' Jamie did not really know Hendor, but he did recognise he was a respected, practical man of few words and many principles; his reassurance was important. His words were kind ones.

The Bishop showed mild irritation at the questioning, 'You wouldn't be my brother's son if you didn't ask. But trust me, nephew. I can only tell you that de Charnay is the key; he is vital in our fight for freedom. You will understand when you find him and discover why I have sent you. In your ignorance lies your protection. De Charnay will understand what you want from him. I am sending you and Will de Irwyne because each of you has special talents.'

Jamie knew he wanted the adventure; his doubts were only natural. He wanted to know what his capabilities were, beyond those of a mason.

The Bishop produced from his pocket a letter bearing the

seal of the Guardians of Scotland and handed it to Jamie.

'This document will give you free passage with any patriot and will be recognised by our friends in Scotland and in France. It should ensure your safety once you reach France and meet with Innes de Mayon; but beware, for if you are caught in possession of this by English agents, you will be treated harshly as a spy and traitor and will receive no quarter. Take ship to France from Leith and be warned: Leith is full of English spies, and taking ship will make the wrong people nosey. I will arrange for Jean de Bretagne to meet you in the Sheip's Heid Inn by the docks in Leith. He will organise a ship to take you and Will across the North Sea to France. Jean will not ask too many questions, and he understands the significance of this seal. Journey as quickly as possible to meet him.'

The Bishop pointed to the apprentice's pouch Jamie carried by his side, which contained his stone-working tools.

'You need a reason to travel, and your story is that you are a mason's apprentice on the way to work in France to improve your skills. I believe Reims and Amiens Cathedrals are under repair and looking for masons, so any nosey official will know this to be plausible. Take your tools with you, as these will add credibility to your story if you are captured. Will is your master and is taking you to his lands in Champagne.'

Jamie listened carefully to his uncle's instructions whilst packing the small white velum scroll with its crimson seal and the amethyst ring deep within the cloth sack.

He had gone from apprentice to spy. He knew the Bishop had not told him everything, but for now the excitement and danger were addictive.

The Bishop grabbed a flagon from the table and gulped down its contents of ale which dripped onto his cassock. Returning the flagon to the table, he placed a purse of gold on the table in front of Jamie. He coughed with a dry rasping sound. 'You will need this to grease a few palms and quiet the tongues of those who would betray you; but use it wisely, and use your instincts, for it is these that I have judged worthy of the trust I place in you, and they will enable you to succeed. Few men have luck and strength, but you are one of God's blessed.'

The Bishop placed his thumb on Jamie's forehead and blessed him with the cross.

'We will leave once the current and tides are in our favour, which should be within the next few minutes. Hendor will travel with me and Brother Geoffrey by barge to Perth via Lanark. I will leave you and Will there. Seek Jean de Bretagne as I have instructed.'

'How will I recognise him?' Jamie asked.

Without thinking, the Bishop laughed. 'Oh, you will recognise him. Look to his feet. He always wears bright red boots. They are like no others.'

Hendor and Jamie wrapped their woollen cloaks tightly around themselves and prepared to leave. Jamie struggled to fasten his brooch, his hands shook with excitement and a little fear.

'The cold makes the fastenings tricky. Don't you think?' Hendor asked as he helped Jamie.

The Bishop walked deliberately towards the external door and gently pushed it tightly shut.

Jamie could hear the English soldiers outside moaning about the rain.

The Bishop threw the woollen sack containing Jamie's belongings towards him and grabbed his own satchel bag, which was resting out of sight beside his carver chair. Then he moved towards the entrance to the tunnel. Jamie did not know the route they were taking. He had always gone via the bridge to the Molendinar.

The Bishop concealed his lamp and gestured for Jamie and Hendor to follow him. They moved silently.

'We will need to go in single file. The way is narrow and slippery.' The Bishop led the way, brushing off insects and cobwebs that had dropped from the tunnel onto his cloak. His feet squelched from the thick mud lining the floor and became saturated as he moved deeper into the darkness.

They turned the last corner and came upon the pale light of Brother Geoffrey's dying torch. The Bishop sighed with relief and whispered a small prayer of thanks. There was a chance that their torches could be spotted from the end of the tunnel by someone watching from the castle keep above. The tunnel came to the surface beneath the undergrowth beside the Molendinar, but they had been lucky, and no alarm had been raised.

'Douse all the torches,' the Bishop ordered. 'Jamie, there is something important you need to know, should anything happen to me.' The Bishop moved himself out of earshot of Brother Geoffrey and Hendor and whispered to his nephew.

'You remember my seal?' The Bishop asked Jamie.

'Yes, uncle. It is also on the parchment you gave to me,' Jamie stammered.

'I want you to take a good look at this.' The Bishop stood so close that Jamie could feel his breath and he held out a small gold seal.

'This seal carries the authority of the Free Guardians of Scotland, and if I ever need your help, I will send its copy. Trust who ever carries it as if it were me'. At this the Bishop showed Jamie a small hidden seam in the collar of his shirt, within which he placed the seal about the size of his thumb. 'Remember it bears a lion rampant, embellished with a double border set with lilies, and words in Latin above the Lion. *"Nemo me impune lacessit"*. You are my arms and ears now, Jamie. You are all I have left.' His tone conveyed the sadness of farewell and they embraced.

They rejoined the others just as the Bishop saw his saviour appear.

A small river barge drifted purposefully but silently towards the riverbank where Jamie, the Bishop and their companions crouched. It was a simple craft, single-masted with a plain sail, four oars, and a manual rudder. These shallow draught barges moved most of the river traffic anonymously and reliably up the rivers and into open water.

Jamie knew now: the Bishop had planned their escape by water. It was the only way, as all the roads would be watched by English soldiers. To get to Perth, the Bishop would slip out to the Irish Sea via the River Clyde and around the north coast of Caithness to meet up with the Bruce at Scone. On the way towards the Irish Sea, the Bishop would drop off Will and himself at Lanark, which lay by the Clyde.

The barge's draught cut silently through the shallows and came to rest by the muddy bank. The lead hand threw the tethering rope towards Jamie, who caught it. He was helped by Hendor, who used his considerable body strength to wrap the rope around his waist and stop the barge's drift. He tied it to a blackened tree stump that stood proud on the bank, intended for this very purpose.

This small quay was used for anchoring river barges that brought stores and supplies to the garrison directly above and the masons working in the cathedral. Rope marks were gouged into its surface.

By the light of one small, well-shuttered lamp, the crew threw a small wooden plank with grooves carved on it onto the bank, which would allow the men to climb onto the vessel. It stuck fast into the mud and previous year's leaves, which had thickened and accumulated into a sticky sludge.

The night was gathering shadows, and a storm was erupting, hiding the escape as they climbed up the plank and onto the barge. Jamie watched the Bishop as he looked anxiously at the windows of the keep.

'Gentlemen our neighbours will be watching us expecting an escape: we need to make haste.' The Bishop held out his hand to Brother Geoffrey and grasped him tightly.

'Hold my hand, Geoffrey,' the Bishop spoke softly. Together, they walked sideways up the narrow plank, one step at a time, onto the boat. The plank was just wide enough for them both.

Up above, the dark sky was lit by pitch torches as the soldiers busied themselves gathering the entourage together for the journey to Winchester. The noise within the keep from the horses and carts obscured the breaking of branches and the scuffing of wood as the Scots readied to leave.

Jamie knew that the English soldiers patrolled the walls every thirty minutes, and any vessel seen leaving at night from this spot would arouse suspicion. They needed to move quickly to avoid immediate danger. The Bishop turned to the barge's captain.

'Stop,' the Bishop whispered. 'We are to wait for one other.'

The captain replied anxiously, 'Your Grace, we have been lucky not to be spotted. We shouldn't push our good fortune.'

'Yes, Captain, I know,' the Bishop acknowledged exasperated. 'Where are you, Will?'

'Please, Your Grace, we must go now.' The captain's tone was full of anxiety.

Jamie could see that the Bishop was struggling to keep his footing in the swell. 'You need to sit down uncle.' The Bishop nodded but refused to sit down, still looking for the elusive knight. Each moment increased the risk of being spotted by the English sentries.

Just as the captain was about to break out the sail, the tall figure of Will Irwyne ran towards them clutching a small satchel in one hand and a saddlebag over his shoulder. He was red-faced but composed.

'Did you get it?' Wishart asked.

Will nodded and jumped from the bank onto the deck.

The barge's captain untied the restraining rope and threw the wooden gangplank onto the deck, then jumped back onto the barge. 'Let us get out of here,' the captain agitation was palpable.

Jamie suddenly saw the light from torches above him. First one and then another, like a beam pointing down illuminating the barge. The first sentry was not yet in sight, but the men on deck could see his shadow shortening as he came closer to the gap in the wall that overlooked the river. The barge was moving but had yet to gain momentum. It was directly below the sentry. The wind engorged the small sail and took the barge away from the bank, assisted by a sharp push from the captain using a long spar.

'Stop! Help! They are getting away! Wishart and his traitors are getting away!'

The sentry's commotion had brought numerous other soldiers and archers to join him on the ramparts.

A large candle holder hit the deck with a bang.

The vessel was now completely in the dark, but it was still under control and was gaining speed. The crew continued to use spars to push the barge away from the bank.

A few poorly aimed but powerful arrows flew past the bow and whistled into the water. More arrows hit the water, their aim becoming more accurate as sentries brought more torches, but the distance between the barge and the castle walls was growing.

The arrogant messenger appeared on the rampart and shouted at the Bishop.

'You won't get far, Wishart! There is nowhere in this realm without an Englishman or someone loyal to His Grace King Edward who would willingly give you up. Enjoy your freedom, for it will be only a short time before I see your head on a spike at London Bridge!'

This was Jamie's first battle, and he was excited. He did not have time to feel scared, but he wanted to survive, and he acted on instinct following the other sailors in using spars to push the barge away from the bank. He was surprised at his strength and courage as arrows crashed around him. Several archers had reached the bank and were firing towards the fleeing vessel with much greater accuracy.

Thump! Thump! Thump! Like drums, the noise of the arrows landing increased until one of the crew was hit directly in the chest. Blood spurted out of his wound. It was a direct hit to the heart, and he immediately dropped to the deck next to Jamie with a thud.

The Bishop rushed towards the dead sailor, heedless of the danger.

'Augh!' he cried. The Bishop dropped to his knees, clutching his shoulder. An arrow had hit him in the back and gashed his shoulder blade.

Flights of arrows continued whining past and drilling into the deck. Jamie and Hendor shoved the Bishop behind one of the wooden crates that littered the deck.

Brother Geoffrey screamed but was unhurt, hidden behind the same crate.

Despite his wound, the Bishop could not resist trying to see what was going on and peeked above the crate. Jamie pushed his head down hard.

'Your Grace, the English have horses, but we are almost at the Clyde, whose swift currents are faster than any horse.'

The wind caught the sail and pushed them further away from danger, and the keel cut deeper into the water, disappearing into the thick haze that had started to blanket the river. The anxious voices of the crew became a softening murmur as they distanced themselves from the garrison.

The occasional arrow whistled harmlessly into the water far to the rear of the vessel.

'That hurt,' Wishart said. He was bleeding from his shoulder wound and remained sitting on the deck, clutched close by the loyal Hendor.

'You will live, Your Grace.' Hendor placed his cloak around the Bishop to offer warmth.

'Where is Jamie? What about Will? Are they safe?'

'Quite safe, Your Grace. They are helping the crew. See?' Hendor pointed.

Jamie and Will had taken two of the oars and were helping to row the ship further into the middle of the water. Each oar was now blanketed with thickening surface fog, which was common for this time of the year. The captain controlled the rudder.

'Get your hands on the oars, boys!' he ordered.

The barge was dark, immersed in river fog obscuring its form with a woollen blanket.

Jamie watched as the torches moved further and further away, but it was the barge that was now gaining considerable speed driven by strong currents. The crew was silent.

The soldiers' voices became fainter. The only sounds were the creaking of the timbers and the lapping of the oars as they cut through the river's tide. It was ten minutes before anyone dared to speak.

The Bishop was shivering as Hendor and Brother Geoffrey lifted him to rest inside the wooden shelter that doubled as the captain's cabin.

The fog was patchier, but it was raining hard, and the wind was increasingly biting and cold. The shelter provided some protection from the elements. It was cosy, lined with dry woollen sacks filled with the fleeces from the cargo of wool bales destined for the Low Countries. In the corner, a small table and four stools were tied to the floor.

Jamie could see into the cabin, but decided that working the oar with Will was the best thing he could do at this time.

'God be thanked, you are alive,' he whispered his uncle's name.

'He is made from iron and has the courage of a lion,' Will replied, surprising Jamie as he didn't think he had noticed him or cared much for the Bishop.

'I think we should just row, what do you think, Will?' Jamie asked.

Will nodded. 'Hendor and Brother Geoffrey are watching him.'

*

'Hendor, next to me on the deck was my leather sack. Please bring it to me.' The Bishop strained to talk. He felt light-headed with pain and in shock. Hendor retrieved the sack and placed it on the table.

The Bishop sank into the soft wooden bales, which gave him a little comfort. Brother Geoffrey lay next to him.

The wound felt like an inconvenience rather than a threat to his life, and the pain was such he struggled to keep awake.

'Your Grace, I need to remove your outer cloak and look at your wound.' Hendor was agitated, and the Bishop knew when he wasn't going to take no for an answer. 'I will fetch a light from the captain.'

Wishart remained still as Hendor fetched a light. He carefully removed the Bishop's heavy woollen cloak, which had a small hole high on the left where the arrow had caught the Bishop's shoulder. The Bishop's undershirt was stained with blood, which had started to dry and had stuck to the wound.

Hendor scrutinised the wound. 'I have seen worse, Your Grace. It will hurt a lot and keep you awake for a few days.'

'I think we should try and sleep.' The Bishop pointed to the far end of the cabin, which was laid out with sheepskins.

Hendor ignored him and tended to the wound, whilst Brother Geoffrey obeyed and covered himself with raw sheep fleeces.

'Master,' I will need to wash this wound clean, and to do that, I need to remove your shirt. It has stuck to the wound. I may need to stitch it.'

The Bishop winced.

'I need to moisten the shirt,' Hendor continued. 'That will loosen the material which is sticking to the wound. I will fetch some water. I saw a barrel by the ship's mast.' He pushed aside the hessian curtain which covered the door.

'Hendor, I will be fine. Forget the water. Please, ask Will to come and see me. I do not wish to be disturbed by anyone else. Ask him to bring another lamp so that I may see the hand in front of my face.'

Hendor left the cabin, leaving the wooden door open.

The Bishop could not resist touching the wound on his left shoulder. He knew he had been lucky today and he had never doubted that God was on his side, but now he was sure of it.

All the oars were in the water now, and the captain took control of the rudder. For the moment, the sail was quickly pushing the barge downstream towards Lanark. It was an untidy sight, but it did not need tending like the oars.

'Drop oars,' the captain said, gesturing. 'Let the sail do its work.'

The remaining crew had wrapped their cloaks around themselves, and they rested over the stationary oars that lay horizontal across their mountings. The tide grabbed the barge and pushed them at pace towards the sea.

Will entered the cabin, a small lamp in hand.

The night was at peace, and the only sounds that could be heard were the voices of two men in the makeshift cabin and the gentle snoring of the exhausted crew.

Chapter Six

Lanark, March 13th, 1306: The Bishop's Tale

'You asked to see me, Your Grace?' Will stooped as he entered the small cabin. He removed his gloves. His long fair hair had been darkened by a mixture of dirt, vegetation, and rain.

Small globules of mud and muck fell to the ground from his hair and jacket as he moved, unconsciously shaking the loose drops over the Bishop and the ground beneath him. The cabin was a claustrophobic six feet by ten. He attached his small, enclosed candle lamp to a makeshift contraption of chain and tatty ship's rope. The light it emitted was just worth the effort.

'You will have to sit down and dry off, my son. Pull up a fleece!' The Bishop joked coughing as he laughed. Will straddled a wool bale; a sodden leather satchel hung by his side, tied to his belt by a narrow thong.

Will looked at Brother Geoffrey, who was asleep at the far end of the cabin.

'Can we trust the old man?' he asked.

The Bishop broke into a wide smile. He said nothing and nodded his head.

'I trust you have brought Brother Geoffrey's book of hours with you?'

'Yes, Your Grace,' Will said, patting the satchel. 'As you said, it was in the cathedral treasury. It is beautiful,' he looked at the book of hours. 'The sort of thing I have only seen in the possession of kings.'

'Yes, it is wonderful. My brother brought it back from the

Holy Land with Brother Geoffrey.'

Will removed the satchel. 'I see you are injured, but I have seen worse, Your Grace.'

Wishart laughed, as Hendor had made the same comment, and it made his painful wound seem trivial.

Will continued. 'You will sleep in some pain tonight, but after that, you'll be fine.' He placed the satchel next to the Bishop and loosened the buckles.

'I know you are the Bruce's man, but we were close once, and I hope we can be close again.'

Will nodded. 'I have fought in bloody battles and slept on sodden grass and snowy fields, but today, Your Grace, I have never felt colder,' he rubbed his hands together.

'Weather like this gave me piles years ago. I see you are not yet afflicted; otherwise, you would be here with me, protecting your poor buttocks with this fleecy armour.' The Bishop laughed as he buried his bum cheeks further into the soft fleeces that surrounded him.

'You have grown into a fine man and become quite the hero; I suspect the twenty pounds of silver for your head has just doubled, thanks to your master Lord Robert and his actions in Dumfries. He has made this a most urgent and serious business, and I need someone with your talents to help me.'

As Wishart spoke, he caught sight of a mouse. It darted across the floor before burying its small frame in a gap underneath the sleeping Brother Geoffrey, but it had missed a predatory eye peering through a crack in the wooden partition.

'I am here to act in whatever manner is required, Your Grace,' Will said. 'Lord Bruce has told me to obey your orders as if they were his, and I will do so. There is no need for explanation.'

Wishart knew that he had chosen wisely.

'You know we have a friend in King Philip of France, and

he controls the Papacy, so our Church is safe for the moment - but we cannot rely on that benevolence indefinitely. I need to control the country, influence the Pope and write the future, and that future is Lord Bruce as King Robert I if we are to be returned to independence and free of occupation. We need our own King. As the Archbishop of Glasgow, I intend to crown the Bruce in Scone as soon as I can.'

Will was silent for a few seconds. 'That is the logical course, the only course. I never doubted for a minute that Lord Robert should be King.'

Wishart's tone darkened, 'I expect you understand the risk we are taking even talking about crowning a King, and it is imperative that we act now before Bruce is excommunicated by the Pope for killing Comyn. Longshanks will have asked for that bull, and it will take about six weeks to issue and make its way from the Poitiers curia to Scotland. The Bruce needs to be the King of Scotland before the end of March, because I can't crown him if he is an excommunicate.'

'I am a soldier, not a priest or diplomat, Your Grace. What will you have me do?' Will asked.

The Bishop held his good arm out, and Will pulled him up from his fleecy bed to his feet. He groaned as he lowered himself onto the bales opposite Will.

'King Philip and the Pope have a few things in common. These men are greedy - avaricious, megalomaniacal robbers. Their greed drives their every action. Once you understand that, everything they say and do makes perfect sense. King Philip is bankrupt, and he has marginalised, persecuted, arrested, robbed, and murdered almost everyone with a sou that he can get his avaricious hands on. His natural targets are always the Jews, but he has so impoverished them that their pockets are now exhausted. They can be squeezed no more - certainly not enough to continue to fund French wars with Longshanks and his other enemy, the Duke of Flanders. He is now helping himself to Church property, but he is having difficulties getting his nobles and the compliant Pope to go along with this. His challenges will only increase if he doesn't replenish his funds soon, and King Philip is not a man to share his good fortune.'

Wishart shuddered with shock. He fidgeted within his cassock, removing a small pottery flask from a hidden pocket, then moistened his throat with a dram of *uisge beatha* before offering the flask to Will.

'This is purely for the pain. Share a dram with me?' The Bishop asked.

Will tipped the flask's contents to his mouth, wetting his lips and tongue.

He handed the flask back to the Bishop, who capped it and shoved it back in his pocket, his hand reaching deep within his cassock, almost down to his knee. The Bishop patted its safe location.

'Pope Clement is like any other pope, measuring his success not in the souls he acquires, but in the sous he personally amasses. When you need someone's help and they are outside your control, you need to find what motivates them, and in this case, we can secure the help of Philip and Clement by giving them a great deal of money. In King Philip's case, we have the added advantage that the money will be used to fight the English, something we cannot do on two fronts but can certainly engineer. Everyone will be happy except the English, of course, and I like any machinations that produce that outcome!' The Bishop smiled, but only momentarily.

The Bishop picked up the satchel Will had recovered. He removed the book of hours from the pouch and, turning the pages, added, 'What money, I hear you ask?'

Will did not respond, but nervously licked his lips, which were still moistened with the spirit.

'My question is rhetorical, my son. Let me assure you, I know where there is a great deal of money, though unfortunately, I have temporarily lost possession of it. We need to find this money, and quickly, if we are to buy the French King and the Pope.'

A crash resounded through the ship, driving Will to almost pull the shabby door off its hinges in his pursuit of its source. The captain had fallen off the rudder and onto the deck, knocking over the wooden pail he had been using as a stool. The captain groaned, but never really woke. He remained on the deck, clutching an empty privy stool like it was a long-lost lover.

The Bishop looked anxiously outside. 'Anything I should worry about?'

'I don't think so, Your Grace.' Will closed the door firmly and sat back on the stool.

'Bit of a coincidence, that noise when I was talking, don't you think Will?'

'Your Grace, the captain fell off the rudder, which he was sleeping on, and crashed into the privy. I didn't see anything or anybody else moving.'

The Bishop wondered if he was hearing things, and the stress was impairing his judgement and scrambling his wits.

'Well, whatever it was, it has gone now. Let me continue.'

Will nodded.

'What I am about to tell you is a tale of treasure - Alaric's treasure - known by few men still alive. Its recovery is vital to our cause, and in doing this, we must make sure it does not fall directly into the hands of the English or the French, who relentlessly covet it. Whoever controls this fortune will have at their disposal the largest treasure in the world and the power to match.'

Will interrupted. 'Alaric? Which land does he rule? Some Eastern or African kingdom, Your Grace?'

'None, my son.' The Bishop's reply was terse. He wanted to tell his tale quickly. 'Alaric has been dead for nearly a thousand years, but he was a great King of the Visigoths.

Like us, he was betrayed by a bully, and when he took his revenge, he humbled Rome and took their treasure. The whole treasury of Rome was paid ransom to stop its sacking. Unimaginable wealth was taken from their temples, villas, and palaces. Alaric's treasure was rumoured to contain ten thousand pounds of gold, a hundred thousand of silver. Pearls as large as quail's eggs, emeralds, rubies, and diamonds, plundered from the four corners of the Roman Empire and beyond. But Alaric never got to enjoy his wealth. Shortly after he received it, he died, and the treasure disappeared, reportedly buried with him in Italy. And it remained hidden there for hundreds of years until the Byzantines discovered it when they occupied Calabria.'

The Bishop looked around for some water, but he could not remember if Hendor had left the water pail in the cabin. He continued, 'With great secrecy, the Byzantine Greeks removed it and hid it within the walls of the great palace of Constantinople, and there it stayed for hundreds of years. This was ironic, as the Byzantine emperors consider themselves the heirs to the Roman Empire and all its assets, so they were rather pleased to get it all back. They had the wealth, but they were weak and poorly led, and they knew that if it were discovered and revealed, they would become a target for the envious and cash-strapped neighbours that surrounded them. They wanted to keep it a secret, but instead of using it to buy an army, the Byzantine emperors helped themselves to its contents along the way. Their plan worked for many years until the Venetians caught wind of it in 1204 and, under the pretext of crusade, stopped off to steal it, sacking Constantinople and removing the treasure for safekeeping to the Templars' keep in Acre. There it could be kept out of the reach of the French and English kings, which was better than if the doge had stored it in his palace, where gossip would have soon revealed its presence. More importantly, the doge's protectors were bankers, mercenaries, and the Grand

Order of the Knights Templar. It would be difficult to decide which of these parties was the most corrupt. The treasure was owned by the perfect team of politicians, thieves, and armed monks.'

The Bishop took another drink from his flask.

'It took near seventy years for the Venetians to steal it all and store it in the Templar keep in Acre, and my brother John found it. He fell on top of it accidentally; to be more accurate, on a treasure barge fleeing Acre. He found much of Alaric's treasure and many other wonderful things.'

'You talked of legend, Your Grace. Are you sure it isn't a fable, and we are being tricked?'

The Bishop shook his head, 'I sent John to Acre to find Geoffroi de Charnay and bring him back. He brought back valuable information, stories of treasure, and Brother Geoffrey.'

The Bishop pointed at the sleeping monk and smiled.

'Brother Geoffrey connects me with the brother I have lost. He has been part of my family for fifteen years, and no one should underestimate how valuable he is to me.'

'I remember your brother, but I never heard what happened to him.' Will looked embarrassed to ask such a personal question.

'In 1298, after Falkirk, when we were in no position to fight battles, I sent Wallace and John to France to meet with de Charnay and recover the treasure, hoping to use it to buy more influence with King Philip and the then Pope Boniface, and bring the rest of it back to Scotland. Wallace and John spent many years in diplomacy with the French King and the Papacy, building support for Scottish independence and avoiding assassination by the English; something happened in France. Only John and Wallace know what, and they are both dead.'

The Bishop felt tears well in his eyes.

'I received a message that John had disappeared in Paris,

and there was mention of him heading to Italy. I was being watched by the English and couldn't travel to France or get to Wallace before he was captured and executed, so I couldn't find out more.'

'Where is the treasure now, Your Grace?'

The Bishop took Will's hand in his. It was not a gesture he manufactured, but his way of exhibiting his sincerity.

'Only four men know where the treasure is hidden. Two are dead; one was John, and the other a knight they found in Acre, who died on a barge escaping the city when it fell. De Charnay is the third, and the fourth can only be found with de Charnay's help. The four men knew that if anyone found such a treasure, it would be their death sentence, so they decided to bury it and only retrieve it when the time was right. Its hiding place remains hidden, unknown except to the men who buried it. The only clues I have are four amethyst rings. When John returned to Scotland, he brought back two of the rings belonging to him and the dead knight; de Charnay has the third and access to the fourth. The treasure ship sailed to France or Italy, and then my brother and de Charnay buried it.'

The Bishop picked up the book of hours and pulled his dirk from the scabbard hanging around his waist. With considerable skill, he removed the binder, and out from the gap fell a large ring with a purple stone. He placed the book on the table next to the ring. The tatty cabin table presented a poor frame for such magnificence.

'You have one ring now, Will, and I have given Jamie the other. When John went to France to meet de Charnay and recover the treasure, he made a copy of both rings because they were engraved with a clue to the treasure's location, and he left the originals with me for safekeeping. He and the copied rings have disappeared, so someone else may already know part of the secret that only the rings can reveal. I suspect the French and perhaps the English have one or both of the copied rings, but what they don't know is that they can't retrieve the treasure unless they have all four, and only de Charnay can provide the missing two.'

'Does anyone know about de Charnay and his knowledge about the treasure?'

'I am sure no one alive apart from me knows the truth about de Charnay. As for the four rings, keep this a secret from Jamie until the time comes. He knows nothing of the rings' significance or the treasure. Remember, only one of the men who found the treasure is known to us and that is Geoffroi de Charnay. He will not need any convincing when you find him, as indeed you and Jamie have the first two rings. He needs you just as much as you need him if he wants to locate it, and that should make him easy to find. De Charnay will recognise Jamie: he looks like John. He has an incredible memory and never forgets a face or a fact.'

The Bishop paused, 'De Charnay isn't the only one who will recognise the rings. King Philip and King Edward know the treasure exists, but they probably do not know how the rings lead to its recovery. Neither do I. You need to find that out from de Charnay. What I do know is that if you are caught with them, it will likely lead to your death or disappearance. Don't show them to anyone!'

Brother Geoffrey turned and cried out, and appeared to still be sound asleep. Startled, a cat ran out from beneath the bales.

Startled, Will reflexively drew his dirk.

'Calm yourself,' the Bishop said. 'Geoffrey is only having a nightmare, and the cat a feast. Neither is eavesdropping. Put your dirk away!'

Will placed the dagger back in its scabbard. 'What would you have me do?'

'I want you to go to France with my nephew Jamie, find de Charnay, recover the treasure, and bring it back to Scotland.'

Will appeared perplexed. 'And you are sure, Your Grace, that the other two men are dead and only de Charnay is still alive? I wouldn't want any other loose ends to deal with.'

The Bishop smiled at the cautious knight. 'Rest assured, Will, that de Charnay is a loyal friend and will provide the two remaining rings and the knowledge on how they can be used to recover the treasure.'

Will smiled. 'Is there any more *uisge beatha* left in that flask of yours? I think I am going to need it.'

The Bishop placed the small flask next to Will, who removed the top and lifted it to his lips, draining the flask with several large gulps.

'Steady, my son. That is the water of life you are enjoying and should be treated with considerable respect.' The Bishop smiled.

'Your Grace, I have no fear of the French, finding de Charnay, or even recovering the treasure, but babysitting a spotty teenager in a foreign land full of danger, with no experience of the world outside of his mother's house is a risk to our success and my life. Does he even know how to hold a sword? I stand a better chance of doing this alone. Please reconsider.'

The Bishop sighed. 'I thought you might say this, and I understand, but the risk to Scotland is greater. This secret is so precious, valuable, and important to our country, that I can share it only with a few hand-picked men. One of these men is you, and the other is Jamie. I need people I can trust, people whose loyalty is unquestionable, and Jamie is a patriot just like you. I need you both on this - and this job is bigger than one man, Will. Can't you see that?'

The Bishop paused again and, practical as ever, asked, 'How can you single-handedly move tons of treasure from a foreign land? Jamie is a mason, and a practical man, you will need someone with his skills!'

The Bishop saw in Will's face that he had not convinced

him, but that Will was still listening, wanting to believe.

'I have arranged for a ship to take you from Leith to Rouen. Seek out the flamboyant Jean de Bretagne. Jamie has the details of where he can be found.'

'He sounds like an interesting character. Perhaps he will attract the kind of attention we could do without?'

The Bishop had often worried about de Bretagne, but over the years, he had proved a reliable if a little controversial member of the Scottish resistance. Will was much quieter and more thoughtful, but it took all sorts of characters to succeed, and the Bishop had no reason to doubt de Bretagne's capabilities - though he still would not trust him with retrieving the treasure.

'The English are used to seeing him taking human cargo across the waters to France and Flanders, so transporting a Scottish mason and his sponsor shouldn't arise suspicion. I have sent a messenger ahead to Innes de Mayon, and de Bretagne will know you work for me, but that is all. It is safer for everyone that he knows no more.'

The Bishop's wound was increasingly drying and tightening around his shirt, and he regretted letting Will drain his flask of instant pain relief. He wanted to scratch the wound, which was itching and tender.

'Will, take the light and look at the far end of the cabin. I believe I saw some whisky casks. Probably the captain's supply, but I don't think he will begrudge us some.'

Will saw a couple of thin-necked, green-glazed pots with wooden stoppers resting in a small wooden crate. They had been secured by their necks to the top slat of the box surrounding them, which had been stuffed with straw to cushion the flagons against the rolling of the ship.

Will dragged the box just far enough that he could reach it with his middle finger. He pulled the box towards him, untied one of the flagons, and lifted it onto the table. There was a piece of cloth sealed with red wax around the flagon's neck. Will removed the wax with his dirk, loosening the wooden stopper, and tasted the liquid.

'It isn't the water of life, Your Grace, but I think it is good enough.' He pushed the flagon across to the Bishop.

The Bishop struggled to lift the bottle with his good right arm. He felt its warmth flow down his throat and rush into his stomach, where its soothing and relaxing effects almost immediately began to balance his humours. He pushed the flagon back to Will.

Will silently gestured to the Bishop and placed his finger on his lips.

*

Ever cautious, Will stood and silently opened the cabin door. It made no sound, and he observed the deck strewn with sailors, wrapped in their cloaks under any shelter they could find.

He could barely see the stern of the ship, where the captain was now sleeping. The peculiar silence of the night was broken by a cacophony of snores, coughs, and breathing of every tone and pitch. Empty flagons of spirits and wine rolled aimlessly across the decks. He smiled as he recognised how inebriated men had to become in circumstances of fear and cold to induce any sleep. Weary men made poor companions and even worse soldiers. The occasional hangover was a small price to pay and, in these times, not out of place.

The barge twisted left and right, arguing with the anchor rope that tethered it to the riverbed. When he had been in the cabin with Bishop Wishart, the crew must have secured the boat in the middle of the river, reckoning that the pursuing English were far behind, and it was safe to stop until dawn. A small lamp hung on the mast, but it gave only a little light, and its brightness was diminished in the dank air that surrounded everything. It swung aimlessly in the cold breeze, generating a pained squeak as the barge's motion pulled it from side to side.

He observed Jamie immediately to the right, curled around a wool bale. He looked as young as he remembered, yet Will could see the face of John Wishart in his features, and the transition from boy to man was well on its way. Perhaps the Bishop was right, and he was the practical man needed for the job. His father would have been.

He returned to the cabin and knelt on his temporary bed. The Bishop looked peaceful as the whisky had taken hold and dulled his pain.

The skin blanket felt cold against him, but it was warming by the second. If the English crossed his path, it would be an opportunity to settle a few old scores and leave a couple on account. That felt good, and he relaxed.

Will decided to read and picked up the book of hours. His breathing softened; he used quiet moments like this to think and reflect. He had more to his character than courage, and he found that clearing his mind of the day's concerns prepared him for dealing with the next day. Reading was his other pleasure – it helped him to think.

He thought of the task ahead and the Bishop's words. What fate had God determined for him and Jamie? Was Jamie touched by good fortune and grace, as the Bishop described? Would they survive or were their fates already determined?

Will knew the power of using the skills God had given you, and he hoped Jamie had wits and charm that outweighed his lack of experience.

As he thought about this, he could feel his breathing becoming shallower and his muscles relaxing. He could sense that he too was snoring, yet still half awake. But it felt good.

*

Dawn was four or five hours away. There was a strange peace now, and the barge was quiet. Small scratches could be heard, and eyes were peering at Will through the gaps in the rough planks that made up the walls of the flimsy cabin. The scratching stopped. People slept - all except one.

Chapter Seven

The Sheip's Heid Inn, March 16th, 1306: Flight to Rouen

Two unassuming horses walked idly along the banks of the River Clyde.

It was the time when dawn was struggling to get through the dark late-winter night, but the moon was almost full and the night sky without clouds. The wind whispered quietly as it cut through the leafless trees, uninterrupted by the faint echoes of men and the voices of beasts.

Distant forms could be seen on the surrounding land as pairs of oxen walked in straight, narrow lines, pulling primitive ploughs through dense clay soil. The plough teams seemed to know exactly what to do with little guidance from their human masters. The accumulated breath of the oxen and the wiry peasants in dark woollen capes and caps rose like a faint mist, betraying their location. The spring was tantalisingly near, and now was a time to plough and prepare to sow.

Will scrutinised Jamie, Bishop Wishart's words still ringing in his ears. The Bishop had ordered him to trust this man even with his life, and Will wanted to believe him. His faith in the Bishop was deep; Wishart was a courageous and cunning priest, and his devotion to Scottish independence was addictive.

He trusted the Bishop's judgement, but he would be lying to himself if he did not recognise his own doubts; they were constantly, uncomfortably in his thoughts. He did not know Jamie and could not trust him yet. At first, he had only sensed an inexperienced lithe youth with fair skin and green eyes, but when the barge had been attacked, Jamie acted with intelligence and courage. He could see well the Bishop in his nephew, in his eyes and his mannerisms, and for a moment he was reassured.

He cleared his throat. A hacking cough came out, but no words.

'Are you alright?' Jamie asked. His voice was almost inaudible.

'Yes. It's just the cold air,' Will replied.

'In such biting weather it's to be expected.' Will did not reply. His small talk was limited in the morning, and he did not try to build any rapport as they escaped the suburbs of Lanark and rode past the English fortifications that ringed the town. Their journey since leaving the ship had been noticeably awkward, but the quiet left him more time for planning.

The barge had stopped dangerously close to the sentry towers on the River Clyde, but everyone had moved silently so that no overzealous English conscript would pick up on their escape. Will and Jamie looked like a lord and his mason on their way to take ship for France.

There had been an uneasy peace for several months, and the English were fat and complacent, thinking the Scots had finally been beaten. The news of the Bruce's rebellion may have reached here, but apparently not its implications.

Will noticed that Jamie was still sick from the water, and he would not be used to long rides, so horse sickness was a distinct possibility. The danger they were now in was enough to handle without having to deal with a motion sick teenager. He sighed in frustration.

'The barge has gone, and your uncle is on his way towards Cape Wrath and an appointment with Lord Bruce at Scone.'

'Yes, I know,' Jamie replied. 'Lord Bruce will be crowned wearing my uncle's vestments.'

Jamie's reply surprised Will. He did not know how much Jamie knew about his uncle's plan, and the reply was bordering on impertinent.

Would he watch my back?

How resilient would Jamie be without sleep, food, and water? He wondered if he could take the mental and physical challenges of their journey. He just wondered.

He also envied Jamie his youth, for he had lived only seventeen winters and had many years left. Will was beginning to feel his age, and his aches took longer to forget. The arrow wound in his shoulder, a souvenir from Falkirk, stung and he had to stop scratching it to blood.

Will had made a difference, and he knew it was now necessary for younger men to continue the struggle and renew the rebellion, but it was a hard role to share. He had earned the right to play a leading role, but what had Jamie achieved?

As far as he could remember, the years of his youth had been full of conflict and battles. He could not readily recollect living a life of normality - sleeping in the same bed each night, partaking of love, sex, women, and the pursuit of the gentler pastimes of a Scottish laird. Like a short chapter in a long book, that part of his memory was buried deep beneath the pages of something else - something much darker. He both fantasised about it and hoped it had been true.

His was a life of fighting and surviving, and anyone he really cared about deserved more than that, so he rarely sought out companionship outside the male retinue of Lord Bruce. Will's family had been at the heart of the Scottish rebellions, and he had learned to grow up fast. His father, Alexander de Irwyne, had been the old King Alexander's chamberlain and had brought the Maid of Norway over to Orkney. His reward had been to die in Longshanks's dungeon, mad with his grief over the Maid's death.

Indeed, the English had given Will many reasons to hate

them, and he had sworn he would seek his revenge at every opportunity.

Will noticed Jamie moving around in his saddle. 'When I took to the horse, I was younger than you, but I never got over the pain of those first few months.'

'I didn't want to complain,' Jamie said, 'but it is rare day that an apprentice mason can ride a horse. I never had the means to own my own mount.'

They continued for a mile. Pauses were a frequent interruption to the stilted small talk.

'Years ago, my father used to take me riding. It allowed us to talk and me to learn, but then he went to France with Wallace, and the learning stopped. You knew my father?'

'I knew him. He was a good man, someone to be proud of.' Will smiled as he replied.

He rode ahead of Jamie, taking him through an undefended and unknown track that led through the hills via Biggar and followed the ancient rovers' trails between the Rivers Clyde and Tweed.

The day was breaking now, and the forested hills were alive with the sound of wolves dining on that night's prey of deer.

Jamie smiled. 'I recognise these lands. My father visited Wallace many times here. His wife grew up in Lamington. We have just passed there.'

'You met Wallace?' Will asked, surprised.

'Yes, though I was young. He was a great friend of my father. He taught me how to draw a bow and use a dirk. He had no children and seemed to enjoy teaching me how to be a fighter. After that, he went to France with my father, and I never saw him again. That was when I was twelve.'

Will laughed. He need not have worried; he was riding with Wallace's apprentice. He did not know quite what to say after that, but it was reassuring that Jamie had learned his weapon skills with the master.

The silence continued, and Will noticed that Jamie rode higher in his mount with a confidence that surprised him. They avoided any villages in case of English soldiers, who were known to arrest any men on horseback as potential Scottish rebels. Jamie did not complain or appear afraid; or he had the good judgement to hide the fear.

They rode on cautiously through the day and night towards the village and harbour of Leith, hoping that their early arrival would not attract too much attention and that they could remain hidden amongst the sailors and traders. The horses moved in silence, almost as if they knew.

There was no one on the outskirts of Leith, and that worried Will. A port was normally bustling with traders coming from the surrounding villages. He felt instinctively that something was not quite right, but he said nothing to Jamie.

He had sensed a presence, and whilst he was not superstitious, he was uneasy whenever his view was not at least a clear two hundred yards - the deadly zone of an arrow.

All Scottish nobles and their supporters were followed by Longshanks's agents at one time or another. There were agents in every town, watching for anything unusual. The barge had docked early, apparently unnoticed, but Will was always vigilant. If these same antagonists knew that they were setting forth after treasure, this would only heighten their peril.

Will worried that their purpose may no longer be a secret. He suspected that they had been followed from the cathedral. But for now, they seemed to be alone.

They had ridden for thirty-six hours without a break and the fatigue was palpable; it was only anxiety and the fear of discovery that, until now, had kept them awake and vigilant.

There was no cloud cover, so the morning was ice cold, and their bones shuddered with the blasts of freezing air that bellowed down the street, chilling the small pools of water that rested at the side of the gutters, changing them into glistening bowls of semi-opaque ice. The distorted reflection of the two men on horseback caught the light of the many lamps that swung outside the wooden buildings strung along the roads and paths.

They had waited until an hour before daybreak to avoid any patrols from the English garrison at Edinburgh castle. Leith was a village some two miles away from the castle and they hoped they would not be observed.

With a crash, Jamie fell off his horse, crying as he landed. He had momentarily closed his eyes and slipped from the saddle. Will had also become increasingly tired, sleeping lightly in his own saddle.

'Are you awake now?' Will mocked as Jamie got to his feet. 'The Sheip's Heid Inn is near the harbour.'

Jamie brushed his clothes free of the mud-covered ice and straw that clung to them. 'We are to meet Jean de Bretagne as soon as we arrive.'

It was now barely six in the morning, but in March by the waters of Leith, there was not even a whisper of daylight, only the reflected light of the moon and the faint traces of light escaping from the lamps and fires that lit and warmed the shops, hovels, and inns that randomly dotted either side of the road from Edinburgh.

Will knew these streets, and neither rider had any reserves for unnecessary discussion.

Clouds appeared, and the temperature dropped. Light snow now blew across the streets, and the wind was increasing in strength, biting and strong enough to sting as it filled the eyes of the two riders with icy particles. Will brushed the flakes away from his eyes, but the snow made them water as they swelled and reddened. With each step, the weather took a turn for the worst. Even the gulls that normally frequented the middens now huddled on the fences.

Ten minutes had passed, and the snow was falling hard

now, blowing directly into his face, and he struggled to see the path towards the harbour. The horses' hooves moved effortlessly over the stones, making no sound except for the whisper of a crunch as each step thrust into the soft powder.

Jamie's horse snorted in the cold air, which was just above the dew point and created a rising cloud of steam from its nostrils.

'Steady, girl,' Jamie whispered. He leaned forward, urging the horse to make less noise, and covering its flared nostrils with his hand whilst gently stroking the flighty mount's ear.

Suddenly, blood and guts fell from the sky and landed in front of him.

Jamie jumped. 'My God,' he cried. Will grabbed his dirk.

Deadly screams could be heard from the side of the road, but not from human voices. Skinny scavenging dogs and cats were fighting with the rats over some animal intestines, which were protruding from the gutter. The soggy mess of filth was solidifying and crusting with frost as it lay in the cold air.

'I thought it was human,' Jamie said.

'This must be the shambles,' Will replied.

The dogs held the rats in their mouths and shook their heads in violent excitement before throwing the stunned rodents to the ground. The cats waited for the rats to fall limp and injured at their feet, and began tearing lumps out of them as they writhed on the snow. The dogs ignored the rats, focusing on the bloody entrails that wept red fluid into the surrounding snow, attracting more passing dogs and cats to the feast.

The welcome scraps looked a ruby-red target against the pale white blanket of deepening snow, and as the animals fought, the mess spread, becoming paler and paler as the snow fell harder.

'I think our mounts have been here before,' Will whispered as the horses moved with little guidance towards the harbour.

'They are following the scent of a comfortable stable and fresh food, as am I,' Jamie replied.

A well-trodden and dirty snow-covered path indicated the direction where Will knew the Sheip's Heid and Jean de Bretagne were to be found, but it was becoming obscured by the deepening snow, which was increasingly hiding the gutters.

Behind the doors of the houses, people could be heard having sex, talking, arguing, and taking their toilet. Jamie just avoided being drenched in a pot of excrement and putrid waste as a door opened and an anonymous hand swung a wooden pail's contents towards the middle of the street.

The contents splattered on Jamie's boots and saddle.

Looking at Will, Jamie rolled his eyes. 'I hope this isn't an indication of how all the folks of Leith welcome visitors,' he commented as he shook off the thick globules that were stuck to the side of his boot and saddle.

The horses turned the corner towards an increasingly loud chorus of gulls that were congregating along the harbour wall, waiting for their breakfasts of carrion. Their impatience was evident in the deafening noise as each bird fought for a prime position adjacent to the fishermen's hovels, where they knew fish was being preserved and salted, where innards were plentiful.

Bang! A solid wooden door slammed against the wall of a wood and stone building. Will and Jamie stopped and looked back.

Immediately their dirks were unsheathed, and both had kicked off their stirrups, ready to dismount.

Above the door, they could see the partially covered sign of a painted sheep's head. Snow dropped to the ground, shaken from the vulgar wooden sign, as the door to the inn banged in the wind again and again. They could just see a fire burning near the opened door, lighting a path towards its warm embrace and the entrance to the inn.

'Here is where we meet the ferryman, my young companion,' Will remarked.

'I don't understand,' Jamie replied.

'You don't have Greek?' Will knew he was rare in having an education.

'Not Greek, Will, but some Latin, and I can read and write,' Jamie retorted proudly.

'Shut the bloody door!' An irate male voice shouted from inside.

A boy of about fifteen or sixteen, wearing tatty woollen tights and a rough plaid cape pulled tight around his face, appeared outside to close the door, which was drawing freezing air into the inn like a giant bellow. He turned to look towards Will, who had dismounted and was walking through the crisp snow, pulling his unwilling mount behind him. Jamie followed, but did not dismount.

The boy's complexion was ruddy and sullen, but he broke into a warm smile on seeing Will and Jamie.

'Gentlemen, you look as if you could do with warm food and some rest at my father's fine ale house.' He gestured proudly into the inn.

The boy grabbed the reins of Will's mount with one hand.

'Let me take your horse, sir. I will get the stable boy to rub it down and feed it the finest oats in Scotland.'

He looked at Jamie, who dismounted and passed his reins to the boy's other hand.

'Please, go inside,' the boy said. 'My father is the innkeeper, and it is his great pleasure to take care of travellers such as those in your condition. Avoid the mutton stew, but do not tell him I said so.' The boy bent over and held his buttocks apart. The gesture was not lost on Jamie, and he would politely avoid any mutton on offer. Will simply laughed, but Jamie guessed he would value the advice and do the same.

'The company within is far more welcoming than the weather outside. Sitting on a cold saddle in this weather will do you no good. Yes, no good at all.'

The boy turned shaking his head and chuckled in self-agreement. He pulled the horses to either side of him and walked away towards the narrow path that separated the inn from the stables, which were tucked down a narrow lane at the back.

'Bound to give even a sainted man carbuncles.' The boy laughed as he walked away.

Amazed at his forwardness and enthusiasm, Jamie and Will watched the boy disappearing before simultaneously massaging their buttocks as they opened the inn door. They both laughed as they walked into the inn.

A large, round, red-faced man of perhaps forty years met them, wearing a well-worn leather apron that smelt of blood. He pointed them towards a dark corner on the far side of the inn that was surrounded by a small wooden stall that went to the floor.

'Please follow me, gentlemen.' He was unusually well built for a tradesman, and his frame suggested someone who had never known famine. He was friendly and accommodating. 'Sit here and get warm by the fire.'

Will, ever suspicious, looked all around them and into each corner. The inn was made up of one large room, and appeared to have three doors: one from the main room to the street, one that led to a room at the back and the exit to the kitchen and stables, and a further exit on the right-hand side of the main room. Behind this last door were probably sleeping rooms that could just as easily hide an ambush, and Will did not like unfamiliar places.

The light in the inn came from the small fireplace and half a dozen small, fat lamps that rested on the benches that stretched along the inside walls of the main room. It was just bright enough to make out forms; he could see angles but not details, tones rather than colours. Betrayal was often subtle and opaque, only discovered in minute detail when it was too late - but this did not feel like a trap.

Will armed himself with a dagger. He noticed Jamie doing the same and thought, *this boy is learning.*

As they got closer, they could smell the sour odour of stale wine, and from just behind the stall, they heard the low growl of an unfeasibly loud fart, accompanied by the snoring of what sounded more animal than human.

As the sleeping man came more fully into view, Will saw that his head was lying off the back end of the six-foot bench, almost striking the floor. It looked like a most uncomfortable position for the man to be sleeping in so soundly. Will suspected that drink had dulled any pain he might have felt from his sleeping position, but it had not dulled the noise. The man was wearing scarlet boots

'I think we have found Jean de Bretagne,' Jamie whispered to Will.

*

'You don't mind sharing a table?' The innkeeper asked, pointing to de Bretagne. 'I'll get the boy to bring you over some warm porridge and ale, and some of my famous mutton stew. Sit, please!'

'No please not the mutton ...'

The innkeeper turned and headed towards the door that led to the kitchen before Will could finish his polite refusal.

The unoccupied bench had been worn by the buttocks of many travellers, and a pattern of wax, pit marks, dagger marks, spills, burns, and mud stains peppered the bench seats as well as the tabletop and the rough, carved legs.

Jamie did not know what to make of de Bretagne, but he felt underwhelmed. He had been expecting someone more impressive. Was this Bishop Wishart's agent?

Will scraped the legs of the empty bench across the stone floor, away from the table, and kicked the opposite bench hard before sitting down and removing his sodden and snow-laden riding cape from his shoulders. He dropped the garment directly on the abdomen of Jean de Bretagne, who was slowly waking. The body recoiled as the heavy garment landed on his solar plexus, and he coughed and doubled up.

'Sit, Jamie. I think Monsieur de Bretagne will shortly be joining us,' Will said as he kicked de Bretagne's impromptu bed even harder.

Thud! De Bretagne fell off the bench and landed underneath the table. He was tall and heavily built, with a mass of reddish, greying hair messily tied into a ponytail with a piece of narrow hemp that was decorated with a tartan ribbon in light blues and greens. A loose woollen cap clung precariously on the left side of his head.

Will looked at de Bretagne, his tone was amused but contemptuous. 'Jamie, can I present the famous Jean de Bretagne, a Frenchman and an adopted Scot, survivor of Stirling Bridge and Falkirk. He had been thought killed by the English in the aftermath of Stirling Bridge, where no prisoners had been taken, and had been discovered tied to a horse amongst an English baggage train. He is often called the luckiest man alive!'

'I have also seen action at Earnside with Wallace in 1304, just a few months before Wallace was betrayed and captured.' De Bretagne growled as he corrected Will. 'And you seem to know a lot about me despite your sarcasm.'

The groaning intensified to a yell as de Bretagne, attempting to kneel, hit his head on the underside of the table's overhang. Will placed his boot on de Bretagne's rear and, as the stone floor was lubricated with all sorts of liquids and greases, managed to push him out towards the open end of the table. De Bretagne crawled out into the clear space between the bench he had been sleeping on and the unoccupied table next to the wooden stall, and fell spread-eagled face down on the floor, groaning and kissing the ground.

Jamie was aghast at his crudeness.

'You woke me most cruelly, gentlemen; just as I was nestling my handsome face within the ample bosom of a woman of amenable virtue, and she was just about to fall for my roguish charm and get on her back. I must have been a great sinner for God to bring such cruelty into my dreams.' De Bretagne sighed audibly as he pulled himself up onto his knees. He turned and offered his hand to Jamie. 'Who the fuck are you two?'

Jamie, irritated by his oafishness, replied, 'I am Jamie Wishart, and this is Will de Irwyne.'

De Bretagne belched as he replied, 'My Lord Wishart sent word that two pilgrims would be seeking me out.' His breath carried an overpowering smell of stale ale and his previous night's food.

'You are aware I am Jean de Bretagne, Breton, sailor, ship's master, brigand, lover, charmer, loyal servant of my friends, and deadly opponent to my enemies. I am at your service. Help an old man up.'

De Bretagne was loud, affable, and crude. This, combined with his long limbs and sturdy build, made him a difficult man to ignore. Despite his impressive proportions and overbearing presence, his most notable feature was a broad six-inch scar down his left cheek. The wound had nicked the corner of de Bretagne's left eye and rendered it dull, absorbing the light from the candles but giving out no reflection. He had no eye colour, only a dark, lifeless pupil. In his efforts to stand up, de Bretagne knocked his woollen cap almost off his head. Jamie moved to rescue it.

De Bretagne's hair clung to the rough woollen threads of the cloth cap and the tartan ribbon, and each hair was raised upwards, exposing his forehead. Above the hairline on the left-hand side, Jamie thought he saw the edge of a birthmark about the size of a silver penny. With haste and purpose, de

Bretagne brushed his thick greying fringe down over that side of his forehead, wrapped the long strands of his hair in the tartan ribbon, and pulled the cap firmly over his head, hiding the mark.

The innkeeper interrupted de Bretagne, bringing a tray with a flagon of ale and three matching goblets. On one large wooden trencher was some dense black bread, surrounded by a whole greasy capon and fat, rough slices of mutton. The juices from the meat were being slowly consumed, sucked into the centre of the bread. The innkeeper placed the tray of food and ale on the table in front of the three men. 'The mutton was meant for my stew,' he said.

Jamie stared at de Bretagne's wound, which still looked as raw as the day he had received it. It was unavoidable that de Bretagne would notice his stares.

'I see you have spotted the only flaw in my devastatingly good looks, my friends. It adds character and defines me. It also explains why I am here before you now - I received this courtesy of an Englishman called Aymer de Valence.' De Bretagne rubbed the scar as he spoke.

De Bretagne sat down across from Jamie and Will, on the same bench where he had been sleeping a few short minutes before.

Jamie could see that Will recognised the name.

'I see you have heard of this man,' de Bretagne said. 'De Valence is like a malevolent sheepdog, nipping at the heels of his king's enemies - only his nipping is fatal. I fought with the Scots against his master, and for this, he decided to torture me with a hot poker to my face before trying to ransom me back to my Breton family. He left me disfigured, half-dead, and tied to a horse's arse. I was saved by a Scottish knight called John Wishart. He found me amongst a captured English baggage train after the battle at Stirling Bridge. Perhaps this man was your kinsman?'

'The man who saved you was my father - he died a few

years ago. He spoke of the man he saved from the baggage train, but I never knew your name. He wept when he described what they did to you.'

De Bretagne moved two of the three goblets towards Jamie and Will, and lifted the flagon, filling each goblet until it was overflowing with frothy ale before filling his own.

'I grieve for your loss. There are few men who, in the heat of battle, wrap a butchered man in his cloak and give up his horse to carry him away from danger. He brought me to Bishop Wishart, who hid me amongst his brother monks, fixed my body and saved my life. Your father risked his life for me, and as a man of honour, I can never forget such a heroic act - you look much like him, and you will be a great man if you have his courage. I have made it my life's work to harm the English King in every way I am able, and I believe helping Bishop Wishart provides the best opportunity to do that.'

Jamie handed over the letter the Bishop had given him for de Bretagne, and watched as de Bretagne studied the Bishop's seal before breaking it open with his dirk. De Bretagne read and reread the contents. Jamie's curiosity forced him to lean forward.

'The Bishop asks me to take you across to Rouen, and at the earliest opportunity.'

'Can you arrange a ship today?' Will asked pointedly.

De Bretagne did not answer the question immediately. He placed the letter on the table and, holding his dirk, cut three large slices of bread and some slices of mutton. He placed the meat, still dripping with juice and fat, onto the black bread.

Jamie's stomach rumbled on cue.

De Bretagne laughed. 'You are hungry and a little anxious, my friend,' he said, pointing at Jamie's belly.

Jamie did not want to complain of hunger, especially as Will had not. He wanted to appear strong like his father, to have a reputation and integrity and be respected by all, and he needed to make a start on that.

'When do we sail?' Will insisted.

'Eat, my friends!' De Bretagne said. 'While you have the chance, for we sail on the next tide. The journey will be a hard one, and at this time of year, the weather can't be expected to be too friendly.'

De Bretagne pushed the bread towards the famished men, who began to cut more slices of meat as they ate, quickly washing each mouthful down with lubricating ale. De Bretagne called out to the room next door.

'Boy! Niccolò, come now.'

They could hear the latch moving as the bolt was pulled back, and a youth of perhaps twenty appeared. His dark hair and olive skin looked out of place amongst so many pale companions. He bowed to de Bretagne.

'Bring these gentlemen some travel clothes! I fear they will look out of place dressed as they are. Quick without delay.'

Niccolò bowed again. He looked at Jamie and Will up and down for much longer than a servant boy should, scrutinising the fighting men before turning on his heels and leaving the room.

Jamie thought Niccolò was not what he seemed. His tatty clothes were there to deceive; he appeared too taut and muscular, the presence of a fighting man.

'My dear friends, men travelling to France will attract much attention, and I need to provide a suitable story to satisfy the harbour master regarding my two extra passengers. His Grace suggests that you pose as two masons on your way to France to work on the cathedral in Amiens, so you must dress the part and look like jobbing artisans rather than soldiers of fortune - which, if you don't mind me adding, is precisely what you look like.'

While he spoke, de Bretagne began to pick the trapped

morsels of food from between his teeth with the end of his dagger. With considerable skill, he managed to avoid any serious injury. This unnecessarily hazardous act amused Jamie, who had never seen someone pick his teeth with a dagger and could not help grinning. His smile became wider as he tried to suppress a nearly overwhelming urge to laugh.

'Niccolò will bring you a change of clothes, and I suggest you hide away any sign of your true vocations, including your swords, and have nought but a dagger on your person. Masons do not own battle swords, and these need to be far away from you. You can store them in my cabin.'

Removing the dagger momentarily from his mouth, he pointed at Jamie and Will and their swords, which stuck out from under their woollen capes and caught the early dawn light that had just emerged through the gaps in the wooden shutters. He placed his overlarge toothpick back into its sheath at his right side.

'Your arrangements for our safety are underwhelming,' Will said with an edge to his voice. 'I expected better from one of His Grace's agents.'

His interruption appeared to surprise de Bretagne as, up to that point, Will had uttered no more than a few words of pleasantries.

'Monsieur,' Will continued, 'do you really think a change of clothes is enough to fool the English garrison that is occupying the harbour keep? The mere suspicion we are on board will be enough for them to fire on the ship. Further, the only time my sword will be removed from me is when I am dead.'

De Bretagne smiled.

The awkward silence unnerved Jamie. Whilst he was inexperienced, he could spot a confrontation when he was walking into one. He agreed with Will: he would not give up his sword easily.

'My dear boy, my advice to you is for your protection,

and this journey is perilous. Your arms may indeed be useful on the journey ahead, but please put on the clothes I offer you, and conceal the swords.' Will and Jamie reluctantly nodded with the worst possible grace.

'My men will be boarding my ship, Nantes, in one hour. They can be found sleeping in the next room - see you are amongst them. Niccolò will show you where the ship is docked and where the harbour boat that will take you to the ship can be found. I have supplied oars.'

At this moment, Niccolò returned with a coarse brown woollen sack in his hand. The sack had holes cut for a head and two arms. It looked as if it had contained grain and smelt like it had been dragged through a midden. He also carried a green hood, which was more holes than wool and appeared to have been woven in one piece before it had been gnawed by rats or even something bigger.

In Niccolò's other hand were a fleece jerkin and long brown tabard, which again had an unnerving aroma as well as evidence of a violent past. Jamie looked at this garment and hoped the stains were soup or stew, but he guessed they were probably blood.

Over his other arm, Niccolò had another long, woollen hood, which was just as dilapidated as its twin.

'Vieni presto, Niccolò.' De Bretagne urged Niccolò towards him and took the garments from his arms and hands. He tossed a hood and cape to Will, and the other hood with the jerkin and tabard towards Jamie.

'Put these on, my friends,' he ordered Will and Jamie. Niccolò bowed and left the room.

De Bretagne turned to Will. 'You are right that this disguise won't fool anyone apart from the stupidest of English soldiers. However, I have a barrel of the finest brandy to dull their senses on a cold day like this, and my animal charm. Bribery is an admiral practice for which the English garrison has a special appreciation.'

He paused and added, 'Oh, and the arrogant English King forgets to pay them from time to time.' De Bretagne winked at Will and tapped his purse, which was hanging off his belt.

'To my friends, I am Jean de Bretagne, and today I am one Jean du Trier, known to the English garrison commander as a rogue, merchant, corrupter of young and old, and bon vivant. For once, we French are enjoying an uneasy peace with the English, so they will think twice about obstructing a French merchant during his business … We are polite now as allies with a barely concealed undercurrent of confrontation but a broken treaty away. No one expects the peace to last, it is just a hiatus between wars as both kings are short of cash and need time to build up their fighting fund. So now, for the moment, everyone simply loves trade, because trade makes everyone rich, from king to peasant. Every cargo pays a tithe to whatever tyrant is in charge, and trade has no integrity. The English think Scotland has no fight left, so they can afford to be on something of a charm offensive with the French - light on the charm but heavy on the offensive. Nevertheless, we can use their current state of torpor to sail out of Leith harbour without too many questions. The spirit will help remove any remaining vigilance they may have. You did not know I was quite the philosopher in addition to my many other talents.' De Bretagne laughed and began to brush away the congealed food remaining in his long untidy beard.

'The English are looking for Scots, and my crew is made up of Frenchmen and Italians like Niccolò. Plead ignorance should anyone in the garrison speak to you. Cover your head and slap some mud on your faces: a fair complexion will be very unhealthy.'

With considerable reluctance, Will and Jamie put on the peasant garb, tying their belts above their waists to hide the ends of their swords. Each of them attached his dagger to his upper left forearm, tightened the leather straps attached to the sheath, and pulled down the loose woollen sleeves to hide its position. In the short time Jamie had spent with Will, he had learned much. Almost without thinking, he followed Will in his preparations, expecting the unexpected.

'*Tout est pret?*' Will said with a certain sarcasm, which made de Bretagne smile.

'Niccolò!' De Bretagne said. 'Take these poor masons to the harbour boat and see that they get to the Nantes in good time and in one piece while I go off to see the keep's captain at arms. Get the innkeeper's son to bring the barrel of spirit I left in his keeping to the garrison.'

'Yes, Captain.' Niccolò bowed and headed to the back of the inn where the innkeeper's family lodged.

*

De Bretagne pulled his cape and adjusted his boots, placing a small, sharp knife down the side of one of them before he walked briskly out the same door Jamie and Will had come through barely one hour before. Will followed him to the door and watched as he turned to walk around the harbour towards the end of the wall, where the harbour narrowed and where a large, simple stone tower guarded its entrance.

The tower was two-storeyed to allow the defenders to fire down on any ship seeking to enter or leave without paying its tithe to the King. The garrison commander also helped himself to his undeclared portion as a small payment for being marooned in a hostile port. The opportunity for corruption in a customs post was considerable and attracted those who were on the make.

The tower was still lit with flaming torches as de Bretagne entered, followed by the innkeeper's son, who had loaded a hand cart with a barrel of what Will assumed to be brandy.

Will hoped de Bretagne would be charming with the garrison commander, but he had his purse and the brandy to fall back upon.

The English were French allies now, and any merchant

bearing brandy would be well received and could easily turn their focus away from the fleeing ship with its valuable cargo of Scottish rebels.

De Bretagne had left behind half of his meal, so Jamie grabbed it and filled each cheek with bread and fatty mutton. He stuffed some more into his pockets before they followed Niccolò out just behind de Bretagne.

'You never know when the next meal will be available,' Jamie commented as he left.

'Venite! Come, please, quickly.' With a very heavy accent, Niccolò urged the Scots to follow him. The crew was awake and assembling at the back door of the inn. There were ten crewmen, and they were all speaking in French and Italian, but Will and Jamie did not have to speak their language to understand their complaints and moans. It did not seem that they had been expecting to sail today.

Several half-dressed whores disentangled themselves from the mass, counting the money clenched tightly in their fists. They waved and kissed their partners goodbye as they wandered away towards the centre of Leith, keeping their cloaks tightly around them as they looked for new boats that had arrived on the evening tide.

'Veloci!' Niccolò urged the men to follow him, and the crew assembled with their bags and belongings in five rows of two. It felt like Will and Jamie were being escorted as they were surrounded by the crew.

Obscured by their companions, Will and Jamie headed towards a large rowing boat that was tied at the bottom of a set of stone steps about halfway between the inn and the tower keep.

'There she is.' Niccolò proudly pointed to the Nantes, which was anchored in the centre of the sheltered harbour about two hundred yards away. 'Gentlemen, over there, see, our ship.'

Will recognised the ship: it was a shallow draught cog

and he felt just for a moment a little safer.

'A fine ship for our journey, broad and stable - the merchant ship of choice. She can navigate the rivers as well as cope with the vile weather that we will encounter in the North Sea. She is short but her wide keel can be loaded with much cargo, which can be brought right up to the weaving towns of France and the Low Countries, such as Rouen and Bruges.' Niccolò's English was noticeably more fluent as if he had previously concealed his fluency with a heavy accent. Will thought this strange and unsettling – were they walking into a trap?

Niccolò and the crew launched the boat by pushing it away from its mooring and, placing their oars in the water, manoeuvred it quickly through the choppy waters of the harbour to the Nantes. The ship's timbers crackled and cried as the outgoing tide pushed and crashed against the keel.

Niccolò grabbed the anchor rope hanging over the side of the ship and, with considerable athleticism, clambered onto the deck. The ship had been abandoned that night, and he had to throw a rope ladder over the side so that the less nimble crewmen could climb on board.

As Niccolò tied the rowing boat to the side of the ship, they could hear singing and laughing in the distance, coming from the keep. It appeared that Jean was handling the garrison as he had promised. In the meantime, the crew was still moaning about the early hour at which they were preparing to sail.

Will and Jamie stood on the deck in awkward silence as the crew busied themselves, pushing them out of the way as they placed long oars in the restraints that lined the deck. There were only ten oars, but as the wind strengthened, Niccolò unfurled the single sail.

A large, dark crewman gestured for Jamie to grab an oar as he went to the stern to take the rudder with a second man, leaving an inconvenient space for Will. The rudder required immense strength and skill to navigate even a small ship safely out of the harbour, and as the single sail was unfurled, they began to move with pace and purpose.

'I wonder how de Bretagne will join us,' Jamie said as he grabbed his oar and Will stood at the adjoining oar.

'I don't think he is coming with us, unless he jumps from the tower,' Will replied.

They started to row, mainly to direct the boat out through the harbour wall, as the sail was taking the wind; and with the tide, they were rapidly heading out towards the open sea.

Niccolò tied the sail down to its mast. 'Captain de Bretagne asked me to get you to Rouen while he deals with the English. It was the only way.'

He turned towards the men holding the rudder and shouted in Italian. Will understood French and some Italian, and was not concerned. He was simply issuing the same orders any sailor would shout when leaving a small harbour, telling the crew to watch the tide and steady the ship.

Nevertheless, it was uncomfortable. Will leaned toward Jamie and whispered, 'I feel I am being guarded. What about you, Jamie?'

Jamie nodded. 'But what choice do we have?'

Will shrugged and slapped Jamie on the shoulder. 'At this moment, none.'

The Nantes passed the harbour wall and was buffeted by the crashing waves, but the tide and wind were in their favour and were pushing them past Leith towards the open sea to the south. They were heading towards the English border.

Will reckoned if they were to be killed, they would have been dead already: why go to the trouble of a long and expensive sea voyage if they were to be handed over to the English? There had already been an opportunity to have the keep's garrison arrest them before they boarded the ship.

Despite this, Will was uneasy. Perhaps it was the unfamiliarity of being within someone else's control that made him feel this way. He was on a ship, and he did not know how to sail. He was relying on the sea and a group of foreign sailors, rather than a horse and the land. Will had to trust these people, yet all his instincts told him to be concerned.

'Smettete di remare!' Niccolò shouted.

The crew stood, bringing up the long oars and resting them on the deck.

'Sit down, my Scottish friends.' Niccolò smiled. Will and Jamie were reluctant to take his advice. The seats carved into the ship's side were now sodden, and the deck was wet with the foam thrown up as they crashed through the waves. They were going to have to get used to being wet.

The rudder was still manned, pushing the ship first to the east and then to the south. The crew had set up a brazier on a spherical bearing that flexed with the movement of the current and undulation of the waves. They placed a pot above it and began to make a pottage of pulses, wheat, and fatty dried meat. The crew threw down sacking for Will and Jamie to sit on and poured some sweetened wine into a beaker for them.

'Tiens,' a heavy-set man grunted in a terse gesture of friendship.

'Jamie, eat some more,' Will said encouragingly.

He realised that Jamie was sweating, and his skin was pale as he put his head over the side for the first time.

'But on second thought, perhaps not,' Will said.

The crew laughed and shouted as Jamie projected vomit downwind to the delight of the gulls. Will smiled; there was no going back now they headed into the featureless sea.

'We will sail just out of sight of land,' Niccolò pointed to a nebulous point on the horizon. 'That will help us avoid the English ships, and before you know it, we will be in France. Sit. Drink with us.'

'Of course,' Will answered tersely. He was now genuinely

concerned by Jamie's constant retching. *You would probably prefer death, my boy.*

Will remained unsettled, but took his place with the crew around the brazier and began to drink some of the sweetened wine Niccolò had offered him. For now, he had no option but to trust these people.

Chapter Eight

Byzantium, Late March 1306: The Revenge of the Emperors

'Andronikos II, the great, the magnificent, God's representative on Earth, Holy of Holies. Defender of the Proper Religion. Custodian of the True Cross.' The priests chanted his litany of titles as he gazed out over his holy church, the Hagia Sophia, without acknowledging the theatre playing out below him.

Andronikos let out an audible yawn. His boredom was palpable; if it had been anyone else yawning, they would have been ostracised from the Church and court - but it was the Emperor.

When will this all finish?

'Remember, it is all about dignity,' he whispered under his breath, maintaining his forced smile.

He had to play the role of God's anointed on Earth. His position demanded that everyone believed in his near divinity, and his relationship with the Orthodox Church was mutually beneficial. As he grew powerful, so did they, making both parties happy and content.

Andronikos favoured philosophers and intellectuals, but later today, after mass, he would meet with the captain of his guard and his joint Emperor to discuss violent acts.

The joint Emperors used a walkway from their palace directly into the upper level of the church, avoiding the commons. They hoped in the darkness they could remain concealed, but that was difficult when each of them was wearing a pallium made of cloth of gold, studded with jewels, pearls, and heavily embroidered with gold and silver threads. They sparkled even in the candlelight that struggled to light up the enormous chancel beneath the huge dome of the Hagia Sophia, the biggest building in the world.

He sat next to his son and joint Emperor, Michael, on the horseshoe balcony well above the holy altar. The incense burner was large, and the fragrant smoke always made him tired and caused his eyes to water, but he tried to hide his irritation.

Emperor Michael was the warrior, whilst Andronikos was the intellectual; they represented both the spiritual and temporal parts of the people's lives. Andronikos understood Michael's role and presumed Michael recognised the importance of religion in controlling his empire: it could not be controlled by the sword alone. One earnest priest was worth a thousand of Michael's elite Varangian bodyguards.

Distracted, Anronikos overheard one of his guards, who was not trying too hard to be discreet.

'Vil dette aldri ende opp med å bli så kjedelig. Jeg trenger en drink og en kvinne?'

I often think the same. A drink and a woman are often on my mind too. But he ignored these thoughts and continued to feign interest.

The Varangians were a distinctive and ever-present force - tall, fair-skinned Norwegians amongst a multitude of diminutive, swarthy Greeks - and their impact served a purpose. They intimidated everyone, and even if their own religious leanings were not for Orthodoxy, they spent each mass in silent acquiescence, only relieving the boredom by scratching graffiti on the upper floor with their magnificent daggers in their own language. They put up with the unfathomable ceremonies every day because they were mercenaries who would do anything for gold and silver.

Emperor Andronikos had an obligation to attend the mass every day, and today he thanked his good fortune that there was no Saint's Day or procession. Being God's representative ate into his day. Today he could not face ceremonies of worship that took any longer than necessary: there were bigger issues to deal with. His empire was in decline, and if he were to leave a legacy, he needed to rebuild the devastation caused by the years of war wrought on his land and his subjects.

He spent these ceremonies dreaming of regaining the lost lands and putting his empire back into its rightful place as the direct heir to the Roman Empire and the line of Saint Peter. The current occupier of Rome, Clement V, was a tyrant and usurper, a fake successor to Peter, and his religion was a second-rate copy of the Orthodoxy that was only to be found in Byzantium.

But what Emperor Andronikos really wanted was revenge on the western powers, and he knew Emperor Michael was demonstratively an angry bitter person and, as such, the right man for the violent jobs that needed doing in any Empire.

Andronikos understood Michael's rage, which fuelled their mutual desire for revenge. Michael had a scar running from the left side of his forehead through to his right cheek from a recent battle with western mercenaries, who had also whipped him out of their camp. He still carried deep scars on his back, and even deeper ones in his psyche.

For a military man, his son Michael was vain. His beard was ornately platted, and he wore his hair in long ringlets that helped to conceal the bottom of his face, but the barber had not concealed the pain. Every time he moved his face, Andronikos could see his twisted back. The dull, throbbing pain must have reminded him of what Bernard Ferrer, the captain of the mercenary Catalan Company, had done to him, and the humiliation that it had brought him. Emperors were supposed to be perfect, but Michael's face betrayed another description. People could not hide their repulsion and horror as they looked at him, such was his disfigurement.

When his son could take the humiliation no more, he hid away in shame, but that was hard when you were joint Emperor. His only satisfaction was that Bernard Ferrer lay rotting in the emperor's dungeon, suffering a living hell, and that reality acted like an opiate. The hate dulled his pain.

Michael had a skill for creating enemies. He had Roger de Flor, the previous commander of the Catalan Company, assassinated for his many slights against the Emperors and his disloyalty to the empire, and he had provoked Ferrer's rebellion. These Catalans had once been mercenaries in the Emperor's pay, but when they decided the pay was not enough, their loyalty had ended, and the Company had spent years stealing and murdering their way through the empire until Michael had stopped them. Andronikos knew he had paid a high price in protecting their Empire.

Now Ferrer was trying to buy his freedom with claims of treasure that had been taken from them - Alaric's gold. Michael wanted his tongue ripped out, but now Andronikos wanted to hear him. Michael's hate for Ferrer was so strong that he could sense palpable tension in the court at the very thought of his name.

Andronikos needed Michael for what he was about to do, as he was not a soldier preferring the power of rhetoric and knowledge, more cultivated in his intentions. This venture required cunning mixed with strength, and Michael had both.

They were both passionate in their belief that it was their Christian duty to take back the land and treasures that had been lost. The irony was that the treasure they had lost had been stolen by fellow Christians. The 1204 invasion had begun this process of plunder and desecration, reducing the population from 250,000 to 50,000; and he was determined to seek his revenge, but that was secondary and for later. He would settle for the treasure.

He hated the West and the Latins, and he hated the Venetians above all his enemies. It was of no consequence that it had been over a hundred years since the desecration; the retrieval of Alaric's treasure was to be his payback.

Andronikos had one further score to settle, a legacy from the so-called Latin Empire. The French had been amongst the most enthusiastic Crusaders, and the Emperors had to deal with the French pretender to the Byzantine throne, the so-called Latin King of Constantinople, Charles de Valois, the idiotic younger brother of King Philip of France. He had married the daughter of the last Latin Emperor of Byzantium and called himself the King of Byzantium, in his eternal pursuit of a crown to call his own.

In 1302, Valois had initiated an ill-planned invasion to claim his wife's empire, and like the fool he was, Valois had looted and robbed his way across Italy and Sicily, and lost the support of the Pope and the papal states, returning to France in disgrace.

But when did a tyrant or a fool ever let the truth cloud a usurper's claim to the throne? If the law meant nothing to Valois, then the Emperors would use something Valois did understand - retaliation funded with the recovered treasure. This was a plan Andronikos had only shared with his closest advisors.

Andronikos stifled another broad yawn. *I hope the Bishop notices my mood and curtails his special aptitude for verbosity.*

Today brought news indeed.

They had learned of something that would help them wreak revenge on all their enemies. He was excited and wanted to be back in the palace.

The Emperor caught sight of his unctuous advisors clasping their hands in prayer as they remained seated on purple velvet cushions resting on a gold scrolled bench. They were magnificently dressed in their heavily embroidered tunics and capes: as his inner circle of advisors, they wielded great power.

They were a pack of traitors, thieves, spies, and scoundrels, and it was only to be hoped that they saw their wealth and prospects as greater in the pay of the Emperors than they would be with the empire's foreign competitors. Amongst the advisors were one or two who thought they should be Emperor. That was why Michael and Andronikos were joint Emperors: there was strength in numbers.

Andronikos had to face facts; the Byzantine Empire was fading: down on its luck, short of money, and at war on all sides. Emperor Michael was leading his armies in battle with the Turks in Asia Minor and the Bulgarians in northern Thrace, and things were not going well. They needed money - a huge amount of money - to reverse their decline.

Finally, the mass was concluding, and the Emperors rose from their cushions. Their retinue got in each other's way as they tried to follow them back to the palace, which was but a short distance away from the great church. Emperor Andronikos shouted towards his son, 'You go on ahead. I need to speak briefly with Theodore Metochites.'

Theodore was small, swarthy, bald, and ostensibly bland; he was completely underwhelming in appearance, and for those who did not know him, he was easily underestimated. He was an enigma, a witty and learned Christian man who believed in the superiority of the Greek world over the Latin one. His loyalty was unquestionable, and both Andronikos and Michael knew this and trusted him. He was no general, but he was the cleverest lawyer in the land and was more valuable than all the fighting men put together. He also ran the empire for both emperors.

As Andronikos walked in procession with Theodore, his Norwegian bodyguards immediately gathered around him. 'Ask Patriarch Gregory to come to my apartments and join Emperor Michael and me,' he told Theodore. 'We have much to discuss this day.'

Patriarch Gregory was part of the Emperors' inner

circle. Mixing Church and State was a fundamental part of the Emperors' power. Gregory's priests and spies were the key to retaining his hold on the empire, and he needed that mutuality of purpose to support the symbiotic relationship that made the empire work successfully.

'Ask Axel Myhre to attend me presently,' Andronikos told Theodore. 'I have an errand for him, and I need his wisdom and wit today. It is time to bring Bernard Ferrer to our chambers.'

'And what about Otto de Grandison and William de Beaujeu?' Theodore asked.

'I do not think they have anything to tell us after so many years. Ferrer is our best chance to recover our gold.' Emperor Andronikos said. 'How long have they been our guests?'

'About fifteen years, Basileus. They have stopped their escape attempts, and are now decaying, both muddled in brain - a ship crewed by the devil indeed. They talk in riddles and are weak in spirit and broken in body. They were tortured and told us nothing but tall tales of murder.' Theodore replied.

The Emperor sighed and rolled his eyes.

'I will bring Ferrer immediately, Basileus,' Theodore replied, bowing low as he turned to walk down the stairs leading from the balcony to the cathedral altar.

The Emperors left the cathedral by way of the Imperial Gate. Only royalty and invited guests were permitted to enter and leave the great church by the long ramp that led from the northern part of the outer narthex to the upper gallery. The route was easy to protect and avoided the congested streets around the cathedral.

The Varangian guards were at every exit and entrance the Emperors used, partly for security but mostly for terror. They were magnificently dressed in scarlet tunics, hose, and capes that were gilded at the edges. Each guard had an iron helmet with a nose guard, also gilded at the edges, and carried a scarlet shield and a double-bladed axe. In their leather belts, each man carried a dagger that was almost the length of a sword, which could be used for closer combat if the need arose, but their preferred weapon was the axe.

The Emperors had a complex of palaces in Constantinople for the guards, government officials, and administrators. The Emperor's rooms were in the section of the complex called the Palace of the Porphyrogenitus, or the Palace of Those Born in Purple. The title created the expectation of riches, but not the reality. The Crusaders had taken over fifty years to empty the Byzantine palaces of their contents, and it was taking a considerable time to replace what had been stolen.

However, even after all the pillaging, the current Emperor's rooms were not a disappointment. These personal spaces had been the first to be restored, and the rooms were numerous. Each room had enamelled religious icons on the walls and enamelled stands. Damask silks draped the furniture, and intricate mosaics and woven rugs covered the marble floors. Gilded bowls full of dried fruits and nuts decorated every table, and engraved flagons and chalices were laid out on gold trays, tantalising everyone who entered; but their sumptuousness betrayed a spartan reality for the rest. The treasury was empty from wars and indulgence, and the rebuilding was now at a halt. Money was power, and power was everything in the Byzantine court.

Emperor Andronikos entered, followed by Michael and Theodore Metochites. A minute later, Patriarch Gregory joined them, and the doors were shut firmly behind him. Slaves stood silently by the walls, and Varangians to either side of the door. The two Emperors were seated, whilst everyone else stood, waiting for them to speak. Andronikos took the initiative.

'I have ordered the dungeon guards to bring Bernard Ferrer to my rooms and summoned Axel Myhre, our agent Aurelian. They should be here soon, and we can begin.'

Gregory looked surprised. 'We aren't alone, Basileus?' Andronikos knew Gregory for what he was and what he could do. He was defined by his own self-importance and had used his considerable cunning to remain Patriarch. Many of his predecessors had been assassinated. That was why Andronikos liked to keep him around.

The door opened again for Aurelian. He removed the helmet as he came into the Emperors' presence, revealing cropped hair, a full, neatly trimmed beard, and piercing blue eyes. He also wore the wrinkles of early middle age, but cared for his appearance and had tried to hide his ageing with excessive grooming.

Aurelian had been born Axel Myhre in eastern Norway and had been a soldier in the army of King Eric II before being sent to Emperor Andronikos to act as one of his personal bodyguards, as was the tradition. After over fifteen years in the Emperor's service, he was one of his most trusted adjutants. His exploits in defending the empire were legendary, so much so that he was called Aurelian, or the Golden One. His methods were a mixture of guile, brute strength, and massive retaliation, and he never left a task for the Emperor unfinished.

Aurelian bowed low to the Emperors and acknowledged the Mesazon and Patriarch.

'Emperor Andronikos, you summoned me, and I am here to serve.' Andronikos winced as he heard his Greek name pronounced with Aurelian's still heavy Norse accent, but that was a small price to pay for such a loyal servant. He was happy to reward him well for his loyalty alone. Aurelian was the nearest thing Andronikos had to a friend.

Andronikos ordered wine for everyone before dismissing the slaves. He knew that was unusual, as slaves were property, and they heard and said nothing. This signalled an unusual audience.

Andronikos focused on Aurelian and ignored everyone

else.

'Aurelian, in 1291 I sent you to Acre to recover some property, Alaric's treasure, which had been stolen by the Templars when they sacked this city in 1204.'

'Yes, Basileus. I remember that my crew had arrived in Acre intent on removing the treasure from the Templar keep, but the Mamluks placed the city under seize as we arrived. We had spies in Acre who told us the treasure was being removed by barge to a place of safekeeping. We followed, but lost the barge off the coast of Venice in dense fog. I had assumed the greedy Venetians had seized the ship and the cargo. Out at sea we found Otto de Grandison and William de Beaujeu adrift, frightened and penniless.'

Andronikos tingled with the thought of getting his hands on his money and returning his forgotten dynasty to power.

The doors opened again, and Bernard Ferrer stood in chains. He looked haggard, miserable, but still had an air of arrogance. Andronikos noticed how thin and gaunt he was, and how he had to be supported by the Varangian guards to either side of him. He was dirty and smelled terrible.

Some of his front teeth were missing, but his eyes were alert, and he was defiant, full of fight. He was dressed in a pale, plain tunic without decoration, and his woollen hose were loose, hanging almost down to his knees. On his feet, he wore overly big sandals that were obviously not his, but covered his bare feet for modesty.

Emperor Andronikos pointed towards a heavily carved pillared chair. 'Put him in that chair and leave us,' he said to the guards.

Andronikos had deliberately waited to reveal his machinations until he had assembled his cabal. It was an uncomfortable but necessary grouping. Emperor Michael could not avert his stare from Ferrer and would have readily killed him, had they been alone. Michael's fists were clenched against his sides, and Andronikos recognised that

Ferrer should not be in his son's presence a moment longer than was necessary.

'By all conventions, this man's head should be on the city gates, but like all his kind, he is afraid of death and wanted to buy his life and his freedom. I don't negotiate with brigands and traitors - I leave that up to the city magistrates - but this man has a remarkable, almost fabulous, story to share with us.'

A prisoner was rarely brought into Andronikos's presence. His dirty work was carried out away from his gaze. He did not soil his hands with such vulgarity, and especially not in front of an audience.

Ferrer looked directly at him and Michael, showing no fear.

'Kneel before the Basileis,' Theodore cried.

Ferrer ignored him. 'You offered me my freedom in return for helping you retrieve Alaric's treasure. I think that was the deal?'

Gregory stepped forward and slapped Ferrer in the face. 'You weren't given permission to speak.'

The blow was so hard that Ferrer's lip bled, and his left cheek reddened. Ferrer could not wipe the blood away, as his shackles kept his hands by his side. The blood flowed into his mouth and down his chin, but Ferrer looked unapologetic.

Andronikos felt no emotion about this slight to his position. He just wanted his gold.

'Indeed, that is the deal on offer, Ferrer, but before we conclude, you said that you have proof that you know where our treasure is hidden. My son tells me you were chained to a soldier who had hidden the treasure and told you the location of Alaric's gold. He also tells me you are a liar and that I should execute you, not give you your freedom. You disfigured a man anointed by God.'

'Please remove these shackles, and I will produce the proof,' Ferrer replied.

Myhre produced the key and roughly removed the shackles, allowing Ferrer to move his hands. Ferrer dropped his hose and, without any consideration, removed from behind his foreskin a gold solidus. He placed the coin in the hand of an astonished Axel Myhre.

'I think you will recognise this,' Ferrer said.

Myhre wiped the coin placing it in front of Emperor Andronikos, who picked it up admiring its beauty and colour. He licked his lips, which made him look greedy and avaricious.

'Pure gold, dated from the reign of Emperor Valentinian II. My grandfather was forced to flee into exile in Nicea, taking a small portion of his treasure,' Andronikos was squeaking with joy. 'These coins are identical to the ones he removed from our treasury. Here we have the first tangible proof of Alaric's treasure in over one hundred years.'

'That proves nothing but that he has had contact with the treasure, or someone near to him has passed it on,' Michael scoffed, speaking with an impertinence Andronikos would have accepted from no other. 'It could have been broken down, dispersed, or stolen since Ferrer came to us.'

Andronikos dismissed his challenge. 'Don't you think we would have heard about it by now if it had been discovered? In any case, we cannot afford to take the risk that the treasure is intact and that our enemies are near to capturing it and all the power it brings.' Emperor Michael scoffed and grunted his disbelief.

'Ferrer, you have kept to your side of the bargain, and I will keep mine and release you into the hands of my agent Aurelian to locate and retrieve the treasure stolen from us.' The Emperor paused. 'Remember, Bernard Ferrer, that my reach is far and that, if you betray me, I will send men to find you and kill you. I am sure my son will volunteer to be your executioner.' The Emperor dismissed Ferrer with a flick of his hand.

Axel replaced the shackles and manhandled Ferrer to the doors. Opening them, he pushed Ferrer towards the Varangian guards standing outside.

'Take this pile of filth back to the dungeons, but see no harm comes to him. I will join him presently.' Upon giving the order, Axel returned to the Emperors and the Patriarch to take his leave.

'Axel, before you leave us, I have one more task for you,' Andronikos said. 'I have brought Patriarch Gregory into our presence because I also want you to put an end to the practice of copying our sacred relics retrieved from our Lord's suffering by Saint Helena. We believe Geoffroi de Charnay and Enrico Scrovegni produce these monstrous artefacts, and we want these fakes destroyed. They are coincidentally also the men we believe are the key to our treasure - at least the intercepted mail we have seen from the spies in France and England believes they are key in finding its location.'

Andronikos turned towards the Patriarch. 'Gregory has taken care of the true relics and keeps them protected in the monastery in Sinai dedicated to Saint Catherine. Now we see that fakes are being worshipped everywhere when the real ones remain with us. The real relics cannot be truly valued and worshipped if their authenticity is called into question by these worthless fakes. It's your Christian duty to destroy those who profited from fakery and blasphemy.'

Patriarch Gregory interrupted, encouraged by Andronikos's rhetoric. 'These peddlers of the Antichrist must be stopped. They attract and deceive pilgrims who are fooled with false hope, and distract them from the real relics. It is to us that these pilgrims need to turn, and to Saint Catherine's monastery in Sinai, within the Orthodox world where we can control their worship and veneration.'

Andronikos turned to Theodore. 'Make the arrangements for Ferrer to be given a horse and provisions, and to be released into Aurelian's custody.'

Theodore bowed.

'Basileis, we leave at first light,' Aurelian said.

'Take advantage of the noisy market to cover your departure. You should assume that the Kings of France and England know as much as we do about the treasure, and possibly more. We have intercepted their dispatches, and there are rumours that they have agents watching us. You should assume you will be followed. I believe Ferrer will take you to the west and the Venetian kingdom: we had word that Charles de Valois was searching for the gold in their lands. Ferrer is unreliable, a traitor. Your adventure will be a most perilous one. Be successful and bring us back the treasure. By doing that you honour God.' At this, Andronikos turned his back on everyone apart from his son, and they took this as their signal to leave.

Chapter Nine

The Court of Philip of France, April 1306: The King's Avarice

In the Palais on the Ile de la Cité, the King of France sat at his small table at the far end of a large reception room, reading documents from his agents in Britain. Large candles stood on wooden stands, creating some light, but the room was huge and intimidating, filled with large painted sculptures and scenes depicting ancient tyrants and dying animals brutally hunted and killed by the King. The coldness of the wind outside leaked through every crevice in the room's structure. The King shuddered slightly from the cold as he studied. Even with the courtiers milling about the palace in their heavy furs and fabrics, the chill was still evident, and many of the servants and courtiers stood as close as protocol allowed to each fireplace.

If the air was icy, Philip's character was colder; he was distant, yet feared. He had made a virtue of being aloof, and the court and its courtiers reflected his coldness. They maintained a distance, allowing him to spend many hours strategising and observing alone. His lack of approachability was just how he liked it.

The documents were tiny parchment rolls that had been smuggled out of foreign courts in extreme secrecy. The King had an extensive network of agents throughout Europe. The men who had taken risks to get their secret messages to Philip were his greatest servants, and many had already been executed for their King, especially those whom he had placed in the English court. King Philip valued few people in his life, but his foreign agents were the exception.

An important message had come from his agent based in Scotland. The King read the decoded words in silence, bringing the velum closer to a small lamp that rested at the edge of the table so that he could see more clearly.

'Sire, rebellion has broken out in the land of Scotland, and Lord Bruce of Annandale has killed King Edward's loyal servant, John Comyn. Scotland is in chaos. Lord Robert was crowned King of the Scots on the 25th of March,' he whispered the last sentence.

King Philip took a great deal of interest in the troubles of his great rival, King Edward of England. He prided himself on never smiling, with one exception: when his rival and brother-in-law King Edward was in trouble. He could barely contain a wry smile as he read the news, quietly mocking his brother-in-law's misfortune.

He had no great affection for the Scots other than the fact that they took the attention of King Edward - and, more importantly, his army - away from France. France was now in an uneasy peace with the English, and the Auld Alliance signed with Scotland in 1295 had been tacitly ignored. The French had done little militarily to help the Scots these past years.

This message had arrived in the French court, so the English King would also be aware of the Scottish rebellion. King Philip suppressed a smile, hiding his joy behind his hand as he thought of how King Edward would have reacted, whilst at the same time wondering how he would take advantage.

He had considered breaking the treaty with Scotland and annulling the Auld Alliance; but now it appeared that the time was close for France to support the Scots and break the uneasy truce with the English. Philip had considered the Scots a conquered people, but this news signalled the emerging shoots of another rebellion. Now was the time to get Aquitaine and Gascony back from the English.

He looked at this trouble in Scotland as an opportunity: if King Edward were busy on his northern frontier, he would have less time to secure his southern one. He wanted his legacy to be the removal of the English from France for good.

The King read the note again and began to plan and scheme. This news gave him an opening, something he could worry about until it became a gaping hole of opportunity to gain the advantage and destroy the English King's foothold in France.

Those who knew him said King Philip was neither man nor beast, but a statue devoid of the normal emotions of a living being. He was lean with narrow features and brilliant blue eyes that were as emotionless as the mind that hid behind them. He was not called Philip le Bel for nothing. His hair was light blond but speckled with white highlights, betraying a man who was leaving his prime and moving towards middle age. At just over thirty-seven, he stood out amongst his courtiers in his stunning blue silks and velvets marked with the fleur de lys. He was known to wear cloth of gold, yet he was not vain. He took little personal pleasure in wearing expensive cloth; the enjoyment came in showing his wealth and power, and the opportunity to display the opulence and majesty of his crown.

His proudest display of that power was not in the clothing on his back, but in the manifestation of his virility: four sons and a daughter, who would be the means to bring his plans to fruition, though they were not without their flaws.

Louis, his heir, who at seventeen was already King of Navarre, took after his feckless and stubborn mother. Next in line after the unremarkable Louis came young Philip, his namesake. At fourteen, young Philip was already tall, and like his father in his coldness and detachment from humanity. His mind worked like a machine with cogs and

140

wheels, and his father recognised in him these unattractive characteristics even though they were his own. Then there was Charles, his lookalike, sometimes referred to as the goose, as his pretty face betrayed a brain as dull as his looks were handsome. Then came Robert - his youngest child, who was not yet eight - and in between Charles and Robert, his only surviving daughter and favourite child, Isabella.

Isabella would have her own throne as the wife and mother of English Kings. Philip had dynastic desires on his rival King Edward's kingdom, and what he could not achieve on the battlefield he would conquer in the marriage bed. He had heard that King Edward's son had inherited none of his father's talents except for his temper, and Isabella had inherited all of Philip's along with the face of an angel. She would rule any man who took her to his bed. King Philip smiled as he gazed upon her.

Looking up, Philip was temporarily distracted from his plotting by the brewing of an argument amongst his youngest children. Isabella snatched a painted wooden horse from the chubby closed hand of her younger brother Robert. He had assembled his wooden toys into two armies, opposing each other at either side of the stone fireplace. Robert cried in protest, but King Philip stopped his servants from responding to the boy's distress.

'Leave him!' he ordered a nurse who had stepped momentarily forward to comfort her charge. 'My youngest son will have to learn to fight for his possessions.'

Isabella was by now ordering her little brother Robert about and intimidating Charles. Charles always did his sister's bidding without objection, and today was no different.

'Charles, put your soldiers over there! No, over there, you goose!' she cried as she pointed away from where her older brother was placing his wooden soldiers. The King watched his children as they played at imaginary war, whilst his thoughts turned to plots of treasure and treachery. How could he break the treaty with the English King and win the real war that would follow?

King Philip was constantly short of the money he needed to make his schemes a reality. He surrounded himself with clever men who were constantly looking for ways of raising money, and he rewarded them handsomely. The circle of service, delivery, reward, and loyalty maintained equilibrium and brought strength and resilience to his kingdom. He used his endless list of noble relatives for certain political issues where position was more important than talent.

He could hear mumbling as his advisors informally assembled.

'Ah, my advisors gather like preening peacocks,' he muttered.

The King spotted Guillaume de Nogaret. An ambitious middle-aged lawyer, de Nogaret only adhered to the laws he liked, and those were the ones that suited the King's will. Philip appreciated practical men with a vision for the future, and he did not care what anyone believed their status was; their purpose was to serve the King. De Nogaret's confidence and influence with the King had made enemies, and chief amongst them was the King's brother, Charles de Valois.

In the opposite corner, de Valois was plotting. He could never be described as a practical man, but he was not without charisma and was almost as physically attractive as his brother. He was not king, however, and he carried this fact like it was a disease that had no cure apart from acquiring a throne. De Valois liked to think of himself as the Emperor of Constantinople, having married its heiress, Catherine de Courtenay. Valois had never set foot in the city and was unlikely to see its walls from anywhere but the outside.

It was clear from the acolytes who surrounded Valois and de Nogaret that they each had different views about what serving the King meant. Charles thought of himself as the beacon of the nobility, while de Nogaret saw himself as the fulcrum of the learned, cunning men whom Philip had promoted on their ability. De Nogaret and Valois distrusted each other and competed for King Philip's attention.

The King gestured to a servant standing behind his table to come towards him.

'Bring me the Scotsman's purse, and ask Seigneur de Nogaret, Brother Valois, and my two oldest sons to join me in Sainte-Chapelle. Tell them to come without retinue. I will need my seal - fetch it!'

'Yes, Sire.' The thin youth bowed and walked towards young Louis and Philip.

The King headed towards the corridor that led out of the Palais to the courtyard. Two armed soldiers, led by their sergeant, walked behind him as he progressed towards Sainte-Chapelle.

The King turned to his escort. 'Stop. Remain here, and send Seigneur de Nogaret, Brother Valois, and my sons to me directly when they arrive. I can be found at my grandfather's oratory.'

'Yes, Sire,' the sergeant replied.

Two more sentries opened tall wooden doors into a dazzling room coloured with the most brilliant wall paintings.

Inside was a kaleidoscope of colour. The room was drizzled with blues, pinks, reds, and the gold of diffused late winter sunlight that cut through numerous tall and elegant stained-glass windows, and seemed to burn their colours into the walls and ceilings. The light was overwhelming in its brilliance.

The interior walls were covered with murals depicting Christ's life, tales of the Old Testament, and paintings and statues of saints. The small private oratories were draped in cloth of gold and silver. The chapel looked like a bejewelled and magnificent reliquary on a grand scale, and that was exactly how it should look, as it contained the most sacred relic of all.

King Philip's grandfather, Saint Louis, had commissioned the construction of the chapel to house the Crown of Thorns worn by Christ on the cross. The chapel's treasure also included a piece of the True Cross as well as the lance Longinus had used to pierce the side of Christ as he hung at the crucifixion.

King Philip marvelled at its magnificence.

You are my family's legacy, and I never tire of you.

At the far end of the nave, he could see the Crown of Thorns contained within the Grand-Chasse, a decorated and engraved silver casket so magnificent that it had cost nearly three times as much as the building that housed it.

The chapel was a place for quiet reflection, but it was still ostentatious and included a large, jewelled golden cross. Hung at each corner of the room were incense burners, which produced fierce smoke and pungent odours.

It was unusual for the King to go unobserved, without bodyguards or courtiers, and he loved it. His world was almost never truly private, and he relished these moments. He knelt before the altar in Saint Louis's oratory and whispered.

'Christ, my saviour, I see your will in these rebellions in Scotland. Please guide me on the right path. Help me in what I must do now.' The King slowly crossed himself as the chapel doors opened. They echoed as a draught blew down the nave, bringing with it the familiar pattern of soft leather-booted footsteps, which crunched on the fine grit that had blown onto the stone flags.

Faint voices could be heard as Valois and Prince Louis exchanged pleasantries. Valois seemed to be enquiring into Louis's exploits of the previous evening with the Parisian courtesans.

The King thought his son's propensity for sharing his exploits undignified and vulgar, even with his uncle. There was never any mystery with Louis.

The King sat on one of the stone benches, which lined the

chapel, and waited for his guests.

De Nogaret and young Philip were not skilled in conversation and followed in silence behind Valois and Louis.

Following Philip and de Nogaret, the King saw the servant carelessly swinging the small purple velvet purse. He stopped at the entrance to Saint Louis's oratory, bowing low to all the lords and princes who now stood in a row by the bench opposite the King.

'You,' the King gestured to the servant. 'Place the pouch here next to me. Away!' he shouted, dismissing the servant immediately. 'And no one is to enter,' he called after the boy.

The King grasped the pouch and carelessly removed the seal, throwing it to the floor. 'Sit, my Lords. We have serious matters to discuss, secret matters of which none but this group must be aware.'

Louis and Phillip sat in silence whilst Valois and de Nogaret competed to get a better view as the King removed a large amethyst cabochon ring from the bottom of the pouch and placed it on top of the velvet cloth.

'Seigneur de Nogaret will remember the tall Scotsman, William Wallace, and his companion John Wishart, who spent time at court a few years ago.'

'Yes, Sire,' de Nogaret said. 'Wallace and Wishart arrived in court around 1299, looking for diplomatic support in maintaining Scottish independence. I remember that Wallace left the court without warning, and his companion remained our guest for a considerable time in our best dungeon in the Chateau Gaillard. He disappeared from there a couple of years ago. He was rumoured to have been with the Templars in Acre and knew the source of their wealth and treasure. He told us nothing.'

The King continued. 'This ring was hidden, sewn in the collar of Wishart's shirt. Wishart did reveal, after Wallace had escaped France, that certain rings would guide their possessors to a treasure and that he was in possession of a second ring. We can presume this contained a further clue to the location of this wonderous treasure and that Wallace removed this second ring when he left for Scotland.'

The King handed the ring to Valois and continued in a quiet, deliberate voice.

'Examine this carefully. It is much more than just a ring.'

Valois twisted the ring between his thumb and middle finger and investigated the large purple cabochon.

'Yes, Sire. It has a strange script hidden within the stone, possibly Greek; and the stone and setting are Byzantine in style. My wife had much jewellery of this type. The stone itself is the colour of royalty. I have many stones of this colour, but none with engraving. But the message looks incomplete.' Valois had been educated, but never worked at anything for long. The King, however, knew he would scrutinise this if there was a chance it gave him a crown.

The King observed Philip looking and listening, whilst Louis continued to pare his nails with his dagger and gave the impression he was there under sufferance.

The King had a short list of things he cared about. His legacy was important, and his major weak spot was his heir, Louis. The King wondered whether Louis would ever show the traits and skills needed to be the King of France. Louis frequently disappointed him as he did now with his disinterest.

'Louis!' The King shouted.

The dauphin jumped, straightened his back, and looked at the King attentively.

'What I am about to tell you, my son, could mean the end of the Plantagenet plague in France forever. Isn't that a prize worth paying attention for? Stop playing with your nails and listen!' The King told Louis off like a child rather than his heir. He struggled to hide his frustration.

The dauphin nodded his head like a toddler, but young

Philip showed much greater curiosity.

Valois passed the ring to Louis. He examined it carefully, holding the ring up to the sharp light which passed through the tall, narrow, coloured window in the oratory. The golden light struck the engraving, splashing its message on the floor, and made it glow as if some supernatural magic had possessed it. Louis studied the letters, mumbling incoherently as if he were trying to decipher the words for the others.

The King knew Louis had nothing to add. 'Impressive, but also mysterious with its hidden script,' the dauphin said.

'I see you are all intrigued.' The King took the ring from Louis's hand and spun it around in his fingers, spreading the text in a continuous circle of light on the oratory floor.

'The words are difficult to interpret because they are not of any language of our lands or our neighbours, and they are not of the Greek or Roman world. The words are in Aramaic, the language of Christ. The unengraved stones came from Saint Helena's cache, brought from Jerusalem. However, Wallace was caught and executed by the English King, so we must reasonably consider that Edward is having the same discussions we are and is in possession of Wallace's ring, and we are in possession of Wishart's.'

De Nogaret gestured towards the platform at the north of the nave containing the reliquary for the Crown of Thorns. 'Sire, what discussion are we having? I suspect you wouldn't have brought us together merely to admire a semi-precious ring amongst so many sacred objects.'

Valois rudely interrupted without waiting for Nogaret to finish. 'Of course, my brother, we understand anything connected to Saint Helena is important ...'

The King held his hand up to stop Valois from speaking further.

'For the benefit of everyone except Brother Valois, the Jewels of Saint Helena were part of a fabulous treasure that our friends the Venetians had liberated from the treasury of

147

the Byzantine Emperor, who had, in turn, found it after it had been buried by the Visigoth Alaric.'

As the King spoke, the sunlight streaming through the windows suddenly darkened, and heavy rain began to clatter off the roof and windows. The iron door rattled furiously in its frame.

The King watched Valois fidgeting uncomfortably on his gilded cushion, as everyone knew he had let the treasure slip away from him in Italy. The King took the opportunity to rub salt into the still open wound.

'This time the gold will not escape me. I have word that the son of John Wishart has travelled from Scotland and is heading here to France, seeking to recover the treasure.'

The King paused. 'De Nogaret - have these men followed. We will locate and retrieve the treasure and it will buy us the armies to push the English out of France for good. I will engage the services of Madame de France to assist in its retrieval.'

Madame was only ever involved in those tasks the King could not even trust to those who guarded his person.

'Whoever finds this treasure will rule all kings surrounding him, so I can only use the most talented people.'

Valois gasped. 'Why use a woman when I am at your service? What of the knights amongst us ... and why Madame?' Valois's face was red with embarrassment.

'The slight is most deliberate, Brother Valois. I cannot risk the Italian fiasco again.' The King was in no mood for a debate on this. He felt uncharacteristic agitation, and he knew it showed. 'My spies inform me they will arrive in France in a few days. We know that no one man has knowledge of the treasure's location. John Wishart told us that under torture, but we don't know how many rings are needed to find it.'

The King held the gemstone up to the fading light again, hoping he would see something he had not seen before. Then he placed it back in the velvet purse, which he attached to his girdle.

'We must find the other cabochon stones to locate the treasure, and I suspect that Wishart's son and his companions possess the remaining stones, or at least can lead us to those who do. We also need to protect them in their quest, as English agents are also amongst us. At worst, if the French crown does not retrieve it, then we need to ensure that the English crown can't benefit from our failure.'

De Nogaret could always be relied on to anticipate the King's wishes. 'Sire, I will contact Madame de France, as our leading agents will be tasked to watch them when they arrive. They will likely head towards Paris. I will have all ports watched in case they leave by sea. It should not be too hard to locate Scottish knights in a strange land.'

The King nodded.

The door to the chapel suddenly burst open, and Isabella ran down the nave, demanding to see her father. King Philip would have normally reprimanded her forwardness, but the audience was finished, and he admired his daughter's confidence.

He wanted to spend as much time with her as he could, as she had been betrothed to King Edward's son. She would leave within the year to be brought up in his sister's household while she waited to marry the young Prince Edward. He was anxious for his daughter, a feeling he would never have for his sons; she would have many foes in protecting her father's legacy.

Uncharacteristically, the King picked up his daughter and stroked her pale hair before walking with her in his arms back to the court within the Louvre Palace. Isabella squealed with excitement. The King was followed by his silenced brother and sons, a retinue of the palace guards, and lastly de Nogaret.

Chapter Ten

Rouen, France, April 1306: Betrayal and Duplicity

The innkeeper had a regular clientele, but today a tall, lithe figure clad in black sat quietly in the tavern, staring without blinking into a dying candle. A plate of bread, cheese, and pig fat lay almost untouched beside a large earthenware jug of wine. The innkeeper frequently poured from the jug, revealing a blood-red rivulet of strong, fragrant liquid, but the stranger was uncommunicative.

Lavender-infused reeds were strewn across the floor, and the smell of dried herbs mixed with the aroma of venison stew and chicken soup hanging above the hearths at either end of the L-shaped room made this inn a popular resting place for river travellers on their way to Paris.

The stranger had a distinguished vaguely familiar face, though it was marked with the years. It was a remarkable face, with light brown eyes and unusually light skin even for Normandy. The man was very handsome, but he was unaware of the attention he was getting from a small group of women travellers who were resting at the far end of the inn.

He had an athletic build, and beneath his dark woollen cloak, he hid a powerful, sinewy frame. He wore a black leather jerkin, cut to reveal a black woollen tunic, and the innkeeper had observed a metal-topped leather sheath concealing a battle sword, which lay beside his left leg. It took a soldier to spy a soldier, and the innkeeper was a veteran of the many French wars. Within the sword's pommel there was an engraved motif, a lion rampant, which was partially obscured by the man's jacket.

These were the clothes and weapons of a soldier, not a peasant or a noble. But he was not the soldier of any French king or duke, for he wore no uniform or coat of arms.

A gold necklace lay carelessly around his neck, its chain obscured by the folds of his undershirt. The man placed his hand on the pendant hanging on the chain, dwelling a little as he held it between his left thumb and middle finger.

The gold pendant contained an emblem, but it was unclear in the candlelight.

Clutched in his right hand was a small piece of partially crumpled parchment on which could be seen a small collection of short sentence - hurriedly scratched words dispatched in haste. He had opened and read the letter several times; after only a few hours in his possession, it was already showing wear, and the sweat from the soldier's hands had distorted the letters and obscured the words. He deliberately sat far away from the heart of the tavern, and his body language repelled any noisy or over-friendly drunk just as his cloak kept out the winter rain, but the women were still captivated and continued to stare.

Not even a small group of the King's soldiers dared enter the man's space, but the strength of the wine they were very quickly consuming was beginning to give them courage. They all wanted a woman that night.

The innkeeper kept looking at the man in black, trying to catch his attention. He sensed that the man was becoming a point of attention. The jealousy of the other men was being fuelled by drink, and the innkeeper had a knack for predicting trouble.

He was a solidly built man, well equipped to handle disruptive patrons, and knew when one drink too many had moved someone from singing to fighting drunk. A former soldier in King Philip's army, he had developed a sixth sense for trouble, but his experiences had taught him how to handle himself, and he was confident despite his unease.

He also kept a large, weighted wooden club close by to prevent trouble. He reached over a beam to where it lay concealed. It was still there.

I may need you later.

The stranger had a familiar look and they had exchanged pleasantries, as he often did with his customers.

He remembered seeing him with the tall Scotsman who had often visited for a little wine, some food, and on rare occasions a stay, but that had been over two years ago. He knew the man was of some station from his clothes and demeanour, which were too fine for the peasants and common soldiers who normally frequented the inn.

The inn was not called L'Auberge du Lion for nothing. It was frequently visited by the men of the lion rampant, the Scots. Since King Philip had allied with the kingdom of Scotland, their business had been good. The innkeeper had fought alongside many a Scottish mercenary, and he knew them as good men with a mutual enemy in the English.

He had bought L'Auberge du Lion with the proceeds of the looting he had carried out in English-held Gascony several years before, and he thought it amusing and ironic that his English customers had paid twice for his good fortune.

The soldiers were now bolder in their talk and louder in voice, and seemed to have grown in number.

They were joined by a couple of men the innkeeper had not seen before. He knew most of the garrison, and whilst these men wore the same uniform, they seemed out of place: their dress too clean and new for soldiers. Perhaps they had just joined the garrison and had money to spend. They did not become involved in the escalating mockery.

The innkeeper stepped outside to see who was on the streets. The April night was unusually crisp and cold, and many a traveller was stopping by the tavern for safety and warmth. Snow had begun to fall, and this encouraged more transients to enter the tavern and warm themselves by the open fire. He lit a line of lamps, which were hanging outside the door. A mist was being carried from the sea to the river, and it would be difficult to find the tavern in this weather without light. The streets were a blanket of nebulous forms in the misty dusk, and strangers could lose their bearings and their purses in this mixture of smoke and fog. The dense, narrow streets hid vagabonds and cutpurses, and an inn was a welcome sanctuary.

It was past the hour when barges and boats had berthed in the town, and the traders knew this was the time to be noticed by the weary traveller. 'The weather's good for trade,' he murmured.

The travellers would fill their stomachs with bread, soups, and stews, which the innkeeper made each morning. The prevailing wind blew the warming aromas towards the harbour.

Rouen was the ideal place to rest for the evening before the travellers, merchants, and men on the make took the river boats bound for Paris or left by ship or road for foreign lands.

The innkeeper could hear many tongues. 'Lots of barges and lots of foreigners with money to spend,' he rubbed his hands together with glee.

Their footsteps heralded the hungry as they climbed onto the harbour walls from their ships. The ships' wooden boards creaked as the travellers dragged their heavy sacks and chests over the decks and towards Rouen, and his business stood between the ships and the centre of the town.

He came in from the cold air, still concerned that there was trouble brewing with the soldiers and the handsome stranger. Inside, the tavern was thick with strangers speaking Flemish, German, Breton, and of course the local French dialect, langue d'oil, as well as the langue d'oc from the south and his own Norman French.

'Welcome, my friends, on this cold night,' he gestured to two men who had just entered. Their faces were covered by hooded cloaks, which were still steaming from the crisp night air meeting with the warm air of the tavern.

Their cloaks were held fast to their bodies as they moved towards the far end of the inn, away from the crowds and near to where the stranger was still sitting. Over their shoulders, they had heavy leather sacks, and tight against their left legs, he noticed through the folds of cloth, they had attached their long dirks to guard them against the many dangers they could face in this town. One of the men appeared unsteady. The innkeeper had seen this many times in inexperienced sailors and rivermen.

*

Jamie still felt sick and light-headed, and his legs were weak. He had not kept much down in over a week. He had confirmed that he truly hated the sea.

Jamie and Will had just arrived on the Nantes from Leith. Dark woollen hoods hid their faces, and their dark leather boots still squeaked from the mixture of seawater and accumulated mud they had gathered on the short walk up the hill, from the harbour to the inn. Their feet were wet and cold, and they both looked forward to a warm fire and a soft, stationary bed.

'Bishop Wishart told us to look for a tall stranger with dark hair,' Jamie scoffed, his voice lowered to a whisper. 'That narrows it down to about half the population of Rouen. Everyone here looks like they could be him.'

He looked around the inn, trying to find someone who might be the contact they were looking for - but how would he know him?

Jamie scanned the room. He was learning from Will, taking in the normal as well as the unusual. He noticed that even though the inn was full, one man was alone, and the

154

target of jeering.

He noticed a battle sword hanging by the man in black's left side. The pommel was engraved. This was no common weapon, but the type of sword one of Longshanks's agents would have tried to conceal.

'How many men do you think come out for a drink wearing a sword like that without men at arms?' he murmured to Will.

'Do you see the engraving on side of the pommel? It looks like a lion or an English leopard,' Will said. 'It's showing off - he reeks of assassin.'

Will glanced at him without making eye contact, but a rotund serving man crossed in front of him, obscuring his view.

'The last time I saw a sword like that was amongst the English soldiers at the cathedral,' Will continued.

A young teenage boy appeared next to them and placed steaming bowls and wine on a shelf next to where they were standing. 'There you are gentlemen - stew, bread, and good red wine. My master, the innkeeper, thought you looked in need of this.'

Jamie had recovered his land legs and was ravenous, focusing on the food presented before him.

'If I do not fill my stomach after five days of emptying it, I will be no good to anyone. I am in no state for intrigue.' His eyes did not stray from the food in front of him as he tore some bread from the pound loaf and dipped it into the stew, overfilling his mouth with bread morsels and thick gravy.

Some women were trying to flirt with the man in black, and as a result, the French soldiers were becoming more vociferous.

Suddenly, the loudest agitator lunged at the man in black. 'You bastard! Can't you leave at least one of these women for us?' The lamps went to the ground, and the far corner of the inn was in near darkness.

155

A flagon of wine smashed on the stone floor. Pottery shards exploded, acting like lethal shrapnel. Food and wine splattered over everyone nearby. Punches flew. More men joined in, increasing the size of the brawl. Four men were fighting the man in black, and he was winning. Bones were crunching and snapping as chairs were turned into weapons.

Through the flailing limbs, Jamie saw the man in black produce a pair of daggers and then let loose in their direction.

Thud! Thud! One dagger and then another landed on either side of their heads.

'Fuck me, that was close,' said Will. 'Get down.' His hand thrust Jamie to the floor. 'Those were meant to kill us.'

There was a crash as a well-dressed man brandishing a jewelled sword broke a chair next to Jamie. A hand grabbed him. Jamie wrestled with the man. He could hear the innkeeper shouting for help.

'Guillaume! Go and fetch the Maréchaussée. Hurry, my boy, before this fight becomes a riot.'

At this, the remaining customers seemed to melt away, disappearing into the streets outside.

Jamie was now on his side. He was trying to fight off an assailant who was pulling at his jerkin. He could feel his hands inside his woollen shirt whilst at the same time dragging him away from the melee and towards the exit. He stabbed the man in the face with a discarded knife. The man fell on the floor clutching his face, before another one in a soldier's tabard kicked the first man away and grabbed Jamie, tightening his hold on his neck. His face was pushed sideways towards the floor, and he was struggling for breath. He felt the cold tip of a dagger brushing his leg as the man attempted to pierce his groin. He was stronger than his assailant, but he was disadvantaged and caught off guard, still faint from having eaten little food in over a week. The shards of shattered pottery were digging into his face and knees, and he could feel the warm, metallic taste of blood in his mouth as he fought for his life.

A thrust to his groin would be fatal, and he would bleed out quickly. Jamie used all his strength to turn himself round to grab the man holding the knife and tried to twist it so that the blade would drop. The tip of the blade had penetrated his hose, but not the skin.

Slowly, Jamie pushed the blade back. He was shaking with effort, teeth bared. The soldier attempted a knee to the groin but hit his thigh instead. Jamie knew he was in trouble, as the soldier still had the knife in his hand and was still on top of Jamie. If he did not do something soon, this day would be his last.

Using the assailant's tactic against him, Jamie drove his knee upwards and thrust it into the man's groin. He connected squarely with the man's testicles. The man screamed. His grip on the knife relaxed immediately, and it fell to the floor. Jamie kicked it across the floor, but regretted it as the soldier rolled away screaming and clutching his testicles. Jamie desperately felt along the floor for his dirk or anything he could use as a weapon. His left hand found a large shard of the broken wine flagon that had shattered on the floor, and without hesitation, he thrust it as hard as he could into the man's neck.

The man recoiled, grabbing frantically at the makeshift dagger embedded in his jugular vein. He snatched at the end of the shard, but the blood spurted out as far as the base of the wall. His strength was gone, and his eyes rolled back in his head as he fell dead.

Jamie pulled himself up onto his knees so that he could draw his sword, which had been trapped beneath him. It was too dark to see whether his assailant had any fight left in him, and he was about to plunge it into the man's chest when he saw the motionless body of Will in the faint firelight - he was bleeding from a wound to his head. A corpse lay over his chest.

Jamie recognised the dead man's face. He had been at the Sheip's Heid in Leith and had manned the rudder on de Bretagne's ship. He was likely in the pay of the English, and Jamie was glad he was dead. He wondered if this was the only treacherous sailor.

Will was very still, his chest not moving. Jamie felt a rush of emotion and a lump in his chest. His friend must have been killed by the man in black. He did not see the lean stranger amongst the heap of corpses. It looked like he had escaped.

There was a lot of blood in warm, dark, sticky pools. It mixed with wine and food and pooled under the swords, daggers, and other discarded weapons spread over the floor. Jamie had been aware of a violent brawl next to him and had heard the clash of metal and the groans of at least four dying men, but he had been more concerned with his own battle and had assumed that the stranger had been overwhelmed by the soldiers who had outnumbered him.

The Maréchaussée would be arriving soon, and they could not be found here with letters talking of Scottish rebellion now that the French and English were friends. He had to escape, dragging Will with him. They had not found Bishop Wishart's agent, and they were surrounded by killers.

'It's up to you now, Jamie.'

He did not know much about this land; at least he knew where Paris was, and that was where he would find the Paris Temple and de Charnay.

Just as he knelt to pick up de Irwyne's lifeless body by the arms and drag it towards the door, he felt the weight suddenly lighten as someone picked up Will's legs and pushed him towards the front of the inn.

Jamie was pushed too fast, and he nearly tripped several times as he scrambled backwards, unaware of who was helping him. All he could see was a dark figure. All the candles lay extinguished on the floor, but the lanterns outside the inn were still lit. Jamie tried to see the man assisting him, but his face was partially covered by blood and hair that had smeared and become stuck across his face.

Jamie's legs buckled - he tripped and fell down the small wooden step leading out to the street. He dropped Will's body to the ground as he fell face-first, twisting to try to catch himself. His face became embedded in a small pile of snow that had accumulated by the side of the path into the inn. The mixture of snow, manure, and frozen mud stung the scrapes and cuts he had received in the brawl, which were still fresh and bleeding. He licked his lips, which tasted of mud and horse shit. He had hit his head hard, and it took a few seconds before he could stand, but he could feel Will's body being pulled away from him. He grasped anxiously at the ground, looking for a limb or piece of Will's clothing.

Before he could groan or curse, he heard the approaching Maréchaussée.

'Arrêtez! Déposez vos armes!' They cried as they unsheathed their swords and charged up the hill from the harbour.

Suddenly, Jamie felt someone tug on his hair, pulling him off balance, and he was thrown into a pile of empty ale barrels that stood on the opposite side of the street, just across from the inn. Rats scuttled away as he hit the first barrel.

Jamie heard someone whispering to him in a soft but distinct French accent. 'Follow me, Jamie Wishart. I am here to help you. De Irwyne is alive. I have no time to explain. Get to your feet and follow me to the harbour.' Jamie tried to get a good look at the man, but he had already moved into the dark shadows. As he disappeared, Jamie saw the bright edge of a battle sword.

Jamie anxiously looked for Will.

'De Irwyne is safe,' the voice told him. 'Move your arse - the Maréchaussée approaches.'

Jamie hesitated for a moment. Was he following a French spy or fortuitous friend in a time of need? He did not take long to think it over: he had no choice. Watching from the shadows, a group of angry-looking Maréchaussée had appeared, clutching torches and swords - they ran into the inn, which lit up with torches and the sound of breaking furniture, broken crockery, and a spate of raised French and Flemish voices.

When the last of the Maréchaussée had left the street, Jamie began to follow the Frenchman as he carried Will, who was beginning to stir. They were heading down a narrow lane that ran parallel to the harbour road.

'Come on,' the Frenchman urged. 'We have no time to hang around dreaming and waiting to get caught. Allez, vite!'

The Frenchman ran further down the narrow lane with Will still in his arms. Jamie followed.

Rats scattered as they followed the contours of the narrow-cobbled lane until it gently declined, tapering to a small exit near the harbour a short distance ahead. The anaemic light of ship lanterns barely lit a path for the fleeing men to follow. The damp fog had begun to freeze on the smooth stones, and it made the men slip and stumble.

'Slow down,' Jamie urged as the Frenchman dragged someone his own height and weight as if it were a minor inconvenience rather than a considerable burden. *He has the strength of Hercules.*

They reached a narrow exit, which met with the quayside. There were perhaps twenty boats tied to mooring irons set into the walls. Large iron rings every twenty-five yards held the huge hemp ropes, and the boats gently swayed up and down with the movement of the river. Their lanterns bobbed with them.

The Frenchman stopped to tighten his grip on Will. Without looking to the side, he stepped to his left and kicked a small wooden door immediately beside him. The door was the side entrance to a small house. It opened, but as the stranger entered, he knocked over a small candle. It fell onto the earth floor, burning on its side. Jamie caught his breath and saw that his rescuer was the man in black. He had lost his dirk and needed its support in getting answers from this man, but if he needed to fight, he would use his fists.

The Frenchman placed Will on the ground and quietly shut the door, carefully picking up the candle from the floor before it was completely extinguished. Even with the lantern lights from the harbour, Jamie found it difficult to see anything in the cottage, but the room felt warm and cosy. It had been prepared; it was not a sanctuary chosen at random as Jamie had initially believed.

The cottage had only one storey and one room, which had a rough square wooden table with a bench on one side and two small chairs on the other. The shutters were closed tightly with a wooden plank.

Jamie noticed a small pail with a wooden ladle. He lifted the handle to see if there was any water to wash away the metallic taste of blood and manure in his mouth. He saw drops of water fall back into the pail, so he took a large gulp to slake his thirst. Perhaps the coldness of the water would bring him around from his mild concussion.

The soldier in the tavern had hit him hard in the face, and he could sense a few loose teeth, which had suddenly started to cause him pain. He did not fear the man in black. *Why save me only to kill me?*

Jamie felt for the outline of one of the chairs and sat down clumsily, almost falling over. He felt for the leather pouch within his jerkin that contained his papers and the ring his uncle had given him in Glasgow.

Jamie and Will had hidden their other belongings in the stables of L'Auberge du Lion, but they were unimportant. The contents of the pouch were all that mattered, and he sighed with relief as he felt the uneven surface of the amethyst ring and his uncle's wax seal attached to the papers.

The Frenchman picked up the drowsy figure of Will de Irwyne from the floor and laid him carefully onto the rough-hewn bench.

Outside, the harbour streets were filled with Maréchaussée voices. With swords drawn, they were now looking for them. The small cottage was hidden from the road and looked deserted. It had been chosen well.

The men inside made no sound, but every breath and swallow seemed amplified, as if they were announcing to the soldiers where they could be found.

Will began to wake. His unguarded movement and groans became louder, as he was unaware of the danger. The Frenchman had been working the failing embers in the hearth with his dagger, and he turned to quiet Will, holding him down with his hand over his mouth.

Jamie had recovered his wits. 'Who are you?'

'Be quiet.' The Frenchman's response was abrupt and aggressive.

Outside, the Maréchaussée were searching the moored ships, their boots clattering on the wooden decks as they went from ship to ship in pursuit of the men. Jamie could hear crates being levered open and cargo being spilt on the wooden decks.

The Frenchman spoke in a whisper. 'I know you have many questions for me, my young friend, but I think that all I need do is show you this and tell you my name. I am Innes de Mayon, and -'

Bang.

Suddenly, as Innes reached beneath his leather jerkin, Jamie heard the purposeful crack of something heavy striking his skull. Will had hit him on the back of the head with the solid wooden ladle, knocking him to the ground.

As Innes fell forward against the table and rolled down onto the floor, an enamelled gold pendant fell out of his shirt.

He lay very still on the ground, blood oozing towards his ear. Jamie was frantic. He could feel his heart racing, his palms were clammy, and he was sweating hard.

He had just been about to find out who this man was, and he feared Will had killed him. 'Damn it, Will.' Jamie could not hide his frustration. He picked up the gold pendant, which was still attached by a cord around Innes's neck, and read: nemo me impune lacessit.

Innes remained still, blood still oozing onto the ground.

Jamie recognised the inscription - he had seen it amongst his father's possessions, and it adorned Bishop Wishart's seal. Nemo me impune lacessit, written in blue enamel under the lion rampant.

The Latin inscription was a token of loyalty to the Scottish crown. No one attacks me with impunity. It was a personal gift of the Scottish King himself to his bravest and most loyal subjects. Will had just attacked and possibly killed Bishop Wishart's most important agent in France: Innes de Mayon. Jamie had heard his name whispered in awe amongst his father's most trusted companions.

Will was still clutching the heavy wooden ladle, ready to hit the man again. He tried to stand and Jamie pushed him back into the bench. 'Stop, I know this man.'

Will stood unsteadily, placing the ladle down on the table. 'Did you not see him in the tavern? He tried to kill us, and I know a hired assassin when I see one. We should finish him off before he finishes us!'

'I think you are correct, Will - he certainly is an assassin, but he is one of ours. This is His Grace's agent in France. The man we were supposed to meet!'

Jamie pointed to the pendant. 'Look at the insignia on the pendant. *Nemo me impune lacessit.* You know what that means!'

Will fell on his knees beside the motionless body and lifted the pendant to review the inscription. 'I saw him aim two daggers at us,' Will argued. Jamie knew he was right but confused. 'He could have killed us in the Inn.'

'Will, you *do* know what that means. He could only have received that from a Guardian or King of Scotland. The man you just hit over the head is Innes de Mayon. He fought at Stirling Bridge with Wallace and Andrew de Morray, and was sent to the court of France as the Guardian's diplomat. I think he is our French contact and the man who will lead us to de Charnay - that is, if he isn't dead.'

'I have heard of him, Jamie, but how do we know this is the real Innes de Mayon? What if he's Longshanks's beast and he stole the pendant?' Jamie had not considered that possibility, but instinct told him this was indeed Innes de Mayon. He remembered how his father had talked about the bravery de Mayon had shown at Stirling Bridge, and how, despite being stabbed in the shoulder by an Englishman's dagger, he had dragged a bloodied Andrew de Morray from the battlefield. Jamie wanted to believe this man was him.

'My father told me about a wound Innes received on the left shoulder at Stirling Bridge. He was stabbed in the back by a knight's dagger, and the scar should still be there. There is only one way to find it out.'

Jamie knelt beside the prostrate body on the floor and attempted to turn him on his front to look for the scar, but as he pushed the body to the right, he felt a hand grab him by the neck, pulling him to the ground. A dagger thrust up against his throat.

Will drew his dagger and lunged towards the two men on the floor. Jamie was unable to move with a knife at his throat.

Will looked like he was ready to stab Innes dead.

'Do you think you would both still be alive by now if I weren't Innes de Mayon?' The Frenchman hissed. 'And further, I take considerable exception to be attacked twice in one night, including once by my own allies. We need to speak no higher than a whisper, or we risk discovery.' He smiled and put away the dagger, giving Jamie a stout pat on the shoulder.

Innes stood up and helped Jamie to his feet. Will returned his dagger to its sheath, keeping his hand close to the hilt.

'I have been ordered by Bishop Wishart to help you in any way I can. Sit down, my friends, and let us talk awhile.' Innes gestured for them to sit in the two chairs before lowering himself onto the bench. He stretched out his legs and rubbed the back of his head. 'The Maréchaussée will be strutting around the harbour pursuing the guilty and punishing the innocent for a few hours yet, so it is best we all lie low here for a time.'

Innes felt the back of his head. 'Will, I commend your strength; you gave me one hell of a bump!' Innes looked unduly relaxed for someone who had killed half a dozen of the local garrison and was being actively pursued by the rest. He continued to rub the back of his head and smiled as he looked at the two men.

'I am sure you have many questions, and I think now we have time to talk awhile and for me to satisfy your curiosity,' he added. 'But first, I think we need some wine.'

Innes wiped the blood from his eyes whilst retrieving a sack from the recess beside the hearth. He removed three earthenware goblets and a goatskin flagon that swished and gurgled as wine sloshed inside it.

He placed the wine and goblets carefully on the table, and took some bread and cheese from a small shelf next to the fireplace. 'I hope you are not in too much of a hurry to get to de Charnay. I suggest we rest here tonight, enjoy the wine and each other's company, and tend to our wounds. We will need our strength, my friends, as I believe your presence here is already known to our enemies in England and France. Foreign spies tried to kill you tonight, and not only English.'

Jamie forgot his pain and remembered his hunger and his

165

interrupted meal at the tavern. The adrenalin had subsided. Jamie cut the food into small bits. His teeth still hurt, so he gulped the wine to dull the pain. He had time now to gather his thoughts and understood he had courage, and it felt natural, instinctive. He had grown up now, fought for his life and won; he had greater strength and confidence, and understood why men sought battle. He understood why his uncle had chosen him.

Innes continued. 'You were followed into the inn. Two of the men who attacked you came in just after the fight broke out, and under cover of that, they tried to make your deaths look like the result of a drunken brawl. You killed one, Jamie, and I slit the throat of the other just as he was searching Will. These men armed themselves with French daggers, but fought like Englishman. I have fought them too many times before not to recognise their ways.'

Innes turned to Will. 'The first man hit you over the head before I was able to get to him; he was looking through your jerkin and was about to finish you. He was looking for something.'

Turning to Jamie, Innes continued. 'And young Wishart, the second was looking through your jerking whilst trying to stab you in the groin. They knew you were both carrying some documents, and they didn't need you alive. It is a shame we killed them, as opening their tongues would have been useful. Tonight, was just the first attempt to stop you, and they will not give up now.'

Will placed the goblet of wine, now empty, on the table. 'There were a couple of well-aimed daggers that almost parted my hair, and they came from your hand. And you could have taken that necklace from the real Innes de Mayon!'

Innes smiled. 'Yes, I am sorry about that. I deliberately missed you, hoping to scare you off, to warn you to leave the inn before you got yourself killed. Bishop Wishart had sent me to look after you, but Longshanks's men got in the way before I could get you out of there.'

Innes continued. 'Your caution pleases me, Will! I could be a French imposter and not the real Innes de Mayon. However, as you were about to find out, I still bear the scars of Stirling Bridge.'

The Frenchman stood up and removed his leather jerkin and shirt. On his left shoulder, they could see a large triangular scar in the shape of a dagger's blade. He moved towards the two men to let them see better. The wound was deep and pink, but the skin was healed and stretched white around it.

'Your wound looks old,' Will acknowledged.

'Yes. You were there too, Will,' Innes affirmed.

'I was, but it was eight years ago, and I don't remember everyone who was there,' Will said.

Innes picked up his shirt, and as he dressed, he looked at Jamie. 'Your uncle sent me this.' Innes placed his hand inside the jerkin and produced a tatty parchment. 'This is in the Bishop's own hand.'

Innes pushed the document towards them. Will picked it up and read it before handing it to Jamie, who recognised the Bishop's handwriting. 'I have a French mother and Scottish father - and have good reason to fight against the English. They killed my brother ... butchered Wallace,' Innes clenched his fists, his rage was clear. 'Wallace saved my life at Falkirk, and we spent five years together in France and Italy. I thought of them when I killed those Englishmen today.' Jamie saw the pain and anger in Innes and recognised that same passion in himself when he thought of his own father.

'I see Bishop Wishart wrote in his note about a traitor within his inner circle, so we must be suspicious of everyone.' Will added before picking up the goatskin wine sack, filling each of the empty goblets that now rested on the wooden table.

'Innes, please drink with me,' he said apologetically.

They all laughed as they picked up their goblets and took a large gulp of wine. Outside, the noise seemed to be more distant. The Maréchaussée had not found what they were looking for this night, but that would not stop them from coming back tomorrow. Innes placed his near-empty goblet on the table.

'The French and the English won't give up looking for you. They do not want us to succeed in getting to de Charnay. Whatever business Bishop Wishart has with de Charnay matters to King Philip and King Edward, and they are doing their best to find you.'

Jamie took Will's lead and said nothing about the treasure. Innes would need to be told when the time was right.

'Not one, but two sets of assassins were after you this evening. The French ones were waiting for you before you arrived, hidden amongst the soldiers of the garrison.'

'How can you be sure they were waiting for us?' Jamie asked. The wine was numbing his pain.

'They looked out of place - they were too clean, and they kept away from the rest of the garrison soldiers. I suspect they are Guillaume de Nogaret's hired thugs, planted amongst the Rouen garrison. But one thing is strange: in the chaos, I was not the only one trying to save you. At least one of the men killed tonight was not killed by me. I saw the flash of a jewelled sword with a fire opal on the pommel. Too ostentatious for English or French spies. Perhaps we have another player here.'

'One of the dead men was part of the crew of the ship that brought us here,' Jamie said. 'He could have been English or French and followed us from Leith - Who is Guillaume de Nogaret?'

Innes smiled. 'He is chief minister to the King of France. He does Philip's dirty work whilst the King looks on. If he is involved, you and Will are big news,' he paused. 'Something else bothers me. The Maréchaussée arrived too quickly too, and it was all of them, thirty or so men. A drunken brawl does not attract that sort of official muscle. I suspect they are interested in you, not some tavern brawl, and they would not have arrived in numbers to save dead men. They were expecting you to be captured and alive. They will surround the town, and tomorrow they will be back. I am guessing de Nogaret wants you alive to interrogate you.'

Innes winked. 'I know a way out of Rouen. We will be long gone by the time they realise their prey has fled.'

Innes took more wine, filling his goblet to overflowing. He mopped the spilt liquid with his cloak.

Jamie liked Innes de Mayon and felt his confidence. He understood a little better why Bishop Wishart trusted de Mayon.

The night was now almost silent apart from the distant noise of drunken travellers and the usual cacophony of night calls from the nocturnal beasts, human and animal, that patrolled Rouen at this time of night. Jamie could just hear the voices of the Maréchaussée as arrests were being made and they carried their prisoners to the garrison keep.

Innes rubbed his head again and said, 'I think we all need to share what we know here. Remember, Philip le Bel and Edward Plantagenet are after something that you know, and your life will only be of use to them if you have what they want. They will show you no compromise or compassion. We will need to work together, so perhaps with that in mind you would like to tell me what is going on.'

Jamie waited for Will to take the lead. He did not know whether he should tell Innes everything or wait.

'Bishop Wishart sent us to France to see Geoffroi de Charnay, and told us you would help us get to him. Do you know of him?' Will asked.

'Yes, I know him. De Charnay is the chief advisor and right-hand man of the Grand Master of the Order of the

Knights Templar, Jacques de Molay, warrior, priest, and chief moneylender to King Philip. If Molay is the figurehead at their heart, the custodian of the soul of the Templars, then de Charnay is the brains. Nothing important happens amongst the Templars without de Charnay's say-so, and that makes him enormously powerful. Half the crowned heads in the known world and even the Pope himself are in debt to the Templars, and that breeds awe, resentment, and envy. Bishop Wishart has done well if de Charnay owes him a favour!'

Jamie pulled out the small leather pouch that was stitched within the seam of his collar, and placed it on the table. He opened the top, which was held tight with a large double knot, and lifted out the contents: a large gold ring with a purple cabochon stone set in the middle, and a parchment carrying the unbroken seal of the diocese of Glasgow.

He placed each item in front of Innes. 'I think this is what they were looking for.'

'I recognise the seal but not the ring. Wallace told me of a purple cabochon from the crusades, but I never saw it.'

'Bishop Wishart gave me this ring from his hand and instructed me that I was to show de Charnay, as he would know what this meant. The parchment is to provide us with free passage, and it bears the seal of the Guardians of Scotland. De Charnay is to give us further instructions. I think His Grace was ever cautious of Longshanks's spies, trying to protect us from knowing too much in case we were captured or betrayed.'

Innes examined the ring. 'It is engraved. I have seen its type in the markets of the East, but its markings are not in a language I recognise.' Innes placed the ring on the table, pushing it back towards Jamie, adding, 'You must show this to no one until we get to the Temple and de Charnay. Today's episode in L'Auberge du Lion is just the start. The English and the French won't stop until they have this.'

Jamie struggled to suppress a loud yawn, which wasn't

lost on Innes.

'We can rest here as long as we leave before first light. The Maréchaussée and the Rouen garrison will tear the place apart looking for us. The night will not keep us safe this time, and I doubt our place of sanctuary will stay secret for long.'

Innes stretched his long frame. 'You need some rest now, my friends. The next few days will be hard, now that we are all wanted men. I have left horses in a small barn outside town so that we can leave without a murmur. You will have to leave your baggage at the inn. I have no doubt it is already in the hands of French or English agents.'

Will lay on the bench, and Jamie stretched his bruised frame on the floor by the glowing hearth, which warmed his aching limbs. He placed his cloak under his head and could feel himself rapidly falling into a deep sleep.

*

At this time of night, the narrow streets were empty of townsfolk. They knew better than to make themselves targets simply by being available.

A motionless frame, curved in its profile, not straight like the ships or the cottages but round and alive, stood looking towards Innes's sanctuary. The face was concealed in a swath of dark woven wool that reached the ground and trailed in the filth.

Rain ran down the cloak towards its sodden edge as a strengthening wind cut through the sails, which hung loosely from the masts of the ships. There was a crossbow over his shoulder and a sword by his side. The sword was neither French nor English. Large drops of water caught on the pommel before they became too large and broke free from the metal, falling heavily towards the ground.

Aurelian needed to follow the knights alone, and he had left his truculent companion, Bernard Ferrer, chained to a stable upright a mile down the road with a Byzantine merchant to keep an eye on him.

The ship's ropes whistled as the wind blew upstream, but Aurelian did not acknowledge any discomfort. He studied the harbour cottage as the three men slept, unaware that they were being closely watched.

He had protected the knights during the attack in the tavern. His concern was that he was not alone. Now there was someone else following the Scots in pursuit of the treasure. There were others trying to kill them - probably the English, maybe French, who would not want any Scot to have access to such wealth. The Emperor had warned him to pay attention.

Tonight, he had saved Will de Irwyne's life by killing that Frenchman. Now his task would require greater guile and caution. The task was as complicated as it was rewarding, and he would relish every minute.

Chapter Eleven

Paris Temple, Late April 1306

Jamie was weary and only held himself on his horse to prove he was as tough as his battle-hardened companions. His youth had prevented him from being involved in the legend that was Stirling Bridge, and he felt left out. Will and Innes had spent many hours discussing those they had lost. It helped them to concentrate and to forget they had barely slept in three days.

Now Jamie was bored with it and felt deliberately excluded by them, as it was all they talked about. He did not have the scars to prove his courage, so he felt he had to be every bit as tough as his companions in overcoming the deprivations and dangers that they faced on their journey to find de Charnay.

They looked prepared and comfortable, familiar with what was ahead. Jamie lacked their ready confidence, but he was less afraid now, growing as he followed in their footsteps.

Will was his friend, and he respected Innes, but was not yet sure of him. Time would determine whether he should trust de Mayon. With Will, he had built an almost subconscious feeling of comfort. He had inherited his uncle the Bishop's instincts in judging the character of a man. He felt an overwhelming sense of safety and success when he was with Innes, but with Will, he also felt trust.

How much further?

He started to doze and woke himself up with a gentle snore. Another fall from his horse would hurt, but the humiliation would be worse.

The morning was foggy and cold, and a light dusting of silver frost covered the surrounding fields, making the ground annoyingly slippery. The horses stumbled slightly on the partially frozen mud and stones, and the visibility was poor, which made it difficult for horse and rider alike to anticipate what was ahead. Forms moved towards them on the road occasionally, but it was only when they were fifty or so metres away that they could be seen clearly and their purpose on the road could be ascertained.

Farmers with carts, merchants in velvet and silk, and the occasional noble with a sycophantic retinue of soldiers, servants, and squires passed the three adventurers. From time to time the sun split the fog, and a brilliant blue sky tempted the travellers with a sense of security.

No one took much notice of anyone else.

'The Temple is not far, maybe an hour from here,' Innes muttered.

Arrogant Templars in their shining chain mail and red and white tabards galloped past them, covering the wagons and horses they passed with frost-covered mud.

They splashed mud onto Jamie as well, but he knew better than to cry out.

'They have a particular way about them,' Jamie said, speaking for them all as he wiped the splatter from his cloak.

'Indeed,' Innes scoffed. 'When you have money and swords, people tend to get out of your way.'

The columns of people knew to pull over and allow the Templars to pass without hindrance - some out of fear, others out of respect. These men were soldiers now - crusades had become a distant memory, and they had moved away from prayer towards the sound of iron and the acquisition of gold.

Jamie knew much about the Templars. When he had been younger, it had been all his father seemed to talk about. Maybe this was one of the reasons his uncle had sent him.

The Templars had been forcibly removed from the Holy Land by the Mamluks and had moved into the Temple, their Paris headquarters. They still plotted further crusades; no one took these plans seriously, but they retained influence with the Pope as a result.

'The Templars dress more like soldiers than monks: money has made them knights with more power than scripture.' Will and Innes laughed nodding in agreement.

'My father always said the Templars attracted two types of men: those with faith and those pursuing power and wealth; that mix made for uncomfortable bedfellows, and the Order's ideals were often at odds with its practice. He believed their money and power brought envy and fear in equal measures, and it was rumoured that the King of France and the Pope were amongst the people who took this view.' Jamie was hoping his information would be acknowledged, but instead the silence from Will and Innes made Jamie feel stupid.

The Scots had avoided travelling by river. Instead, they had ridden to Paris. They had travelled by night, avoiding the expected inns and resting points, using places to change horses that were only known to Innes. They had slept inside barns or in uninhabited hamlets to avoid detection. Sleeping during the day was difficult, as they knew they could be discovered, so they all slept lightly with one hand on their swords, ready for fight or flight. Any spies who might be following them probably guessed the men would head for Paris, but were unlikely to know who they were meeting.

Jamie had learned much from watching Innes. He had a charisma, a natural way with him seeming to know the right thing to say at almost every occasion. Like Will, he had an instinct for things that looked out of the ordinary. He analysed every fellow traveller for a threat, but did not arouse their suspicion. He told an initially cynical Jamie that he could tell any of King Philip's or Edward Plantagenet's men by the way they wore their swords and rode their horses. Jamie was now believing him.

Will was much like Innes. They were cut from the same cloth, and it was exciting to be around them.

The mist began to reveal more and more of what it had hidden.

'Look over there: walls, towers. It must be a King's palace.' Jamie pointed to a shape emerging through the clouds. He could see a high crenelated wall flanked by disorganised rounded turrets. There appeared to be numerous stone layers covered by a terrace, upon which could be seen a handful of sentries in bright red and white surcoats. The light wind brought with it the concentrated smell of the midden and steaming manure, which combined with the damp, sweet odour of the moat that surrounded the entire structure.

'Not built for kings but for the Templars, and far more ornate than any castle,' Innes replied.

As they approached, the stone building rose even higher until it became overwhelming; the rest of the walled city of Paris was dwarfed and obscured by its profile. 'Takes your breath away, doesn't it?' he added.

Jamie was unprepared for the astonishing building before them. He had seen grand buildings before, but nothing like this. He gasped in disbelief. Innes stopped his horse and turned to them.

'Gentlemen, welcome to the Villeneuve du Temple, residence of the Grand Master of the Order of the Knights Templar and home of the man we seek, Geoffroi de Charnay. As we have travelled all this way, I do hope that he is at home.'

Innes spurred his horse onto a gallop. He disappeared towards a small stone bridge, which led into the esplanade. Jamie and Will galloped after him.

The Temple's courtyard was alive with industry. Knights, horses, and a myriad of squires, servants, and serfs bustled about. It was easy for Jamie to know the wealth and position a man held by the colour and quality of his clothes, but seldom their measure.

The serfs were dressed in rough, dark woollen tunics and tatty hose that showed the evidence of their labours, and the ingrained stench of manure firmly confirmed their status at the bottom of the social order. Servants wore uniforms embellished with the crests of their masters. The squires, arrogant and aloof, wore tabards with emblems of rank and were more position-conscious than the lords they served.

Lastly, there were the Templar knights, proud and arrogant, dazzling in the white tunic and red cross of the Order. They sat astride their tough, stout warhorses, which were covered in the same brilliant white cloth embroidered with the cross.

The knights' war swords caught the early morning light, but few of these men had seen much combat. Jamie was astonished at the extent of it all. He had never seen such splendour. This was a different life than the one he had led these past seventeen years. His life had been so mundane, and now he was truly awake to the world outside Scotland. He was in a foreign land, amid a legendary order of knights, surrounded by the international elite. He was part of a plan to change his country forever, and he was about to meet the man who could make this happen. He did not like to think of the pressure of this responsibility: it scared him, excited him, and made him nauseous.

Innes was about fifty yards ahead and had already dismounted. A young novice of the Order ran towards his horse and gathered up the bridle in his hand.

'Greetings, traveller,' he said to Innes just as Jamie and Will arrived.

'I am a Breton working on behalf of the Norwegian court, and my companions come presently,' Innes told the novice. 'Make haste. I wish to see your master. My companions have luxurious furs to delight even the most demanding customer.'

'My master will likely be found in the chapter house or justice room, or one of the many meeting rooms which can be found on each of the floors within the main tower. Leave it to me, Sirs.' The novice was so chirpy he bordered on the familiar.

'Do you see how easy it is to defend this place?' Will murmured to Jamie. 'The Templars learned much from the Holy Land. Two or three knights could fend off hundreds. It is rumoured King Philip keeps his treasure here. A siege here would be from no foreign army - more likely a peasant mob. They have much to riot about.'

Jamie was perplexed. 'What do you mean?'

'This King is a thief and a scoundrel. His coinage is debased, and starvation rife.'

'How do you have such insight?' Jamie was surprised at Will's knowledge.

'Reading,' Will replied.

Jamie and Will brought their horses to a halt beside Innes, who was now impatiently waiting for them at the steps to the north entrance of the Temple.

Around them, the business of the day was continuing. A few fur traders should go unnoticed amidst so much activity.

The novice who had greeted them reappeared whilst a stable boy removed all the horses and took them to the stable block.

'The Order is delighted to welcome you to the Temple! We do not often extend our hospitality to King Haakon's subjects.' His disposition was exuberant and cheery, but after such an uncomfortable journey, his charm was wasted on Jamie.

'Please step inside, Your Honours! I will take you to the Templar chancellor. He likes to meet all our new merchants and will help you become familiar with the workings of the

Order.'

He urged the three men through the door and slammed it tightly shut as they entered a small hall with a circular staircase on the right, leading upstairs.

The room was small, lit by two wall-mounted torches and a brazier, which gave a comfortable feeling of warmth as the men waited. A stained-glass oriel window above the entrance cast a rainbow of light onto the stone floor. The sun was strengthening, and its rays shone through the glass, projecting gold, rich reds, and blues towards the base of the circular stair that led to the floors above.

Jamie noticed a solitary sentry standing motionless by the circular stair, his face obscured by the coloured light, a war sword with a golden jewel on the pommel by his left hand, and a spear in his right. The only feature Jamie could see clearly was a recent deep scar that led from the left side of the guard's forehead through his now missing eye. He had been lucky, as the wound could easily have been mortal. Jamie thought he looked familiar, though the sentry stepped into the shadows and turned away as they entered the room, preventing further scrutiny.

The steps were damp and narrow and turned always towards the right. Small slits had been cut in the walls, just large enough for crossbows. The wall also held tall, tar-laden torches that encouraged them further upstairs towards the chapter reception room. The novice led the way, followed by the Scots, as the stairs were too narrow to climb in anything but single file.

'Your master mason is a clever man,' Innes said, unable to conceal his admiration. 'No hostile force could climb these steps and survive to the top.'

'Yes, Your Honour, very clever - as are all members of the Order. Ironically, a trick learned from the infidel, I believe.' The novice cheekily rolled his eyes. 'My uncle Pierre is the secretary to Order Preceptor de Charnay, and you can present your credentials to him.'

The stairs appeared to narrow and become steeper as the four men climbed forty and then fifty steps. Innes's sword scraped on the stone stairs as he led Jamie and Will up, flight after flight of granite steps. Just as they felt the climb would never end, they arrived at a wooden door, which was set just off the staircase. The landing was wide enough for everyone to stand together.

The novice knocked on the door with the metal handle of his small dirk. The door was plain apart from a round handle carved with the face of a smiling Saracen, which made Jamie smile. The stone frame was decorated with carvings and writings, which extended the entire length of the arch. Jamie stopped to look more closely, but was interrupted as the door moved ajar and the overly familiar voice of the novice encouraged them to enter.

'Come inside, Your Honours, please.' The novice entered first and waved them in. Two more sentries stood inside, armed the same way as the one downstairs.

They stepped into a large room, which echoed with the creaking noise of the heavy wooden door as it unwillingly swung on its hinges. A large fireplace faced them, fuelled by several wooden logs, which crackled and burst into flames as they caught the fresh air that blew through the open door.

Jamie had never seen such ostentatious buildings.

Identical arched windows filled with the same brightly coloured glass lay to either side of the fireplace, and Byzantine baldachins and tapestries woven with richly coloured thread covered the main walls.

Innes appeared enraptured by the tapestries, and his eyes studied each one.

Jamie thought they showed vignettes from the Garden of Gethsemane and the Last Judgement. His theological education had faded, and he wondered why Innes was so interested as he and Will drifted towards the table at the opposite end of the large room.

Jamie's head turned again and again as he took in the decorated ceilings and walls depicting scenes from the Bible. This matched everything he had heard about the Templars. They were vulgar and had the wealth of legend, and this display of gold and silver leaf had more than made up for the understated nature of the tower's reception. He remained silent, and even the cheery, forward novice was quiet.

In the far left of the chapter room, a figure could be seen moving soundlessly from behind one of the tapestries. A tall velvet-clad chair and a wooden table obscured a stout figure whose presence was only betrayed by his echoing footsteps.

'God dag, herre,' he said in Norwegian.

He was a balding, middle-aged man of average height. He pulled the chair from beneath the desk and sat behind it. Immediately, a small group of clerks and servants appeared from nowhere and joined the man, who was obviously in charge. Each of the servants bowed in turn as they entered from behind the tapestries.

The novice immediately marched towards the man, almost running in his haste. Jamie and Will quickly followed. Innes remained by the tapestries, ignoring the footsteps of the others.

'Please, Your Honour, will you join us?' The novice did not conceal his annoyance with Innes.

Innes joined them before the long table at the left-hand side of the chapter room.

'Gentlemen, may I introduce to you Brother Pierre de Nogaret, secretary to His Honour, Preceptor de Charnay.' The novice bowed towards the stout man as he spoke.

Pierre de Nogaret gestured for the men to sit down as the servants brought three backless, padded stools.

De Nogaret wore the surcoat of the Templars, white linen with a red cross. Upon his head, he sported an extravagant red fox-fur cap, as even with the huge fireplace and numerous braziers, the late winter's day still had the chill of the morning frost.

Underneath, he wore a pair of fine woollen hose and a woollen shirt. His face, wrinkled and flabby, showed his age - probably fifty or more - and although he was stooped slightly, he held his form well.

He was a Templar, but he did not look like the type to live a warrior's life: he had likely held a pen rather than a sword; and he had the presence of one who was in charge. His hair was shaven into a tonsure, yet he wore a large dagger. The dagger drew Jamie's attention, as it was on his right side rather than his left, and he was right-handed. In a fight, he would be unable to take it out of its scabbard.

Pierre de Nogaret spoke very slowly in Northern French. 'Gentlemen, I apologise that my three words of Norsk are all I have to greet you! Our Order does not often offer our hospitality to merchants from the Norwegian court. I hope my nephew, Guy, has made you welcome.'

Jamie and Will spoke some French as well as Gaelic, Latin, and English, but the etiquette of the Templar court was more foreign to them. They were silent and let Innes do the talking, conscious of their heavy accents and Innes's expertise as a diplomat.

*

Innes bowed to de Nogaret and spoke. 'Your Honour, I am Innes de Mayon, and as you have already gathered from my voice, I am a Breton acting as agent for these gentlemen. King Haakon has sent these merchants to offer a proposal on setting up a trade route for furs and amber using the Order as our sole business partner. I have with me a letter from the King in Bergen, and its contents are for the eyes of His Excellency Preceptor de Charnay only.'

A cold silence followed: Innes needed this man's help to access de Charnay and he looked for some common ground. Flattery was normally an ice-breaker. 'Are you related to

Guillaume de Nogaret, the great legal scholar and influential Conseil du Roi of King Philip?'

Pierre de Nogaret merely nodded, as if he were not happy his brother had been mentioned as a means of introduction.

Guillaume de Nogaret was the head of the King's secret agents and coercive forces. If the King needed something done which he wished to distance himself from, he got Guillaume de Nogaret to deal with it. No scruple restrained de Nogaret when the royal prerogative was in question. He was totally ruthless, devoted only to the enhancement of the King's power and wealth.

Anyone connected to Guillaume de Nogaret, especially his brother and nephew, had to be treated carefully.

The secretary gestured to one of his servants, who took several documents from a leather pouch and placed them on the table in front of him. Behind de Nogaret stood another servant, who provided further documents. These too were placed on the table. Innes wondered how the servants appeared unseen, as no other entrance was in evidence. He suspected some secret stairway extended through the middle of the Templar tower.

'May I impress on Your Honour the importance of this trade agreement for the Order and the gratitude you will receive from my master King Haakon,' Innes said. 'Anyone who sponsors this arrangement will receive much patronage in gold from all concerned. I am sure your master will be most pleased with your help in bringing this to his attention.'

Innes turned to Will and urged him to place in front of Pierre de Nogaret the small pouch which Bishop Wishart had sent with him to bribe those who required encouragement. Innes had picked up on the barely veiled touting from Guy de Nogaret.

'Your Excellency, I have been asked to offer to you a small token of the gratitude of the merchants of Bergen.' Innes pushed the small, sealed red velvet purse towards de

Nogaret, who barely acknowledged the bribe as he continued to scrutinise the papers his servants had placed on the table. He placed the large parchment he was reading on top of the purse as if to conceal it.

'Monsieur de Mayon, I am of course a monk first, a soldier second, and a merchant third. However, the pressures made on my order's purse for charity to continue our godly work are considerable, and we have to espouse our spiritual needs to more earthly ones, such as trade.' The secretary pulled the parchment and purse towards him and continued.

'We are all at heart but poor knights of Christ, but my earthly needs are nothing to remark upon. It is the Order that must thrive and continue its work, and we will use your gift to continue our mission to rid the Holy Land of the unchristian heathens who currently rule where they should not. I am grateful to your master King Haakon for this gift.'

Innes knew the poor and needy would receive no benefit from today's transaction.

'I see you were taken with the splendour of our tapestries, my Breton friend,' de Nogaret said. 'They were designed by Florence's most famous artist, Giotto di Bondone, and were a gift to my master Geoffroi de Charnay from his good friend Enrico degli Scrovegni.'

De Nogaret continued. 'Perhaps you have heard of the Scrovegni's family? Enrico's father, Reginaldo degli Scrovegni, was of great assistance to my master in his escape from the fortress of Acre in 1291. Strangely, the tapestries are of no Templar or hero of Acre but likenesses of the Plantagenet family. The shocking red hair and red boots are unmistakably Henry II of England and his five sons, but I probably shouldn't say that so near the French court.'

'Your Honour, I am aware of the Scrovegni, as is most of Christendom,' Innes replied. 'Their wealth and power bring considerable attention even in the remote villages of Brittany, and certainly in my master's court in Bergen, but I am not of their particular acquaintance.'

De Nogaret gestured to one of his servants, who picked up the purse, leaving the parchment without concealing it behind. De Nogaret would recognise the Scottish seal. Innes knew he was taking a risk, but he reckoned that Pierre de Nogaret's loyalty would be to the Templars and not the French or English Kings.

De Nogaret paused long enough to confirm he recognised Bishop Wishart's seal.

'You have asked me to facilitate an audience with my master. Access to the Preceptor and his advocacy is a privilege. Your master is indeed a wise man to seek his patronage: King Haakon knows the strength of the Order and has given you the best advice in coming to us. I will speak with my master and see whether he will meet you. I will send my servant later today with his response.'

De Nogaret rubbed his nose with his index finger, and immediately the one-eyed sentry left through the hidden door.

Innes was concerned. He was not convinced he could trust Pierre de Nogaret. He had a sense that what was being played out before him was dangerous. He had spent the last few days watching for the unusual, and this struck him as odd, as if de Nogaret knew the real reason why the Scots were there. His hospitality might be a trap.

'Guy, please find some rooms for our guests in the visitors' house. Make our travellers from the North comfortable.'

Innes was about to reply when de Nogaret stood up, licked his fingers, and extinguished the small candle. He had made his point: the audience was at an end. With this, he turned on his heels, walked behind his chair, and disappeared in the same manner he had appeared from behind the tapestries. He was followed by all his remaining servants apart from Guy.

The hostile atmosphere demanded silence.

'Your Honours, please follow me to the visitors' house,

which is outside near the stables,' he said. 'Hurry, please.'

Innes lagged at the rear. He tapped Will and Jamie silently on the shoulder and slowly drew his sword halfway from its sheath - he was warning them of danger.

Guy de Nogaret was unaware that they were still on the landing. He was already half a flight below.

'The visitors' house will be most comfortable for men who have come so far. We, Templars, are sometimes known as the Hospitallers, such is our care for strangers. Our cook is exceptionally fine.' The Scots had reluctantly followed as he chatted, not listening or concerned with their stomachs - it felt like an arrest.

Guy reached the bottom of the stairs, and the light from the brazier lit the way to the tower entrance. Innes expected a hostile reception, but all that was waiting there was the same one-eyed, battle-scarred Templar veteran.

As Guy led them to the visitors' house, they became aware of a small group of sentries that were following them. Leading the group was the one-eyed veteran. It was not clear whether these men were an escort or a guard, but Innes suspected the latter.

'I will have your belongings brought up from the stables to your rooms,' Guy added.

This was to prevent them from returning to the stables and possibly escaping. Innes suspected that something had alarmed the Templars, but he was sure they had left nothing incriminating within their belongings.

He relaxed his sword grip, and as Jamie and Will looked on, he shook his head. Even if they fought off the guards, they would need to get to their horses and past the guards on the bridge.

There were too many guards and sentries to fight their way out, and it was broad daylight.

It was not clear whether Pierre de Nogaret was always this cautious in protecting his master when he had unknown visitors, or whether de Nogaret knew their true identities and was in the pay of the French or English.

*

Guy de Nogaret reached the building on the far side of the Temple esplanade, known as the visitors' house. It was small in relation to the rest of the Temple, only being three storeys high, and had two tiny, shuttered windows on each of the four sides which allowed light in and minimised the cold, but could be defended easily by crossbow or longbow.

Guy opened the door. 'Please, can you leave your swords outside the door and step inside?'

They looked shocked to be disarmed so easily. Will contemplated a fight but knew there was no winning that battle.

Their escort followed closely, but remained outside as they stepped into a reception hall, which had a rough-hewn table at its centre surrounded by four carver chairs. Each chair had a cloth with the emblem of the Order draped upon its slatted back. A glowing iron brazier gave the room warmth and some light, and a large lamp stood proud on the table.

'You were expecting us?' Innes asked.

Guy looked confused. 'Sir, we always have the visitors' house prepared for guests, expected or unexpected.'

Will's attention was drawn towards the far-right corner of the room, where there was a spiral staircase leading up towards the remaining two floors. One room was just off the reception hall to the left. The door was fully ajar, and he could see three wooden beds in parallel against the left-hand wall. It was obvious now that they had been expected. Will was annoyed with himself. The possibilities of a trap were clear, and he had done nothing to prevent it.

'Please, make yourself comfortable.' Guy de Nogaret ushered the men inside as the remaining sentries stood outside on either side of the door. 'Some refreshment and

187

food will be sent from our kitchens, but I am sure that after your journey, you will need to sleep and refresh your tired limbs.' His tone was patronising; Guy knew they were prisoners and his haughtiness irritated Will.

Guy left, and the door slammed shut before being locked and barred from the outside.

There was now no pretence that they were guests who were free to come and go. They were under lock and key, and subject to whatever justice Pierre de Nogaret deemed appropriate.

'This is the first hospitality house I have been locked in.' Will's tone was mocking. He had observed everything and understood the situation perfectly. 'Pierre de Nogaret knew who we are and knew we were coming.'

Innes nodded. 'Of course, but he didn't know we came from Bishop Wishart. The seal of the Guardians of Scotland, which I showed him when I gave him the bribe, was a surprise.'

'I think so. The one-eyed man with the bejewelled sword looked familiar; it was strange how he tried to hide his face from us. I recognised him from L'Auberge du Lion.' Will rubbed his head.

'He was one of the men who tried to kill me,' Jamie said. 'I left him with that scar and no eye.'

He paused. 'I was at the Bishop's house when the English came to arrest him,' he added. 'I am sure I saw this man or someone with a similar sword on that occasion. He is a mercenary.'

'I only caught a glimpse,' Will said, 'but I am certain Jamie and I were followed from Lanark to Leith as well, and that the person following us wore a jewel on his sword. I think I saw it catch the sun, but I was not sure. Now I am.' Will knew these events were connected, but was it the French, the English, or someone else? He did not know. The one thing he did know was they were after the treasure.

'I wonder if Pierre de Nogaret knows that, or whether this man works for him.' Innes scoffed.

The door flung open with a crash. They all got to their feet ready anticipating a confrontation, but almost immediately relaxed.

A kitchen serf appeared along with an armed sentry. The servant carried a tray covered with bread, cheese, and ale, which he placed quickly and precisely on the table before hurrying out of the room.

Will laughed in embarrassment whilst he quietly thought of how they would escape.

*

Pierre de Nogaret was happiest amongst his papers and his plots. He did not appreciate distraction, and outside the noisy esplanade was now full of theatre as the Preceptor of Normandy, Geoffroi de Charnay, arrived with his extensive entourage. Over a dozen heavily armed knights had ridden in, and the tradesmen and servants had scattered like scared rabbits to the four corners of the main courtyard.

The noise had attracted Pierre de Nogaret to the window. He could see his master displaying the grandstanding he had come to loathe. Nothing was subtle or restrained about Geoffroi de Charnay, and it irked de Nogaret to recognise his popularity.

Bastard, he thought as de Charnay strutted across the esplanade.

De Charnay had ridden into the Temple in full armour, the Order's emblems liberally displayed on his horse and tabard, his flags flowing in the spring wind. They were not at war with anyone apart from themselves, and Pierre de Nogaret shook his head in disgust at the ostentatious display. He was just as committed to the Order as de Charnay, but he saw commerce as the best protection rather than dreaming of a fighting force that was past its best.

De Nogaret returned to his desk, which was piled high

with parchments and scrolls. A small glass carafe of wine and two small glasses were the only diversion from the bureaucracy and the only token of the good life that de Nogaret allowed. Without looking up, he gestured to the ever-present one-eyed guard, Gaston de Bezier, to come closer.

'Gaston, you were gone many weeks and have put me at considerable inconvenience by getting into a fight with these men in Rouen. You were to follow them only. Find out why they were here and what they knew.' His tone was edged with rage, his fists gripped and relaxed in frustration. 'Questions are being asked at court, and there are rumours of Alaric's treasure. The intercepted diplomatic dispatches from the Byzantine court are full of talk of gold. King Philip can almost taste the money. You know we cannot let King Philip or his allies get hold of such wealth. Now it is clear the Scots are here to meet Geoffroi de Charnay, something the King does not know, and they must not meet him.'

De Nogaret dropped the purse of money Innes had given him into de Bezier's hand. 'Interestingly, in addition to bribing me, they carried the bribe in a purse containing the Bishop of Glasgow's seal. He must know about the treasure, but does he also know where it is? I wonder how much he knows.'

De Bezier had been handsome and was still strong and muscular even in middle age, though Jamie's well-aimed dirk had cost him an eye.

'I have been in your service these many years, master. I did not fail you or our cause.'

'While I may accept your loyalty and good intentions, we have a greater purpose,' de Nogaret said. 'We must ensure that the Cathar cause is foremost in our actions. The King of France is our greatest enemy; he must never acquire this wealth.'

Gaston scoffed. 'It wasn't me trying to kill them. There

were others trying to do that, and if those heathen Scots had only realised, I was trying to protect them, but here is the mystery … I do not think I was the only one trying to protect them: I am sure there were other swords working for them …' he brushed his hair away from his deformed eye. 'And I got this for my trouble. If I get an opportunity, I will kill Jamie Wishart and Will de Irwyne.' De Bezier smashed his fist into the table in frustration, making de Nogaret jump.

De Nogaret ignored him, only nodding in acknowledgement rather than agreement with his servant.

'Also, the French King isn't the only one determined to get what doesn't belong to him,' de Bezier said. 'I waited for them to disembark from the ship in the harbour. They might think they left the ship first, but that is not the case. A man slipped into the water before the ship docked and headed away into the darkness.'

'And did you see who it was?' De Nogaret asked.

De Bezier wiped the discharge from his withered eye.

'I was watching the Scots until the fight broke out in the inn, and I know whoever it was went straight to the Maréchaussée. They arrived too quickly, you see. But someone was in that inn to kill Innes de Mayon and knew he was there. Four men pounced on de Mayon, and I do not think De Irwyne and Wishart were their targets for killing. Chaos erupted: men appeared from everywhere; they spoke in French and English, with some trying to kill the Scots, and one golden-hair individual protecting them. I think your brother's agents were amongst the dead men and the English. In their dying, they stopped concealing their origins.'

De Nogaret nodded. 'So, it seems the English wanted the men dead because they were Scots supposedly conspiring with the French, and someone summoned the Maréchaussée to capture them alive to steal their treasure or kill them. Neither the English nor the French are aware of the other's intentions.'

He was sure he was the only one with this insight and must be ahead of the rest of the pack pursuing the treasure – that gave him an advantage and he smiled with satisfaction.

'The Scots want the treasure for rebellion, we have known that since 1300 when Wallace and Wishart were at King Phillip's court, and we need to stop everyone else from getting what they are seeking.'

'How delicious this is,' de Nogaret said, laughing. 'We can get our revenge and thwart the French King's plans, and whilst we have no love for the English, they are the lesser of the two evils so perhaps we should let them capture de Mayon.'

'Master, I don't understand.'

Pierre wanted the English to get the treasure. 'The old King would die soon, and the younger Prince Edward was reputedly very malleable, especially when money and young men were involved. I will bring the new English King to the righteous path of Catharism, and the treasure would lubricate that path. If Edward II did not see my point of view, I could buy another one who would. With all that money, I could afford a usurper or two.'

He thought for a moment. 'Tell master de Charnay that I wish for an immediate audience with him.'

*

Gaston de Bezier headed down the internal staircase that led to the receiving room. He stopped at the bottom of the stairs and anxiously removed the sword with the fire opal in the pommel that had been given to him by his real master, the English King. He had lied to Pierre de Nogaret, and he had been one of the men trying to kill Innes in Rouen and capture the Scots and the papers they carried. He had followed Jamie and Will from Glasgow to find Innes and had hidden on Jean de Bretagne's cog, with the help of one of Jean de Bretagne's sailors, but his flamboyance had been his undoing. He should not have worn the sword so prominently; the young Scot,

Jamie, had placed him, and he could not risk exposure to Pierre de Nogaret. Gaston might be a Cathar, but he would take money from whichever side paid the most, and in this case, the English King had been most generous. He would not share his good luck and his bribes with anyone even if de Nogaret was for the English. This was about him and not the Cathar cause, which he did not believe in anymore.

He wondered who had tipped off the Maréchaussée and how many others were involved.

The Scots were dead men now.

He would do as Pierre de Nogaret asked and would hide his plans for murder amongst his master's machinations.

*

Preceptor de Charnay was removing his riding clothes and catching up on all the latest gossip and plotting, and it would not be long before he heard about the visitors from Scotland. There seemed to be a lot of chattering today.

The reception room was candlelit, as the days were still short. De Charnay's arrival had been sudden and unexpected, and the servants were anxious not to keep him and his entourage waiting. In the absence of Grand Master Jacques de Molay, de Charnay was the most important Templar in France.

De Bezier entered the room and found de Charnay was stripped to his tunic and undershirt, still sweating from his ride.

'Preceptor, excuse me.' De Charnay was attaching his cloak when he caught sight of de Nogaret's servant. He belied his middle age by carrying himself with joie de vivre and enthusiasm that younger men often found tiring. The only clue to his real age was a greying mop of tonsured hair, his one acknowledgement of his holy orders.

He barely concealed his contempt for de Bezier, who behaved more like a reptile, silent and slippery, never knowing his place.

193

'I see you have been in a fight,' de Charnay said. 'Who poked your eye out? Was she drunk? I have been on the road for many days, so make it quick.' He picked up a full cup of sweetened wine from the reception table.

'Preceptor de Charnay, Master de Nogaret wishes for an audience at your earliest convenience.'

De Charnay wanted to rest, but he thought this was probably important. He knew of the riot in Rouen and the rumour of foreign agents, and his instincts told him that de Bezier's injury, the killings in Rouen, and his meeting with Pierre de Nogaret were not unrelated.

He emptied his goblet and handed it to the servant who was adjusting his cloak.

'Tell Brother de Nogaret I will see him in my rooms,' he said to de Bezier. De Charnay paused. 'And I hope he is brief. I am in no mood for long-winded anecdotes.'

Pierre de Nogaret was a necessary evil, as far as de Charnay was concerned. He had no experience with battle, but he did keep the Order in order, as it were, and every powerful entity needed bureaucrats like him. De Charnay turned away from de Bezier, who was now scurrying away to find de Nogaret.

With his usual panache, de Charnay took his leave of his entourage. 'Farewell, dear brothers. *À tout à l'heure,'* he cried.

Everyone raucously toasted him with the remains of the sweetened wine as the Preceptor walked up the central staircase, followed by his servant and the laughter of men glad to be home.

On the second floor of the main tower, two armed guards stood at the entrance to de Charnay's chambers, a burning torch on either side of them. A servant opened the door into the reception room and bedroom and followed close behind. The rooms felt cold and smelt damp, having been uninhabited the last few weeks as de Charnay had progressed through the

Templar lands in Normandy.

'It is good to be home,' he whispered as he warmed his hands at the fireplace.

He was tired and yearned for some sleep in a comfortable bed, having spent several weeks sleeping in strange beds. He hoped de Nogaret would be brief, but he never was.

He sat clumsily and awkwardly on the large carver chair that dominated the reception room. He slumped into it, trailing his leg over the side of the chair, and leaning against a side table that was adjacent to it. He could feel the sweetened wine hit his brain, making him drowsy.

'Let Brother de Nogaret in when he arrives,' he winked at his servant. 'And don't let him stay longer than fifteen minutes.'

The servant busied himself preparing his master's bedroom as the heavy oak doors creaked open and Pierre de Nogaret stepped over the threshold. He bowed his head to his superior as the doors slammed shut behind him, and the servant brought them wine that had been hidden in the bedroom awaiting de Charnay's return.

The servant served the wine before leaving the two men next to the fireplace, sipping wine, and avoiding conversation until they were alone.

'To what do I owe this pleasure, Brother Nogaret? I assume it is an urgent matter?'

De Charnay did not want to hear the latest court gossip. He knew that de Nogaret liked to play him with his knowledge of the court's inner secrets, which he gleaned from his brother Guillaume.

'We have some guests from Scotland. They claim to be Norwegians, but I know that is a cover. I had them followed.'

De Nogaret paused, expecting some acknowledgement or some expression of interest. De Charnay said nothing: he would not reveal anything until he knew de Nogaret's motivation. 'Go on, Master de Nogaret.'

'They arrived about a week ago on Jean de Bretagne's cog, the Nantes, and were joined by Bishop Wishart's agent, Innes de Mayon.'

De Charnay had not heard the name of Bishop Wishart for many years, and it came as a bittersweet surprise. He knew that his great friend and Bishop Wishart's brother John had disappeared. The rumour was that the French King had had him killed.

'Do you know what they want? I heard there was some trouble in Rouen.' De Charnay tried not to betray his thoughts, especially to someone as duplicitous as de Nogaret, for he knew well why they had come. He did not want to show his concern, and he hid it by gulping another large mouthful of wine.

'Master, I rather hoped you could help me in that matter.' De Nogaret was displaying his usual arrogance. 'They are here for the treasure - Alaric's treasure - and they want you to tell them where it is.' De Charnay was surprised by his frankness. It seemed vexatious.

There was a discernible pause before de Charnay laughed at de Nogaret's abruptness and his astonishing statement.

'So, the mythical treasure is the goal of these desperate fortune hunters,' de Charnay scoffed. 'I had heard the Scots were on their knees, but I did not think they were so desperate as to resort to fantasy and fabulous tales.'

'Oh, I think there is a bit more to this than mere fantasy. They were careful and determined to reach here, which suggests to me they are chasing more than a fable.' De Nogaret was digging, but de Charnay was not going to be tricked into revealing anything about John Wishart and Acre.

'I see their determination in your servant's face,' de Charnay replied. 'You had them followed?'

'Yes. My servants got caught up with the Maréchaussée. We had intercepted letters stating that the English King had sent assassins to kill Innes de Mayon, servant of Bishop

Wishart; and in your absence, knowing the great affection you had for him, I sent Gaston to watch over him, and we ran into the treasure seekers meeting with de Mayon.'

He paused and showed de Charnay the seal of the Guardians of Scotland. 'This confirms who they are, and I was right to help them.'

De Charnay made no comment condoning his actions. 'And where are they now?'

De Nogaret paced towards the small window overlooking the esplanade. 'They are locked up together, enjoying our hospitality in the visitors' house and probably wondering how they will escape.'

De Charnay expected that the King of France would soon hear that the Scots were at the Temple and would come to him, asking awkward questions about his involvement and the treasure. The King had been like a rabid dog whenever he had heard of its presence ever since he had interrogated John Wishart over five years ago.

'Their presence is too well known amongst our enemies. I heard about the fracas in Rouen, and if I did, then we can assume King Philip has as well, and we can do without our name being part of that dispatch. Neither of us wants King Philip meddling in our affairs.'

De Charnay could see the risk and he wanted de Nogaret to understand how this was a real threat to the order. 'He is a poverty-stricken King looking for money. Our businesses in money-lending and relics need to continue unregulated by the King or your brother. The Order needs to distance itself from talk of treasure.'

De Nogaret nodded before continuing what was turning out to be more like an interrogation. 'Master, what shall we do about the rumours of the treasure within these walls? King Philip and the English King will have agents camped at our door before nightfall if they know these men are here.'

De Charnay paused and did not reply, creating an

awkward silence.

'We don't want them here, so we shall send them away, and in doing so divert any investigation by a nosey King and his avaricious courtier,' he said at last. 'They do not know I am here so let us tell them what they want to know. They are looking for Alaric's treasure, and it was last rumoured to be hidden in Padua, so that's where we will tell them to go.'

De Charnay sensed de Nogaret was being deceptive; he was hiding something. His instincts screamed out not to bring him in too close. For now, he would play all his enemies against each other whilst he worked out what he would do.

'I will write a command; you can deliver it to the Scots and present it as instructions I left for you to pass on only to Bishop Wishart's trusted servants. I will tell them to journey to Padua and look up my dear friend Enrico degli Scrovegni.'

De Charnay called to his servant. 'Fetch me a pen and parchment!'

The servant arrived and laid a silver vial of black ink and a parchment roll in front of de Charnay, who hurriedly scratched out a message.

Without looking up, he addressed de Nogaret again. 'Make sure you give them all the assistance that the Order can provide - horses, food, and an escort that makes certain they head to the border - and give them this. They will know the letter is genuine if they have this.'

De Charnay removed a large amethyst ring from his purse and placed it on the table next to the note.

De Nogaret picked it up and could see a bright stone marked with a scribbled engraving which he could not read. He had stopped listening to de Charnay. He would pass on the note to the Scots as soon as the ink was dry.

'Master, I will see them out of the Temple as you wish, without fanfare or fuss.'

De Nogaret bowed. De Charnay sensed his anger in his

silence as he turned and left the room, but for now he could not risk bringing him into his confidence.

*

Jamie was angry at being locked up. The windows were small and barred, and only he seemed to be thinking of escape. It was a prison - perhaps the plushest they had ever seen, but nevertheless, they were trapped within its walls, locked behind impressive and impregnable doors.

Will and Innes were resting on the beds. They had thrown off their wet boots and were enjoying a nap, curled up in the warm blankets and resting, but not in a deep sleep. This lack of action upset Jamie, who was reconnoitring the house, looking for ways to escape. Gaps in the corners of the stones and the roof offered the best route for escape if they could work away at the beams. They still had their dirks to carry out the deed. Perhaps in a few days, they could loosen the wooden frame sufficiently to squeeze through a small gap and disappear into the darkness.

'Gentlemen, I believe I have found our way to escape,' Jamie announced, expecting immediate gratification and thanks. Instead, he heard nothing but the sound of gentle, shallow snoring. He coughed once, and still there was no reaction, so he coughed louder. The only acknowledgement he received was even louder snoring from an unmoved Innes.

'We would be dead before we got out of the window,' Will muttered without even opening his eyes. 'We would be incredibly lucky if they didn't shoot us by the time we got to the rooftop. There are sentries overlooking us, stationed on every roof, armed with crossbows. I spotted them as they invited us in here. Rest awhile. There will be a time, just not now.'

Jamie felt stupid as he looked out of the window and spotted a raft of inquisitive sentries overlooking their quarters, brandishing armed crossbows.

'Do you think they are deciding whether to kill us or

not?' Jamie asked.

'Probably, but there is little we can do about that, locked up in here,' Innes said. 'We need to wait until we are outside, hidden from the sentries by darkness. They need information, and they have not finished interrogating us.'

Despite Innes's words, Jamie looked at the frame around the window again and wondered how he could work loose the bars. At night, the window would be obscured by the shadow of the overhanging buildings, hiding them from the view of the sentries.

The door flew open and slammed against the stone upright, scattering dust and the mice that had been cowering under the beds.

Will and Innes jumped immediately to their feet and half-drew their dirks. Jamie stood behind them by the window, his dagger drawn.

Two Templar guards accompanied Pierre de Nogaret, who was grinning as he entered. In his right hand, he held a folded parchment embossed with a large red seal. The guards stood by without drawing their swords; it did not look like they were preparing to murder Jamie and his companions.

'Dear friends, I hope you have been enjoying our hospitality. Please put away your daggers. I bring you good news.'

He urged the Scots to sit at the table, which was strewn with discarded food and empty wine containers.

'Please sit with me for a while. I have news from Master de Charnay.'

'Can we see him now?' Will said, interrupting de Nogaret and ignoring the letter.

De Nogaret continued to smile, but shook his head. 'Master de Charnay is now on his way to see the King at the Louvre Palace and can't be delayed.'

De Nogaret broke the seal and unfolded the parchment. 'Master de Charnay asked me to read this note to you and offer all assistance with your quest.'

De Nogaret read the short note. 'He asks that you journey to Padua and contact Enrico degli Scrovegni. He can be found at the Arena Chapel. You are to make the acquaintance of Giotto di Bondone, who can make the necessary introductions. Master de Charnay asks that you take heart, for the Scrovegnis can offer the help you seek and can direct you on your journey. You are to leave immediately.'

The Scots were about to contest the instructions when a larger armed escort arrived within sight of the door. One of the soldiers was carrying their swords.

Jamie saw that neither Innes nor Will wanted to fight despite accepting their returned swords.

'Master de Charnay has provided an escort to the southern mountains near the border. They will take great care to see that you all come to no harm on your journey.' De Nogaret threw a purse full of gold onto the table. It was so ostentatious that it came across as a bribe to go away.

'This small contribution from his coffers will help make your journey more comfortable. There is also this,' de Nogaret opened his palm showing an engraved cabochon. This was identical to the ring Bishop Wishart had given him and he knew its significance. De Charnay was giving the treasure up, and this gesture confirmed it was real. He looked at Will who seemed to recognise it - but how could he. What did Will know?

'The Preceptor added that this is given with his best wishes for your good luck and fortune.' De Nogaret placed the ring in Will's open palm.

'I will keep this ring and associate it with the Templars and the help you have given me.' Will tightly clenched the ring in his palm.

Two servants appeared from amongst the crowd that was now gathering outside the door. They pushed themselves past the escort, stood next to de Nogaret and bowed.

'My servants will help you pack, and my grooms are saddling fresh horses for you as we speak.'

Will placed the money and ring from de Charnay within his jerkin.

'You will have an armed escort of six of my finest knights, all of whom are familiar with the road through France to Padua,' de Nogaret said. Six heavily armed knights stepped forward as the servants continued their frenetic packing. They had obviously been instructed to pack as rapidly as they could.

Jamie realised that they would not be seeing Geoffroi de Charnay any time soon, but they were at least away from the prison, which he had seen little opportunity to escape by their own means.

'I see you have thought of everything!' Jamie said, still hostile.

'Follow me to the stables, where your horses will be ready,' de Nogaret added contemptuously. 'My servants will bring your belongings and join you in a few minutes.'

The Scots pulled on their boots and grabbed their riding cloaks as they were politely but forcefully taken out of the guest lodgings and marched towards the stables.

'Perhaps once you have completed your journey to Padua, you can return to the Temple and call on Master de Charnay. You have been unlucky to have missed him.' His tone was disingenuous and he didn't appear to care.

Outside the large stable block were three sturdy mounts, saddled and waiting for their riders. They had been provisioned with food sacks and pottery flagons. Nearby were six more beasts covered with the dress of the Order, no doubt for the escort. The knights mounted in columns of three and moved to either side of the horses that had been set aside for the Scots.

'Mount up, sirs,' de Nogaret urged the knights. 'There is light enough for you to travel two or perhaps three leagues before nightfall. Every league will count on such a long and arduous journey. I would make haste in the winter sunshine.'

The Scots looked around anxiously for their belongings, but the two servants appeared almost immediately with three saddlebags over their shoulders. The Templars had provided food supplies and changes of clothes, which were pushing out of the top of the saddlebags where the leather straps had been crudely fastened.

They tightened their cloaks around their bodies and mounted their skittish horses, which seemed to have been chosen based on their desire to be away from this place. Jamie calmed his horse, arranged his sword to sit at his left side, and leaned forward towards de Nogaret.

'We will return to this place very soon, Monsieur de Nogaret, and repay your many kindnesses,' he whispered. 'And when you see Master de Charnay, tell him the same.'

In his anger, de Nogaret smacked the back of Jamie's horse, causing the animal to stumble before galloping out of the Temple over the lowered drawbridge, followed by the surprised escort, who had been caught temporarily off guard. This was no escape, as Innes and Will followed close behind. They couldn't escape their escort, but they wouldn't be cowed by them.

*

De Charnay drained the last dregs of wine as he watched the Scots disappear. He was not proud of his deception, but he was probably saving their lives. It was only a matter of time before the English and French spies caught up with them. Nothing that happened in the Temple stayed secret for long, and he did not trust de Nogaret to be discreet. He had a direct route to the French King through his brother, and de Charnay simply did not trust him.

As de Charnay watched, the Scots galloped towards the southern road. Gaston de Bezier rode out of the stables shortly after, a mounted figure amongst the chaos of traders, merchants, and off-duty soldiers.

De Bezier did not see that he was being watched from two floors above his master's office. His face was covered, but the Preceptor of Normandy recognised the rider as Pierre de Nogaret's loathsome servant, de Bezier, and he allowed himself a wry smile.

'Good luck and Godspeed to you Scots,' de Charnay whispered as he turned away, crossing himself as he returned to his bed to rest.

*

De Bezier turned his mount slowly and walked his horse towards the diminishing figures, who were now almost out of sight. He looked up towards the oriel window where Pierre de Nogaret had his offices and nodded, lifting his hand in acknowledgement. His face was swathed in a woollen cloth, hiding the long scar. De Nogaret had instructed the Templar sergeant, Argentan de Houdain, to make sure the Scots got no further than the French border, and de Nogaret had sent de Bezier to ensure that happened - but de Bezier was working according to his own agenda. He would follow Aymer de Valance's order and kill Innes de Mayon; and proving his loyalty further, deliver the treasure to his English paymaster.

Chapter Twelve

Paris by Notre Dame, Late April 1306: The Tale of Two Cathars

'I am the King's counsellor, yet I have to skulk around at night, walking through this shit.' Guillaume de Nogaret minced gingerly through the middens and open sewers, but it was difficult to avoid the inch-deep mud. He had had the good sense to cover his fine clothes with a plain woollen cloak, but it was getting sodden and heavy, and the weight pulled it further off his shoulders, exposing the rich velvets beneath. It was raining hard, and a small river was running through the middle of the streets, washing filth everywhere.

He knew this area of the Ile de la Cité, which was not far from Notre Dame. He had worshipped many times with the King, but he had never wandered alone outside the cathedral at night. He marvelled at the magnificent lady, even if she was surrounded by foul smells and dirt.

Sensible people are inside on a night like this.

He stepped on a large turd, which squelched onto the top of his boots and onto his cloak.

The smell is overpowering, and most of it is coming from my cloak.

He pulled a gold vinaigrette filled with lavender oil from his cloak pocket and held it under his nose.

Perhaps displaying such an item is not such a good idea in an area full of thieves and whores, Guillaume. I will be filleted if I do not move quickly.

'Why did I agree to meet here?' Guillaume muttered. 'I wish I were a million miles away.'

He heard shouts from the Maréchaussée as they tried to keep order in a place where chaos was the order. He should know - he made the laws, and he set the culture. But what he did not acknowledge was that he was walking through his own creation, and it was dirty and violent.

He struggled along narrow streets where the overhanging houses almost touched, blocking out the faint light. The darkness concealed the lawlessness within.

Why would Pierre want to meet in the Moor's Head Tavern? It is home to transient undesirables.

Then he understood why. It was not a place where a member of the establishment would willingly be found. He had intentionally left his guard behind.

This meeting needed to be secret, and he did not want anyone from the court, especially that greasy capon Valois, to know that he was here.

He approached the inn and heard theatre, singing, the voices of drunks and raconteurs, boasting soldiers and brigands, and the cries of harlots mixed with the poetry and bawdy songs of students, minstrels, and sailors. Suddenly the door of the inn flew open.

He saw a huge, burly innkeeper throw a body into a midden. 'Get out, scum. Those who order food and wine here must have the means to pay for it. My inn is not a fucking charity.'

The innkeeper stepped out into the street and checked the man, who appeared unconscious.

De Nogaret glanced back and saw two men purposefully heading towards him. They had unsheathed daggers in their hands.

The innkeeper called out to de Nogaret and waved at him.

'Hurry, *monsieur.* Hurry! A warm welcome to the Moor's Head Tavern!'

De Nogaret stepped nimbly over the threshold and glanced back at the two men, who ignored him and walked on.

Just inside the door, mummified and resting on a wooden shelf, was the dried but recognisable head of a Moor, complete with his Arab turban. De Nogaret shuddered in surprise, even though he had seen executed men before.

'Ah, *monsieur*, I see you are wondering who this was. He was -'

Disinterested, de Nogaret brusquely turned away and ignored the innkeeper, who followed him inside.

He removed his brown woollen hood; his scarf was wrapped around his face so that only his eyes could be seen. He quickly snatched the crimson hat from his head and stuffed it in his pocket. It showed the royal insignia and would draw attention when none was wanted.

De Nogaret felt the warm air against his face, but his mood had not improved. He stopped to warm his hands at the open brazier that stood in the middle of the room, and peered into each nook, seeking out Pierre.

In the far corner with his back towards him in the darkest recess of the inn, he spotted his brother nursing a flagon of ale. He could see the pale white tunic exposed beneath a dark woollen overcape that covered his attire and draped on the wooden floor.

Guillaume checked to see if he was being watched before he moved towards his brother, who was sitting on a stool, resting his drink and his dagger on a small, rectangular table directly in front of him.

'My dear friend and brother!' Guillaume whispered in the langue d'oc as he placed his hand on his brother's shoulder and gripped it warmly.

Startled, Pierre jumped slightly, but he relaxed when he saw it was his older brother. They embraced and kissed.

Pierre then bowed to Guillaume. 'Your Honour,' he whispered with a smile.

They were brothers, within a few years in age, and they

looked both similar and dissimilar. Guillaume was tall for the district, while Pierre was stouter. Both had greying beards and the frames of recently retired soldiers or well-fed nobility, strong backs with broad chests, and just a hint of relaxed muscle around their middles. Pierre was the younger, and his demeanour was staid, narrow, and dull. Guillaume and Pierre did share a mutual superciliousness which sucked the atmosphere dry and made enemies.

Pierre was displaying a tonsure.

'I see your hair has thinned, but not your scowl,' Guillaume said with a laugh.

The innkeeper placed another warm flagon of spiced ale and a goblet in front of Guillaume, who had sat down across from Pierre so that he could watch the door.

'Do you want me to remove Fallone?' The innkeeper gestured towards the brothers' smelly neighbour, who was sleeping a few feet from their table. 'Fallone is a bit of an institution around here and does no harm, especially in that state.'

Guillaume took another sniff from his vinaigrette to stave off the strong odour of the women draped over the table nearest to them. The body looked more like a bundle of clothes haphazardly thrown together. The clothes were unique in that nothing matched in colour or fabric, as if each garment had been chosen on impulse and through opportunity rather than selection. Most likely, it had all been stolen. In a place of unpleasant smells, the odour was overpowering. A mixture of stale sweat, manure, sour ale, and rancid food emanated from its direction.

'If it keeps away other customers like the flies, then it serves some purpose. I see it offers no harm,' Guillaume said to the innkeeper.

'Whatever it is, it is asleep and doing no harm,' Pierre added.

On passing Fallone's table, the innkeeper kicked the

occupant's stool hard. The bundle fell off and rolled under the table, unharmed and still asleep. Guillaume relaxed again.

Guillaume looked on his younger brother with the warmth he could never express at court. He had no time for relationships and was driven by ambition and power. He sensed his brother was his weakness and his joy, and seeing him generated feelings that made him uncomfortable. He hated feeling this way, and it scared him. He thought it made him like other men, and other men were vulnerable and weak.

Pierre began to fidget nervously with the ruby ring on his middle finger, as if it were providing inspiration. 'It is good to see you, even in these surroundings. I was surprised you accepted my invitation. Guy recommended the location.' Pierre sounded nervous as he spoke.

Guillaume looked around at the peeling paint and leaking roof. 'Interesting place for a meeting. I could not wait to get here. Lovely neighbourhood too.' Guillaume smiled, and Pierre laughed, his nervousness gone.

Guillaume smiled as he thought about Guy.

'There is perhaps more of a man within Guy than I suspected,' Pierre said. 'Nevertheless, I wanted to find somewhere we could meet and talk in private without too many prying eyes and curious courtiers,' he paused. 'How is the loathsome King you are so loyal to?'

Guillaume's voice darkened. 'Be careful, Pierre. Remember my office. I came here to see you at your request. I know your opinion of the King, the realm, and the Papacy. You would strike at them all if you could, but that is a powerful trinity of enemies to choose in such times. These are dangerous thoughts that need to remain private, and should they become known to the wrong people, even I could not save you - I am not here to lecture you, but we need order.' Guillaume was angered by his brother's complacency and stupidity when the stakes were so high; his loose talk would threaten them both.

Pierre sipped his ale, wetting his dry lips. His tone was less measured.

'I didn't choose these enemies - they chose me. They chose us, though you hide behind your office!'

As he spoke, Pierre's face reddened. Guillaume could see the meeting was already heading in the wrong direction, and they had barely spoken a few dozen words to each other.

'Guillaume, everything you now represent destroyed everything I held dear. Your King, your realm, and your religion killed our family. They burned our father, mother, and sister alive for being Cathars - or have you sold out so much that even your memory has erased everything that does not fit with how you want it to be? You may consider what happened to them as an inconvenient truth in your quest for power, but I do not. I will not forget, and I don't want to forget.'

Pierre's voice faltered as he slammed the goblet down hard. Guillaume understood the frustration and anger, but had moved on. The noise brought the attention of those nearby, but only momentarily. Their conversation was drowned out by singing and rhetoric from the *comédiens* who had arrived in numbers. It looked as though a group of bargees had just landed a large cargo and were spending their wages. Drunken singing had taken over, and the noise increased. Guillaume struggled to be heard without shouting.

'I do not forget, but we have to move on. The past is something we cannot change. We must influence the future by grabbing power and holding onto it. I have chosen another way to right the wrongs.'

Guillaume could see his brother was not listening, merely waiting to speak. He had to get Pierre to think in a different way and cut out the cancer of revenge that was defining him and destroying their relationship. He did not consider his position at court flawed in any way.

'Have I not proved that my way works and gained our private revenge on all those who persecuted us?' Guillaume preened with a tone so self-righteous he could see it was irritating Pierre. 'I have humbled the Papacy. I have humiliated two popes and have another under house arrest. I influence the King and control his council, and through that, this realm. Have I not harvested a terrible retribution on those who helped murder our parents? Is this not enough for you, brother?'

Pierre sighed heavily, and Guillaume took the hint and stopped lecturing him. Pierre had not contacted him for the first time in five years for nothing.

'Pierre, it gladdens me to see you after so long, and I sincerely do not want to argue with you. Let us drink a toast to one another, and to Languedoc and our long-dead friends.'

Pierre filled his goblet to overflowing and urged Guillaume to do the same. Guillaume poured a full goblet of ale and toasted his brother and the occasion of their meeting.

'Pierre, I was intrigued by your request and your invitation to an inn in an area of Paris I doubt you would send your dog to visit, so please tell me why you wanted to see me. I am sure it wasn't just to mull over old times and indulge in family nostalgia.'

'Guillaume, we have many envious men around us who seek to destroy us. When either of us is weakened, then so is the other. In one's destruction lies the ruin of the other. I am here to seek your counsel and your help, and to warn you. Remember, we both have Cathar heritage.'

'You brought me over to this hovel to ask me to keep your Cathar sympathies secret?' Guillaume could scarcely keep his irritation hidden.

'No, brother. It is not the discovery of our origins that I fear. I have heard that the King is looking for Alaric's treasure. You know what the King is thinking and doing, and

I believe he thinks the Templars are involved. Should the Order feel threatened?'

Guillaume could see warm beads of sweat began to emerge from just below Pierre's hairline. His mind returned to the secret meeting with the King in Sainte-Chapelle and the actions he had taken to find Wishart's agents. He tried to conceal his interest.

'My master, Geoffroi de Charnay, often talked of Alaric's lost treasure,' Pierre said, 'but I thought of it as no more than a legend, a tall tale from an ageing Crusader reliving past glories.'

Guillaume knew his brother well; he was a cold character, measured and controlled. Now, after all the years of silence, he wanted something - he recognised deceit and duplicity when he saw it.

'Pierre, like all good legends, it is one of unimaginable wealth, questionable ownership, and avarice. The King likes fables and tall tales, but Alaric's gold is a legend. Rumours of its existence ebb and flow like the Seine. There is much violence, betrayal, and death associated with this prize; but should it be true, King Philip would pursue it as rigorously as the next man.'

Guillaume did not believe in coincidences, and the fact that his brother had called this meeting after five years of estrangement, so shortly after the meeting with King Philip in the chapel, was no coincidence either. Pierre's questioning confirmed King Philip's instincts that the treasure was nearby, and that Guillaume had to help the King retrieve it. Regardless of how much he cared for his brother or what platitudes Pierre now gave, Guillaume had no intention of allowing any Templar near the treasure, even his brother.

'In truth, Guillaume, my interest in this matter is somewhat academic, as every time my master discussed the treasure, the story became even more fabulous. My place in the world has benefited from facts, the brutal reality of life and death, not legends. It seemed like no more than talk, as I never saw any evidence that the treasure had ever been found, and that could not be kept a secret. The acquisition of that wealth would attract considerable attention, and it must be clear that the Templars are not involved and should not be part of any investigation by the King.'

Guillaume found Pierre's dismissiveness unconvincing - he was certain he knew much more.

'Whoever found the treasure would rule over all the other kings in Europe and King Philip would always seek to be that King if he could, and I would be at his right hand as his noble council.'

Guillaume had gripped Pierre's hand so tightly it reddened, as if Pierre held the keys of the treasure in his palm, and Pierre grimaced, on the threshold of real pain.

'It was thought to have been hidden in Italy until that idiot brother of the King, Charles de Valois, went chasing after it with all the finesse of an ancient tyrant,' Guillaume added.

'Duke Charles was never renowned for his subtlety or his finesse, but he has always been a friend of the Order,' Pierre said.

'I agree, Valois never acquired his brother's guile. Instead, he marginalised precisely the people he needed to help him find it. Charles de Valois is vain and always comes second.'

Guillaume added, 'You should never place faith in Valois. He is only reliable in being unreliable. When his loyalty to the Templars and self-interest clash, the latter always comes first - he would destroy the Templars if it got him a crown.'

On such a damp, inhospitable evening, the inn continued to fill with more river travellers. Put off by the rank smell of the sleeping Fallone, the new customers left the two brothers isolated and crowded around the braziers at the far end of the U shaped room, where an impromptu party was now in full swing. A musician entertained the crowd with his *vielle* to

213

earn his supper, accompanied by out-of-tune drunks singing themselves hoarse.

Guillaume was determined to trick Pierre out of all his information. 'We pick up lots of intelligence going from one court to another. We recently intercepted a Byzantine courier. He was put to torture, but whilst he talked of treasure, it was all very non-specific. We can't investigate every piece of gossip coming from foreign courts.' Guillaume deliberately downplayed the news. 'Their agent Aurelian is somewhere in Paris, and he is chasing a ghost.'

Guillaume knew the information from the Byzantine court would get some reaction from his brother, especially the news that Aurelian was in Paris. Aurelian was a respected and feared legend who had ended the life of many Catholic Templar knights on the orders of his Orthodox masters. Pierre hated him because he had blocked his many machinations by assassination.

'What else do you know, Pierre?'

Pierre remained silent.

Guillaume sought to reassure him about keeping Templar involvement away from the King's view. 'Jacques de Molay is Princess Isabella's godfather. Why would the King work against you?'

He was interrupted as a gust of wind caught the door, pulling the Moor's head off its plinth and onto the floor. The head bounced and rolled as if alive towards Guillaume, Pierre, and the smelly drunk.

The innkeeper raced forward and stopped the head with the side of his foot as though he were playing some macabre ball game. He replaced the Moor back on the plinth, mumbling of his intention to nail it down in the future.

Guillaume's throat was dry. 'More mulled ale,' he called. The innkeeper provided it within seconds, slamming it onto the table.

'Should you know more, you must tell me now. If the

Order helps me find it, and once I have the treasure, I can protect the Order and remove your enemies. I will have such power with the King that no one will ever be able to challenge me. There will be no council, just King Philip and Guillaume de Nogaret. Just think what the patronage and the treasure would do for the Templars' influence and power.'

'Your King has a reputation for breaking agreements,' Pierre mumbled in barely concealed contempt. 'I know you believe the King is ordained by God and the word of a prince is worth more than that of an ordinary man, but forgive me for injecting a little cynicism. I have my doubts. Your King has an unmatched pedigree in twisting agreements and breaking treaties. I can do nothing in helping you without discussing an arrangement with de Charnay.'

Pierre removed a small gold coin from his purse and thrust it towards Guillaume. 'This is a *masse d'or,* already devalued and known by everyone, peasant and noble alike, as *royal dur,* and in this particular district of Paris as *royal merde.* It is 22-carat gold sold as 24 carats. The King skims off nearly a tenth from every man. The only men who trust your King sit round his council table. Walk outside your cosseted fantasy world, Guillaume, and you discover that no one, high- or low-born, believes in your King.'

Guillaume accepted the point, but it did not matter. 'Trusting the King is neither here nor there, and fairness is not how this world works. The King is the King. You do not have a choice; you must deal with him. But you can trust me, Pierre.' Guillaume spoke with genuine sincerity.

In the main room, the atmosphere was growing in heat and energy as a brawl began. Bodies with flailing arms and legs were pushing towards the quieter corner of the inn where the two brothers were seated and Fallone still lay on the floor.

The fight was spilling out onto the street, but it was also threatening to involve the de Nogaret brothers.

215

'I will speak with my masters at the Temple,' Pierre said, 'but for now, I suggest we leave this place. The Maréchaussée will be called if it gets any worse. Remember, Guillaume, I wanted to meet you to protect the Order, not further involve it with plots that will only ensure its demise, but if helping you protects us, I will think more carefully.'

Pierre stretched his arms out, leaning down towards his brother. Guillaume ignored his affection and remained seated, but Pierre remained standing, expecting them to leave together.

'Master Geoffroi has returned to his estates in Normandy,' Pierre said. 'I will require his agreement if we are to help you, so I must wait for his return.'

'Don't make me wait too long, dear brother,' Guillaume said.

Pierre pulled his cloak tight over his head and around his white tabard, covering any sign of his order and protecting him against the weather outside. He embraced his brother and, holding him tightly, kissed his cheek and whispered, 'Never forget, if I do help you find the treasure, I will hold you to your promise to protect the Order.'

'I promise,' Guillaume whispered back.

Pierre kissed Guillaume again, turned abruptly on his heels, and, without a look back, walked briskly towards the door.

Guillaume considered what remained in his goblet and appeared to have no great desire to leave after what could be supposed to be the conclusion of his business. He leaned towards the table to the far left and could just grip the small tallow lamp that still burned there. His fingertips rolled the metal holder towards him, and finally taking it within his grip, he placed it on the table in front of him.

He sighed with gentle resignation and took one last long drink from his flagon, almost tipping the remaining dregs onto his face. His attention focused towards the still-sleeping drunk, Fallone, who had snored loudly but moved little throughout the entire meeting.

He thrust the candle towards Fallone's face, so close that her dirt-clad features were lit up in its flame. Beneath the mud veneer, her skin was clear and her eyes a brilliant blue. Strands of dirty blonde hair were stuck across her face. She tended to scowl to look haggard and unattractive, but there was a strange attractiveness to her, which de Nogaret found intriguing. He gently kicked the pile of rags as he spoke.

'Sorry about the kick earlier,' he muttered in a matter-of-fact tone. 'Did you get all that?'

The pile of rags moved abruptly and replied in a soft, feminine voice. 'Yes. The innkeeper was a little too enthusiastic with his boot, but I consider such acts an occupational hazard.'

As Fallone sat up, she clasped her left side and rubbed where the innkeeper had kicked her. 'My layers of pauper's rags not only keep the cold from my bones, but also protect me from the leather boot of Gilles de Bruyere, our friendly host,' she chuckled despite the obvious discomfort she was feeling.

Fallone stood up and sat clumsily opposite de Nogaret on the stool vacated by his brother. She was slim but not skinny and was tall for a woman, about five feet and four inches, so she hunched her shoulders and walked with a stoop to appear aged. She was no more than twenty or twenty-one years old.

She wiped the perspiration and mud from her face with the back of her hand, and her unexpected beauty became apparent. She removed the woollen hood and pushed the matted hair away from her eyes, tucking the unruly strands behind her ears and licking a small nick on her lips, which de Nogaret noticed as she swept her tongue across the wound.

He found the act vaguely erotic and was momentarily aroused.

De Nogaret coughed as the odour emanating from Fallone's clothes overwhelmed and permeated the clean air. He removed the small vinaigrette from his pocket and breathed in the sweet fragrance of wild lavender.

'Apologies for the smell, my lord. I had forgotten how sensitive you nobles are, but I needed to be convincing, and around these parts my odour doesn't set me apart - quite the opposite.'

Fallone scrutinised de Nogaret's aristocratic attire. 'It's astonishing that you made it to the inn alive. A man wearing those clothes in a district like this has a fat purse and a short life. I am surprised you didn't get gutted.'

De Nogaret pretended not to look offended and failed. He was not used to his judgement being questioned, especially by a woman who smelled like rotting fish - but then again, she was the King's most trusted agent. Deep down, he knew she spoke the truth, but it did not mean he had to like it.

'My clothes are of no importance,' Guillaume retorted. 'What about my brother?'

'You want to know what I think? Your brother is cunning. That was pure theatre - a sizeable act of deception mixed with a huge narrative of farce. He played you rather well. Did he dominate you when you were growing up, even though you were the older brother?'

De Nogaret found Fallone's familiarity unnerving: she did not fear him and treated him bordering on contempt, and he knew it.

'And your brother was lying. Geoffroi de Charnay rests his head within the Temple walls this very night, and three Scottish nobles left the Temple this afternoon, escorted by your brother's personal bodyguard, heading to Padua and a rendezvous with the treasure.'

Guillaume was astonished at how easily his brother had deceived him. 'Don't be so surprised and stiff-necked,' she scoffed. 'I bribed the guards at the Temple. So much for the brotherhood of the Order.'

De Nogaret had difficulty dealing with women and had never understood chivalry or the romantic code of the French court, but he knew that Fallone had King Philip's trust, and if her sex maintained her anonymity, that was good for the realm and the King. They shared little except their mutual respect for the King.

The noise in the inn was now more subdued. The money and drink had gone. It was well after midnight. People were heading for home, as even the hardiest would need a few hours of sleep before another day of hard work and a chance to do it all over again.

Fallone was no longer obscured by the crowds and noise. They would look like a mismatched pair in a poor district in Paris, and that would not remain unnoticed for long.

Noticing his distraction, Fallone took control.

'Monsieur de Nogaret, we should not dwell too long on what should be done here. I think we should follow our instincts and accept that your brother is hiding something that could help in our pursuit of Alaric's treasure.'

She pulled the rags tied around her head down over her forehead and her neckerchief up to just below her bottom lip.

'I need to find out more about what your little brother is up to,' Fallone said as she stood. 'Tell the King that Madame de France is in pursuit of the fortune that is rightly his, and I must follow the Scottish knights. They are heading to Padua.'

'Madame, will you follow them and report back to me? I have some trusted men who can assist you.' Guillaume knew she did not need any protection, but although her loyalty was to the same King, he did not want her having direct access: it must all come through him if he was to control it, and control was everything. Whilst he needed Fallone's help, he would not let her take all the glory.

Fallone smiled. 'I will follow them, and I don't require any of your thick-footed and even thicker-headed guards. I work alone. I will send word to you when I know something.'

Fallone stood up to leave. She had taken on the appearance of the lowest tier of poor souls and could now operate freely in this part of the city, unlike Guillaume de Nogaret, who suddenly felt very exposed. The inn was empty, and he was being sized up by the local villains.

He clasped his dagger, which hung hidden beneath his cloak, and quickly followed Fallone into the darkness. The watchmen could be spotted with their flickering lamps, announcing the hour, and fleecing the drunks who were strewn unconscious over the filthy streets.

*

Fallone found it strange that she was protecting a middle-aged man. His confidence in her only enhanced her belief in her ability and her contempt for him.

Behind him, the cutpurses lurked, watching them walk briskly towards the River Seine and the relative safety of the Louvre Palace and its environs. They were too far behind to pose a threat, but their continued interest, unnoticed by de Nogaret, was not a secret for Fallone. They were dressed as villains, but she doubted that their real purpose was to rob them. They were following de Nogaret; she had seen them in the Moor's Head. Their eyes had not left him throughout his meeting with Pierre.

Guillaume was chasing a fortune and a secret. There was too much at stake, and she mused that they were probably foreign agents - likely English, she thought, for they were rather too comfortable in the rain and mist. Her own assessment made her smile.

She would make sure de Nogaret got back to his escort in one piece, not because she cared about him, but because he cared about her father the King, and for the moment that was good enough.

Chapter Thirteen

Cupar Castle, June 19th, 1306: Aftermath

The Bruce could feel his horse dying underneath him as it gave its final scream. A warm, sticky concoction of flesh, manure, and blood covered his face, got into his mouth, and bathed his hands as the horse crashed to the ground. Through the chaos, he saw the livery of Baron de Mowbray. He would not forget it.

His head bounced off the horse's skull, dislodging his helmet as he followed the beast's journey to the ground. He fell hard, and for a few seconds his senses escaped him. His hands slid through the mud as they tried to find purchase, but he was held fast, pinned under the horse's leg.

Swords and axes swung around him, creating an audible vortex. He had to get free of the stirrup and pull himself out from under the dying horse. A whirling mass of limbs, blood, flesh, and metal were getting closer.

A blade swung at him, but as the horse breathed its last, it struck Bruce's assailant hard in the head, opening his skull to the brain with its hoof and shifting the targeted blow away from the Bruce's torso and into the ground. The Bruce wiped the creamy matter from his eyes. The ground was spinning.

The Bruce had to gain his wits very quickly. His hand was dislocated badly or had been broken such that his fingers were bent the wrong way. He was concussed and had to swallow back vomit as it rose in his throat. He gagged and choked, forcing the foul-tasting liquid back down into his gullet. The dragon banner was predominating amongst the English standards, and he knew that there would be no quarter given. He was a King and would never submit. There were six thousand Englishmen with instructions to kill him on sight.

I must get up.

Where are you, bastard?

He felt the ground for his battle-axe, but he could not find it. It had been hidden by the twitching body of his fallen assailant. He grabbed at his left hip, grappling to remove his dirk from its sheath, but it too had been knocked into the mud and battle wreckage which lay thick and fresh around him.

A hand appeared from behind him and pulled hard at his left arm, and he immediately expected a blade to his ribs. The adrenaline hit him like a warm river flowing rapidly into his stomach. *Is this where it all will end?*

In that moment, his sense of danger faded away, and his thoughts turned to his wife Elizabeth. She had been right: he would only be remembered as 'King for the summer days.' It had been barely ninety days since his coronation in Scone. If he died now, his legacy would be one of inglorious defeat and failure - his head on a spike, his mutilated body hanging beside Wallace's on London Bridge. This public display would be the end of independence and a clear sign of Plantagenet victory and Scottish defeat.

He was a King, yet Robert the Bruce had been fooled by a false sense of chivalric honour and belief in English integrity. The English had attacked without warning despite agreeing to a parlay with Aymer de Valence. He was sure now that the English would take terrible revenge on him, his family, and his people. There would be no honour under the backdrop of the dragon banner.

He could hear the strain and exertion of men fighting for their lives and felt the sweat of hand-to-hand fighting behind him. He was being pursued and he could hear his name being called as men hunted him.

He waited for the final blow to strike, but none came. The hand on his shoulder pulled him harder, not towards a blade but to his feet, and for a moment he feared that his saviour was seeking a ransom.

The Bruce swung his fist at the figure behind him, but failed to connect. A familiar voice could be heard above the screams of battle.

'Robert, it's me - Seton. Don't hit me.'

Sir Christopher Seton was the Bruce's brother-in-law.

Seton effortlessly lifted the Bruce and set him onto a horse, his face decorated with the blood of the man he had killed. The horse was held by a familiar figure. It was Hendor Robertson.

The King grasped the reins as best he could, though the fingers of his right hand were barely able to close. *The Bishop must have sent these men.*

'Sire, we must run now and live to fight another day.' Hendor smacked the King's horse in the rear with the flat of his sword, and it took off.

Hendor and Seton grabbed their reins and furiously kicked their horses into motion, galloping after him.

Four hundred yards distant, the Bruce saw a corps of pursuing English infantry. Having routed the Scottish troops, they had now turned their focus on the fleeing Scots.

The Scottish army had been preparing their dinner and had not been expecting to fight a battle that day. The Scots had been outnumbered, outsmarted, and unprepared. They had been scattered and then massacred in one charge.

Now the English soldiers pursued for gold, not just for blood; a dead knight's armour and sword would be a decade's income, and the prize money would set an infantryman up for life.

Spears and arrows were aimed towards the fleeing Scots, and the English screamed their promises of victory and revenge for Comyn.

'Where is your crown now, you traitor? Lord Valence will flay you alive, kill your entire family!'

Bruce knew the day had been lost and that to fight on would mean their destruction, so he kicked harder.

Hendor rode up to the side of the King. Gathering his reins tightly in his remaining hand, he leaned forward and shouted.

'Sire, the Bishop is at Cupar Castle, and he must speak with you.'

Bruce nodded, but his mind was more focused on keeping in the saddle. He was still concussed, and his vision was blurred. Seton rode beside the King, steadying the Bruce's horse as he encouraged it to increase its speed.

The sun was fading but still bright as they rode without further conversation.

'We must make speed, Your Grace,' Seton shouted as he slapped the King's horse again with his hand. 'Plunder and drink will only keep the English occupied for a few hours - soon they will be after us. Cupar Castle is three hours' ride, and we should arrive just before nightfall. The English will not follow at dusk, as the country is still hostile. For now, they will enjoy their victory, but tomorrow is another day. Ride fast Sire!'

The three hours passed quickly, and the exhausted horses slowed to a walk, slipping on the damp cobbles with each step into the dark castle courtyard. As they entered Cupar Castle, the men could see the signs of the recent siege. Piles of weapons were strewn around the perimeter of the small esplanade. The stench of burned wood and riven flesh permeated the air, and the taste of acrid wood metal was palpable in their throats. At the far end of the esplanade, some of the Scottish garrison were huddled around a brazier, roasting meat on spears. It was summer, the night skies were clear, and the air was cool. And the English were coming.

In the middle of the square were the remains of a siege

engine the Scots had used to knock down the walls. By the wall, under torchlight, several soldiers were putting back the stone blocks that these very engines had just knocked out. A few soldiers were bringing in grain sacks and driving uncompliant pigs and chickens to the castle keep. The indignant cries of the animals stood out in the charged atmosphere. No one was making idle or gossiping, and all actions had a purpose. Their work needed to continue despite the danger, as word had now reached the castle that the Scottish army had been routed by the English, and they would be next.

Those in the garrison who were not working were lying bloodied from the siege, grabbing some sleep, and sharing their crude beds of damp hay with the castle vermin. The rats were aggressively fighting one another for space and the morsels of grain still not foraged in the hay. They too were preparing for the siege to come.

Hendor dismounted first, followed by the King and Seton, who handed Hendor their reins. A small, dark figure strode towards them, carrying a torch that lit up his face and vestments, which to the Bruce's surprise included a breastplate. Bishop Wishart's cheeks were ruddy and swollen in contrast to his pale skin and short-cropped white hair.

'Sire!' he cried as he bowed. His voice was hoarse but full of warmth.

'Your Grace?' Seton and the King replied in unison. The King's voice was full of surprise, relief, and gratitude. They were the lucky ones. Many of the Scottish army's best soldiers were either dead or fleeing for their lives, pursued by a vengeful English army under the dragon banner and the command of Aymer de Valence.

Hendor took the horses towards the stables, which were to the left of the courtyard; the animals were white and steaming with the sweat of their ride, and Hendor wiped them down with a handful of straw.

'Join us in the guard tower when you can,' the Bishop called after his servant. 'And hurry, Hendor. We have little time!' His stress was apparent in those few words.

The Bruce felt the pain in his forehead. His eye was swollen, forcing his eyelid closed, and he was struggling to see clearly. Everything was blurred and misshapen. The Bishop held the torch to the King's face.

'Nasty bruises, Sire - but you are alive, and we have no time for sympathy. The day may be lost, but not the war.' He slapped the King on his back and brusquely walked towards the guard tower, which stood at the entrance to the castle just in front of the drawbridge, within the safety of the keep. But its height had exposed it to the siege missiles, and it was severely damaged, displaying the evidence of many tragedies etched into its stone walls.

'What about my hand,' he cried waving his dislocated fingers at the Bishop. The Bishop scoffed.

The guard tower was tall and narrow, and the ground floor was cramped, as it contained a small room for the keep sergeant as well as the gears and levers that drove the portcullis.

Concussed as he was, the Bruce's first thoughts were for his family. He had left his wife, Elizabeth de Burgh, along with his ten-year-old daughter Marjorie and his two sisters, Mary and Christina, with the Bishop and his brother Niall Bruce for protection.

'Where are my family?' The Bruce's speech was slurred.

'They are safe with your brother Niall and the Countess of Buchan - one day's ride ahead, on their way to the Norwegian court.'

The Bruce was confident they would be safe in the hands of his brother and the countess.

A large ditch ran around the keep, and the tower stood thirty feet above: whoever controlled this guard tower could see three hundred and sixty degrees around the keep, and could fire on anyone who attempted to climb the grassy bank with a well-timed spear or arrow.

Two sentries stood at the entrance, and as the Bishop approached, they bowed their heads.

'Tell the garrison captain to let me know immediately when the English troops are close.' Bishop Wishart sounded less like a Bishop and more like a commander; he was more than the garrison's spiritual advisor. He was leading the defence.

King Robert saw that the sentries were visibly shocked when they recognised him as the King. Kings were not supposed to show injury or be covered in blood. He saw the look in their eyes - he needed to appear invincible. He was the Nation.

The guard tower was made of stone, but its roof had been holed in the siege, and the top floor was near collapse; however, the bottom floor's small receiving room was largely intact, with only a small hole in the roof to show the destruction of the siege. It was a good place to talk. It was the only place to talk.

The other buildings within the keep had been made of timber and had been severely damaged or destroyed by the fire that had helped dispatch the English garrison.

The Bishop urged the King and Seton to follow as he led the way through a short, narrow corridor towards the receiving room.

'Quick, Sire, my lords, please hurry!' The Bishop's anxiety was clear.

The room was dimly lit with torches attached to iron finials and cluttered with mismatched chairs and a table, which were too large for the space. As the torchlight hit the wall, a small, thin figure could be seen huddled next to a brazier. The shadow against the stone floor was that of a monk, his figure gaunt and ethereal. He stood up and acknowledged the Bishop before sitting down on a rough, narrow stool. He almost lost his balance, steadying himself with his hand against the cold stone wall.

He uttered a garbled greeting, and it was obvious from his informality that he did not recognise the King or Sir Christopher Seton. His eyes were fixed on the Bishop and no one else.

'Don't be afraid!' The Bishop reassured the elderly monk.

The King recognised the figure as Brother Geoffrey, who seemed to be perennially at the Bishop's side. The Bruce found his presence annoying; the Bishop's attachment to him was distracting and difficult to make sense of in someone so astute. The King needed strong, clever minds with stout hearts, and his most trusted advisor should not be distracted by a feeble-minded monk languishing in the twilight of an unremarkable life. His holy brothers should take care of him. Dispensing charity was the reason these orders existed, so they should look after their own.

'Please sit, Sire and my Lord Seton.' The Bishop almost pushed the men into their seats.

With Brother Geoffrey's back to them, the three men sat down on the small chairs that had been placed against the wall. The brazier left little proper space for anything else; it had obviously never been a fixture in this room.

A small table was covered with a haphazard collection of daggers, swords, and axes, their edges caked with dried blood. Next to the weapons were tatty, scorched sheets of velum and parchment, many of them affixed with a heavy red seal. Below the brazier was a large pile of ash and partially burnt parchments. There had been an attempt to burn the castle archive.

'I have been reading these documents, which were amongst the belongings of the former English commander of this garrison. He was killed before he could burn them properly. Leaving many of them intact was very careless of him. If we had not dispatched him to God, I think King

Edward would have done the same if he knew the intelligence his loyal lord had left for us to find.' The Bishop laughed, holding up two documents. 'And he had the good sense to decode them for us first.'

The Bruce rubbed the gash on his forehead and wiped the caked blood away from it. His left eye was swelling further and was now completely closed, and the gash just beneath his hairline was crusted and scabbed. Each time he moved his face, he opened the wound and winced. Even a king was only flesh and blood. He was sure his pain was evident in his twisted features.

'I would have hoped, Your Grace, that the recent battle and the impending arrival of our enemies would be more pressing than supply lists and gossip from the English court.' The King barely concealed his impatience.

The Bishop ignored the King. Instead, he opened the door and ushered one of the sentries inside. 'Let Abbot Maurice know I have need of him. Hurry! He can be found in the chapel. And wake up my Lord Sinclair. He can be found in the stable barracks.'

The Bishop continued. 'Sire, it is true that much of this intelligence is tedious tittle-tattle. However, amongst the dross there are some crumbs of pure gold. Amongst other things, they tell us that the English King is unwell and likely to die soon. His enemies and his son are already circling around his kingdom like vultures waiting for an animal to die, jostling for the best position to stick their talons into his realm and rip off chunks of land for themselves whilst his body is still warm, but he is not dead just yet. As you saw today, he is still strong enough to really hurt us.'

The King tried to open his injured eye. The English King was a formidable enemy, but he was a tyrant, a duplicitous aggressor, and Bruce despised him. In Edward's mind, Bruce was a traitor who had murdered his cousin and snatched the Scottish crown, and he would receive no mercy. They had one thing in common: both would kill each other without hesitation or regret.

The Bishop ordered the sentries away from the door and continued, 'The English King's demise isn't what I want to talk about, though it is an unexpected bonus given our current situation. His son will be easier to deal with when the time comes, but our time is not yet.' The Bishop was speaking extremely fast, unable to control his excitement. 'I wish to talk with you about other matters - matters that will further improve our position.'

The door handle rattled, and Hendor came into the room. Having watered the tired horses, he filled the air with the smell of sweat, manure, and wet horse.

Immediately and awkwardly, the Bishop changed the subject. 'Today reminds us that we won't win if we confront the English the way they want us to engage. Falkirk and now Methven have taught us that we need to fight the way that brings *us* the advantage, and that is not a pitched battle. The English want us to fight pitched battles because they have more of everything - more men, more equipment, more experience.'

Normally, the King and Lord Seton would take advice from no man, but the Bishop was right. The Bruce said nothing.

'I am a Bishop and not so skilled in the arts of war, and you recognise we won at Stirling Bridge because we fought on our terms. The English commander that day was foolish and overconfident, his army arrogant and complacent. The current English commander, Aymer de Valence, is arrogant but experienced. Today he chose when to attack you, Robert, and you were complacent!'

The King's face became flushed. 'Bishop, I was tricked by the word of a charlatan. I will never trust an Englishman's word again.'

'Robert, we have always known Valence was duplicitous.

You allowed yourself to be tricked under some chivalric code, when Valence had ripped the rule book up years ago. Now we need for circumstances to favour us again, and to do that, Sire, we need you alive to wait for better times. We need you to wait for the English King to die. I need to get you away from this place before the English find out you are here and kill you.'

King Robert and Seton sat uncomfortably on their chairs, embarrassed to be lectured by a churchman on the art of war. 'Kings don't run away, even on the instructions of a Bishop.' The King's words were sincere.

'Sire, indeed, that is not what we expect of kings: it is not honourable, but it's the smart thing to do. These are desperate times, and desperate measures need to be taken.'

'You are impertinent, Bishop Wishart, but I will take advice from you, as you risked everything to have me crowned and to make me King. You shielded me from the full force of excommunication, and I know you had much to lose by doing so.'

'In that case, you must do as I ask; if you don't, you will be captured and executed in the most horrible manner. If you don't want to do this for yourself then you must do it for Scotland. I have planned for you and Lord Seton to travel with Henry Sinclair and Abbot Maurice of Inchaffray Abbey to stay with the Laird of Halcro in Orkney. The English will never find you hidden in the Norse Isles. There are places in this world where they fear to tread, and Orkney is one of them.'

Orkney was remote and under Norwegian control, and the King's sister, Isabel, was Dowager Queen, so if they could get there, they would be safe. There would be immense challenges, they would be hunted, and all the ports would be on alert for them. The King had a King's ransom on his head.

The Bishop turned to Brother Geoffrey. 'And you, brother, will also go with the King, whilst Hendor will take ship to France. Hendor, I need you to find Jamie and Will de Irwyne and bring them home. They can be found via our agent in France, Innes de Mayon.'

'I know Innes very well, Your Grace!' Hendor smiled. It was obvious that there was warmth between them.

The Bruce did not want their escape to include Brother Geoffrey. He doubted the monk could hold a Bible, never mind a sword.

'Your Grace, if I must run away, I think that it would be better for Brother Geoffrey to remain within your protection. The days ahead will be tough and hard - certainly too much for a simple monk of sixty years. It would be better if he remained here within the safety of the castle, surrounded by the garrison. His cowl will save him from harm, but only if he stays here.'

The Bishop placed his arm around Brother Geoffrey, who seemed to be deaf to the King's rejection. The old monk clenched the Bishop's hand within his, kissing the conjoined fingers.

'I understand the great affection you have had for Brother Geoffrey these many years, and charity is a virtue of the Church,' the Bruce said. 'But in forcing him to come with us, you place an elderly man in great danger and put us all in danger as well.'

One of the Bishop's servants brought in a wooden tray with meat, bread, and a green pottery flagon, allowing the Bishop to ignore the King for the second time. The servant poured the ale and left.

The Bruce drank heartily, not knowing when he would be able to drink and eat again.

'Lord Seton, Hendor, can I please have a few minutes alone with the King to bless his journey and to hear his confession?' The Bishop said. 'You must take Brother Geoffrey with you.'

Hendor was just stuffing a large morsel of bread into his

mouth, and Lord Seton was drinking a second beaker of ale. The King gestured for them to leave. Hendor handed some of the food to Brother Geoffrey and, helping the old monk to his feet, took him towards the door of the guard tower.

'Your Grace, I will prepare the horses for the King and his escort in readiness for their departure,' Hendor said.

Hendor helped Brother Geoffrey outside into the darkness of the courtyard. He was followed by Lord Seton, who had taken with him one last beaker of ale. The King scowled at Brother Geoffrey as he left the room; his resentment was transparent to Bishop Wishart.

The Bishop checked that the door was closed, and he listened as the gentle chattering faded into distant, distorted murmurs.

The Bishop smiled, but it seemed forced, less natural than normal. 'I think for just this night, Sire, you and I are with friends. Tomorrow you will be away, and I must face Aymer de Valence, and give him good reasons why he should not hang me. Brother Geoffrey is a distraction, and he will be tortured. You know how vindictive the English King can be.'

The King returned the smile and relaxed, even if it was just for a fleeting moment, as he took some of the ale that Lord Seton had grudgingly left behind. It lifted his mood, rushing through his empty stomach and strengthening his spirit. Just for a moment, he forgot the intense pain in his face.

The Bishop pulled his chair towards the King until he was so close that Bruce could hear his rapid breathing, and his tone took on a new seriousness.

Chapter Fourteen

Cupar Castle, June 19th, 1306: Saving the King

'You must take Brother Geoffrey with you and take great care of him,' the Bishop said emphatically. The Bruce was King now, and he was no longer used to being ordered around or the language of 'must' - but he would allow it from Bishop Wishart.

'Sire, I know he means nothing to you, and you think it simply the charity of one man for another, but he is more valuable to me than you could possibly comprehend.'

The King sighed with frustration.

'We need to hide him from everyone,' the Bishop said, 'the English will kill him to get to me. He is one of the few connections I have with my brother, and they will not take long to understand he is my weakness.'

The pain in the King's head was dull and unrelenting, and whilst he normally understood the Bishop's machinations, today was not a day to unravel the man's plots and deconstruct his strategies. He needed willow water; it would ease his pain.

The Bishop paused for a moment. The background sounds of activity were gone except for the lonely, distant resonance of metal hammering on stones as the masons completed their work on shoring up the castle.

The curtain of night had brought with it a brief respite from the stresses of the day, and most of the castle keep was quiet as the garrison took its last chance for sleep before the English attack. Even the crows seemed to sense the peril and ceased their cackling out of respect for those who faced the night for the last time.

'I know such things about the legitimacy of the English King that need to be kept secret, and that's why everything dear to me such as you, Brother Geoffrey, Jamie, Hendor need to be away from me - hidden where they can't be used by the English to loosen my tongue.'

The Bruce did not immediately understand.

'What if there was someone with a greater right to the English throne? What if we can prove to the Pope and to all the crowned heads of Europe that someone else should sit there, and Lord Edward's self-righteousness is nothing but a sham?'

The Bruce interrupted. 'I don't think anyone will listen to us. King Edward has been King of England for nearly thirty years. These questions are all fanciful suppositions, and we do not have time for this! The English King is ailing but alive, and we saw today he can still hurt us. His throne seems secure, much as we would like it to be different.'

'Sire, Edward Plantagenet and his line are usurpers. I can expose their illegitimacy. The Plantagenets have many enemies; there is always someone in Edward's court who is ready to revolt, and the storm we can create at his court will be biblical. It will force him to spend all his energy fighting his nobles instead of us. He will be so busy trying to hold onto his own throne that he will have no time to steal yours.'

The Bruce recognised the Bishop's sincerity. He would do whatever it took to remove the English from Scotland, but perhaps the old man was losing his judgement. It was Bruce himself who had been hit on the head and had his senses pummelled, not Bishop Wishart's.

Bruce relied on the Bishop's counsel to maintain his sense of reality.

'Bishop, if one thing was real, it was that the English King was his father's heir, and his right and legitimacy had never been questioned. Every court in Europe would ridicule us for making up audacious lies, and we Scots need all the support we can muster now. You would be thrown out of every court in Christendom and be a laughingstock even beyond. Do you have some evidence?' The King could not think of anything that would convince him.

'Trust me, Sire, but I must keep my counsel and not be threatened by torture or treachery into revealing what I know. I will use this knowledge when the time is right, and that time is not yet. We are not powerful enough. Our army is defeated, and you must flee to preserve your crown.'

The King sighed in disbelief. 'If there were any truth in your tale, it would be well known.'

The Bishop could see that the King was still unconvinced.

'In 1209, our King William the Lion sent two of his daughters, Margaret and Isobel, to King John as hostages. King John held them together with his cousin Eleanor of Brittany, the daughter of Geoffrey of Brittany, King Henry II's fourth son. And they became friends, confined, but in some luxury. King John was Henry's fifth son, so Eleanor of Brittany came before John and had a better claim to the English throne than any of John's descendants, including the current King. Why else would he keep her locked up?'

The Bishop was talking quickly, and the Bruce could tell he was anxious. 'The women kept in touch, and William's daughters married English lords. They kept their Scottish escorts, but remained in England and maintained their acquaintance with Eleanor, who was still under close confinement. Familiarity with the comings and goings of the princesses made Eleanor's captors lose sight of their job. In 1216 King John had died and was succeeded by King Edward's father, Henry III. He only needed her jailors to do one thing: to "Stop her producing a child."'

He held his index finger up to his lips. 'Shush. Did you hear that?'

'Hear what, Your Grace?'

'Footsteps. I thought I heard footsteps. No one should be outside the door. I sent the sentries away.' The Bishop was acting agitated in a way the Bruce had not seen.

The Bruce checked outside. 'There is no one here, Bishop.'

The Bishop turned the large garnet ring on his left hand around and around his middle finger.

'Come back, Sire. Sit. Let me continue.'

The King took the opportunity to move closer so that they could speak in whispers.

'You see, Eleanor was past fifty years - thought incapable of bearing a child,' the Bishop continued. 'Henry III's interest in whom she saw became no more than passing; he failed to appreciate that Eleanor's namesake and grandmother had produced King John at near fifty herself. And bear a child she did, and the father of the child was a young Scottish knight called Knox de Mayon, who despite his youth had fallen in love with her gentleness and her beauty. She wasn't called the Fair Maid of Brittany for nothing.'

The Bishop put great emphasis on his next point. 'The child was no bastard. Eleanor had married Knox. The priest, Father Donal Machair, was a distant relative of mine and left record of the marriage. I have in my possession a written record of the marriage and the birth witnessed by the two Scottish princesses.'

The King interrupted again still showing his impatience. 'Your Grace, you have told me that there is an old man somewhere who is the legitimate son of the granddaughter of Henry II of England. Where is he?'

The Bruce saw the Bishop's eyes roll.

'Sire, Eleanor understood well enough that if the English King knew she had married and had a child, he would kill her, the baby, and the baby's father. But her brief happiness was to end in tragedy. She became deathly ill shortly after her child's birth. The child carried the birthmark of the

Plantagenets and would be easily found. Eleanor turned to the only people she could trust. The child was hidden by the Scottish princesses, who came and went at Corfe Castle and were above any suspicion.'

The Bruce began to believe and contextualise what he was being told.

'As Eleanor weakened, her captors didn't suspect for a minute that her indisposition was because of childbed fever, but she had enough reserves left to make plans to get her son and her husband out of the country.'

The Bishop emptied the last few drops of ale.

'She sent the boy and his father out of the reach of the English. Helped by the Scottish King and his princesses, Knox and his son left for the Holy Land, where they could hide amongst the endless and secretive religious orders, and there the boy grew up, not knowing who he was but surrounded by clerics and monks.'

The King stood, opened the door, and shouted to the nearest sentry, who was about a hundred and fifty yards away. 'Boy, bring me willow water and gauze.' Wearily he pulled shut the door, which was disintegrating more each time, another victim of the siege. 'Please continue.'

The Bishop scowled at the King's interruption.

'After many years, Knox returned to his lands in Scotland, leaving his son in the hands of the Eastern Orthodox monks in Jerusalem,' the Bishop said. 'The Greek priests had no allegiance to the Catholic world, and believed his son would be safe in Jerusalem, hidden far away from the European courts. But unfortunately, there were enough men amongst the knights in Jerusalem who would recognise a Plantagenet, and the rumour of the boy's existence and claim grew amongst the soldiers of the Crusade, especially the Templars, who were diplomats and travelled widely. These rumours came to the attention of the English King, Henry III, and importantly the sainted Louis IX of France. They were considered so reliable that Prince Edward himself came to Acre in 1270 under the pretext of a Crusade, hoping to find Eleanor's son and kill him, but he was himself subject to an assassination attempt and left. The French King came too, but to find him, not to kill him. He knew the value of a legitimate living heir who could topple King Henry III!'

The Bishop tried to pour some ale, but the flagon was empty.

'Fortunately, Louis found him first, and Eleanor's son was held safely in the castle keep in Acre, no longer in the hands of the Orthodox priests, but in the custody of French-born Templar knights. Knox had tried to find his son but was told by the Templars that the boy was dead. Louis died a few months later, and the care Eleanor's son received became confused in the chaos of the umpteenth Crusade. The secret of the boy's identity was so carefully hidden that good King Louis had forgotten to pass it on to those looking after the boy, and he became like any other Templar hostage of many years. He disappeared, but I know where he is, and I can't allow the English King to find out that I know he isn't the true King of England.'

The door screamed open, and a servant entered, bringing with him a large, green-glazed jar of steaming hot water in one hand and a smaller flagon of willow water in the other. Over his shoulder was a longer cotton diaper for wiping the King's swollen face.

The Bishop picked the swaddling cloth off the servant's shoulder. Placing it on the table in front of the King, he gently manhandled the servant to the door and then outside. 'I will tend to the King.'

The King picked up the cloth and began to dab his crusted head with one hand as he gulped straight from the flagon of willow water. They waited for the servant to leave.

'God, that tastes horrible.'

The Bishop ignored the King's wincing as he cleaned his

wounds. Outside, the garrison was moving again.

'Sire, the willow water will dull your senses as well as your pain,' the Bishop warned as the King consumed more of the pain-relieving water.

'I think it is clear from the noise outside that our remaining time is short, Your Grace.'

'Sire, you should go easy on the willow water.' The King felt mildly scolded.

'I understand it would be fortuitous for a challenger to emerge for the English throne, especially if the old King is dying. To press the claim and give it legitimacy, we need Eleanor's son, and to my reckoning he must be over sixty years old now. Where is he, Your Grace?'

There was noise outside. They could hear people shouting that the English army was on the move, and the anxiety was pulled into the room.

The Bishop adjusted his breastplate and dirk in anticipation of the next siege.

'After our King died without an heir and the English invaded, I went looking for Eleanor's son, sending my brother John to Acre to find evidence of him. He was first to enquire with our Templar kin and my good friend Geoffroi de Charnay. I could trust no others, but he is away from here and only I know where he is.'

The King knew Bishop Wishart would not make up a story at a time like this.

'Ok, I will remove anybody that the English can use to make you reveal your secret.'

'Precisely - and that's how it needs to remain. The English sent assassins to Acre in 1291 to kill Eleanor's son, but he got away. The English and the French have been trying to find him ever since, the English to kill him and the French to parade him.'

The Bishop pointed again at the documents that were languishing at the end of the table.

'Amongst the papers they tried to burn is one that tells us they know Eleanor's son is here in Scotland, and that means we have a spy amongst us. I must find out who that is, but until I do, I must cut off all contact and all my dearest friends must go with you to ensure their safety.'

Outside, they could hear the echo of hooves and familiar voices as Hendor, accompanied by Lords Seton and Sinclair, Abbot Maurice, and Brother Geoffrey drew up outside the wooden door. They did not enter, but the Bishop and the King knew that they only had minutes before they needed to leave; otherwise, they would risk being caught by the approaching English army. The garrison was now preparing for the inevitable siege, and Bishop Wishart was needed to lead the garrison and command the defences. He was driven to tell all to Bruce, not knowing if they would ever meet again.

'King Edward wants to kill Eleanor's son before that wastrel of a son of his becomes King. He does not think Edward the younger would survive the inevitable rebellion a rival King's existence would cause. The old King knows his boy is weak and is trying to help him before he goes to his grave. If we weaken the English crown, we will strengthen your hold on the Scottish one, but we must time when we produce Eleanor's son.'

The door opened, and Lord Henry Sinclair entered. He was older than the King, over sixty years and his body displayed the signs of his years. His hair was speckled grey with red, and a scar ran down his left cheek extending from his forehead, a wound he sustained at Acre, but he carried himself with the confidence of someone who was extremely comfortable with who he was. His family ruled much of Orkney as well as Roslin Castle and lands around Edinburgh. The King knew him as a brave man, trusted friend of the Bishop and a veteran of the crusades. On the journey, he had much to ask this man who had been in Acre for many years,

241

including the siege, and he would have to be discrete.

He bowed. 'Sire, Your Grace, English scouts have been spotted in the hills. We must leave now whilst darkness hides our tracks. We must make great distance away from here and towards Orkney.'

The Bishop helped Bruce fasten his sword and placed his chain mail over his woollen shirt. He covered both with a stout woollen cloak. The Bishop embraced him and bowed. 'Sire, remember I have a spy inside the English court: he will keep us informed of any new English plots. I will write to you.'

'I know, Bishop, but your spy can't be everywhere,' Bruce whispered.

Outside, Lord Seton, Abbot Maurice, and Brother Geoffrey were already waiting on their mounts. The Bishop came outside as they prepared to leave.

The Bruce climbed on his horse and glanced at Brother Geoffrey, who was embracing Bishop Wishart. He was still resentful in taking such a liability with him.

They were ready to leave as the Bishop shouted to Hendor. 'Get to Paris and find your old friend Innes de Mayon. Find him, and you find Jamie and Will. Get them home.'

The Bishop removed a small scroll from his cloak and handed it to Hendor. 'Read this when you are alone, and then destroy it. I have explained everything. Take ship at Leith, but not with our regular captains. Make use of one of the Norwegian boats.'

'Goodbye, Your Grace,' the King said. He nodded, almost bowing to the Bishop, and kicked his horse into a canter. He was closely followed by his companions as the Bishop turned and walked away.

*

From the hills above the castle, a small English army was advancing. They had drawn up about a mile away from Cupar Castle, and the commander, Aymer de Valence, had

242

dismounted from his horse and was pacing some distance away from his escort. He made no pretence of measuring or concealing his anger.

A terrified royal messenger was lying prostrate, having been punched and kicked to the ground. The earl read the dispatch and screamed out in frustration.

The message had come from the King's chamberlain and was therefore a direct command of the King. It could not be ignored.

You are to execute the Scottish rebels except Robert Bruce, whom you are to bring for trial in London. You are to incarcerate under close quarters anyone over the age of sixty and spare Bishop Wishart. Once captured, bring these traitors to the Tower of London for imprisonment and interrogation. Allow them to speak with no one.

The earl spat, threw his gloves into the grass, and kicked the ground in anger. 'I was to raise dragon, give no quarter, no chivalry, no mercy. The dragon does not pardon traitors. But I am to capture Bruce and Bishop Wishart alive and bring them back to England.'

The Church is protecting Wishart again.

The small, mounted escort stood still. Even their horses sensed the danger and dare not move. There were few torches lit, and each man looked anonymous, covered in mud, and clad in dark leather jerkins and hose.

The earl gestured to one of the men, whose face was covered with a woollen scarf; only his eyes were visible to his comrades. 'You, dismount and follow me.' His voice trembled in fury.

The unnamed knight dismounted and walked the ten yards to where his commander stood. He carefully removed his gloves, revealing hands pitted and reddened by work.

The earl had turned his back on the rest of the escort and was staring towards Cupar Castle. The man stood next to him, his face still covered by his woollen mask. The earl was breathing heavily as he tied to calm himself. He turned to the man. 'You are sure Lord Bruce and Bishop Wishart fled to the castle?'

The man removed his mask to reply. 'Yes, my lord. I know that Lord Bruce fled there after the battle. I followed Bishop Wishart from the cathedral. I know his plans. The Bishop brought him there and is preparing for our siege.'

'I hope you are right, Master Mathew.' The earl dismissed him with a wave. Bishop Wishart's head mason now rode with the commander of the English army in Scotland.

Almost as if embarrassed to be barefaced, Master Mathew covered his features with the scarf again and mounted his horse. The earl threw the parchment down on the ground and ground his heel into the words before mounting his own horse.

'Let us go finish off our job and those rebels!' The earl cried as he kicked his horse hard with his spurs and galloped into the distance.

Chapter Fifteen

Padua, July 1306: The Last Judgement

Hendor felt like his bones had shattered into thousands of pieces. He was not a sailor at the best of times, but staying hidden amongst the barrels and crates of a merchant ship had broken his back and removed his posterior from any sense of connection with the rest of his body.

The Bishop had told him to leave from Leith using a Norwegian boat, as English agents would be looking for him, so he had stowed away on a trawler amongst the pickled herring and bales of unwashed sheepskin. Even now, after four weeks in pursuit, he could not get the mixture of sheep dung and fish from deep within his nostrils. He had repeatedly washed, but he still caught a reminder of his sea journey in stressful moments like this.

Hendor hated the warm stickiness. It was a hot day, hotter than it ever got in Scotland. He liked Scottish summers, when for a few short months the rain was warmer and the temperature amiable.

The sweat trickled into his eyes as he hid amongst the damp grass, watching the Scots and their Templar escort meander through the fields and hills, heading towards the coastal road to Padua.

The evening smell of the lemon groves temporarily removed the stench from Hendor's clothes. After weeks on the road tracking, he had found his quarries resting at a small, abandoned farm.

The wooden buildings were utilitarian, made up of

unfinished wood that had been baked dry in the sunshine. The owners were probably in the alpine pastures above the coastal plain and would be back when the first snow arrived on the mountains next month.

As he had followed them, he had observed no sense of purpose in the path they took. They had avoided every major route between Paris and Avignon. Hendor wondered what they were doing.

Now he was just outside the small town of Menton, and he could see them at last. The escort were just outside the Republic of Genoa, which was no friend of the Templars.

Hendor doubted that the Genoans had ever heard of Scotland, never mind whether the Scots were a threat or not. But they had heard of the Templar Order, and everyone in this group was in danger by association.

His old friend John Wishart had spoken about Padua, and they were now on the coastal road towards the plain of Veneto - the route to Padua.

There are six Templars and three Scottish knights, plus me. When the time came, four Scots could master twice their number. I like those odds.

It was the evening now, and even though there were still a few hours of light left, days ended quickly in the late summer.

They would rest here tonight and make for the town tomorrow.

The Templars began to make a small fire whilst others removed their saddles from their horses and took out their bedding, ready for the overnight stay.

Just beyond the Templars, he saw Innes, Will, and Jamie sit upon some wooden crates. They remained still as a Templar ordered them to prepare to rest for the evening.

One of the other Templars placed two pitch torches into iron holders that had been hanging from either side of the outside door lintel. He then pulled them out of their door fitting and stuck the iron spikes into the ground on either side of the small fire.

Another brought two very full wine skins, one slung over each shoulder, and held three pottery goblets in between the fingers of each hand. He placed them next to a blanket which lay on the grass, then fetched another three goblets from the wooden building. Next, he removed all the stools and chairs from the wooden house and organised them next to the fire and wine goblets.

No one was going anywhere now, so Hendor left his vantage point and returned to the horse to retrieve his woollen blanket and the small knapsack he had packed with bread, wine, and cheese for just such an open-air feast. Hendor had left his horse in a small copse about four hundred yards away. He did not need his horse crying out in the still evening and giving his position away.

It made him anxious that the Templar knights were with his friends. The Scots were not in chains, but neither did they look like they were there voluntarily.

He hoped that tomorrow the Templars would not cross into Italy but would instead return to Paris, leaving him to make his rendezvous, but perhaps that was wishful thinking. Tonight would be dark, silent, and lonely, with a numb arse and only the stars and his horse for company. It was not the first time he had done this since he had left Scotland, but he knew that it would be the last night alone.

Hendor crept up towards the precipice of the hill to take one more look at his friends, who were still sitting together on the wooden crates. He slid back down about six feet to remain hidden and enjoy his sparse meal in peace. If there was any trouble, he was not too far away to get involved.

*

The Scots watched as the Templars prepared some food. Innes made sure he could not be overheard. 'I know these lands. We could have been here in a few weeks, yet we have taken ten. These men are not helping us, but they certainly are hindering us. Today, we had no less than six thrown horseshoes requiring a farrier; yesterday, a Saint's Day, so no travel. All excuses to make sure we travel six miles a day rather than thirty. Have you noticed they haven't removed their swords this evening?'

'Yes, it is summer, and the roads are good. Every night they repeat the same ritual - remove their bedding from the horses, remove their swords, feed the horses, prepare for eating, make a fire, eat, take their toilet, and go to bed; and you are right about the swords.' Will and Jamie nodded: Innes's suspicions were not alone.

'We are within walking distance of the Genovese border, and these Templars won't want to cross that threshold. This should be their last night with us. They are planning something.' Innes sensed things were not right as he studied the escort, looking for more changes in behaviour.

The pots for cooking were set out and the fire prepared. As well as the sword, the Templars were still wearing their armour, and their daggers remained in their sleeves.

It was not unusual for the Scots to gather and sit apart from their escort, so their association was of little interest to the Templar knights - at least for the moment.

'Don't look at them, just smile,' Innes whispered. 'Anything else you picked up, Will? I noticed you were riding along with their commander?'

'He was different today. He could not look me in the eye. He was distant and curt.'

'We need to be ready. De Charnay wanted us out the way and has prepared this charade to stop us.'

'Didn't he have his chance to finish us at the Temple?' Jamie asked.

'There were too many people in the Temple who saw us arrive. A quiet death on a long journey is a long way from de Charnay and leaves little to explain. Gentlemen, tonight our genial hosts will ply us with drink and slit our throats.' Innes thought de Charnay would prefer the messy business of murder out of sight and removed from any scandal.

The Templars were waving. 'Come join us for some food,' one of them called. A fire had sprung into life, and they had set a tripod with stew over it.

Will smiled as the guard beckoned him to sit and join the feast. 'Soon, *monsieur*, but we must wash away the dust and sweat of our ride.'

Will walked towards the well, which was behind them on the opposite side of the yard to where the Templars were sitting. He pulled up the bucket, and its slops dampened his shirt and hose as he placed it precariously on the side of the well. Jamie and Innes joined him.

Innes spoke first. 'We have our dirks, but we are outnumbered two to one. We should play along with their plans to dull our senses with wine, but make sure when they take a full cup, we take a quarter. If they take some food, we eat twice as much. They will attack us when they think our senses are dulled.' Will nodded but before he could speak, 'We need to separate them and pick some of them off,' Jamie said. 'I think I know how we can do that,' he continued. 'I offered later to share some of my remaining flask of uisge beatha. I gave them a small taster, and they kept asking for more. The whisky is in my saddle, over the rail at the back of the house. If you can keep them busy and their goblets full, they will not notice that people are missing. I will lure two away and finish them behind the stable. That will leave us with three Scots and four Templars.'

Innes could see that Jamie had matured over the past few weeks. He had kept his own counsel but had shown intelligence in his engagement with the Templars. Now would be the biggest test. Innes would rely on Jamie to cover his back and maybe save his life. They were outnumbered and were only going to beat the Templars if they worked together.

Jamie coughed and sheepishly added, 'My timing is not the greatest, but I think I ought to tell you both that whilst I fought and killed that man in Rouen, I was defending myself - he was trying to kill me, not the other way around. How should I kill them?'

Innes looked at Will in disbelief. He had never considered that someone needed to learn to kill. It was not a natural state for many people and obviously not for Jamie.

'Jamie, forget your fear because that's precisely what you need to do. Invite them one at a time and use your dirk between the shoulders from the back through the neck, and use your hand to stop them crying out. You must kill them quietly and without a sound! Will and I will deal with the other four.'

Innes understood how Jamie would be feeling. The reality of assassination was probably something Jamie hoped to have prepared for, but there was never going to be a time when he would be ready for this. Innes saw him swallow hard, clearly anxious.

'You will not be alone when it came to the killing. I will be there too.'

He would leave Will to deal with the others. Will nodded.

'After dark, and when they have consumed more than their fair share of the wine, we will act.'

The Templar knights had already started the night's drinking and were shouting again for the Scots to join them. Their complacency was apparent. They would be thinking they outnumbered the Scots and that, even inebriated, they could butcher them easily.

The Templars were pressing again. 'Come now, Écossais.'

'Monsieurs, we are coming.' Innes smiled and waved at the knights. 'Drink some more wine. There will be plenty for us once we have finished here.'

Will joined in with the encouragement. 'Drink, my

friends, for tomorrow we reach Italy.'

He wanted to make sure the Templars suspected nothing. Instead of the Scots falling for de Charnay's ruse, it was the Templars who were the prey, wandering into a trap set with the bait of drink and complacency.

*

Gaston de Bezier watched from the animal byre that was just beyond the stable. He was obscured by its roof, which had slipped and blocked its entrance in a recent summer squall. The Templars had ignored it for shelter and had tied up the horses in the yard outside the stable, which was too small for the twelve or so horses and pack animals.

He had followed the Scots knights and their Templar escort for weeks now, knowing the escort were to delay and obfuscate their journey as far as the border into Genoa and Venetian lands. The Scots must not be killed. He needed them alive to lead him to the treasure, and only then he would make them disappear.

He recognised the Templar sergeant. He was an unpleasant piece of work. He had orders to kill the Scots and would probably take his time and torture them first. De Bezier hoped the Scots would not try to barter for their lives with the treasure. As he watched and plotted, he wondered how he would get the treasure to his master in England. The glory of this deed and the reward, he would not share with de Nogaret.

De Bezier did not relish killing fellow Templars, but he had to make sure his treachery with the English remained secret. The murder of the Scots would happen tonight, once darkness and the effects of the wine had kicked in. It looked to him as if the Templars had drunk much wine already. Any efforts from them would be messy.

He noticed all the horses and pack mules were tied together, and it would not take too much to spook them and have them rampage through the yard. He had a trick up his sleeve in the black powder he had acquired from a Cathar priest, Olivier de Pau. He had been a soldier in the Holy Land and had learned about the magic of this powder from the Mamluks. Pau had taught him to pack the powder into a hollow reed and light the end; he had called it flying fire. These could be thrown from a distance and created mayhem in close quarters. They would be perfect for the job. He removed a dozen from a long bag next to him on the ground.

If the Scots did escape into the hills, he would pick up their trail later. They were heading for Scrovegni, and there was only one way there - through the Venetian Plain.

He watched as the Scots sat with the Templars and started to drink wine. They had finished one skin and were well on their way through another. The noise of voices became louder and louder, and there was an acrid edge to the conversation as the wine began to talk. De Bezier knew he would have to act soon. His flying fire would panic a sober man and terrify a drunken one. He would wait an hour for a drunken melee.

*

Hendor was finishing off his spartan meal, but he had allowed himself a treat in a small tot of whisky, and he lay back on the lush grass and looked at the stars as they began to pop through the dark canvas that was the night sky. He could hear the laughter of the Templars mixed with the familiar sound of the Scottish accents, and he could sense an argument was brewing.

He crept back up towards the top of the hill to see what was happening below. Perhaps he would need to interfere sooner than he thought.

Suddenly, a flashing light flew towards the horses. It had a flaming tail and hissed before landing right in the middle of their huddle. The horses pulled and hauled at their tethers, straining the leather that held them fast on the wooden upright. One of the horses reared up and stamped repeatedly on the crossbeam, smashing fragments of rotten wood away from the core, shattering its fibres, and loosening the ties.

The noise was deafening. Four of the horses pulled themselves free of the others and darted in all directions, trying to get out of the yard - but all the gates were shut, probably closed by the Templars to stop the Scots from running away when they were attacked.

The drunken Templars stumbled around, not comprehending what was happening and trying to escape from the panicking horses that ran across the yard. Men and horses fell into the cooking fire, kicking hot embers and throwing boiling stew into the air. As they ran, more screeching missiles flew across in front of them, and they turned and ran in the opposite direction. One torch was thrown onto its side and spread hot tar across the ground. The other somehow remained upright and burning in its holder, giving the only continuous light amongst the flashes and explosions.

Another fire-tailed missile flew towards the remaining horses; they stamped and pulled harder before they too broke free.

Hendor grabbed his sword and ran towards the chaos. He did not care if he was seen now. He needed to save his friends from whatever was attacking them. He had read about magic weapons with fire tails that sounded like thunder, but this melee would attract everyone in the area with the noise.

As he approached the farmyard, he could see that the horses had burst through a gate and were galloping away. He caught flashes of people moving and running, but he could not find Will, Jamie, or Innes.

He tripped and put his hand down to break his fall - and felt the warm, sticky consistency of blood oozing out of the obstacle that had toppled him. Another flash of light showed him the bodies of two dead Templars. A rusty axe was sticking out of one's chest, and the other had been bludgeoned with a metal pole that was still embedded in his skull. *That was quick work by the boys. Two down, four to find.*

Hendor got up and ran behind the byre. He only made out men's shadows. If there were two dead men there, where were the others? He began to panic.

Where are you, boys?

One further flash lit up the sky, and he caught sight of Innes raising his arm to fend off an attacker, but there was another Templar knight behind him. He was too far away to help without a bow, which was the only immediate way to take the man down. Suddenly, two bolts flew into the Templar's chest, and the brief light was no more. Hendor dropped his sword in shock, and he heard it clatter and bounce on the ground below.

Hendor recognised the sound of a crossbow, and he knew it had been fired by someone very skilled. Will and Jamie had no such skill. There were more people present than he had seen. He thought quickly.

Who would want to protect them? Had Bishop Wishart sent someone else?

He felt his tunic being tugged hard, pulling him forward. He fumbled for his sword, but it was not there. His face hit the stones, and he could taste the blood oozing from his lip. He pulled out his dirk from his left sleeve and thrust it in the direction of his assailant.

A familiar voice swore. 'Hendor, old friend, put that pig sticker away. It is me, Innes. Quickly, come with me.' Hendor did not wait to be asked again, and Innes's hand pulled him to his feet and pushed him away from the byre. One of the startled horses had kicked a hole in its wooden wall.

'Jamie and Will are waiting for us beyond the hill. We spotted you in the flashes that created this diversion, allowing us to get away. We owe you our lives. But we must hurry. There may still be some Templar knights alive around here.'

Innes dragged a startled Hendor with him, and they ran up the hill towards his waiting friends.

'It wasn't me that set off these fire sticks, and I don't know who it was,' Hendor said, wheezing as he climbed up the incline.

'Well, if that's the case, we'd better get out of here.'

Innes was heading to the very copse where Hendor's horse had been tied. Hendor could just make out two figures holding horses and a pack mule. He could not see their faces but was sure it was Jamie and Will. There seemed to be no one else around to halt their escape.

'Hendor, it gladdens my heart to hear your voice,' Will said, welcoming his old friend. 'All the noise and the light in a dark sky will bring the Maréchaussée from the town in minutes.' He had never seen weapons that lit up the sky and if he had not, he was sure that provincial Maréchaussée would be ignorant whilst annoyingly also curious.

Hendor was quickly recovering his breath. 'The Maréchaussée will be after us, but curiously none of the Templars. They are all dead and the Templar sergeant body has a couple of crossbow bolts through his chest. None of us has a crossbow - I fear we are not alone. I saw two bolts hit him, so there is either one mighty skilled crossbowman or two people out there dispatching Templars. I don't think we should hang around and find out.'

'It was too easy for us to escape,' Innes said. 'Will even had time to recover our saddles from behind the bothy whilst the Templars seemed to vanish from around him. He killed one with an axe, and Jamie used an iron bar, but where there were two knights, there should have been six. We do not have time to work out what happened to the other four. We need to get away. Follow me.' Innes climbed onto his horse. 'We will head to the mountain pass and over the border.'

Jamie helped Hendor up onto his horse, which was still tied where he had left it. Hendor nodded in agreement, but he was worried about the anonymous protector. *Who is out there?*

255

'To settle my own curiosity, where are we heading?' Hendor asked.

'We are heading to Padua to find Giotto di Bondone and Enrico degli Scrovegni,' Innes replied.

Hendor looked at him blankly. 'I don't understand.'

'We'll have time enough to explain.' Will moved his horse to stand next to Hendor's.

'Innes, how many days' ride to Padua?' Will asked.

'We will need about a week. The roads and weather are good at this time of the year.'

Innes turned his horse and started to gallop away, followed by Jamie, Hendor, and Will bringing up the rear.

The Scots were directly above the farmyard and watched the torches and commotion as the village Maréchaussée were examining the carnage. The Scots were well hidden in the shadows above the valley. It would not be long before their path was followed, but the Scots had a head start.

The sky screamed and lit up again, and there was a large explosion where the Maréchaussée had assembled, throwing up soil and dispersing the crowd to every corner of the farmyard. The Maréchaussée dived through the gaps in the fence, and their torches flew into the air. The noise was deafening and echoed across the valley like thunder. The people below cried that the world was ending, but Hendor and his friends knew better. Hendor sighed. 'Our guardian angel wants to make doubly sure we escape.'

The Scots took the opportunity to quicken their pace. As they climbed, their path was lit by the moonlight, which had appeared from behind the clouds. In silence, they headed over the mountains towards Padua.

Chapter Sixteen

The Arena Chapel, Padua, July 1306: Giotto and Scrovegni

Seven days later, they arrived in Padua in darkness. They had waited in the hills nearby to enter the city after sunset. Jamie was amazed by the size and sumptuousness of a place he had only heard about. He was enchanted by the colours of the buildings in terracotta and ochre. In comparison, Glasgow seemed so colourless and dark.

They were to find Giotto here at the Arena Chapel. Jamie was disappointed: it looked stoic and singularly unattractive. Its only characteristic was its dullness and rigidity, and the warm, damp night made the building look even less appealing.

'Hendor, I seem to remember you breaking into a certain English baggage train without leaving a trace. Perhaps you can do the same here.' Innes smiled at his recollection.

The wooden door appeared to be closed as Hendor examined its lock and gently pushed the latch to see if it would open. There was no one around, but he could not afford to be seen. He pulled his cloak around his face.

Jamie watched from the lane opposite the main door as Hendor gently worked and manipulated the latch loose. He had thought of Hendor as past his best, but on the journey, he had appreciated his wisdom. Jamie had seen that he had many talents, from skinning a rabbit to shoeing a horse, all useful for the obstacles they would have to overcome. Breaking into a locked building was just another of many skills Hendor possessed despite his missing fingers.

257

Hendor waved at them to follow. Jamie was clutching the only lamp. As they entered, they could hear singing and humming, which echoed to every corner of the building. Someone was still in the chapel, even at this late hour.

The candlelight flickered in the darkness as a sudden wind taunted the flame, twisting it to the left and right as the door to the chapel closed quietly behind them.

Jamie did not have a spiritual side - his relationship with God had been broken when his father had disappeared - but for a moment, he felt a level of kinship with the Church and his uncle, which he had been missing. He was amazed by the fabulous sight that met his eyes. Everyone stared with their mouths open, but no one said anything in case they were discovered.

The chapel's dull exterior hid its incredible inner beauty. Jamie nearly dropped the lamp hidden under his cloak as he looked around him.

At the west end of the chapel, Jamie could just make out what he thought was a depiction of God shimmering in the faint light. He raised the lamp slightly to see more. He stood further and further up on the tips of his toes, almost falling over. It was heaven in his eyes - wall after wall of beauty in brilliant colour depicting the last days of Christ.

A shadow lay across one wall, cast by the light of numerous candles. High up on a scaffold next to the candles was something that looked like a statue, but it moved.

Silently, they crept around the corner to the source of the candlelight.

Jamie could see it was a small figure, possibly a child. In faltering Italian, Will called, 'Boy! Boy!' The figure was lying on his back, a small brush held between his teeth.

A piercing reply rang out through the quiet darkness. 'I am no boy,' the small figure replied with arrogance in his voice. He looked down at the dishevelled knights and coughed, clearing his throat. He climbed down the scaffolding he had been perched on, which was lit at every level with an individual candle, but at that height, they could not distinguish his face.

'I am more of a man than someone who arrives in my chapel with a wet crotch and an even wetter backside. I smelt all of you before I heard you, and I heard you speaking English. Your Italian stinks as much as your clothes.'

As he descended, he grew larger, and his head appeared to be out of proportion to the rest of his frame.

Jamie quickly sniffed his armpit and had to grudgingly admit that the rude stranger was not wrong. They were a bit high, but it had been several weeks since they had bathed.

Jamie was not going to let a few insults get in the way of finding Scrovegni. His skin was too thick to be offended. He still did not know the full extent of their task, and he hoped Scrovegni would answer the questions that Will and Innes could not.

Will had told him that if anything happened to him, he was to carry on and that the treasure would be found by getting the fourth ring as Bishop Wishart had told him.

When de Nogaret had given them de Charnay's ring, Will had admitted he had the same amethyst ring, and at that point Jamie had owned up to a third ring - and they were all identical except for the engravings which differed. Scrovegni would probably have the fourth.

The shadow belonged to a small, angry-looking man wearing a pair of rough woollen hose and an overly large smock, which had numerous pockets within it. Scraps of paper, sticks of charcoal, and numerous small brushes could be seen sticking out the tops of the pockets. Stuck to his hair and beard were flecks of paint, gold leaf, and feathers. His face was not attractive, and he displayed an arch-shaped gap in his teeth from holding a brush in his mouth. Jamie suppressed his surprise. *We have risked our lives to get to this man.*

Just as Jamie was about to speak, he heard the small, hurried echo of steps coming towards them. He moved his right hand towards his sword, but almost as quickly, the words 'Papa, Papa' broke the tension. A young boy came around the corner and rushed towards his father, carrying a small bundle that appeared to be his supper tied up in a small woollen sack.

Jamie was astonished by their close resemblance.

The painter smiled and wrapped his arms around his son in a warm and loving embrace. Kissing the boy softly on the forehead, he turned to look at Jamie.

'Sirs, I am Giotto di Bondone at your service,' the painter declared, quite unmoved by the four-armed men in front of him.

The Scots looked at this strange looking family, open-mouthed but silent.

'And I know what you are thinking. In God's light, I create all the beauty you see around you, so how come Giotto is so ordinary?'

Will thrust the letter of introduction from de Charnay into the little man's hand. 'I am looking for Messer Enrico degli Scrovegni. I was asked by Geoffroi de Charnay to seek him in the Arena Chapel.'

'Well, you have found the artist Giotto, and I am pleased to meet you.' The artist held out his hand to Jamie, and then everyone in turn enthusiastically shook his hand. His small son stood shyly by the artist's side.

'Some men call me Giotto and some the maestro who paints the walls of the chapel for Scrovegni, but I consider all men my dear friends unless proven otherwise. Please, excuse my somewhat impersonal welcome, but you all smell,' the artist pointed out.

Giotto examined the animal dung and muck decorating the front of the Scotsmen's cloaks. 'What have you been up to?'

'We have been sleeping in animal byres and gutters with our horses as mattresses,' Will replied. 'I see you have some food in hand. We would like to eat and then make the acquaintance of Messer Scrovegni.'

The artist turned to his son. 'Take my supper back home and tell Mama I will be bringing four guests for supper and a bed for the night.' Giotto gently tapped the boy on the bottom as he ran out of the back door into the courtyard behind the chapel, swinging the cloth sack with his father's supper still intact.

Jamie was still in awe of the brilliant colours and figures that covered almost all the chapel. Since he had arrived in Italy, he had seen more colour than he had seen in the rest of his life. Everyone was looking all around them, marvelling at how each wall was covered in even more splendour than the next. The frescoes extended as far as the eye could see. The building was bursting with vibrancy, even in the dead of night.

Jamie glanced at Giotto, who had the look of somebody who knew just how good he was.

'Scrovegni is all around us,' the painter said. 'This is Scrovegni's penance, his act of humility to purge him of his great burden of immense wealth. If only we could all suffer from such misfortune!' Giotto laughed.

'He seeks to gain God's favour and forgiveness for becoming the richest man in all of Italy, including the Kings and the Pope. His father before him was arrested for making money from usury, and his son has lost none of his father's charm and avarice despite his father's imprisonment.'

Giotto looked upwards to heaven and crossed himself.

'And his shame has kept me in work these past few years, but he is still not sure of the value of his soul and how much God will require of him, so he asks me to paint more and more, and I am happy to oblige.'

Jamie could see that Giotto was a good-hearted, if

261

arrogant soul. His paintbrush seemed to give him tremendous courage and confidence.

'Perhaps you can share your anecdotes after you have cleaned yourself in my stable,' Giotto said. 'There is a water trough you can use, as I fear to introduce you to my wife in your present condition.' Giotto held his nose and shook his head.

'You look tired and hungry. I am sure the business you have with Enrico degli Scrovegni will make a good story over dinner, and I invite you to stay and dine with my wife and family tonight.' He clapped his hands, put one arm around Jamie's waist, and squeezed it.

'Take a look around the walls. You will see Messer Scrovegni's portrait there. He is the skinny and worried-looking one, like all moneylenders. Look in the *Garden of Gethsemane.*'

'But there are hundreds of paintings!' Jamie said, as if Giotto had not known that already.

'Yes, there are. The search will keep you busy whilst I finish up here. But do not let that worry you. We will meet up with Scrovegni tomorrow. His palazzo is close by.'

Giotto left the knights to marvel at his work as he climbed up the scaffolding and then back down, extinguishing all the candles. Jamie watched as he cleaned his brushes with oil and water before leaving them neatly on a table beside his final fresco.

'I think I have spotted him,' Innes said. 'The rich man amongst the peasants. You can tell from his clothes. He is offering the chapel to the Madonna.' He pointed to a man with a red cap and a rich cape handing a model of the chapel to the Madonna and two angels.

'Yes, that's him - but not a portrait, just a likeness,' Giotto said, confirming Innes's choice. 'I have toiled here for many years, and this is my last fresco. It's called the *Lamentation of Christ*,' he wiped his face clean of the paint that had dripped on it.

With the last remaining lit lamp in his hand, he walked towards the rear entrance and the enclosed courtyard at the back of the chapel.

'Come, gentlemen. My work here is done, and we need to get you fed and watered. Bring your horses around the back.'

Hendor and Innes went out the main entrance to retrieve the four horses and pack mule, whilst Jamie and Will accompanied Giotto, walking on either side of the artist.

'My wife will prepare a fine supper, my friends. We have not far to walk, just a few hundred yards or so across the courtyard to my home. We can drink some wine, and you can tell me all about yourselves and how you come to me in Padua from so far away. Your accent is Scottish, so I know I will drink plenty of wine with you tonight.'

Will laughed out loud as they opened the door and went out into the night.

Chapter Seventeen

Scrovegni Workshop, July 1306: New Enemies or Old Friends

The dreich weather of the previous night was forgotten as the sun rose quickly and steeply, warming the damp bones of the Scottish knights. They had been half resting and half hiding in a stable next to Giotto's workshop and home, but a stable was a stable, and this was no different from all the others, frequented by the same unwanted vermin and permeated with the smell of manure and urine. But the previous night's wine and good company had dulled the discomfort of the hay bed.

The horses kicked at anything that moved, farting, and chattering as the morning warmed and the stable's inhabitants stirred.

The smell of warm bread was permeating the air as Giotto's wife sang a local folk song. She was preparing breakfast for her visitors and seemed unfeasibly cheery. Her younger children could be heard in the courtyard directly in front of the stable, crying, shouting, and demanding attention from their mother. She was wearing a shift of green fabric with shimmering thread woven within it, and her golden hair was plaited like the women in Giotto's frescoes in the Arena Chapel.

Will had woken early and dressed and was now reconnoitring the courtyard. A very thick stone wall surrounded the house, stables, and outbuildings. The courtyard could only be entered from the Arena Chapel or through an arched gate, which was protected by an overly large stone portcullis and barred wooden gateway that would not have looked out of place on Scrovegni's palazzo.

Palazzo degli Scrovegni was next to the Arena Chapel and was grand; it was too grand for even a moneylender, and its ostentatious display of wealth was eating away at Will. He suspected that the treasure was not waiting hidden for him, but could be instead found in the stone and lime mortar of Palazzo degli Scrovegni and here at Giotto's house. No wonder Giotto's family were so cheerful.

Last night, the amiable Giotto had plied them with wine and tall tales. But they had to complete their business with Scrovegni fast, and leave: Will's gut told him that their pursuers were not far behind, perhaps a day or two. Hendor had told him he felt a presence as if they were being shadowed as they travelled through France. It was just a feeling, a glimpse of metal catching the sun or a familiar horse, so Will felt he had reason to be anxious.

He was a soldier, and he understood the politics of wealth. The treasure could purchase the Papacy and the Church, which was the only entity able to wield power with more strength than money, but over the years it had become a market stall. Even a place in heaven could be bought and sold; the only negotiation was the price. The price of eternal life was a terrestrial deal, and this treasure could buy countries and souls: it was that powerful.

Will understood French politics, having spent many months at Lord Bruce's lands in Normandy. Philip the Fair had spies everywhere, and there would be someone in Padua who was willing to give them up. Will was sure the French were in pursuit, but so were the English, and neither would let them live once they had tortured them for the location of the treasure.

Perhaps Enrico degli Scrovegni could reveal its secret location, but he was being unhelpfully elusive.

Will knew Messer Scrovegni's likeness, as he had

indulgently placed his portrait amongst the saints on the walls of the Arena Chapel within Giotto's fresco. Perhaps he was painted amongst the saints so that they would intercede on his behalf.

Padua was full of dark, narrow alleys and opportunities for ambush. If they disappeared so far from Scotland, no one would ever find out. It was as if Giotto knew of the danger and had kept them hidden last night at his home, away from the town and its gossip. Nevertheless, no one had slept deeply that night.

John Wishart had trusted Geoffroi de Charnay, but Will could not fathom why a man of considerable judgement would trust such a charlatan. They had experienced nothing but duplicity from the old Templar. He paced around the stable, fighting his instincts. It just did not feel right, and it was probably because he was not seeing the full picture. So much had happened since their arrival in France that he could not piece everything together yet.

Ever since they had left Scotland, it had felt like they were being followed. The entire journey had been full of shadows and hidden figures. He was sure that the only reason they were still alive was that they had not found the treasure yet.

If the treasure had been spent on a palazzo and a church, then he had failed the Bishop and Lord Robert. Since Hendor had brought the news about Bruce becoming King, he had felt an even greater motivation to succeed for his King.

Will observed his sleeping friends and wondered what would happen next.

Giotto's wife, Ciuta, appeared at the open stable door with a wooden bowl in her hands and a white diaper over her shoulder. She was a small, elegant, buxom figure with pale skin and plump cheeks. Her beautiful dress was now covered with a white apron and attached to the hem was a small child pulling at his mother's side and demanding attention. They had been introduced the previous evening, but still Will could hardly believe this beauty was the wife of the plain-looking artist.

She spoke to Will in Italian. 'My dear Scottish friends, I have bread, meat, and much wine to break your fast!'

There was little response from Will's companions apart from the inaudible grunts of men who have had little sleep and have been drinking wine most of the night.

'Please complete your toilet and join me in my house,' Ciuta said. 'I have laid out some food for you to enjoy. We will meet Messer Scrovegni after you have filled your stomachs. A full stomach makes a man reasonable and sane. People are always nastier when they are hungry, don't you think?'

Will understood but was struggling to respond. She turned and picked up the child, who was no more than two years old, and kissed him on the cheek before walking briskly back into her small house.

'What did she say?' Jamie asked.

'If you get up, then you might find out,' Will replied. 'That goes for all of you.'

Hendor stood up, stretched his limbs, and groaned.

As Will looked on, a fully clothed Hendor stuck his head into the bowl of water.

'No wonder you smell in those clothes if you never take them off,' Will remarked.

Innes and Jamie were dressing now, attaching their swords to their left hips, and adjusting the dirks which were concealed in the sleeves of their woollen shirts. They preened and finessed their silhouettes whilst Hendor looked on with disdain, preferring to wear his clothes like a sack.

'You two take longer than lassies to get ready,' he muttered.

Will watched as Jamie tucked away the small leather pouch which contained the engraved amethysts from Bishop Wishart and Geoffroi de Charnay. He retained his own cabochon to protect them from discovery.

Will was remembering the previous night. After Giotto had retired, they had talked and shared their thoughts and intentions.

The dynamics of the group had been settled and any doubts about each other resolved. It was time to explore why they were in Padua, and the wine had lubricated their tongues and relieved them of the burden of their silence. They had all experienced so many dangers: the escape from Glasgow Cathedral, the journey to France, rioting in Rouen and the Templars' attempt to kill them. Hendor had told them about the Bruce's coronation and how his army had been routed by the English at the Battle of Methven.

After much wine, thought and discussion, they were determined that Scrovegni must have the fourth ring and they would use whatever means to get it from him. They wanted to go home as heroes. Will remembered Bishop Wishart's words: 'Its hiding place remains hidden, unknown except to the men who buried it. The only clues I have are amethyst rings. When John returned to Scotland, he brought back two of the rings … de Charnay has the third and access to the fourth.'

The Bishop was right. They now needed Scrovegni to provide his, and then they would have all the information required to locate the treasure.

There must have been four men who had been on the barge that escaped from Acre or had been involved in hiding the treasure - Enrico degli Scrovegni, John Wishart, the missing hostage, and Geoffroi de Charnay - and no one man had enough information to find it. Any three out of the four rings were not enough.

Will waited impatiently as Jamie fastened his leather jerkin and cleaned his face and hands in the water that remained in the wooden bowl.

Finally, they were all ready.

They walked together across the yard towards the open door that led into Giotto's house. Will observed that the yard was framed on all four sides by the Arena Chapel, Giotto's cottage, and one further L-shaped stone structure which appeared to be built into the wall. This building was plain and dull and had not been painted ochre or covered with terracotta roof tile. By trying not to attract attention, it did exactly the opposite for perceptive eyes.

'Don't you think it's odd that a painter's house is so well fortified, but there are no guards?' Will murmured. He believed that there were more people around than Giotto's wife and children.

'I thought the same,' Hendor replied. 'It's almost as if he has something valuable to protect and is trying just too hard to be discreet.'

'Like treasure, you mean?' Jamie said. 'The defences around this house would require deeper pockets than any artist should have, even one as good as Giotto di Bondone.'

The smell of fresh bread enveloped their senses. Before them was a table covered with bread, radishes, onions, cheese, and dried sausage. Four green-glazed plates had been laid out with four small, tubby goblets as companions. A dark crimson leather flagon was standing awkwardly in the middle of the table, its uneven sides looking like they were about to collapse, but its tough construction belied this impression. The small child who had been clinging to his mother's skirt ran outside to join his brothers and sisters and was swept up in the arms of the boy they had met at the Arena Chapel. He had not been in the courtyard when they had walked from the stable and seemed to have appeared from nowhere.

Ciuta gestured to the men. '*Sedetevi. Buon appetito.*'

'We are invited to enjoy the food,' Will translated.

Ciuta did not sit amongst them, but remained scrubbing at some linen in a pail with a wooden paddle. A baby slept quietly next to her in a woven basket. She sang to her child and ignored the men as they started to eat.

'Scrovegni is not the only one captured in Giotto's frescoes,' Jamie said. 'Do you see how her hair is plaited? She looks like one of his angels. How could such a beauty have such a plain husband?' Jamie's appreciation of the art around him surprised Will. He appeared enchanted by Giotto's wife and the murals.

'Money, perhaps?' Will replied.

Hendor poured some of the liquid from the flagon and tasted it. 'Wine! I love wine. But peasants drink ale, don't they?'

'Not in Italy,' Innes said with a laugh. 'They drink wine on weekdays, Saturdays, and even Sundays. Did you see the acres of vineyards we passed?'

'I could get used to that.' Hendor placed the filled goblet to his mouth and drank rapidly.

Just as Hendor was about to fill his goblet for a second time, the noise outside grew as the children started laughing and shouting.

Will stood to look out of the door, which was still ajar, letting in the gentlest of breezes. July in Italy was hot during the day and wet at night, and the humidity was uncomfortable. He saw Giotto surrounded by his small children and accompanied by a man in early middle age, wearing an oversized royal blue damask tunic edged with gold and a matching hat, which would not have looked out of place on any king.

In addition to dressing like a king, he walked like one; the gold threads on his tunic caught the sunlight and sparkled. His face was thin and gaunt, and his skin as dry and wizened as the salsiccia they had consumed. His features were fine but angular, and his nose was hooked. He looked like all his charisma had been sucked out and his face was caught in a moment of perpetual disdain.

Like many Northern Italians, his hair was brown and his eyes blue. He had bearing, but he was not attractive and had a meanness in his presence. Whoever he was, he dressed and swaggered with a tangible air of self-importance. In contrast, Giotto's clothes were covered in soot and silver paint.

Hendor, Innes, and Jamie were tense around strangers, and their hands covered their left sleeves, where their daggers were concealed, but Will gestured for them to remain sitting and to be calm. Will knew fighting men when he saw them, and the playful Giotto and his fop companion did not strike him as combatants.

'They don't look like assassins,' he whispered in English. 'He might get blood on his blue silk, but he looks like a man who would care.'

Will watched as Ciuta spotted the men and ran out through the door. Before she acknowledged her husband, she curtsied to the gentleman in silk. It was a low, humble curtsy, and more than mere manners. It was a sign of submission and humility, as if she owed a considerable debt to him. The man stood above her, almost blessing her.

'Ciao,' Giotto bellowed as he entered the cottage, standing to one side as the magnificently dressed man entered.

Giotto spoke in English. 'Brothers, may I introduce to you Messer Enrico degli Scrovegni.'

Will could see the suspicion and annoyance in Scrovegni's demeanour. He had the air of aloofness of someone who was not used to be pressured into meeting with commoners.

He looks like his picture, Will thought, remembering his likeness from the frescoes in the chapel. Scrovegni had the bearing of someone who cared for no one.

The Scots acknowledged Giotto and Scrovegni.

'You asked me to bring Messer Scrovegni to meet with you. I know you are Scottish knights, but we are alone now, and I think it is time you made plain why you are here.' Giotto's tone was less amiable than it had been the previous

271

night.

Ciuta removed the sleeping child from the straw crib, gently putting the tight bundle over her left shoulder before taking the other children to the far end of the courtyard. She spread her cloak over the tiled floor and began to sing to them, and they clapped their hands in enjoyment.

Scrovegni and Giotto sat down on the other side of the table.

Will was the first to speak in English. 'My name is Will de Irwyne, and my companions are Innes de Mayon, Hendor Robertson, and Jamie Wishart. We have been sent here by Geoffroi de Charnay. I am sure Messer Scrovegni is familiar with his name.'

Scrovegni's expression did not change; he gave away nothing, and it was clear that Giotto did not recognise the names or understand their significance.

Will turned to Jamie. 'Please show Messer Scrovegni our evidence.'

There was an uncomfortable pause as Jamie nervously ran his hand around the collar of his linen shirt. For a few seconds he panicked, and Will hoped he had not dropped the pouch in the stable.

Jamie felt again for the leather pouch and found it caught in the collar's seam. He retrieved it and placed it on the table, which was still strewn with the remains of their breakfast.

Will cleared a path through the crumbs and daintily untied the leather thong that fastened the pouch. From inside, he removed a folded black silk cloth and placed it on the table. He unfolded the cloth to display the two engraved amethyst cabochons.

The third remained in his jerkin for the moment. If Scrovegni attacked them, Will did not want him to have all four stones and go after the treasure himself.

Giotto leaned towards Will and looked at the jewels with curiosity, but his interest appeared to be no more than good manners.

Will watched Scrovegni closely. He noticed that his pupils became bigger, and his frown changed to an expression of surprise.

Will spoke directly to him. 'I see that you recognise these jewels, Messer Scrovegni. You knew this day would come, and I am told you are an honest man. Please provide us with your stone, which I know to be in your possession, and we will take our leave of you.'

Scrovegni said nothing. The only sound that could be heard was the children singing with their mother. Will waited, but after twenty seconds, he wondered if Scrovegni was struggling with his language.

'No, no, no.' Scrovegni added no other clarifications.

Will was surprised at the brevity. He expected denial, excuses, duplicity, some sort of disclaimer, something more convincing. He had not expected Scrovegni to hand over the stone and the location of the treasure easily. He had never expected this would be a straightforward task. There was an embarrassing silence.

Perhaps the Italian does not speak any English, and these are protestations of ignorance.

'Giotto, does he understand me?' Will asked in Italian.

'Are you asking if he speaks English, or if he understands why you are here?' Giotto sounded agitated, but Scrovegni spoke before he could say anything more.

'I understand who you are and why you are here,' Scrovegni answered in thickly accented English as he removed his silk cap, placing it on the table. He took from its lining a third cabochon, which he placed on the silk cloth next to the other jewels. 'I learned your language from the Scottish knight John Wishart.'

Scrovegni pointed at Jamie. 'I didn't recognise you immediately with your beard. I see your father in you. Please understand my suspicion: I have come across so

273

many thieves and charlatans that I needed to be sure who you were. Giotto di Bondone told me what he knew, but I needed to see you for myself.'

Scrovegni unexpectedly grabbed Jamie's hand from the table and placed it between both of his with a warmness that Jamie had not been expecting, and he moved his hands away. He grabbed Jamie's hand and shook it vigorously. Scrovegni's mean face transformed, and he broke into a smile. 'I am so incredibly pleased to make your acquaintance, Messer Wishart.'

Will knew the welcome was genuine, but where was the gold? They had to get the treasure back to Scotland as soon as possible. Moving tons of gold in secret would require time and help, and he was not sure how they could do it without Scrovegni. They were too far away from home to get any help from Bishop Wishart.

If he had to, Will would manipulate Scrovegni's obvious rapport with Jamie to get that help.

'I met your father over fifteen years ago, when he came to visit my father with Geoffroi de Charnay and that odd little monk,' Scrovegni said. 'They arrived in the middle of the night, having navigated a barge up the River Brenta. My father was an acquaintance of Messer de Charnay and thought nothing of helping out an old friend to hide his boat.'

Will was nervous, as he did not know how far they could trust the genial moneylender. 'Should we be talking so openly about events that should remain secret, Messer Scrovegni?'

Giotto immediately realised it was his presence that was in question.

'You need not be concerned about Giotto di Bondone,' Scrovegni said. 'There may be no uglier man in Padua, but there is also no more honest one. In any case, he is aware of how I got my wealth.'

This was not what the Scottish knights wanted to hear.

Will could see the anxiety in everyone's face.

Scrovegni picked up one of the engraved cabochons.

'I know what happens when you shine a light behind these and display them in a mirror. I was there with my father Reginaldo, de Charnay, John Wishart, and the monk when they were made, and I know the need for secrecy. The engravings are written in Aramaic on the Jewels of Saint Helena. Oaths were made that the treasure's location was to remain a secret until everyone who had hidden it agreed to its retrieval. The stones gave instructions on retrieving the treasure from its hiding place, but that is of no matter now.' Scrovegni paused.

Will felt a knot in his stomach. He had fought hard to get so far, and Scrovegni was so nonchalant about the treasure slipping out of his grasp. He knew everyone else would feel the same.

'The rings have more value on your fingers,' Scrovegni said. 'You need to ask Geoffroi de Charnay where your treasure is. He has it!'

Scrovegni stood up, and immediately the Scottish knights did likewise as they reached for their sword hilts. The atmosphere had darkened in seconds.

Giotto remained sitting.

'Your dress and your chapel tell us something different,' Hendor scoffed. 'You have benefited from great wealth from some source, and we haven't travelled so far not to demand an explanation. We won't be dismissed so lightly.'

Will's indignation was tinged with rage, and he struggled to keep calm as his voice trembled. He could feel his mouth drying and his face redden. 'We aren't going to go back to the person who sent us to you. You must know we won't leave until we have the treasure.'

'Honoured gentlemen, please follow, and I will show you that I don't have your money and tell you the secret of how I made my fortune.' Scrovegni walked to the door.

'Please come and walk with me awhile. I will take you to my workshop, and it will explain everything.'

Scrovegni walked across the courtyard towards a set of steps, which led up to the upper level of the perimeter wall.

They all reluctantly followed Will. This was not what he had anticipated. He expected the treasure or a fight for it, not the disappointment of a pointless journey risking their lives for nothing. Will felt stupid at how easily he had been deceived, but they had no option but to follow Scrovegni.

Scrovegni looked as if he were going to climb the steps, yet there were no rooms on the upper level, just a walkway that went around the entire courtyard where defenders could shoot arrows or throw spears down upon anyone attempting to enter the building uninvited.

As Will approached, he could see a small door deliberately obscured by the steps. Scrovegni opened the door and went in, followed by Giotto and then the Scots.

'Please follow me, Gentlemen.'

Will saw that the corridor descended inside the wall and then under the main outbuilding. The descent was gradual, and the corridor looked never-ending. The way was lit by several small, covered lamps that barely gave enough brightness to see where they were going. Will's throat became desiccated by the dry air, which became hotter and hotter the further they walked. There were no windows or openings for air, and in the summer heat, the air inside was hot, sticky, and full of flying insects.

Will listened attentively as Giotto talked incessantly to Scrovegni in Italian, but it was a conversation not of treachery but of money and his demands for completing the frescoes in the Arena Chapel. Giotto was animated, as if he were still painting each scene as he explained.

Will was increasingly concerned that Scrovegni had tricked them, but as the tunnel turned a corner, they could see a door and hear the gentle rumbling of lathes, hammers, and voices. There were people at work.

Scrovegni opened the door, and the rest followed cautiously. The room they entered was larger than Will had imagined. It was a cellar lit by hundreds of beeswax candles, which gave off little smoke and were usually a luxury of the rich.

The room was unbearably hot. The temperature was fuelled by braziers and fire pits glowing with charcoal embers. Signs of metalwork were everywhere, and gold, silver, ivory, and bone lay in piles on tables along the walls. Plain, undyed linen cloth stood in bales next to barrels of dye.

Suddenly, the voices from the main room became louder, but the tone was one of appreciation. Will looked on. He had not seen that some of the artisans were monks, clad in woollen habits and with their hair shaven in tonsures. An old monk had staggered to his feet from behind a large, dark curtain and was displaying a long linen cloth coated with a dark powder. Other artisans were patting him on the back and proclaiming their appreciation.

'Brother Albertus, you have proved it doesn't just cure the pox!' The monk was covered with blackened silver powder.

Scrovegni smiled. 'We are working on a shroud, and as it happens, it is destined for Messer de Charnay. Brother Albertus studies the philosophy of Aristotle at the University of Padua for love, and the properties of powdered silver for me for money. It captures the shape of the human form when exposed to light. I think we will have many uses for it in our work.'

'So, the piece of the one true cross, the finger of Saint Peter, and the nail that pierced our Lord all came from this manufactory?' Jamie asked.

Scrovegni nodded. 'Most likely.'

'That's wicked,' said Jamie. 'But brilliant.' He looked again to see how the monk's face had been captured on the linen. It was as if Giotto had drawn it in charcoal.

One table, the biggest, was covered in bones - hundreds of them, like an ossuary. It would have been unremarkable except that it had a pile of human skulls at the back, so these bones were likely human. Giotto and Scrovegni continued to talk, but Will remained quiet as his gaze fixed upon the skulls.

The smell all around them was unpleasant and caustic, and everyone except Scrovegni gagged to repel the acrid taste in their throats. Will had a bad feeling about this, and he could see that everyone else was horrified and fascinated.

He marvelled at two sets of huge leather bellows that were fixed through the ceiling. They were being worked hard by a team of labourers, who were trying to increase the airflow through the oppressive heat. Small, perforated ceiling tiles let in more fresh air, and he could not help being in awe of the creativity.

Will was sure there had to be access through the first floor: he could hear voices and footsteps above them. Those upstairs must know what lay beneath.

'Messer Scrovegni, what is above us?' Will asked nervously as he peered down and saw a pile of finger bones with their nails still attached.

'My offices are above us. They are full of bean counters and lawyers, and to a man, their professions mark them out as cowards. Fear not: they are too busy counting the money. But I can see from your face that my workshop isn't what you were expecting.' Scrovegni started to chuckle. Will could not see the joke.

'Please follow me.' Scrovegni moved on, having acknowledged the tradesmen who stopped briefly to bow and scrape and show their respects. The room turned slightly to the right and had a small recess where a table had been laid out with wine and olives. Will could see that the area had been recently cleared. There were visible signs of damped-down fires and half-finished work. The artisans had retired into the main room and seemed preoccupied with their work, ignoring Scrovegni and his guests.

They sat on the small chairs that surrounded the table and waited for Scrovegni to explain.

'It is easier for me to speak in Italian, with your permission,' Scrovegni said.

Will nodded, apprehensive and unsure of his capabilities in such a stressful situation. 'I will translate for my friends.'

'I wanted to show you my workshop, and I know you are surprised by what appears to go on here, but your imagination and the reality are at odds. I am no servant of the devil. Indeed, I am quite the opposite - I help the religious world to maintain its control.'

Will still did not understand why they had been brought here. There was gold and silver, but not in quantities that suggested a treasure was close by. What game was Scrovegni playing in showing them this place?

'Messer Scrovegni, we have come a long way to find the treasure, which was left with you for safekeeping.' Will paused. 'Why are you showing us this place?' His tone was not complimentary. The workshop was like a charnel house.

'I don't have your treasure. I needed to show you this place to provide an explanation for my wealth. Otherwise, you wouldn't believe me when I told you.'

Giotto interrupted. 'Messer Scrovegni is the greatest forger of relics in the whole world. I design them and he makes them. He produces what we term genuine fakes, so good we doubt the Holy Trinity could tell the difference.' Giotto laughed as if his blasphemy amused him.

Will could see that Scrovegni appeared increasingly anxious, and he stopped Giotto from talking further. 'I take great pride in the work I do here. I have the greatest minds and forgers from all over Europe, and no one knows what I do. Creating relics needs to be a secret, and I need an international group to distribute them. Geoffroi de Charnay and the Templars provide both services - anonymity and distribution.'

The self-serving excuse was all Will heard; he did not listen much past that, knowing that the treasure was gone. 'So, you traded the treasure for Templar protection so you can continue to steal people's hope and sell them forgeries? You need to do much better than that.' Will's Italian was just adequate, and it was tested to the extreme, as he simultaneously translated in English for the others and back to Italian. He lost some of the nuances in doing so; his interrogation was hostile and Scrovegni's squirming proved this.

Will could see that this did not appear to bother Hendor or Innes, who took an equally hostile stance and stared at Scrovegni; Jamie appeared more reserved, and gazed at the ground as if he were embarrassed or afraid.

'You don't believe me so let me convince you. Five years ago, Charles de Valois, the French King's brother, was near to finding the treasure. He needed money to buy the Byzantine throne. He had married Catherine de Courtenay, daughter of the last Latin King of Byzantium, and as the saying goes "What is hers is mine", he took on her right to that throne. Unfortunately for Valois, there was already someone on the throne in Byzantium, the Greek contender Emperor Andronikos. Andronikos, being a poor incumbent, felt threatened and sent his agents to find the treasure - or at least stop the pretender Valois from finding it.'

'The history lesson is not convincing me, Messer Scrovegni,' Will said, his irritation unchanged.

'Please, be calm,' Scrovegni said. 'Drink some wine.' The table held fine glasses filled with rich ruby red Paduan wine.

'It may seem strange, but when my father helped hide the treasure with the others, he wasn't planning to steal it, and neither am I. In any case, we did not know where it was hidden. And if I am a charlatan, as I believe you think I am, I would not waste my time showing you my workshop. I would have likely killed you all and had done with it. You are in my land now, and I would have gotten away with it. No one would ask questions about Scottish spies on the run.'

Will knew Scrovegni could have had them stabbed in their beds or taken prisoner, and there was no reason to tell such an elaborate lie. If he had stolen the treasure, he did not need to explain anything. Killing them would have been the logical action. He hurriedly translated, unable to hide his frustration and disappointment. Hendor and Innes bristled, and Will could see them grasping the pommels of their swords, but Jamie remained quiet.

'At the same time as Valois was ravaging the area, my family was under investigation by the Inquisition for usury. I could not let anyone know that our money came from forging relics: that would have guaranteed my imprisonment and execution. But to my surprise and relief, in the summer of 1301, de Charnay turned up. He came for one reason - to move the treasure. If we did not move it, the grasping hands of Philip the Fair and his brother would find it, or the Byzantine Emperor would. Can't you see I never needed or wanted your treasure?'

Scrovegni nervously gulped down a whole beaker of wine, spilling drops from his mouth. 'Do you think if I had all that money, I would be risking my neck forging relics?'

Will could see the logic, but he was struggling to see past the anger of disappointment and failing Bishop Wishart. The explanation seemed to fit with the duplicitous nature of de Charnay, who had already tried to have them killed. Valois had indeed invaded Italy in 1301, and the timeline fit. It sounded plausible, even believable, but it did not change the fact that what he had travelled so far to find was now out of his reach. Will's face told the others everything: he did not need to translate.

'Shall I finish this now?' Hendor spoke curtly: it was clear he had heard enough and was ready to slit Scrovegni's throat. Will grasped Hendor's right hand preventing him from pulling out the sword hanging on his left side, whilst Innes watched anticipating a fight or flight. Scrovegni did not flinch, which proved one thing – he was certainly a brave man and perhaps a truthful one.

'You don't have the treasure, and de Charnay does. How did he find it without all four rings? They were created to stop just one man from finding and taking the treasure away.'

Messer Scrovegni anxiously stared at Innes and Hendor, adding, 'I will answer your questions much better if your friend does not threaten me – don't you agree?'

Will nodded, understanding they were all courageous men, not rash ones. 'We need to hear Messer Scrovegni out.' Innes and Hendor grunted reluctant agreement whilst Jamie remained silent, simply nodding his approval.

'I see why you are so cynical. You obviously do not know very much about Geoffroi de Charnay. He was used as a diplomat by the French King, and for good reason. he has a considerable memory. He never needed to write anything down. He didn't need to have the location of the treasure encoded on amethyst stones in ancient Aramaic; he simply read the stars and remembered where it was.'

Will could see the change drink had made in Scrovegni: it had turned him from a measured businessman into something more vociferous and indiscreet.

'My father came up with the idea of the stones. De Charnay and his companions arrived in the summer of 1291 in a boat filled with gold. Even then, the Scrovegni's family were in trouble with the Inquisition for usury, so my father helped de Charnay partially out of friendship and partly because he was under investigation by the Church, and the Templars could use their influence with the Inquisitors. The treasure was buried by the Trappist monks of Drumziel within the hidden waterways and caves on the Venetian coast. On the instructions of de Charnay, the rings were engraved by Brother Scotus, a trusted Scots monk who understood Aramaic and would remain silent. You just needed to know the starting point and that was Padua, then the rings would guide you to the precise location.'

Hendor could barely wait for Will to translate before he interrupted. 'Did you not know that de Charnay also understood Aramaic from his years in the Holy Land?'

'He never mentioned that he could, but he did tell my father, Reginaldo, that he had been the Templar garrison commander and would have been exposed to Aramaic script.'

Jamie interrupted. 'What I don't understand is how he assembled the instructions when they were fragmented to keep them hidden from any one man.'

'Once the treasure had been hidden, I know the stones were only held together once: the night before John Wishart and the old monk left to return to Scotland, and de Charnay to Paris. They were placed in gold settings by one of my illiterate craftsmen, so de Charnay could have seen the whole script, but only for a few moments.'

Scrovegni paused for a moment and exclaimed realising his stupidity, 'The engravings are celestial locations written in Aramaic. It must have been then. De Charnay was always boasting he could read the heavens. I thought he was being religious, but he was signposting his plan as if he always intended to come back for the treasure alone.'

As Will translated, he could not help affirming Scrovegni's conclusion. 'So, de Charnay didn't need you to find it. He knew where it was all along. So much for sending us here and talk of secret codes.'

'It appears so; in truth, I had thought no more about it these past five years. But mark my words, no good will come of having such a bounty. There is such a thing as too much wealth, something the Templars must not ignore. It will draw the attention of the greedy French King, who does not like to share his fortune.'

Will could not understand why Scrovegni, or indeed any man, would be afraid of the treasure. After all, having access to that much gold was the dream of every man.

'Ask Scrovegni why he didn't steal it in 1291, when he had the chance. That must have been tempting.'

Innes asked the obvious question, which Will carefully translated.

'As I said, my father needed the Templars' help; and to be truthful, we did think about stealing it - but we gladly gave it to the monks because it would have overwhelmed us, and we were already under the suspicion of the Inquisition. Possessing this money would have condemned us. Only a state or the Church could transport, guard, and benefit from it. We had to keep it from the very organisations that could exploit it.'

Will was old enough to remember the chaos in Europe at that time. Scotland had been ripped apart by the English. No wonder John Wishart had not come home with all that gold.

'I remember those times, but now it appears the treasure is with the Templars and well within the French King's reach. I think we need to thank you for your hospitality and go pay de Charnay another visit.'

Will finished his last translation.

'We should leave this place right away and pay another visit to The Temple,' Innes spoke with a resonance that seemed to define their mood.

'Giotto and my servants have prepared for your departure, and fresh horses are in the stables waiting for you,' Scrovegni said. 'Take care, and I wish you good luck.' Scrovegni remained seated as the knights stood and shook his hand.

They headed up the secret corridor and out through the hidden door in the courtyard, followed by Giotto and Scrovegni a few seconds later. Giotto's wife and children waved and shouted greetings before returning to their games under a canopy that looked like Ciuta's apron.

*

On the other side of the wall from where the Scots were mounting their horses, two men lay dead, their lives extinguished without a sound. One, the scar across his eye still fresh from a recent fight, had been stabbed clear through his heart without so much as drawing his dagger. The other, one of Scrovegni's guards, had likely come to investigate. His curiosity had brought him torture and the grooves of a garotte around his neck.

The dead men had been carefully hidden in the bushes that surrounded the town side of the wall. Next to them, a shadow stood silent, watching the knights cross the courtyard and saddle four horses in the stable. They would leave very soon.

Aurelian could see Scrovegni and Giotto talking through the open drawbridge, which had been left down. There was no point in entering, however. He did not have to: now he knew the treasure was not there, as the Scots were leaving empty-handed. There were no ox carts weighed down with gold and silver.

He would follow them, and at some point, they would meet up with the treasure. He just had to be patient. He would wait and see if they rode towards the river or the road.

The Scots were waved out of the courtyard by Scrovegni and Giotto. Aurelian watched the guards around Scrovegni's courtyard immediately double. *Something must have scared him.*

He had watched relics come in and out of the secret door and had tortured Scrovegni's guard before he killed him. He had a sack of gunpowder over his shoulder and a fuse in the other hand ready to blow up Scrovegni's workshop, but he had no time for that now. The Emperor would have to wait for a while. He had to follow the treasure for now. At the very least he now knew who the heretics carrying out this work were, and revenge demanded more theatre than simply destroying their workshop. He would demand compensation for his masters, and Scrovegni was rich. Later he would enjoy killing everyone involved – but later.

The Scots rode past Aurelian, but did not see him as they turned and headed away from the river. He knew where they were headed, and he had time now to slide off to hide amongst the tradesmen of a busy town. The Scots were heading onto the main route out of Padua, northwest towards the French border. *They are heading back to France. I wonder if de Charnay double-crossed them.*

He mouthed the Templar's name, almost announcing it as he walked unnoticed, dressed as a poor artisan, towards the taverns and whorehouses. First, he would find some wine, some food, and maybe even a little love.

*

He passed a bundle of rags without observing that he was being watched. The form was only just discernible as human, but it was lifeless and smelled of rotting flesh, so anyone passing would think it was a dead body rotting on the street. The blue eyes were peering through some threadbare linen that concealed Madame de France. A crossbow covered in rags laid close by within grasping distance, ready to kill anyone too curious or unlucky. She was patient and had reached the same conclusion: the Scots had found nothing yet and she would follow just like this man. She wondered who he was. She would have to kill him, but only after she found out what he knew and who he was working for.

Chapter Eighteen

Paris Temple, August 14th, 1306: The King's Avarice

Geoffroi de Charnay was standing in his bedroom, waiting for a particularly important visitor, and as he hurriedly dressed, he could not help vainly admiring himself.

'You cut a quite stunning figure.'

Not far from his fiftieth year, his skin tanned from constant exposure to the sun, he gazed at his looking glass as he preened his immaculate white hair.

He may be a man under holy orders, but that did not mean he had to let himself go: appearance mattered to him, and to those who mattered. He had to look the part as one of the most powerful Templars in France, not like some mealy-mouthed cleric who had studied his way to the top. He had been a warrior in the Holy Land, the garrison captain at Acre. That made him legendary, a respected soldier for Christ, and had earned him his position of leadership. The Order was everything to him, and he owed everything he had to it.

He enjoyed moments like this, when he had time to think, as he was rarely without a crowd, always in the thick of some machination. This felt like the calm before the storm, when he could reflect on the outcomes of actions he had taken and plan for the Order's future.

His servants adjusted his tunic, girdle, and hose and straightened his tabard. They pulled the ornate, jewelled gold belt buckle around to sit at the front of his waist.

'Pass me my purse,' he bellowed at his servant. De Charnay considered himself fair but strict with his servants, but they feared him, and he was comfortable with that because it was the way of the world.

The L-shaped receiving room was filled with chairs and tables at one end, and a large wooden double bed was hidden in the narrow side of the room.

The servant removed a purse bursting with gold coins from a small wooden trunk adjacent to his master's bed.

The trunk concealed a treasure trove; it was full of purses and loose gold coins. Its exterior was rough-hewn oak and would not have looked out of place in the poorest peasant house. Inside the outer wooden frame was an inner iron frame and a huge, complicated lock to secure the valuable contents and support its very considerable weight.

De Charnay attached the purse to his girdle, which was adjacent to his right hip. 'Pass me a *royal dur.*' The servant opened the purse and picked out a few coins before handing his master a bright, button-sized gold coin. He carefully returned the others to his master's purse.

'Come closer - do you see this coin stamped with the image of Philip the Fair sitting on his throne? It states along the top, "Philip, by the Grace of God, King of the French".'

The servant barely looked up, appearing awkward with what de Charnay was showing him. 'Yes master, I see it, I have never owned such a coin and I likely never will. It is five years' wages – an unattainable fortune.' He looked down at his tatty boots, which were not a pair but did have matching holes at the front.

De Charnay rubbed the coin between his thumb and fingers. 'It is important that you know of the venality of the man who rules this realm. This King should have been called le Voleur Batard of the French people. He has debased the coinage and replaced the 24-carat gold double florin with this 22-carat gold coin; thus the royal treasury, which is the King, had pocketed the difference and expected no one to notice, but the copper he had used made the coin harder, hence the derogatory term *royal dur*, or royal hard.'

The servant answered meekly, 'I don't understand, master.'

De Charnay smiled and let out a loud belly laugh.

He believed that finding novel ways to take other people's money gave the King and Guillaume de Nogaret an erection every time they thought about how clever they had been. It was a royal hard in more ways than one.

'*Batard, le Roi. Nous avons faim!*' Cries echoed through the open windows. The noise could be heard even in the inner Temple.

Now there were riots all over Paris because of the crippling price of bread driven by debased coinage, and the Parisian mob wanted to take their anger out on the King and his advisors. The King had fled the Louvre Palace and was heading to the better fortified Temple for refuge until the rioters had vented their frustrations, satisfied their hunger, and cooled their tempers. No doubt the merciful King would take his revenge on their ringleaders later.

De Charnay recognised that the King knew that the Templars had lots of money, but he could only guess at how much - and none of it was debased with copper. It would make the Order even more powerful when used correctly, but timing was everything, and it was not yet the time for spending it. Its very ownership was dangerous.

De Charnay had to be careful not to reveal the source of the Templar wealth to the King or anyone linked to his entourage. Faking relics would open them up to a charge of heresy and give the King the excuse he needed to go after them.

It was only a question of when, and not if, before the King and Guillaume de Nogaret would come after the Templars, but he was determined the Order was not going to be another victim.

De Charnay had a plan, but he could not put it into place until he had word from Pierre de Nogaret. Pierre gave him a glimpse into the mind of the French King, and he knew he could rely on him if moves were being made against the Order. Pierre hated the French King and his advisors; de Charnay merely distrusted them. He could not fully trust someone as emotionally broken and devoid of empathy as Pierre, but he was an effective co-conspirator, and many of their goals were aligned. Both men were concerned with the continuation of the Order and sought to increase its influence. Their relationship was built on accomplishing tasks that benefited them both, rather than on warmth and trust; so they were not friends, but they respected each other. De Charnay had tantalised Pierre with hints of the treasure's existence, knowing he would want to use it to benefit the Order, but had not given its location.

But can I trust you now, de Nogaret? De Charnay had considered taking de Nogaret further into his confidence about Alaric's treasure, but he still had not decided. He felt that circumstances were forcing him to take a risk with Pierre. The French and English Kings, the Byzantines, and the Scots were getting closer to finding out the truth about the treasure.

The French King had an insatiable thirst for money. Perhaps if his ancestors had been more prudent, he would not have so great a need. De Charnay smiled when he thought of the funds the Templars had liberated from the sainted King Louis for the Crown of Thorns. Three times the King's income for a worthless thorn bush that could have been picked up on any piece of Jerusalem's scrub ground.

That was too good to simply smile about, Geoffroi, he thought, and he laughed out loud. But his mood was only lightened for a moment. It was late afternoon, and the Temple had visitors. Great visitors. The King was coming to stay.

'When will King Philip arrive?' he asked tersely.

The servant looked uncertain. 'I believe within the hour, master.'

I wonder why that bastard has chosen to come calling now. Mobs have rioted before, and he stayed home then. What is his game?

He looked at the large ruby on the girdle around his waist and thought better of it. The avaricious King would not miss the implication of accessible wealth. 'Boy, change this girdle and give me my plain belt.'

De Charnay stood as the servant removed the jewelled girdle and placed it carefully in a velvet bag within the iron-lined oak trunk. He replaced it with a plain leather belt from another trunk under a stained-glass oriel window depicting Saint George and the dragon. The summer sun drove its rays through the red, green, and yellow glass, and the colours danced on the tiled floor.

The King would not arrive by horse. His hubris would not thrive in Paris's hostile streets with the jeers, insults, and shit that would be thrown in his direction. The King would travel by boat, using a covered inlet from the Seine and arriving at a small pier hidden under the Tour de Caesar.

The Temple was made up of three large and associated smaller buildings - the Grosse Tour, the Tour de Caesar, and the Temple Church - all enclosed by a high wall. De Charnay would be there to greet him and profess his unconditional loyalty and hospitality.

There was one problem, and it had been his biggest concern since he had sent the Scots to Padua to retrieve the treasure. Once they found out it was not there, they would be back, and that time had come. They would be looking for Geoffroi de Charnay with short tempers and long knives.

He had been right to send them to Italy: they had been attracting too much unwelcome attention to themselves and the Templars. With Aurelian and Madame de France on their trails, it would be only a matter of time before the location of the treasure was discovered and they all ended up dead, including de Charnay.

'Master, a message has arrived from Gervaise de Houdain.'

He read the note to himself. *The men you seek have been spotted close by, hiding amongst the mob.*

De Charnay scrutinised the note, hoping that its contents would change if he read it again.

This was inconvenient timing, as it coincided with the unexpected arrival of the King; he did not want to have to deal with both these issues at the same time, and he certainly did not want the King's party to meet the Scots, though he suspected the King already knew they were in France.

The meeting at the Moor's Head had not been so secret. Pierre had told him, however. Guillaume had brought along Madame de France to eavesdrop, a fact Pierre had only discovered when he had had Guillaume followed after the meeting; and his spies had reported them leaving together. She would be close by under the orders of Guillaume de Nogaret, and she would be totally ruthless in pursuing the treasure.

It would be awkward to explain to the French King what the Scots wanted with the Order, and torture would free up the tongue of even the most stoic brother.

Gervaise was watching the river and the roads, so he should have sufficient warning if he needed to keep apart those who should never meet, but these Scots had been hand-picked by Bishop Wishart to find him and the treasure, so they would be unpredictable.

They will come tonight under darkness, covered by the confusion of the mob.

De Charnay was still pleased with what he had delivered for the Order over the past few years. He was distributing the relics manufactured by Scrovegni and was making money for the Order by taking a hefty commission for their distribution. He had hidden the gold from the avaricious tentacles of King Philip and his equally greedy brother, Charles de Valois. He had also deprived those unholy Greeks in Byzantium of the chance to get their treasure back and use it to replace the Catholic world with an Orthodox one. He was satisfied with how well it was all working out.

Power is better than gold. Clever boy.

He had played everyone for fools, but he told himself it was all for the Order. He had convinced himself that the richness of his surroundings reflected the power of the Order and was not for personal gratification.

He chuckled again when he thought of all that gold beneath his feet, hiding in plain sight.

Today he would flatter and grovel when the King arrived, pretending to show total submission. He wanted the King to think there was no threat to the crown's power and to return to the Louvre Palace as soon as possible.

Outside, he could hear a rising tide of rage and panic, which signalled the arrival of the King.

'Fetch my summer cloak,' de Charnay ordered.

The servant placed a long silk cloak with the red cross of Saint George around de Charnay's shoulders and fastened it with a plain bronze pin. He bowed and handed de Charnay his sword and scabbard, which he fastened onto his left hip.

The captain of the Templar guard, Esquieu de Floyran, entered as de Charnay was ready to leave. The captain was fully clad in his Templar regalia, which was emblazoned with the cross of Saint George.

'King Philip's barge has been sighted, and he will be at the pier presently.'

De Charnay's response was curt. 'Make sure we make an impression and have twice their number to greet him. Order the guards to escort the King and his friends to the Grand Master's quarters, unless they want to go to mass first. Either way, I will be there to greet him.'

De Charnay paused. 'Make sure no one wanders around the Temple looking in places they shouldn't and making themselves too much at home.'

He bowed low, and when he rose his face was determined and serious.

Esquieu de Floyran had once been a rising star in the Order. He had been a sharp politician with smart rhetoric, but preferred boys and had had an equally rapid fall following the killing of a sous-prieur who had turned down his advances. He had been the Templar commander at Montfaucon and had been saved four years ago from execution through the intervention of Pierre de Nogaret.

He was older than most of the Templar captains at over forty, but he was astute and cunning. For several years now, he had been de Charnay's most trusted captain and was at the very heart of the Order, protecting the Temple.

De Charnay watched through the window as de Floyran walked away from the Grosse Tour and de Charnay's rooms out into the huge esplanade that separated the Temple buildings. He could see and hear that the advance party of King Philip's lackeys had already arrived, including Guillaume de Nogaret and Charles de Valois. Court trumpeters were heralding their arrival. The noise was deafening and unsubtle, so de Charnay knew Valois was amongst them.

De Charnay scoffed as he caught sight of Valois, but he knew the value of observation. *What a vision in deep blue velvet, a whirlwind of self-importance and pomposity.* He spotted a less vulgarly dressed man behind Valois. *And you must be the King's chamberlain, Guillaume de Nogaret. I have not seen you in years. I remember you as young and untrustworthy, now you look old and sinister.*

De Nogaret hung behind Valois. *De Nogaret might be behind you Valois, but he got the deeper bows – how interesting. I now know who has the real power.*

De Charnay laughed. *Your face, Valois, would turn milk sour.*

Among all the men bowing and scraping to anyone of a higher status, Esquieu de Floyran appeared to be in deep conversation with Valois. The conversation looked cordial, de Floyran relaxed, and Valois touched his shoulder.

De Charnay considered the gesture strange, as royalty never touched anyone unless the relationship was a special one. *Now, how do you know each other so well?*

The King's personal bodyguards came next and lined up from the pier's entrance to the courtyard, pennants flying in the gentle summer wind. As instructed, the Templars had more than doubled their numbers, extending almost as far as the door to the Grosse Tour.

De Charnay did not want to be seen and took a step back from the window, but as he did this, suddenly all the escorts and sentries stood straight, looking dead ahead.

That must be the King.

A tall blond man of early middle age, dressed in blue velvet, and wearing a small gold crown, strode up the stairs and walked briskly past the assembled men. Valois and Esquieu de Floyran followed close behind the King and Guillaume de Nogaret, flanked by the King's personal guards.

De Charnay watched as Esquieu de Floyran looked fleetingly back up towards the oriel window. He furtively caught de Charnay's eye before turning away to follow the King, who headed towards the Temple Church instead of the Tour de Caesar and the lodgings of the Grand Master. He was off to take mass like the devout monarch he was.

De Charnay was thoughtful about what he had seen and who had been speaking to whom as Valois again placed his hand on Esquieu's shoulder and they stepped through the church entrance.

De Charnay had observed enough. Now he needed to join the political theatre and play his part. 'Boy!'

The servant reappeared from the shadows where he had

been hiding and bowed before his master.

'Let me know as soon as the King finishes hearing mass and is within the Grand Master's lodgings, and fetch me Pierre de Nogaret. Immediately! Run!' he waved the servant away.

De Charnay and Pierre de Nogaret were rivals, but Pierre's connections with the French court through his brother were valuable to the Order, and they both knew it. For the time being, this made de Nogaret one of his closest confidantes.

*

Pierre de Nogaret did not like being ordered around by anyone, and he grudgingly placed the manuscript on the table adjacent to him before following the servant upstairs to the first level, where Geoffroi de Charnay was waiting for him.

He entered the room as de Charnay ordered the servants stationed in his receiving room to leave.

De Charnay placed a pair of dark oak carver chairs together. 'Please sit down.' Pierre's curiosity was piqued by the fact that he had been called here today of all days, when the King's visit would normally be all-consuming for a political animal such as de Charnay.

The oriel window was open, as the late summer heat made the air heavy with humidity. When the King was resident, protocol insisted that everyone dress in their most impressive clothes, even when the heat was stifling.

'Guillaume is here with the King and his tactless brother Valois, hiding from the mob. They are telling those ignorant of the true facts that they are paying a long-overdue visit to the Temple, but you and I know better, Pierre.' De Charnay wiped the sweat from his brow.

'That is what happens when you debase the currency, and a livre becomes worth a sou.'

'You are ever the businessman, Pierre. You might like to consider the poor and the meek occasionally - remember we are soldiers of Christ, and show some compassion.'

De Nogaret scoffed. 'These are not the times for sentimentality: money and power will more surely protect us.'

'Pierre, you and I both know why he is here. He is looking to dine on Templar gold, and we need to make sure he goes away hungry.'

'What gold are you talking about, ours or Alaric's?'

Pierre waited, hoping de Charnay would tell him where the treasure could be found. They were allies in keeping this fortune out of the hands of the French King, and that was good enough for now.

'Gold from any source. I do not think Philip cares. Secrecy is important: we must ignore any talk of treasure; and to that end, I see you have selected Esquieu de Floyran to head the guard.' De Charnay seemed to be interrogating him, his tone was pointed.

'Yes, he owes me a great debt of gratitude for saving him from the hangman at Montfaucon and has shown himself to be incorruptible.' Pierre's response was defensive. 'Moreover, he has had no previous contact with the King or my brother. That would suggest his loyalties lie elsewhere.'

'What about Valois?' De Charnay asked. 'I saw him out the window in deep conversation with him, and de Floyran looked embarrassed when I spotted him.'

'Geoffroi, in truth, most people are uncomfortable being cornered by Valois, and despite what you may think of him, he is the King's brother and tough to ignore. I understand the need for secrecy in such times - and on that topic, why were you so keen to send those Scots knights to Padua?' De Nogaret interrogated de Charnay hoping to put him on the defensive whilst at the same time trying to trick him into revealing more about the treasure.

'I sent them to Scrovegni and the location where Alaric's treasure was said to be hidden. That is what they wanted. I am expecting them to arrive in Paris any day now.'

'I don't think they found it. I think we would have heard through our spies in Padua. Do you think they will come to the Temple looking for you?' De Nogaret enjoyed pointing out problems to someone who considered himself untouchable.

'Yes, they will. Despite my good faith in the matter, they will be disappointed and angry, and that is why I called you here. We need to get them away from here and back to Scotland, and I need your help!'

Pierre watched as de Charnay wiped his sweated hair out of his eyes.

'Preceptor, I can't understand why you spared them and sent them to Padua. I would have killed them when we had the chance. Now they will be returning, and I imagine they will be even more determined to find you. I won't be able to fob them off this time.'

Pierre wanted the same thing as de Charnay - to keep the treasure out of the hands of the French King. He preferred dead Scots to live ones, but for some reason, de Charnay did not want them dead. This was strange: even though de Charnay was no tyrant, he did not flinch from removing anyone who threatened him or the Order.

'The Scots must go home empty-handed. As King Phillip's allies, they are likely to pass on some of the treasure to him. You do not want that any more than I do, Geoffroi.'

De Charnay nodded, but only in acknowledgement rather than in agreement.

Pierre wanted revenge for the Cathar persecution, and he would do whatever it took to help the English find the treasure and use the wealth to destroy the French realm and avenge his family. He was not going to let anyone hand it to the French or the Scots.

English agents were close by, waiting for Pierre to alert them. He would tell them everything if he had to, but not yet.

He did not know where the treasure was; he had yet to get the information out of de Charnay.

'I know you wondered why I let the Scots go,' de Charnay paused. 'Let me tell you why. I owe everything to Bishop Wishart and his brother John. They rescued me from Acre when all my brothers had perished or run away.' De Charnay hesitated, and it was clear to Pierre that he didn't want to trust him, but perhaps circumstances were forcing him to share a secret he was struggling to reveal.

'Whilst the Scots may think I am a liar and a thief, it was for good reason that I moved the treasure from Padua. My silence kept it safe, kept them safe. I moved it away from the avaricious Valois. It belongs to John Wishart, Brother Geoffrey of Brittany, and their heirs as much as it belongs to me. They are due their share now. How they obtain that share cannot be allowed to focus attention on us, and now there is plenty of attention from the Kings of France and England and the Emperor of Byzantium. They are all looking for the Scots and the treasure.'

De Charnay paused and hesitated to emphasise his conclusion. Pierre could not suppress his joy – he sensed its presence in de Charnay's voice.

'If any of them found the Scots and the treasure, they would discover what we did to keep it away from the French crown, and King Philip and your brother are notoriously vindictive. It would give them the excuse they needed to kill us and destroy the Order.'

This was a side of de Charnay Pierre had not seen. He was a principled and loyal man, especially when it came to the Order, and it was surprising that he would keep such a promise to an aged Bishop, a missing agent, and a group of unimportant Scottish knights. De Charnay intended to give the Scottish knights a substantial portion of the treasure, and Pierre could not allow that: this would renew their rebellion against the English King and embolden the King of France, who was ever the opportunist. He would use the help he received from the Scots to seize the English lands in France and increase his power.

'For now, we need to keep the treasure and the Scots knights hidden until things quiet down, but circumstances in Scotland mean they need their gold soon,' de Charnay said. 'Moving it anywhere is going to be tricky, and I need your organisational skills to get them and their portion of the treasure back to Scotland, as I promised all those years ago when we buried the treasure in Padua.'

Pierre tried not to betray his excitement. His heart raced with anticipation, his mouth became dry, and his throat tightened. He would be part of the legend, the greatest secret in Christendom - the location of Alaric's treasure. He would finally surpass his brother. His chest was tight; he could hardly breathe at the thought of the power it would give him. After all these years of wondering, he was moments away from being part of the enigma.

Pierre had to ask, 'What do you want me to do?'

'The treasure is nearby, but I need you to speak with your brother and find out how close King Philip is to connecting it with us. I will look after the Scots knights when they arrive.'

De Nogaret could feel the surge of disappointment flow through his veins. He tried not to give away just how much he needed to know. The damage to the French King's ambition and power, should the English possess Alaric's gold, would be devastating. The English could reconquer their historical lands and reduce the French King to the Ile-de-France and the days of Louis VII. The Cathars would be allowed to practise; such would be the gratitude of the English, and the Scots and Geoffroi de Charnay could not be allowed to get in his way.

In seconds, Pierre de Nogaret had sufficiently composed himself to conceal his true feelings.

'I will do anything I can to protect the Order, so of course,

I will speak with my brother. But wouldn't it be advisable to share the burden of the treasure's location in case one of us should be taken?'

'The less people know, the better. Our safety is better served in limiting those who know. We need to deal with Philip, your brother, and the Scots before we talk more.'

Pierre sensed that the location was not a question to press, and de Charnay had never spoken so transparently about a secret he had kept for so many years. De Nogaret was tantalisingly close, and he needed circumstances to help him. He knew better than to spoil the new openness between them. A promised conversation with his brother should do the trick, and then he would watch de Charnay.

'Geoffroi, I will meet with my brother and find out what he knows. I will ask him to meet this evening after we have dined with the King. Wine always helps lubricate the mind and makes the mouth careless, and my brother is no different.'

De Charnay shook his hand and pushed back his heavy oak chair before leading Pierre to the door.

'It is good to have a man such as you in the Order.'

De Nogaret left the room with knowledge he could not have imagined he would have when he arrived. He knew he was close to the money, and he just had to push de Charnay a little more. And he had no intention of speaking with his brother. The mere mention of the treasure to Guillaume would energise his suspicions and desire to pursue the Order for its location.

*

Night had fallen, and the esplanade was dark except for the spasmodic splashes of light that the pitch torches provided.

A rising crescendo of voices and clattering metal began at the church before enveloping the esplanade. Soldiers streamed out of the church, covering the main esplanade as they moved away from the church entrance.

A tall, well-built figure dressed as a royal guardsman moved into the church just after the King had left. The figure heard approaching footsteps; he was sure he had not been followed, but he could not afford to be discovered, so he had to find somewhere to hide quickly. He spotted a large stone altar in the chancel; it was just long enough to hide his long torso and limbs if he contorted them to fit behind the stone. It was the height of summer, yet the stone was strangely cold, and an icy draught blew up through the joints in the stone slabs.

Just as he concealed himself, he heard the door of the church open. Its hinges creaked with the weight of the wooden and metal door.

A man in a rich blue velvet cape and blue silk tunic entered alone. He had to be a high-ranking aristocrat to be dressed so lavishly, but he had not called out, so the man hiding assumed he had not been seen.

The church was dark, and the well-dressed aristocrat was carrying an iron lamp, which barely lit the way to the east end. He was alone, with no guard or servants, and he was furtive and distracted. The tall man thought it unusual for someone so wealthy to have no entourage. Perhaps he was there to pray.

The man took up position on the shriving bench in the chancel. Only the stone altar separated the two men, and the tall man could barely breathe, as he was sure at any moment he would be discovered. He could hear his heart beating so hard that he was sure it must be audible.

He thought he had recognised the man, but he was not sure: he had only caught a glimpse of him. He was curious why he was sneaking into the Temple Church at this time of night, out of breath and looking anything but noble. He could hear noises outside and wondered if soldiers were coming in. He worried that he might be discovered.

Chapter Nineteen

Paris Temple, August 14th, 1306: An Unexpected Confession

The soldiers had moved away from the church, so there were no torches lit to show the way. A man approached, hidden under a long, dark hooded cloak that covered his clothes and obscured his face. There were no sentries around to see him, so he stood back, watching, and waiting, trying to remain unnoticed.

There was considerable noise coming from the Tour de Caesar as the King and the Templars ate and drank, and drank some more. The noises were those of friends, not of enemies, and the soldiers outside were relaxed. Their night was still young, and neither guards nor dignitaries would be retiring for a few hours yet.

Valois sat uncomfortably on the cold shriving bench. The church still reeked of expensive frankincense mixed with the smoke of a thousand candles. King Philip was a passionate Catholic and insisted on spectacle, even when he heard mass five times a day. Some said his devotion was so spectacular because he needed God's intervention more than most.

Valois had received a note. Someone had slid it under the door of his bedchamber just as he had arrived at the Temple. He pulled the anonymous note from his sleeve and read it again.

I invite you to come with all haste to an urgent meeting within the Temple Church, which will help you retrieve the treasure you seek. Please come alone.

He would normally have ignored such pleas, as he

received pleadings all the time. Although he was not the King, he was the King's brother and had daily access to him, and that influence was worth paying for. However, this note had added that the author knew where Alaric's gold was located. This was something that would attract his attention. He had been chasing the treasure for so long now.

Valois was obsessed with acquiring it, and this was the first solid lead in five years. His brother, King Philip, would demand his share, but Valois would find it first and work out how to deal with Philip later.

He stood up and rearranged his cloak to create a cushion to keep the dampness from his hose. Valois was not used to being kept waiting. He never lacked a sense of his own majesty, and he began to wonder how long he would have to sit on this stone bench. As he waited, he considered current events at court.

I wonder if the charlatan Guillaume de Nogaret is testing me: he can never play any situation straight, always been gnarled and warped. If he wanted to test my loyalty, this seems a strange way to go about it, but you never know with that snake. He is obtuse about everything. I have nothing to seek forgiveness for. My brother asked at Sainte-Chapelle for a commitment to look for the treasure, and that is what I am doing.

Valois's gaze remained on the door as it trembled. There was a gentleness in how the iron latch was lifted and the door moved gracefully open.

A figure stepped inside the barely lit church, where the only brightness came from Valois's anaemic lamp. Like Valois, the man wore a cloak and hood, hiding his identity. He almost ran down the nave towards Valois, which made him nervous. The stranger's demeanour had the hallmarks of an assassin, and Valois wanted to flee.

The stranger loosened his cape and removed his hood. Valois still could not make out who it was, and he had nowhere to run. He stood straight and drew his sword, ready to fight for his life. But as the man came closer, he could see that it was a familiar face, someone he knew very well. It was Esquieu de Floyran, and he felt foolish for greeting him with his sword drawn.

Valois quickly replaced it within its scabbard and greeted his friend. 'My dear Esquieu, it is good to see you - but why meet under such circumstances and in secrecy? We could meet in my comfortable lodgings in the Grosse Tour.'

Valois's tone was not entirely friendly, and Esquieu must have had a clear sense of his irritation.

'Your Grace, it is important that we aren't seen together. I have kept my long-standing links with you and Guillaume de Nogaret a secret from the Order. Were they to know we were more than acquainted, they would have sent me to some isolated flea pit of a garrison, guarding manure-spreading peasants!'

'Your note mentioned Alaric's treasure, and that's what I want to talk about.' Valois was curt and impatient. 'I don't appreciate being kept waiting, but if you can retrieve the gold, I can put up with this cold bench and my impatience. You have my undivided attention. Please, tell me more.' De Floyran looked embarrassed at this ungrateful reprimand.

'In 1302, I was incarcerated in the Louvre, awaiting the King's justice; and in the dungeons, I met other Templar transgressors - specifically one brother who had served as a mason of the Paris Temple. The mason had been involved in constructing a secret chamber with a workforce entirely composed of convicts who had had their tongues cut out. That was not the only strange thing about this: he did not work with any of the other masons and took his orders directly from Geoffroi de Charnay. No plans existed, and no record of the chamber was to be made. The entrance channel had to extend from the River Seine and had to be deep enough to accommodate a seagoing barge.'

Valois could not understand the connections being made.

'Monsieur de Floyran, what has this got to do with Alaric's treasure? Keep to the matter at hand!'

'The point is that the treasure is kept in the chamber. It was moved here on a seagoing barge so that it could be hidden in the chamber and transported at a moment's notice. That is how de Charnay was able to move it from Padua to the Temple without anyone noticing. And now?'

Valois looked astonished. This news was indeed positive.

'In 1301, de Charnay summoned the mason and forbade him to enter the completed chamber,' de Floyran said. 'And further, the Preceptor told him that he was sending him away to the court of the Rus. The mason's entire convict labour force had suddenly disappeared without a trace, and he clearly understood he would never return from the Muscovy court. Before he left, curiosity and considerable suspicion made him take one more look at the chamber, and what he found inside amazed and overwhelmed him. There were chests full of gold and silver and piles of jewels, all waiting patiently on a barge. He helped himself to pockets full of gold coins. He found the coins hypnotic. He knew if he spent them, he would be discovered, so that's why I have them now.'

De Floyran dropped the purse from his belt onto the bench in front of Valois. The coins burst untidily out of the leather pouch. They sparkled brilliantly, even in the dim light of Valois's lamp.

Valois picked a coin from the top and examined it. 'Now, where would a humble mason get a gold solidus of Emperor Valentinian II, I wonder?'

He smiled as he held it up against the lamp. It had the look and feel of pure gold. Valois marvelled at this small treasure and could barely contain his excitement.

'Continue, Esquieu,' he said, suppressing a broad smile.

'The mason had enough sense to flee and took this gold

with him. If Geoffroi de Charnay found out, he would end up dead like his convict labourers, so he deserted, hid his identity, and joined up with the renegade Roger de Flor. It was ill fortune that he ended up in the Louvre dungeons, but good fortune that he ended up chained to me.'

Valois realised that the mason would be a danger to his plans.

'What happened to the mason? What was his name?' Valois asked anxiously.

'He was called Bernard Ferrer and he is dead. He was released from the Louvre and left with Roger de Flor's mercenaries to fight for the Byzantine Emperor against the Ottoman Turks. Nothing has been heard of him in a couple of years.'

Valois started to count the gold as it lay on the confessional bench. He placed it back in the purse before attaching it to his belt. 'Where is the rest?'

Valois could barely contain his greed. He must know where the rest was. The purse tantalised him.

'My lord, I don't know where the chamber is, but it is nearby. That is why I need your help.' Esquieu was interrupted by the sound of voices approaching the church.

The church door opened, and a servant entered and bowed. The servant was followed by Guillaume de Nogaret.

Damn him, Valois thought.

'I noticed you had slipped away from the banquet, and I was concerned for your safety,' de Nogaret said. Valois despised his smug tone.

'I was discussing the matter of the King's security with the captain of the Templar guard. I am reassured by his arrangements.'

De Floyran turned to leave, hoping to evade de Nogaret's questioning. 'Thank you very much, Captain,' Valois said. 'I now know the King's safety is in sure hands.'

Valois turned to de Nogaret. 'The drunken mob

307

surrounding the King's residence is an unusual situation that presents unique security risks, which de Floyran only felt comfortable in sharing with me.' Valois hoped that de Nogaret would be fobbed off by his answer, but as usual, he was quick with his challenge.

'Any threat to the King's security is a matter for the captains of the Templars and the King's guards, and not one for the King's brother.' Valois knew de Nogaret was right and was certain he did not believe him. 'Lord Valois, I am sure that the King's safety is foremost in your mind as it is in mine, but I have ultimate responsibility for his person, so I need to know. Is there a specific threat to the King's life?'

'There is no specific threat. The Templar captain had a serious concern about the small number of palace guards inside the Temple's perimeter wall and the many angry peasants on the outside. There are only a handful of the King's bodyguards, and de Floyran recommends more palace guards - an issue he didn't think he could comfortably raise with their captain, who selected that number in the first place!'

Valois was pleased with himself. He had been caught, but this explanation was sounding more and more plausible. 'Guillaume, I intend to speak with the captain of the palace guard immediately.'

To avoid further interrogation, Valois stood up and walked briskly towards the church door, followed by a sceptical Guillaume de Nogaret and a frustrated Esquieu de Floyran.

Valois would have further dealings with de Floyran, but he would need to do so later, away from the gaze of de Nogaret. The treasure was safe for now within the fortified walls of the Temple, assuming it had not been moved again - but he sensed de Charnay would not risk its discovery by doing so. He was satisfied that in a few short hours, he would have all the gold he needed to buy his crown. He would need to include the King in his good fortune, and he would use its glory to totally crush de Nogaret.

The meeting in Sainte-Chapelle had shown to everyone present how important the treasure was to the King's ambitions, and when Valois brought its location to the King, his position, value, and power would be unchallenged. The King would be particularly happy that the English King had failed to take the treasure, so he would be doubly obliged to his brother.

The time was right to surround the King with men of noble birth according to the proper order, and geld the upstart's endless ambition. Valois would take his news seated at the right hand of his brother the King.

He would return to his rooms and start plotting. It had been a wonderful day after all. He could barely contain his smile.

*

Geoffroi de Charnay had noticed the absence of Charles de Valois and Guillaume de Nogaret from the King's banquet and thought it was unusual. Where one was, the other could normally be found close by, and they always stuck to the King like a brace of competing loyal dogs.

He took a quick look outside the main door and decided he would return to his rooms, where he could see the whole Temple. The esplanade was still quiet, but there were plenty of places for people to hide.

Most of the Templar garrison were surrounding the Tour de Caesar or looking out from the battlements towards the drunken mob. There were only a handful of stationary sentries on the ground floor of the Grosse Tour.

He temporarily left the King with Gerard de Villiers, the Preceptor of France and the Order's treasurer. He was an amiable host, and as unusual as it might sound, King Philip was rumoured to like him. Gerard had considerable charm, and many believed the King liked him because he lent him money at very reasonable rates.

309

De Charnay climbed to the second floor to look out of the top oriel window. He wanted to see who was outside the banquet and suspected Valois and de Nogaret were together.

On his way, he crept past Pierre de Nogaret's room. Pierre's door was shut, but the lights from his lamps were still visible under the door. No doubt he was still at his desk, hard at work and making a point of ignoring the King.

His room was in darkness, but now that night had properly fallen, the moon was bright, and it covered the esplanade with its muted light. He opened the oriel window and could see across to the entrances of the Temple Church and Tour de Caesar.

Just as de Charnay settled at the window, he saw the Temple Church door creep open, and Valois came out of the narthex followed by the ubiquitous Guillaume de Nogaret. A servant followed close behind, and they headed towards the Tour de Caesar and the King. He looked back at the church door, and a few seconds later, Esquieu de Floyran came out of the same door, adjusting his helmet. He looked around him, and de Charnay stepped back further into the room to avoid being seen in the moonlight. However, Esquieu looked everywhere but above him. He admonished the sentries at the entrance of the Tour de Caesar for some minor infringement before following Valois and Guillaume de Nogaret to the King.

De Charnay sighed and wondered why the two most powerful men in the kingdom would meet with de Floyran in such a secretive manner. He did not have to think hard, but now he had to think fast.

*

Below him, Pierre de Nogaret paced up and down his room.

I cannot let de Charnay hand over a tranche of the treasure to the Scots, and it must not fall into the hands of my brother or King Philip. I need the English King's help, and there isn't much time.

310

It would be impossible to take the treasure from its location, which was nearby according to de Charnay, without being seen. It was probably in Paris or even in the Temple itself. He could not simply steal it without help, and there was nowhere safe to hide it in France, so he needed to move it somewhere else.

If the rumours were correct, the treasure was too large to transport except by water, so that was how de Charnay and his Scottish allies would move and secure it. The best route back to Scotland would be back up the Seine to Rouen and then by sea, taking a barge via the North or Irish Sea. He did not have to locate the treasure himself, he simply had to steal it from the Scots. The best place to steal it would be as it left France and headed out to sea.

He began to scribble down a message to the English agent in Paris for immediate dispatch. The English had agents along the Seine and up along the English Channel to Scotland. They could appropriate the treasure there in the open sea.

'Boy, come,' he cried. A weary servant came in from the anteroom.

'Take this right away to Monsieur Hubert de Lacy at the College de Sorbonne and place it into his hands - no one else's. Do you understand? Only give it to Hubert de Lacy!'

The servant bowed and headed out towards the pier. He would take a boat along the Seine to the college: it was quicker and safer, and he was unlikely to be challenged by anyone who might seize the note.

*

De Charnay knew he needed to counteract Valois and de Nogaret's duplicity.

'Boy!'

'I do wish you wouldn't call me that when we are alone.' De Charnay's servant straightened his crooked back and shook out his hair, which had been dressed in a pomade of

311

water and flour to make it appear grey.

'My dear Hugh, it's for appearances, as you well know. I need you to be around me but unnoticed, and disguise is the only way.' De Charnay smiled. 'Please, take a seat.'

Hugh de Verneuil was dressed to look like a peasant in late middle age, with a Templar tabard draped over his shapeless clothing to denote his status as a servant, but his clear, unwrinkled skin betrayed his relative youth: he was no more than thirty. No one who mattered ever took much notice of servants or the lower classes unless they stuck out, and Hugh de Verneuil wanted to blend in with the mass of mediocrity that kept the Order functioning.

Despite his attempt to conceal his age and build, his upper body was strong and muscular. He did not carry the signs of malnutrition, which were normal for ageing peasants, and his stoop was manufactured. He was of above-average height and had large, thick hands that could either mean he had held a sword or ploughed the land. Verneuil had been in de Charnay's service these past ten years, part bodyguard and part confidante, and he had never tilled the soil. De Charnay needed someone loyal to him within the Order, and Verneuil was that man.

'Tonight, we will be visited by the Scots knights we sent to our good friend Scrovegni,' de Charnay said. 'You remember them?'

Unknown to anyone but de Charnay, Verneuil had hidden in the loft in the guest quarters when the Scots had visited the Temple, and he had spied on them. He knew all about Bishop Wishart's plans and why the Scots had been sent.

'I recollect them well. I remember freezing my bones listening to their conversations about treasure.' De Charnay had told Hugh about the threat to the Order if the Scots were found by the French King, and he understood they must never meet.

'I need you to help me secure the treasure and get it away

to somewhere safe, out of the reach of the major powers who would do great harm, were they to acquire it. We can't allow the Kings of France or England or the Byzantine Emperor to control this wealth, as it will give them unimaginable power.' De Charnay paused. 'They will use that wealth for ill, and we both know that none of the men that lead these countries are fit rulers. The best option is that it goes to Scotland. They will keep our share safe until we need it.' He coughed as he took a large gulp of wine that went down the wrong way.

'Geoffroi, I have dealt with life-and-death situations, but not one directly involving two Kings and one Emperor,' Verneuil said.

'Hugh, Madame de France is also involved. I remember what good friends you were. I need you to watch out for her presence.'

De Charnay could see that the normally calm Hugh looked unsettled at the mention of her, and he nervously removed his woollen cap. Madame de France - or as some called her, Fallone - was elusive, and few knew who she was. But Verneuil knew her well.

'The treasure is here in the Temple, in a secret chamber, and now we have to move it,' de Charnay said.

Hugh looked surprised. 'I never guessed it was here and I thought you trusted me in all things.'

De Charnay could see Hugh was disappointed that he had not included him in his secret.

'Hugh, you know now, and we have no time to talk about hiding secrets, as we have to act quickly. The Scots knights were spotted by my spies amongst the mob outside the Temple walls, and I am sure they are watching me. If they are caught and the French King finds out the son of John Wishart is in the Temple, he is bound to order a search. Whatever happens, we must move the treasure tonight, even if I have to help crew the barge myself!'

De Charnay was waiting for the obvious question - the

313

location of the secret chamber. 'When the Scots are here, I will share its location. For the moment, all I can say is that it's well hidden.'

Hugh looked quizzically at de Charnay, who repeated himself. 'The treasure: it's hidden in plain sight, but you will only find it if you know it's there.' De Charnay understood how his riddles would irritate his friend. He was being secretive not to goad him, but to protect him in case their plot was discovered.

'How can I help you retrieve it if you don't tell me where you hid it?'

De Charnay had been right: he could hear the frustration in Hugh's voice.

'I need to keep some secrets, even if only for a short time. It's safer that way,' he smiled. 'Leave me now. I will call you when the Scots are ready to leave.'

*

In the Temple Church, Aurelian had lain quietly, listening to the machinations around him. He had remained still for an hour now and had had to empty his bladder. His dignity was damaged, but his life was intact. He was still face down on the cold stone floor and had been waiting for all the noise to die down outside before he attempted to leave. The floor was still very cold, and his trousers were wet and smelly.

Ferrer had led him to the Temple, but had not revealed the treasure's hiding place. Aurelian doubted that the former mercenary would be waiting for him outside the Temple walls as arranged. He had always known Ferrer was unreliable, but it looked like the treasure was indeed somewhere in the Temple as he had claimed.

There was a real danger that de Charnay would hear of Ferrer's return or recognise him, and then Aurelian's efforts to retrieve his master Emperor Andronikos's property would be unravelled.

If Ferrer did runaway, Aurelian would find him and kill

him later. Emperor Michael had ordered him to do this once the treasure had been located, and he never let his Emperor down. Ferrer was no fool and had guessed his life was only worth something as long as the treasure was missing.

He sat up and was surprised to see that, after only a few minutes, the place where he had been lying was bone dry, as if his piss had soaked through the stones and been evaporated by a breeze from below. He took out his dagger and pushed it between the stones. The lime gave way like damp chalk, allowing his blade to push deeper and deeper into the stone. He could move the hilt of the dagger from side to side, as if the stone lay on top of a hollow; and as he shifted it, the faint, damp smell of the river touched his nostrils. There was a space beneath him, but he could not see how he could get down there, unless it was the crypt. Curiosity flooded him as his mind began to race at the possibilities. Could he have found the lost treasure as easily as pissing himself?

*

Outside Geoffroi de Charnay's sturdy wooden door stood Will, Jamie, and Innes. Hendor was downstairs, disposing of both sentries. With their removal, they would knock on the door and wait until the servant had opened it, and then they would force their way in, taking de Charnay prisoner.

They could hear footsteps on the wooden floor from within the room and held their breath. If de Charnay called out, they would be caught in the staircase and slaughtered by the Templar guard. They needed to surprise and silence him before he had a chance to raise the alarm. Innes stood on one side of the door and Jamie and Will on the other, swords in hand. They dared not breathe as the latch rattled and the door creaked open.

Chapter Twenty

Paris Temple, August 14th, 1306: An Audience with the King

Gerard de Villiers had considerable charm, and his repartee was engaging, but Philip the Fair was becoming weary of talk, and it was late.

'Brother de Villiers, the day has been a long one, and there are only so many old tales of the Crusade and Saint Louis I can digest in one day.'

Travelling by boat never sat well with him, and the formalities of the King's progress made him weary - and to end the day on a low point, his brother Valois wanted a late audience. He loved his brother, but he would rather listen to his grumbling tomorrow. He was the King, but sometimes his brother's sense of entitlement outweighed his own, which was considerable.

I need to meet with you immediately. Valois. The note had been thrust into his hand.

The King was glad he had left the atmosphere of the temporary court and got a few moments to himself before his brother arrived.

The King kicked off his shoes as his servant removed his overshirt, revealing a silk undershirt.

He sat on a large, intricately carved oak chair covered in cushions and a damask silk throw. Next to the chair were his beloved books. He did not like people, but books were a different matter. He loved them and went everywhere with them. He considered himself educated rather than learned.

He had an illustrated copy of Tacitus's *Histories* and had

read again and again the chapter on the expulsion of the Jews from Jerusalem by the Romans. He had just expelled the Jews from France after taking their money, and he felt vindicated.

'Wine!' he called, avoiding eye contact. The servants kept their heads bowed as one fetched the wine. Philip liked it when people acted like they were not there.

The servant placed a pair of decorated silver goblets and a decanter on the table by the King. This room was the Grand Master's and was hung with fine tapestries, but the furniture was utilitarian and suited for an order of armed monks. Philip looked at some scuff marks on the floor, as if fine furniture had been moved away and replaced with this peasant façade.

Monsieur Jacques, you are trying just too hard to look poor. This was not the first time the Templars had tried to mislead him about their wealth. They were always pleading poverty and claimed to be unable to contribute to his wars unless they attached a healthy interest rate to their terms.

He considered it strange that Geoffroi de Charnay had been absent for most of the evening, leaving him with Gerard de Villiers. Political animals like de Charnay normally pursued the King's attention, and in the Grand Master's absence, it was his duty to flatter and obtain favour; yet de Charnay was still skulking in his room. There were always machinations going on around him, and he wondered what it was this time. He was sure de Charnay was up to something he did not want the King to know about, but Philip was a patient man.

He drank carefully from his goblet, not wishing to dull his wits - and within seconds, his brother burst in.

'Sire. Brother.'

Charles was King Philip's only surviving brother, and they were vastly different in temperament as well as physical appearance. Valois was larger, darker, and muscular with the pugnacious physique of a self-indulgent wrestler. King Philip was fair and blond, blue-eyed, and fine in features and proportions. He was as ethereal and clever as Valois was bulky and impetuous.

'What crisis drove you to have a note thrust in my hand and demand I leave a very convivial dinner with Gerard?' The King was still sitting, relaxed on his chair with his long legs perched on top of a cushion-topped footstool. If Valois's energy was on fire, the King's was almost extinguished.

Valois looked so excited he could not even sit down to talk. He paced the room.

'I bring you the most exciting news. I have found Alaric's treasure!' Valois almost shouted his news, and the King sensed in his tone that this was not Valois's usual bluster and exaggeration - but he did have the habit of overstating his point, so the King needed to know more.

'Sit. Calm yourself.' The King urged his brother to sit by him and share some wine. 'It would be great news indeed if our crown were to come into possession of this treasure. Please, explain your news.'

Valois sat on an adjoining seat, fidgeting like a small child who had been ordered to be quiet. He took some wine straight from the flagon, ignoring the second cup. It dripped messily down his chin.

'Sire, do you remember Esquieu de Floyran, the Templar de Nogaret arrested for killing his servant in a drunken rage?'

The King thought a little. 'The name has a tinge of familiarity. Was he the one who was saved from Montfaucon?'

'He was reprieved to act as an agent for the crown and report on the Order's activities to the King's council.'

'I remember the crime, but not the man. Wasn't he working as an agent for Guillaume de Nogaret?'

'Yes, and he came to me this night in the Temple Church under great secrecy to reveal the treasure's location, but we were interrupted by de Nogaret.' Valois paused.

The King was always sceptical when his brother said anything about de Nogaret. Their differing attitudes often brought them into conflict.

'Before we were interrupted, Floyran told me that the treasure lies here within the confines of the Temple.' Valois was stammering as he stumbled over his words. 'Sire, my brother, the treasure is greater than we can imagine - so large it is stored on a barge so that it can be easily transported.'

King Philip always sought to simplify the issues, stripping them down to the bare facts, while Valois was more impulsive, filling his speech with elaborations and ornamentation. The King was not keen to plod along and wait for further details. The treasure belonged to the crown, and his focus was on how he would capture it. Before he could speak, Valois interrupted.

'Sire, I need your help to get it. The palace guard can search the Temple this very night, and we can be back in the Louvre Palace with the barge in tow before daybreak.'

The King wanted to act, but he was not as impulsive as his brother.

'Brother, we are within the Temple walls, and seriously outnumbered by the Templar guards. We are also under siege by an angry, drunken mob. Even if we had a force to equal the Templar guard, I can't imagine that the Order is simply going to allow us to tear their Temple apart looking for it.'

The King could see the colour rise in Valois's cheeks. He was obviously infuriated by Philip's measured response.

'Sire, I accept that our position is weak, but we must act! The treasure is here, and we can't let it slip through our fingers.' Valois tried to look in control, but he had a familiar look of desperation. The King believed his sincerity.

Even though they were brothers, the King never let Valois think he made the decisions. 'First, we must find where it is hidden, and it will be difficult to move when we do. Our weakness is only temporary; we cannot act right now, as we will be overwhelmed by those defending the Order. We need to wait and watch and be patient.'

Valois's face was contorted with disappointment. He was not someone who understood the language of patience and cunning, preferring direct action led by sword or axe.

'I want you to find out from de Floyran where the treasure is hidden,' the King said. 'I will instruct our spies on the Seine to watch for any barges originating in Paris. I am sure Madame is on its trail and protecting our interests.'

The King did not want to further involve Charles in finding Alaric's treasure now. Valois's reputation for being indiscreet was legendary, but here it seemed by coincidence that the treasure had found Valois.

'We need to act with wisdom and stealth,' Philip said. 'God is on our side: how else can we explain such luck?'

Emboldened, the King was already planning how he would use the fortune to crush his rivals.

'Fetch de Floyran, and I will summon de Nogaret and contact Madame. We shall wait for the morning to enact any actions. We do not want to aggravate our defenders and rouse the mob. Be discreet and keep blood off the walls.'

'Yes, Sire. I can be found in my rooms below, should you need me.' Valois turned and left.

The King smiled and demanded more wine before picking up Tacitus with a smile.

After being driven out of his palace by an angry mob and forced to take shelter, now he was about to become the richest man in the world. He felt his smile growing, and he acknowledged that it was a significant departure from his norm.

'Today didn't end so badly, after all. My brother is a most brilliant fool,' he announced to an empty room.

*

The English spymaster in Paris, Hubert de Lacy, was oblivious to the lateness of the hour. His pale complexion and flabby body did not thrive when the sun was strong, so he hibernated during the day. He liked the late summer, when Paris became cooler, and the nights became longer. Today there had been noisy rioters in the streets, but now in the night hours, the curfew was in force and he could work and read the dispatches from his master, King Edward.

He had excused his servants for the evening so that he could work uninterrupted and unobserved. He had reports that Scottish agents were in Paris, and the French King was whipping up treachery. The reality was that there was no truce between England and France, just a pause between wars.

Now he was reading that Aurelian was in Paris in search of Alaric's treasure, and Madame de France was, in turn, searching for Aurelian.

To make things worse, he had no answer for King Edward, who had demanded to know what de Lacy was doing about finding the treasure and stopping the others from finding it first.

He had a large, half-eaten pound loaf and a plate of meat and cheese beside him, which he pulled at as he wrote.

He dipped his bread into the goblet of watered-down sweetened wine to his left, grateful for the large jug just behind it. He always ate when he was stressed, which was all the time.

He was overweight and always sweaty, but he convinced himself that corpulence coupled with the experienced life had brought him charisma. As an ambassador to the French court, dealing with King Philip and working for King Edward at the same time, he needed to be personable.

The two Kings deserved each other, and his job was to smooth out the rough edges and somehow make their interests accommodate each other even though they were in opposition. That required a clever man, and he believed he was very clever.

He heard a scream followed by a groan just outside his window in the street below. Quickly, wiping his fingers on his hose, de Lacy grabbed the candlestick and looked out the window. His heart was pounding, and his hand started to shake, but he was more likely to flee than to fight - he was a diplomat, not a soldier.

There was no one there, just the scuttle of rats raking around in the gutters. Screams and violent noises were not unusual in the streets near the College de Sorbonne. Drink and intellect could be a poisonous combination.

Nothing to see here, Hubert.

He relaxed back into his chair.

Suddenly, there was an anguished scream, followed by a crash as the door held fast, but only just. He heard a thud and the rhythm of something heavy tumbling down the stairs.

For a few seconds, maybe ten, Hubert de Lacy dared not move. He remained sitting in his chair, using the table as some basic protection. He pulled the dagger from his left sleeve and stabbed it into the table.

A murder outside the home of the English ambassador would create a diplomatic schism. The noise would have attracted the attention of his neighbours, so he would need to find out what had happened before anyone else came to see what all the noise was about.

He pulled the dagger out of the table with one hand and held a heavy lit candlestick, which could also serve as an impromptu second weapon, in the other. He looked nervously out onto the staircase; it was pitch dark, and only a sliver of light from the candle pierced the darkness, but he could not see anyone hiding.

Then he saw him. It was dark, and the form was ill-defined but human in shape. He looked around again and, seeing no one around, proceeded gingerly to the bottom of the steps.

He could see that the man's eyes were bulging, and his

face was turned to one side. He was warm but not breathing, and his clothes were wet with something - blood, judging from the smell. It was mildly sticky on his fingers as he examined the dead man.

It was a Templar servant from the torn tabard, and his clothes looked as if they had been rifled through. His murderer had been looking for something - his full purse was still hanging at his belt; this was not robbery. The murderer had certainly been looking for the message he carried, but secret dispatches between the Templar agent and the English King's spy were normally held in the agent's shoe, somewhere a rushed assassin would not look.

De Lacy removed the shoes and searched the inner soles, from which he retrieved a small, rolled parchment. He furtively pushed it into a pocket within his jerkin before dragging the body outside to throw it into the midden, which ran behind his lodgings. It was several feet deep as well as wide, and the body would soon be covered with the mess thrown from the overhanging buildings and concealed from the nosey Maréchaussée.

De Lacy had seen death before, but this was the first time anyone had died in front of his lodgings. He did not possess that sort of courage and disregard that soldiers seemed to require. He was shaking as he moved the body, and he struggled to stand, fearing his legs would give way.

He returned to his rooms and pushed the damaged door closed. His heart raced with anxiety, and he could feel that the warm stickiness of the man's blood had soaked into his hose.

He removed the message from his jerkin and held the candle fast against the letter, almost setting the parchment alight, so faint was its light. The letter was unsigned, but he recognised the hand, and it surprised him. It was a note to King Edward from Pierre de Nogaret.

This message contained the most profound news.

Monseigneur, Alaric's treasure can be ours. It is to be found within the walls of the Paris Temple, and an attempt will be made to remove it and place it in the hands of England's enemies. It is my only objective to ensure His Grace, King Edward, is in possession of this wealth as God has guided me. Watch all river ports and harbours for a river barge crewed by Scottish rebels. Act immediately or the prize will be lost.

Your humble and loyal servant – Pierre de Nogaret

Someone did not want the English King to know. De Lacy knew Alaric's treasure was more than enough reason to murder the bearer of the message.

He held the parchment in the flame until it was no more, then he felt around for his quill and ink and frantically started to write, concerned that the assassin could still be hiding outside.

There was another way out of his rooms avoiding the main staircase - through the merchant's house next door via a connecting staircase from this room into the merchant's attic. An outer staircase led from the back of the merchant's house directly to the square and away from the river.

The merchant was away and his house unlit, so Hubert could leave unnoticed and get this note to his servants, who were sleeping in a dormitory in the quadrangle behind his and the merchant's houses. They could leave quietly by the back routes and be in Rouen in two days.

His note was to his master's agent in Rouen, as the treasure barge would have to travel via Rouen to reach the sea if it was heading to Scotland and the rebels. But they should also cover all the main waterways out of France, including westward via the Rhone to La Rochelle. He addressed the note with a flourish to a certain Jean de Bretagne.

King Edward would be unforgiving if Hubert did not stop the Scots from escaping with the treasure, but together with Jean de Bretagne, they would seize the treasure for their master.

Hubert crawled to the adjoining door and surreptitiously moved into the adjoining house. The only light was the diminishing candle he clutched in one hand whilst he stuffed his note into his shirt. His knees were sticking to the rushes, and he collided with solid chairs and tables as he crawled through the darkness.

His heart raced again as he stopped breathing and listened against the outside door. There was no shadow under the door, and he gauged it safe to open, and gingerly creep outside. But he could barely lift his shaking hand to open it.

It is now or never, Hubert. Carpe diem!

There was no one there. He breathed a sigh of relief as his stomach turned over and vomit filled his throat. There was no arm above him clutching a dagger ready to plunge into his back, but he had to move quickly and get the message on its way.

He blew out his lamp. The moon would light his way to the dormitory where his servants slept. The message would be leaving for Rouen, and when he got back, he would wash the blood from his hands.

*

In the alley behind Hubert's house, Madame de France clutched her side. She knew the wound was bad, but it was not mortal. Pierre de Nogaret's servant had fought like a soldier and had caught her in the ribs with his dagger. She had not found his message, so perhaps he had intended to deliver it to the English spy orally.

She had followed the servant from the Grosse Tour, which held the offices of the Templar leadership, but he was no novice, and rather than hand the message over, he had fought with her.

His wound had been mortal, and he had died at de Lacy's door, but not before he had cried a warning. The noise had attracted attention from the surrounding houses, and where there had been darkness, there was now the flickering of candlelight, even though it was after curfew. The risk of discovery was high, and her usefulness to the King would be compromised. She could not follow, so she would patch up her wounds and return to the Temple. The boatman was close by, and she could rest for a few hours. She was sure now that the Temple was the centre of this conspiracy, and she would be rested and waiting to act.

She slunk off down the alley towards the river, still sore and a little embittered about being bettered - but she had learned a valuable lesson today: she had underestimated her foe and the situation, and it had nearly cost her life. She would not make this mistake again.

Chapter Twenty-one

Paris Temple, August 14th, 1306: Flight to Orkney

De Charnay and Hugh de Verneuil sat silently at the far end of his receiving room. They were hidden in a dark corner, obscured from anyone who entered through the main door. They were waiting for someone.

The lock clicked open, and the frame of the door shook gently. The latch followed, gliding upwards out of its fastening. De Charnay knew it was them.

The Scottish knights snuck in, one after another, with their daggers drawn. Hendor pushed the door shut and, clutching a small lamp for light, flicked the latch closed with his dagger. Innes looked around the main room, which appeared empty and silent. 'Hendor, you said he was still in the Temple, but the bird appears to have flown.'

'He's here in this tower for sure, hiding somewhere.' Hendor's voice was confident.

'Yes, remember last time we were here, when we met Pierre de Nogaret?' Jamie added. 'People appeared from behind tapestries. This place is a labyrinth.'

'I won't forget his duplicity, his treachery, and his greed,' Will said. 'He will get one chance to tell us where the treasure is before I beat its location out of him. We should check the far end of his rooms for hiding places. Hand me the lamp!' He started to walk to the end of the large L-shaped room to look around the corner.

De Charnay could hear the footsteps and knew he would soon be discovered, but he was not hiding, only waiting.

'I have been waiting for you.' He walked into the

main room, accompanied by Hugh. They were expecting resistance and came prepared ready to fight de Charnay's guards, but there were no guards in view, just de Charnay and his unarmed servant.

'We expected you would have company.' Will pointed his dagger between de Charnay's eyes, ready to strike.

'I recognise you. You were one of the men who arrested us the last time we visited the Temple.' Jamie moved his dagger and pressed the point gently into de Verneuil's belly.

Innes searched them both. Finding Verneuil armed, he removed his dagger and handed it to Hendor.

'My friends are being cautious, Hugh; they mean you no harm.' De Charnay had no intention of fighting. That would be pointless. For now, the Scots wanted him very much alive, despite their boasting.

Innes stood by him and pushed him back into one of the chairs. 'Sit down - and if you cry out, it will be the last noise you make.'

Will spoke for them all.

'I'm sure you are surprised and disappointed to see us back. You must realise that we are not here to talk of friendship. You destroyed that when you had Pierre de Nogaret send us on a futile journey to Padua and arranged for our murder along the way.'

De Charnay understood their anger, but he had not ordered any murder. He was shaken by this allegation. He may have engineered their trip to Scrovegni, but he had ordered that no harm should come to them. He had been clear on that to Pierre.

He understood betrayal. He had seen it all around him, and yet he had trusted de Nogaret, knowing he was a flawed man. 'You are wrong. I am no murderer.'

He had been mistaken in believing Pierre would always work for the best interests of the Order, not realising other interested parties were in play, probably the English.

'I walked you into greater danger, and if I were in your position, I would feel as you do: betrayed, threatened, and vengeful.'

De Nogaret had known about the treasure for years, so why chose now to betray him? Unless it was because he knew the treasure was nearby and he would soon not need de Charnay anymore. De Charnay had been right not to share its location.

'I have been betrayed too and I cannot undo what has happened.'

De Charnay knew he had not assembled the full picture of de Nogaret's betrayal yet, and until he did, he would say nothing. The only certain thing was that de Nogaret was not working alone and would need help to locate and remove the treasure.

Jamie's and Will's daggers were still drawn, and it did not look as if there was any possibility of the Scots giving him the benefit of the doubt.

'I can make amends if you will listen,' de Charnay knew he was pleading for his life. 'I had my reasons for sending you away, but I ordered that none of you were to be harmed. I understand that you do not believe me, but give me a hearing before you decide to kill me.'

De Charnay was certain that Bishop Wishart's servants had been chosen for their wits as well as their ability to fight, and they would be more sophisticated than armed thugs. He hoped they were open to reason.

'You mean you had *our* interests at heart in sending us to Padua with people tasked to kill us?' Jamie scoffed as he lowered his dagger from de Verneuil's stomach.

'Yes, Jamie,' de Charnay said. 'Your well-being was at the heart of my actions.'

De Charnay's arrogance infuriated Jamie. 'Every time I hear the name Geoffroi de Charnay someone is trying to kill me: does that suggest well-being to you?'

'Your father was one of my dearest friends. I owe my life to him when he saved me at Acre: how could I hurt the son of John Wishart and the nephew of my dear friend Bishop Robert?'

'I am flattered but not fooled,' Jamie said. 'Sole ownership of Alaric's treasure could make any man forget his principles and his friends. I would say that would be motive enough for anyone to get rid of us. Wouldn't you?' De Charnay appreciated his candour. Bishop Wishart chose men with some wit, even if it was tinged with impertinence.

De Charnay needed to regain control of the conversation and convince them he did not want them killed.

'Bishop Wishart must have a traitor in his camp!'

Will interrupted. 'Yes, and the bastard stands before us.'

'You want my blood, and I understand that. If Bishop Wishart were here, he would listen.'

De Charnay held his hand out to Will, who remained still with his dagger pointed at him. Will did not even look down at his hand.

Hugh de Verneuil rose to support de Charnay, but Innes pushed him back into the seat of the chair.

'The diplomatic letters that came to the French King were full of information about you before you even arrived here. You landed at Rouen on Jean de Bretagne's ship, the Nantes. The King of France knew when you were coming and for what purpose. So did the English King and the Byzantine Emperors. The only thing they did not know was where you were heading, and that would not have remained a secret for long if you had stayed in the Temple. Nothing is a secret for long here. I knew you would come to me, followed by those ordered to find the treasure. Let me lay out what they had planned for you.'

Hendor, who had been quiet until now, spoke at last. 'Let me have ten minutes with him, and he will tell us what we want to know.'

'I am not taken in by him, but a dead man tells us nothing: I think we should hear what he has to say.' Will argued. 'Carry on.'

'Firstly, they would let you go through the effort of finding it, and then they would take it from you and killed you. I have no need for personal wealth, as you can see. I have a sumptuous roof over my head, and today the King of France is a guest under my protection - I do not need this treasure, but I do care whose hands it falls into, and it cannot be the Kings of England or France or those delusional heretics, the Emperors of Byzantium. If any of them gets his hands on that wealth, he will have the means to destroy the other two, and a few smaller kingdoms like Scotland will get swamped in that wave of destruction. I know you share these fears, and you can see the damage these tyrants would reap. You also have another right. John Wishart and I found the treasure - or should I say the treasure found us. Part of it is yours by right. So, you see, we really should be working together.'

'You made a lot of decisions on our behalf,' Will said. 'Just tell us where it is, and we will be on our way. It is in the Temple, isn't it?' he continued to pressure de Charnay, but the Templar was quick with his response.

'Do you think you can just sail away with a ship full of gold, silver, and jewels and transport it halfway across France unnoticed? You will not get half a league before the French King deprives you of the treasure and your lives. You need my help to get home.' De Charnay could see that his arguments had made them stop and think.

They all nodded.

'All right, you have our attention,' Will said.

'Paris is full of spies and gossips. I am the only man in France who will watch your backs. You need to trust me: you have no choice. I knew you would come back here from Padua because what you were looking for was not there, and if I had wanted to kill you, I could have ordered your assassination at any point along the route back or waited for you in some alley outside the Temple walls. You find me here alone with only one knight for protection and all my servants dismissed. Do you think this is an accident?'

'I want you to take us to the treasure now,' Will said. 'I want to see it and know it is not a myth. Where is it?'

De Charnay hesitated. He had seen Esquieu de Floyran plotting with Valois, so he could not take any chances. The French King and Valois were probably aware of the proximity of the gold, and palace guards would soon be searching the Temple, so he needed to act now.

'I will, but as I told you, we have the King of France as a guest, and we need to act with caution. We need to scout the esplanade and pier for palace guards and spies, and once we are sure we are not being watched, we need to head for the Temple Church. The entrance to the treasure chamber is there.'

'Jamie, Innes, and Hendor will go and see if there are any overzealous guards hiding out in the esplanade,' Will said. 'They'll check the pier and the church too. Until I believe it is safe by their signal you and your friend will stay here with me. I don't want you to get lonely.' De Charnay had expected that he would not be allowed to leave until he had gained their trust, and he would now remain with Will and Hugh until it was safe to go to the chamber where the treasure was hidden.

'One last thing before you leave,' de Charnay said. 'Moving the barge at any time would be dangerous, but today we have an advantage. I intend to start a riot!'

Will looked perplexed. 'To what end?'

'To cover your escape. We are surrounded by a drunken mob that, if given the correct motivation, would conceal the second coming, but I have more modest plans. I intend for chaos and noise to cover us as we remove the treasure ship under the noses of King Philip and Valois. The players are around us, prepared to make fire and brimstone, to take their anger out anywhere the King is. All we need to do is throw in a match, which is why Hugh is here with me.'

De Charnay could sense he was winning their respect. They appeared more relaxed, their weapons were lowered, and they were taking his orders. He was sincere. This was their only way of getting out of Paris alive and with the treasure.

'Make sure the route to the Temple Church is clear of prying eyes,' Will told his companions. 'We will believe Brother de Charnay once we have seen the treasure with our own eyes.' He pulled up a stool and sat down.

De Charnay pointed to the large tapestry hanging in his bedroom. 'Take the back stairs, which are behind that tapestry.'

Jamie took the solitary lamp which had been burning in de Charnay's bedroom to guide them, leaving Will, Hugh, and de Charnay in the dark. The only light was that of the full moon, reflected into the room from the walls of the other towers.

'Now tell me: how you propose to start a riot?' Will asked.

De Charnay stood and walked towards the chest under the oriel window. 'May I?' he gestured to the lid. Will nodded.

De Charnay unlocked the chest and removed a hefty sack, which fell onto the floor with a thud. He dragged it towards Will and Hugh.

'You asked to see the treasure, Will? Come and see, for this is but a minuscule fraction. There are numerous other chests - some with coins, others with jewels!'

De Charnay lifted a handful of the glistening gold coins and placed them on the table next to Will.

Will picked up one of the coins. They were astounding. He had never seen gold of such quality.

'This sack of gold will have to be sacrificed for the riot. It is a small price to pay and cheaper than hiring mercenaries. I propose to distribute the gold amongst the crowd that surrounds us, as well as in the taverns. Once they know that the King has all this gold but still shaves and debases their coinage, they will be even angrier. They will pound these gates and create hell everywhere except on the river. Unlike the Lord, they cannot walk on water, and that's how we will leave.'

De Charnay turned to Verneuil. 'Hugh, I want you to take this money outside and into the mob and tell them where it came from. Spread it around the taverns and brothels and throw some off the walls. Make sure everyone thinks it is part of the King's hoard. Throw Guillaume de Nogaret's name into the mix, and make sure they know he has his snout in the trough. If that does not get the mob on the warpath, nothing else will. They will want to tear that money-grubber apart.' He turned to Will. 'Can Hugh leave? With your permission, of course.'

Will nodded in agreement.

Verneuil carefully removed the coins and replaced them in the sack.

'I assume that your men will have cleared the courtyard?' De Charnay asked.

Will smiled. 'You shouldn't concern yourself about that.'

Through the window, de Charnay saw Innes, Jamie, and Hendor outside the Temple Church. The esplanade was quiet, so he assessed it as safe for Hugh to leave.

De Charnay watched Hugh struggle with the sack of coins. He slung it over his back with difficulty, almost knocking himself over with its momentum before he left de Charnay's quarters by the hidden stairs.

The silence between Will and de Charnay was excruciating. This was no surprise to de Charnay: there was bound to be resentment and distrust. The coins were evidence that the treasure had been here, but no doubt Will needed to see the rest before he would fully trust him.

Will checked every few minutes for a sign it was safe to move towards the Church, whilst de Charnay nervously waited, fidgeting with his belt and twisting the garnet ring on his finger.

'Give Hugh half an hour to do his work,' de Charnay said.

After ten minutes or so he saw a lighted arrow skim the sky. It embedded itself in the door of the Church, briefly lighting up its entrance before running out of fuel and fading into darkness.

'There is our signal,' Will said. 'I really hope for your sake this is not another trick.'

De Charnay pointed towards the tapestry and the exit. 'Let us head to the Temple Church and see.'

'After you, brother,' Will said, pushing de Charnay ahead.

*

Inside the church, Aurelian could smell the sour water from the river and guessed from what Ferrer had told him that the treasure was still on the barge, hidden in a chamber underneath him. He wondered how seaworthy the vessel was after so many years and thought that anyone hiding such wealth would use at least a little of it to keep the barge watertight.

There must be a small canal leading from the Seine, and he suspected it extended further than the first pier. He could not work out the mechanism for opening the entrance, but if it were easy, then the treasure would have been long gone.

He looked around the private chapel for something out of place. He held a small, flat candle in his palm to prevent the light from being seen outside, but the weakness of its glow forced him to examine every inch of the stone. He touched each point, pressing for loose stones that might reveal hidden labyrinths, but everything looked and felt solid and original.

Suddenly the church echoed as the lumbering wooden door rattled open. Aurelian blew his candle out and hid behind the open door into the chapel. He dared not shut it, fearing he would be caught.

Three men came through the door, but he did not recognise them in the darkness. The men lit the line of candles that stretched along the nave and began searching each nook and corner along the inner perimeter of the church. Aurelian's heart was racing, as he expected to be discovered at any moment. One of the men entered the chapel, but did not look behind the door. Aurelian recognised him as one of the Scots he had seen in Padua. There had been four of them then, and now they were only three. That made it easier for him if he needed to eliminate them. For now, he would listen and watch.

Having completed their search and found no one, the Scots sat on the confessional bench. Aurelian listened intently, hoping to pick up information.

'And what do we do now? We have been lucky not to be spotted, and the longer we stay in the Temple with the King of France in residence, the stronger the possibility that we will be arrested.'

'Patience, Hendor. They will be with us presently. Sit, relax. They must create a riot, and from the noise outside it sounds like it has started. We have signalled to Will: he will soon bring de Charnay here.'

'Ever the pragmatist, Innes.'

Aurelian was no longer worried about being discovered. He commended the Scots on their ingenuity. *Starting a riot to cover your escape. I wish I had come up with that myself. First-class thinking, boys.*

*

Outside the Temple, there was a discernible change in the pitch and sound of the mob. Instead of distant, muffled drunken screaming, the noises were getting louder and more coordinated, and people were chanting. The guards were preoccupied with what was going on outside the walls and ignored what was happening within.

'Death to the King! Death to de Nogaret!'

'Bread, not blood!'

The crowds were stamping on the bridge over the moat and banging the portcullis gate, which was closed. They would not break through the metal gate, but that did not stop them trying to set fire to it. Archers on the perimeter fired warning shots to keep them away, but they could see that the mob was growing and becoming angrier.

The Temple was framed with a wall of torch fire on three sides. At the main entrance, in the centre of the mob, a dishevelled and filthy man was egging on the others. His face was dirty, and half-covered with a cloth. Hugh de Verneuil had been quick in following his master's orders, and he had been pushing against an open door. Demanding the King's death was a crime that carried the death penalty, but the mob had no fear because they had nothing to lose: the punishment was no worse than starvation that would consign them to anyway.

Hugh was pleased as the mob's chanting became louder and more vicious. He saw that the palace guards were more anxious and their aim more erratic. Several arrows hit the moat just below them. He was sure their nerve would fail, and someone would be shot, and then there would be a maelstrom of violence. The people outside the walls were not some foreign army: these were the sentries' own people, possibly relations; and the soldiers were panicking.

He saw that more guards had been ordered to the walls as missiles flew from the mob. Most of them missed, but occasionally one would creep over the wall and smash into the esplanade.

The Tour de Caesar was on the side nearest the river and safe from attack, but Hugh was sure the King must have

337

heard the noise outside and questioned coming to the Temple for his safety.

Now it was not looking so safe after all, and knowing the Capet brothers, they would return in secret to the Louvre Palace tomorrow and leave the Templars to quell this melee.

*

The guards looked outwards towards the mob. They had now taken several hits from an impromptu catapult that was firing pots of Greek fire onto the walls, temporarily setting the stone itself on fire. Pierre de Nogaret watched de Charnay stop, turn, and smile, looking more smug than usual. He must have played a part in this chaos. He would not be smiling if he knew what awaited his Scottish friends in Rouen.

A diversion to help you remove the treasure from the Temple won't change a thing. Indeed, it will hasten your meeting with the English, he thought as he watched them. He had wondered how they would transport so much gold away without alerting half of France. His allies in England would be pleased with this turn of events.

He watched them enter the Temple Church. 'It's in there!' he exclaimed before returning to his paperwork.

In celebration, he took a large glug of wine from the goblet next to his quill, more than pleased with what he had achieved. The King of England would soon be in possession of the wealth necessary to crush the King of France and would owe that success to him.

He would extract the price of vengeance from King Edward for this service on behalf of all Cathars. If King Edward disagreed, this treasure would end up at the bottom of the North Sea. He picked up the latest list of letters for his perusal and began to write as if today were just like any other. The first letter would congratulate Edward, King of England.

*

Jamie rushed to the door as he heard the latch click, closely followed by Innes and Hendor, their swords drawn for combat. They stood to either side of the door.

Jamie had heard the growing commotion outside and was confident that would consume the attention of any nosey guards. 'We should be prepared for the Temple guards coming to pray for God's protection.'

'You are right, Jamie. Good thinking, and highly likely.'

Jamie had been a follower, but now he was beginning to lead their actions, and the others were starting to follow.

'Brothers, put down your swords.' De Charnay paused, but Jamie could see his anxiety - or was it perhaps excitement?

'Come quickly!' He ushered everyone towards the altar, carefully shutting the door behind him.

De Charnay lit the beeswax mass candles, which brightened the entire chantry and extended as far as the private chapel. These lights sparkled in front of the stained glass.

'We need to act fast, my friends.' De Charnay looked up to the window and acknowledged the increasing noise and chaos outside.

Jamie could feel the excitement of the moment as de Charnay's clever plan was coming together. Bishop Wishart had asked them to put their trust in de Charnay, and now Jamie had found that faith, and his suspicions were disappearing. Following de Charnay no longer felt like a leap of faith.

The altar was carved with the Shield of the Trinity, the Scutum Fidei, inscribed with the words: God is the Father, God is the Son, God is the Holy Ghost. Its stone was decorated in muted greens, blues, yellows, and reds. Underneath the shield, in its own *cartouche*, was an inscription in Latin: *In hoc signo vinces. Amen.*

With this sign you shall conquer. Amen.

'Now, stay close and follow me down into my labyrinth,'

de Charnay said. 'I warn you: touch nothing surrounding the ship, as the walls are dusted with belladonna and studded with razor-sharp metal spikes.'

De Charnay stood close by the altar and wiped away the accumulated dust from the shield and the cartouche with the bottom of his knitted tabard, whilst Jamie watched him in silence, a little perplexed. Everyone else mirrored his silent fascination. De Charnay worked on, quiet in his purpose.

He then pressed the stone words on the Scutum Fidei with his fist: first the Father, then the Son, and thirdly the Holy Ghost. Finally, with both palms, he pressed Amen. Then he stood back.

Suddenly, the stone groaned, and dust quietly exploded into the air as the altar descended into the stone floor. Slabs continued to grind, stone against stone, as the top stone slid back and a spiral staircase emerged, leading down into a dark cavern. They could hear water lapping and hitting some sort of stone-lined channel, and there was a smell of rotting vegetation and suppurating mud, bubbling in the summer heat.

'What magic is this?' Hendor muttered in astonishment.

'It's not magic, but it is fucking incredible,' Jamie blurted.

De Charnay lit the lamp he had brought from his rooms and took the first steps. 'Remember, be careful.'

De Charnay led the way, followed by Jamie, then Innes, Will, and finally Hendor. Gingerly, Jamie placed his foot on the first step of the staircase. It was steep and slippery, with an unpleasant, slimy green covering. He took a second step and then a third as he gained confidence. De Charnay did not seem to have the same difficulties negotiating the slime, which surprised him. He was beginning to realise his youth did not make him an expert at everything.

As de Charnay climbed downwards, Jamie could not see him clearly. There was light coming through the opening above him, but it was insufficient for him to see anything.

This tunnel was built to deceive with twists and bends. De Charnay would soon be out of sight, and the anaemic light generated by his lamp would be lost in the pitch darkness of a dangerous labyrinth. 'Hendor, pass us some of those large altar candles.'

Hendor had been on the first step and easily reached back to grab the beeswax candles. He passed one down, followed by a second and third, holding on to the last one for himself. Armed with his own light, Jamie tried to suppress his rising excitement and focus on the stairs. They were so close now.

De Charnay called up to them. 'Brothers, remember my words and touch nothing until you reach the barge.' He sounded anxious, as if proximity to the treasure had increased the stakes.

Jamie held the large candle in his left hand. He had to concentrate hard to neither fall nor use the poisoned walls for support.

'How long is this corridor?' Jamie was keen to keep pace with de Charnay, eager to outrun any danger, but struggling not to lose his footing and fall against the wall. From the quiet behind him, he guessed the other men were similarly torn between a propelling sense of urgency and the desperate need to concentrate.

Suddenly, Innes slipped, knocking into Jamie's knees, and causing him to stumble backwards. He grabbed Innes to stop himself from brushing the walls.

Jamie took his sword out of his sheath and used it to support his weight as he stood up.

'Come quickly. Quickly!' De Charnay shouted, nearly out of sight. In the seconds it had taken to topple over and catch themselves, he had made nearly double the distance.

Jamie slipped and tripped down twenty steep steps before landing on a platform beside a shallow stone-lined channel, which was perhaps half a man's height in depth and three in width. De Charnay was waiting there.

Jamie clutched his sword and candle, conscious to avoid slipping into the dark, murky water of the channel that ran next to them. He was soon joined by the others, who were covered in cobwebs and detritus that had dropped from the roof onto their cloaks and hats.

'Now I think we need some proper light, and we had better close off the entrance to keep out any overzealous meddlers.' De Charnay reached above the heads of the knights and lit a wick finer than a length of gossamer thread. A cascade of pitch lamps lit up with an intensity and speed that was totally unexpected.

Jamie raised his sword in shock. 'I was wrong - this is magic!'

The chamber was carved out of the stone foundations that supported the church. The walls were coal-black, except for an unhealthy dampness, which made them glisten in the light. Large moulds were growing above their heads, and somehow, numerous insects had got into the sealed chasm and a new colony of life was flourishing. The insects swarmed towards the lights, swirling across their faces, and tangling into their hair and clothes.

'Have we arrived in hell?' Innes asked as he brushed insects from his shoulders and inside his tunic.

Behind him, Jamie watched as de Charnay pushed a stone that was not flush to the walls like all the others. The pinhole of light that reached the bottom of the stairs from the church upstairs disappeared as the stone mechanism snapped shut. Dust rushed down the staircase, and almost immediately the air became damper and staler. It smelled of burning pitch.

As the insects settled, Jamie looked around the cavern. He had been expecting the light to present the form of a treasure barge, but instead he saw a hollow, empty cavern hewn out of solid rock and blocked with a wooden gate that contained a small door. The door sported a large padlock, and Jamie sensed everyone's frustration. He was getting bored and angry with de Charnay's riddles and duplicity.

'Where is the barge, Monseigneur?' Will's voice was cold and direct, betraying their rapidly fading patience in de Charnay as he strode away from them towards the next section of this seemingly endless labyrinth.

The gate extended the full depth and breadth of the channel, and the only way through the gate was by the padlocked door.

De Charnay appeared to take no notice of Will's pleas. 'Come quickly, before this foul air overwhelms us.' De Charnay appeared to feel no stress, and his tone was reminiscent of a church liturgy. He produced a large iron key from a cloth pouch attached to his waist. 'Pull your tunics up over your mouths. The air is poisoned, but we will be safe on the other side of this air-proof gate. We still have time. Don't let this little barrier frustrate you: it is nothing more than a little extra security to discourage anyone who might get past my other devices.' Jamie sensed that de Charnay enjoyed showing off his deviousness.

Jamie watched closely as de Charnay pulled the padlock towards him and placed the key in the lock. The lock looked rusty and difficult to turn, and it squeaked as it resisted. De Charnay's powerful hands were forcing the lock open, but the device was reluctant. At last, de Charnay's strength overwhelmed it, and the mechanism clicked and turned. The robust iron loop came away, and the padlock fell apart onto the floor. The noise echoed around the chamber and distracted everyone apart from Jamie, who pushed the gate ajar, eager to be first through it.

He felt a sharp tug on his jerkin as de Charnay grabbed his neck and pulled his head back so hard that he threw Jamie and himself to the ground, almost slipping into the channel.

Hendor immediately placed his sword at de Charnay's throat just as a large axe flashed across the inside of the open gate. It was large and split the air with such force that it created a vortex. All the candles were extinguished except de Charnay's lamp.

The axe would have chopped him in half. Jamie felt stupid, as his impulsiveness had nearly cost him his life, and it was a valuable lesson he would never forget. De Charnay had saved his life.

Jamie stood back up and wiped the sticky green slime and dust off his tunic and hose.

'Sorry, my dear boy, but this was my last trick to deprive any undeserving fortune hunter of the treasure.'

'You are sure it is safe now?' Will asked, looking amused and amazed at the ingenuity of the old Templar. 'Bishop Wishart said you were a resourceful man!'

The door was narrow, and only one man at a time could enter. Inside was another space cut out of the rock. It was dark, lit only by the light penetrating from the adjoining space. It was just enough to expose the edge of a stone walkway surrounding the channel.

Will led the way, and Jamie, his dignity almost recovered, followed him through the doorway. In the darkness, they could just make out a fat, bulbous shape. The shape seemed to move very slightly.

'Once you are through the gate, remove your masks, and don't forget to bring in a torch,' de Charnay ordered.

Hendor and Innes grabbed three of the pitch torches from the wall, lighting them with de Charnay's lamp and passing one to Jamie. De Charnay entered last and stood back, allowing the Scots to assemble.

Each torch added to the intensity of the light; they framed and then defined the shapeless form. Ten steps away was a creaking wooden barge with a shallow draught, lying heavily in the water and straining against the walls of the narrow channel.

The decks were covered with rough woollen cloths and animal skins. Jamie felt a bitter disappointment rising within him.

'So, this is what we have risked our lives for?' Hendor said. 'I see no gold, no jewels, just a few sheepskins and the smell of rotting fish.' Jamie knew Hendor would always be the sceptic amongst them.

He had believed de Charnay - believed they would save Scotland. But this was not a treasure barge. It was … just a barge. Just another step in the Templar's twisted game.

De Charnay placed his torch in the holder by the inner door and stepped onto the deck first. He put his hand out to help Jamie on board, followed by Innes, Will, and Hendor. 'I am remembering Acre. In this light, Jamie resembles his father and brings back the memories of our escape to Padua.'

He paused and looked down at a gash in the deck. 'It has been fifteen years since Acre, but I remember every moment, every gash and bruise of our escape.' Jamie saw him wince and knew this experience was real and still with him.

'I know you are impatient, and my memories are of little interest, so may I introduce Alaric's treasure.' With characteristic flamboyance, de Charnay threw the coverings off the barrels and chests towards the knights like ethereal missiles, and they landed in a chaotic pile on the walkway.

Jamie gasped in wonder. Even Hendor could not find a suitably sceptical comment, blurting out, 'Well, fuck me!'

Innes and Will were silent, overwhelmed. What they saw was fabulous. They had all agreed the tales of the treasure were born out of legend, and like all legends, they would only be based on a soupçon of truth. But the reality was greater than the legend. The gold glowed as if it were alive and breathing, and the jewels were as large as goose eggs.

'Sweet Jesus,' Innes murmured. The others said nothing. They simply stared in astonishment.

Like children, they grabbed handfuls of gold coins and precious gems and let the coins fall through their fingers like water returning to a well. They pushed their swords as far as they could into the chests to see where the fill started and finished. Each chest was overflowing.

Will shouted with delight and threw jewels and gold into the air. Innes tried on a circlet studded with rubies and diamonds. It was like they were drunk, but with wealth instead of wine. Innes grabbed Hendor and they danced like drunken women screaming without inhibition.

No one noticed that the noise outside seemed to be much louder now, as if it was only a few feet away - and indeed it was. The gurgling of the river echoed as the waves lapped against the stones, but there did not seem to be a way out from the chamber to the river.

'Boys, can you hear outside? They will be tearing the Temple apart within the hour.' De Charnay's tone was calm and controlled. He displayed little emotion around the treasure, unlike the others.

'Brother de Charnay, this is beyond our wildest imagination.' Jamie ignored de Charnay's comment. He was still exuberant about the riches around him and could not contain his smiles and laughter. If only Bishop Wishart could see what they had achieved. It was like the joy of the gold had taken over his self-control. Everywhere they looked, the barge was covered in chests and barrels creaking with the weight of their golden cargo.

'How do you plan for us to get it out of here?' Hendor looked around the chamber. 'The barge had to have floated in here, but I can't see any exit.'

Jamie was still cheering, but Hendor's comment made him stop in his tracks and drop the handful of gold in his fist back into its chest. Innes and Will did the same.

'Other than manhandling the barge's contents back up through the church, I can't see any way out, and that wouldn't be practical with the rioting above us,' Innes said. Will nodded.

De Charnay moved some wool sacks that were piled on

one side of the deck. 'Take these sacks and spread them over the chests and barrels and bring the woollen covers and sacking back onto the barge. You need to become English wool merchants.'

'English?' Jamie, Hendor, Will, and Innes cried in a chorus of disapproval.

De Charnay gave out a huge belly laugh. 'Yes, I thought that description would stick in your craw, but it is necessary. There are many English merchants plying their trade up and down the Seine, and you will fit right in.'

Jamie and Hendor took the cloths that de Charnay had thrown at them and re-covered the barrels and chests.

'Aren't we moving ahead of ourselves?' Will said as Innes started to help Hendor and Jamie. 'We still don't appear to have an obvious way out; other than the way we came in.'

'Patience,' de Charnay said as he continued to prepare the barge. 'We have to arrange the boat, oars, and mast, and then I will show you my final surprise.'

He started to straighten out the sail, which was crumpled in the ship's stern and still clung to the wooden beam, which was attached to the upright in the bow. Jamie quietly stepped forward to help him. A beautiful emerald fell out of his collar as he leaned over and bounced to the other side of the deck - a deck that was now decorated with gold, rubies, and diamonds.

Jamie thought the mast was broken, but then it became obvious that it had been dismantled to get the ship into the chamber. The wooden poles that made up the mast and rigging were robust and stout enough to support the sack cloth.

'Place these four oars into their holders. You will need them to push the boat onto the river, and I will need all of you to put this wooden mast in position - but not until we are ready.'

De Charnay continued to pace around the deck as

the Scots lifted four oars into iron holders. He checked the rudder, then reached into a chest stored next to it and produced a small, rolled parchment, which he untied.

'Gather round and see this river map. Come here, quickly!' De Charnay rolled his map out on one of the covered chests and placed his lamp on it to help flatten it down. 'I have made arrangements for Hugh de Verneuil to hire ox carts and spread the word he is heading to Chatillon-sur-Loire. He will make sure those following you think you are heading for ships out of Saint Nazaire. That should divert some of the attention you have gathered, but in fact, you will be in the North Sea before anyone realises they have been tricked.'

The map was beautifully illustrated with the mythical gods of the sea - Nereus, Proteus, Glaucus, and Phorcys - hand-drawn on vellum and coloured in gold and blue. Jamie was used to plain mason's sketches and was momentarily distracted, wondering why something so utilitarian should be decorated so well.

'I have marked out where there are robber barons who are likely to demand a tax for passing on the river unhindered, so you need to pass these at night.' De Charnay pointed to the route up through Rouen to the mouth of the river at Le Havre. 'The key to your escape is speed. You must be out of the river and on the sea by the day after tomorrow. You can't be stopped by these self-appointed tax collectors!'

'Innes grew up in Normandy,' Jamie said.

Innes nodded. 'I know the Seine and its currents well and can get every ounce of speed out of the barge.'

De Charnay put his arms around Innes and Jamie on one side and Will and Hendor on the other. He pulled them closer towards the map. 'You mustn't travel through Rouen's harbour: everyone who isn't at Chatillon-sur-Loire looking for you will be waiting in Rouen. Travel in silence and in darkness. Hide amongst all the other river barges transporting wool. Don't stand out, and you should be at Le

Havre before anyone realises you are at sea and on your way to Scotland.'

De Charnay rerolled the map and handed it to Innes. 'Finally, my brothers, I wouldn't let this treasure go with you unless I knew you would use it wisely to help your country remove its occupiers and maintain its independence. Remember, whilst it is yours by right, a share of this treasure is the Order's, and I would ask that you take care of it and keep it for such time as we should need it. We will call on you then.'

Will took a step forward and grasped de Charnay's hand in his. 'You have our thanks, and on our honour, we will use this great fortune wisely and retain your portion for a time of your choosing.'

De Charnay embraced Will. 'I am sure, as you are a man of honour. Now, my friends, we must part. I return to the Order and you to Scotland, King Robert, and His Grace Bishop Wishart.'

De Charnay walked to the stern of the barge and, using a pulley, pulled on the anchor chain.

Jamie could hear and feel the water rushing in. It pushed the air from the chamber and made his ears pop, such was its force. The gate separated from the entrance to the church, and the channel began to fill rapidly with water, lifting the boat up. At the bow of the barge, the rock began to separate like the parting of the Red Sea. The rock made a low groan as it moved. Small stones danced and splashed into the water as the barge continued to rise, lifting the back slightly higher than the front. The barge started to float very slowly forward.

'You must assemble the mast once you are clear of this chamber and row away from the Temple without one glance back,' de Charnay shouted from the pavement. 'Remember, not one glance back!'

De Charnay smiled and added, 'Give my warmest regards to Bishop Wishart and King Robert, and speak fondly of me to them.'

As he spoke, the barge gathered momentum, and the rocks finally parted and came to rest within what remained of the outside wall. The gap was just large enough for the barge to pass through. Innes carefully steered the barge out of the chamber, as it was now on the same level as the river, and with incredible grace, the bow glided onto the river without a splash.

Standing by the exit, de Charnay shouted, 'Goodbye, my dear friends, goodbye and good luck.' He paused for a moment before adding his final words. 'And send me word of Geoffrey de Mayon.'

'Geoffrey - Geoffrey de Mayon did he say - Who is he?' Jamie shouted back glancing at Innes, who seemed to be preoccupied with steering the barge, but Jamie was sure he heard him.

The others looked at Innes who remained quiet whilst manipulating the heavy rudder; Jamie wondered what other riddles and plots his uncle had not told him about, and which he was soon to uncover. He saw Hendor nod at Innes as if he knew what de Charnay meant, but he remained quiet. Jamie preferred to focus on the situation at hand: the greatest treasure in Christendom amidst a riot as they sailed beneath the windows where the King of France was probably watching them.

The entrance to the river closed as suddenly as it had opened, and de Charnay's lamp could be seen no more.

*

Madame de France saw a barge creep into the river. It was unlit but was headed downstream to the north and towards the sea. It slowly built up speed as oarsmen and sails were assembled. This boosted their speed, and they accelerated away from the Temple.

The Temple was surrounded by chaos: fires burned, and men shouted and screamed. The chaos was uncontrolled and random. She had seen mobs run riot before and survived; indeed, her profession thrived in such an environment.

The treasure barge slipped quietly past, unnoticed by the rioters. The oars lapped quietly in the water as the current pushed it out into the centre of the river.

On the other bank was a small rowing boat covered with barrels and cloth. It bobbed in an ungainly manner in the swell created by the barge, which due to its weight shifted a considerable draught of water. Inside the boat, Madame peered out from under a cloth, scarcely breathing. She had observed the Scots knights and heard de Charnay as they had parted.

The barge was heading downstream at full speed, but she did not dare follow immediately, or she would risk being seen. Her boat was smaller and more agile than the barge, and what she lacked in brute strength, she could more than make up for with the nimbleness of her boat. All she needed was to recruit a couple of stout hearts at the nearest tavern who could row.

The barge was heading towards the open sea, so she had an hour or two to rest her wounds and hire her crew. She did not have time to seek guidance from Guillaume de Nogaret or the King, but she knew they would want her to prevent the boat from leaving France and falling into the hands of a foreign power, and that was what she intended to do.

*

Aurelian knew he must get away; he took a minute to think. Even if the Scots knights and the Templar de Charnay had disappeared beneath him, the vibration may attract others to the Church, so he should make himself scarce. He had heard the staircase disappear as the altar moved back over the opening and hid its secrets, but he would not attempt to follow them that way. He had felt the vibrations as though the foundations were creaking under the weight of the Temple walls, and he suspected that the barge had left by

351

some secret route. It had nowhere to go but the River Seine and would be heading to the sea: he would be right behind it.

The treasure had been down there, he was sure of that now, but there had to be another exit, and he needed to get out of the church and down to the river. In all the noise and the chaos, he would be well hidden and would arouse no suspicion. He decided to risk discovery and moved out of his hiding place and crept down the nave towards the door. The light from the stained-glass windows helped him find the door, and he moved swiftly and lithely.

Just as he was about to lift the door latch, he heard the same grinding of the altar stones. De Charnay must be coming back. He had no time to return to his hiding place: he must leave the church now.

He lifted the latch and hurriedly pulled the heavy door open, just enough to squeeze through before pulling it closed behind him. He stood outside for a few seconds to compose himself before joining the Templar and palace guards who were putting out fires and removing objects that had been raining down on them from outside. Terracotta grenades were smashing on the ground, ejecting Greek fire. There was so much confusion that Aurelian simply walked down the side of the church and out towards the pier. He could see that a heavy boat had just left; the wash it left behind was so large that it had covered the pier and was rhythmically rocking the wooden supports and eroding the mud bank.

He watched a large, dark vessel move out towards the far side of the river. The moon reflected off the water, and he could just make out Innes at the stern, holding the rudder as the sail was unfurled. 'Damn it - it was moving faster than I thought,' he muttered. He started to plot the best way to intercept them.

There were many small boats tied to the pier, which the Templars used to transport messages and goods. Aurelian looked around and decided he would liberate one and follow the barge to the sea.

He stepped onto the nearest one and untied the restraining rope. The boat was half full of the water that had been thrown in when the barge had left. He straddled the keel, tipping the boat to one side, and emptied this unwanted ballast back into the river before he pushed away from the pier with his oars.

Aurelian was the Emperor's most trusted captain and spy, and he was also Axel Myhre, the Viking adventurer; he could outrow any man, and certainly a gold-laden sea barge, but he needed to keep a distance behind them. He could not take the barge alone, so he would head for Rouen and contact the Byzantine agents there.

He breathed heavily, partly out of relief that he now had the Emperor's treasure in his sight; but he was also alone and had barely escaped from the Temple, and he was deep in hostile France.

He started to row, cutting the water without making a sound. He glanced at his side and saw his small dagger was missing. It had been a gift from Emperor Andronikos, made of the finest Damascus steel and decorated with a large sapphire. He scanned the boat to see if he had dropped it, but he could not see it - then the realisation hit him: he must have dropped it in the Church as he rushed to escape. It did not matter: once he had the treasure, the Emperor could afford to buy him hundreds of such daggers.

He started to row and found that the rhythm of the oars relaxed him, and he quickly forgot about the valuable dagger.

The last time he had rowed a boat was in Norway, near his home on the great Sognefjord. He thought of those days and mused that it had been an eventful few weeks, and he knew that the real adventure was about to start.

*

Above him in the dark recess of the Temple Church, Geoffroi de Charnay sat alone. In his hand was a curved dagger, decorated with a large sapphire and attached to the remnants of a torn leather belt.

The door had been closed in a rush and had ripped the valuable possession away from its owner, leaving it right by the opening of the inside of the door. It wasn't there when he had entered the church with Will, so he was certain the knights had been overheard; but by whom? He had been as careful as he could to conceal their escape, but he had to assume that someone knew everything, and the knights were in peril.

He would wait for Hugh de Verneuil to return tonight, and then he would reveal the treachery. They had another traitor to find, and they had to get word to the Scots. They had not escaped in secret, and they were in great danger.

THE END

To find out what happened next in this engrossing saga, see *Revenge of the Tyrants* by L.A. Kristiansen to be published by Ringwood Publishing in 2022.

Acknowledgements

I wish to personally thank the lovely people at Ringwood Publishing, specifically Sandy Jamieson who placed great faith in a first time author. I would also like to thank my very kind, patient and supportive editors, Bianca Procacci and Kirsty Walker, who offered great insight and professionalism to make an idea something printable; Nicola Campbell for her artistic cover and Rachel Campbell for her marketing advice and support, as well as all the Ringwood proofreaders and back room staff.

I would also like to thank the following people for their contributions to my inspiration and knowledge and other help in creating this book: Emma, Hans, Steven and M for helping in my other life and giving me the time, love and space the book needed; Ralph Appleby and Lynne for believing the book 'had something' and editing my first draft; Maurice Druon and my funny, and kind history teacher Peter Duckhouse.

I would like to give my warmest thanks to the following people and organisations for their contributions to this book: Tonya Mitchell, whose free advice on editing was given at my lowest point and made all the difference; Jennifer Quinlan, Aaron Redfern and Anna Bennett of 'Historical Editorial' for development and proofing my early work, giving a rough diamond just a little sparkle; and Tamian Wood of 'Beyond Design International' for just having great design ideas.

About the Author

Born and brought up in Glasgow, author L.A. Kristiansen discovered a passion for Scottish history and, through her interest in genealogy, uncovered her close family ties with many of the leaders of the wars of Scottish Independence such as Bishop Wishart, Robert Bruce and William Wallace. During her research she discovered how their bravery and courage played a significant part in the historical events of the 13th and 14th century. She decided to write about them weaving a plot of fact and fiction leading up to the acknowledgement of Scotland's sovereignty in 1328 and Bruce's death in 1329. She is a full time writer, spending her time in Scotland, France and Norway researching the new adventures of the characters first found in this book and the seven others to follow.

Other Titles from Ringwood

All titles are available from the Ringwood website in both print and ebook format, as well as from usual outlets.

www.ringwoodpublishing.com

mail@ringwoodpublishing.com

Embers
Stephanie McDonald

When the shy and mild-mannered Graham meets the confident Angie at university, he is instantly besotted. The two soon embark on an all-compassing love affair, later marrying and settling down together.

But Angie has a past unknown to Graham – one which threatens to shatter the loving family they have created together.

An intimate and heart-breaking story of the complexities of modern relationships.

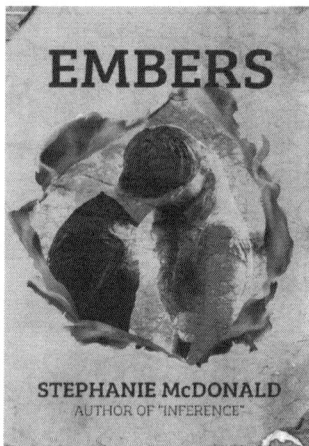

STEPHANIE McDONALD
AUTHOR OF "INFERENCE"

ISBN: 978-1-901514-99-5
£9.99

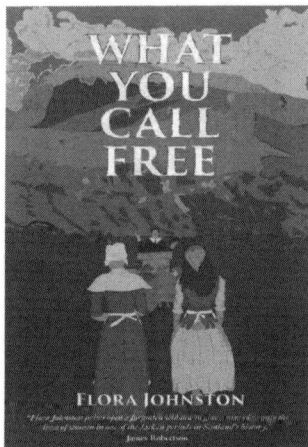

FLORA JOHNSTON

ISBN: 978-1-901514-96-4
£9.99

What You Call Free
Flora Johnston

Scotland, 1687. Pregnant and betrayed, eighteen-year-old Jonet escapes her public humiliations, and takes refuge among an outlawed group of religious dissidents. Here, Widow Helen offers friendship and understanding, but her beliefs have seen her imprisoned before.

This extraordinary tale of love and loss, struggle and sacrifice, autonomy and entrapment, urges us to consider what it means to be free and who can be free – if freedom exists at all.

Not the Life Imagined
Anne Pettigrew

A darkly humorous, thought-provoking story of Scottish medical students in the sixties, a time of changing social and sexual mores. None of the teenagers starting at Glasgow University in 1967 live the life they imagine.

In *Not the Life Imagined*, retired medic Anne Pettigrew tells a tale of ambition and prejudice that provides a humorous and compelling insight into the complex dynamics of the NHS fifty years ago.

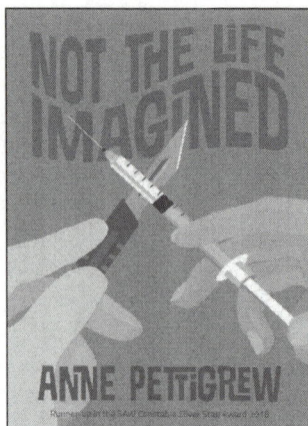

ISBN: 978-1-901514-70-4
£9.99

Not the Deaths Imagined
Anne Pettigrew

In a leafy Glasgow suburb, Dr Beth Semple is busy juggling motherhood and full-time GP work in the 90s NHS. But her life becomes even more problematic when she notices some odd deaths in her neighbourhood. Though Beth believes the stories don't add up, the authorities remain stubbornly unconvinced.

Is a charming local GP actually a serial killer? Can Beth piece together the jigsaw of perplexing fatalities and perhaps save lives? And as events accelerate towards a dramatic conclusion, will the police intervene in time?

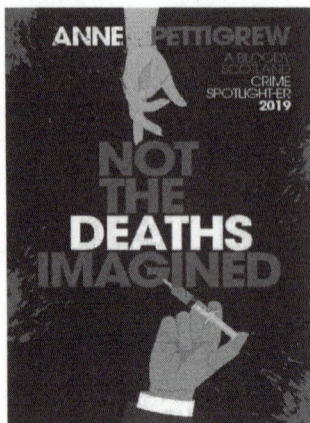

ISBN: 978-1-901514-80-3
£9.99

Murder at the Mela
Leela Soma

DI Alok Patel takes the helm of an investigation into the brutal murder of an Asian woman in this eagerly-awaited thriller. As Glasgow's first Asian DI, Patel faces prejudice from his colleagues and suspicion from the Asian community as he struggles with the pressure of his rank, relationships, and racism.

This murder-mystery explores not just the hate that lurks in the darkest corners of Glasgow, but the hate which exists in the very streets we walk.

ISBN: 978-1-901514-90-2
£9.99

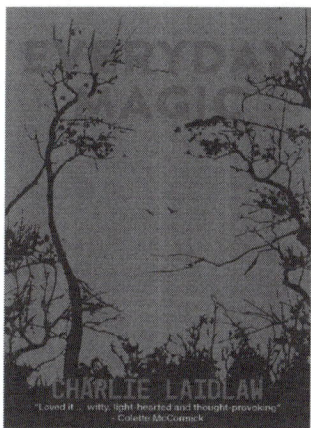

ISBN: 978-1-901514-77-3
£9.99

Everyday Magic
Charlie Laidlaw

Carole Gunn leads an unfulfilled life and knows it. But in spite of her mundane life, Carole has decided to do something different. She's decided to revisit places that hold special significance for her. She wants to better understand herself, and whether the person she is now is simply an older version of the person she once was.

Instead, she's taken on an unlikely journey to confront her past, present and future.

Everyday Magic is an uplifting book that reminds us that, while our pasts make us who we are, we can always change the course of our futures.